The author wishes to thank The   Council for its generous support during the writing of thi manuscript. Also, to Jan Whitford, agent and friend, for overseeing its nativity, James Lumsden for his careful attention to the initial sections, Leslie Donnelly for hearty encouragement after twelve pages and Richard Ford for kind words and the power of example. Most of all, to Don Sedgwick, Kathryn Exner and John Pearce of Doubleday, my ongoing gratitude and admiration for patience, guidance, compassion and faith.

AUTHOR'S NOTE

Some of the events pertaining to native political history did occur — Oka, Alcatraz Island, Wounded Knee, Anishanabe Park. I have been as accurate as memory allows with the dates. However, Ted Williams's book *The Science of Hitting* was published in 1971. I've used it out of time here for the benefit of the story. It is still the epitome of how-to books, especially for hitters.

For Tom Gilbert,

a great friend,

and enduring example,

a warrior

in the truest sense.

You are told a lot about your education, but some beautiful, sacred memory, preserved since childhood, is perhaps the best education of all. If a man carries many such memories into life with him, he is saved for the rest of his days. And even if only one good memory is left in our hearts, it may also be the instrument of our salvation one day.

Fyodor Dostoyevsky
The Brothers Karamazov

PROLOGUE

We are born into a world of light. Every motion of our lives, every memory, is colored by the degree of its intensity or shaded by the weight of its absence. I believe the happy times are lit by an ebullient incandescence — the pure white light of joy — and that the sadder times are bathed in swatches of purple, moving into pearl gray. When we find ourselves standing against the hushed palette of evening, searching the sky for one singular band of light, we're filtering the spectrum of our lives. We're looking through the magic prism of memory, letting our comforts, questions or woundings lead us — emotional voyageurs portaging a need called yearning. Because it's not the memories themselves we seek to reclaim, but rather the opportunity to surround ourselves with the quality of light that lives there.

The muted grays of storm clouds breaking might take you back to the hollowness you found in a long good-bye. The electric blue in a morning horizon might awaken in you again that melancholic ache you carried when you discovered love. Or you lay on a hillside in the high sky heat of summer, the red behind your eyelids making you so warm and safe and peaceful, it's like the scarlet a part of you remembers through the skin of your mother's belly when you, your life and the universe was all fluid, warmth and motion.

—

The qualities of light are endless and our entire lives are immersed in them. That's why we go back. That's why we use the gift of memory to sift through it all, seeking answers in the people, places and things we inhabited once, hoping we might find there a single quality of light that defines us.

My name is Joshua Kane. I am an Ojibway and the word that brought me to light was *Indian*. It was carried on the reed-thin shoulders of a boy who lived most of his life in darkness but who shone with the mantle of a hero. I became an Indian because of Johnny Gebhardt. When he walked into my life in the early spring of 1965, my life was sheltered, peaceful, predictable — and white. My parents, Ezra and Martha Kane, had adopted me at birth and I was raised in the staunch Protestant tradition perpetuated in the furrow and fallow of the farmlands they sprang from. It's a sad irony that my mother would be barren given the fertile soil which nurtured her creation. Still, it was the same measure of love that spawned my adoption as would have gone into the immaculate joining of seed to womb in my parents' marriage bed. I know this today as surely as I know that the earth is Mother to us all and we come out upon her breast to learn the motions of the dance that connects us. The cosmic dance driven by the music we learn to hear through the soles of our feet.

We lived on my grandfather's farm outside a small southwestern Ontario town called Mildmay. Our friends and neighbors bore names like Hohnstein, Dietz, Schultz and Schumacher, with a smattering of Ringles, Conroys and Leach. In that rich tradition of hereditary farms, the idea of family was more important than its definition, and I was accepted, quite simply, as Joshua Kane because that's all I had ever been. That I was the only brown face in Kane family pictures was never questioned. I was born and I lived as a Kane. My parents had never kept the truth from me and I'd known about my tribal blood from the moment I could understand. They told me of my mother's inability to conceive and how they felt the need for the love that they felt for each other to be rendered more completely through a child. The Ontario Children's Aid Society had directed them to a very young Indian girl who was pregnant and had no means of raising a child. They told me that they wanted to bring into their lives someone who would be theirs from as close to the beginning of life as possible. Someone whose history could begin and end with them.

They told me how happy they were when the arrangements had been made to pick me up at the hospital and how they waited, almost like they were pregnant themselves, with all the anxiety, anticipation and joy that birth parents feel. And how natural and right it felt to finally hold me, like a circle closing, their lives and mine coming together as fat and full of promise as a harvest moon. They told me of the tremendous love they felt for me from that first moment and of the gratitude they held for the Lord for bringing us together as a family.

Family. I suppose I understood from my earliest days that it's something far greater than simply blood and chromosomes. It's belonging. Fitting. Wearing other people's lives around your shoulders easily, casually, as a loose and familiar robe. A comforting weight, resplendent in its weft and warp. A fabric compelling in its texture. Yes, I was a Kane, and the Indian in me lay somewhere underneath all of that, an anonymous subtext in the book of my life.

"You've got all the chapters and verses," my father would say. "The only thing you don't understand is the begats. And believe me, son, no one ever reads the begats."

I remember the mornings of my boyhood as the basso rumble of my father's voice through the darkness and then the soft scraping of wooden spoon against my feet. "Joshua, son, it's time," he'd say and I would emerge from sleep, tousle-headed and grinning, rested and ready for the day's journeys. That's how my days began for as long as I can remember. So that now, on the cusp of middle age, I can almost swear some mornings I hear the creak of his step across the floorboards, just as I did all those times I faked slumber so that the dulcet bass of his voice would become the hinge my world swung open on.

In that spring of 1965, my world was three hundred and twenty acres of farmland. We lived in the three-story brick house my great-grandfather Nathaniel Kane had built with a horse, pulley and swarm of neighbors just before the turn of the century. It stood on a long slope overlooking sixty of those acres running west from Highway 9. With the small apple orchard behind and the long graveled driveway lined with pines leading up to it, the house stood like a sentinel against morning skylines, windows gazing outward like pale yellow eyes — wide-eyed, curious, benign. The creaks and shiftings of that house were the lullabies I remember most, and the shadow creatures that agrarian moon conjured in the corners became the purple hills themselves, calling me forward into dreams and then the soft awakenings of my father.

I'd walk into the kitchen to see him stirring oatmeal, and my mother, face as pale and quiet as an egg, absently buttering toast with one hand and following the words in her Bible with one finger of the other. The sun would be a mere suggestion against the lush plum of the skyline. When we'd seated ourselves around the table my mother would bow her head and pray and then read a verse or two from the Good Book before we'd spoken a word to each other. Then my father would wink covertly at me, grin at my mother and begin the farmer's good-natured litany of chores and destinations. I'd sit and listen, watching as my mother bent over her Bible, engrossed in her verilies, begats and whosoevers, as my father would say. When we'd eaten, we men would rise, clamber into our coats and hats and gloves and begin the formal procession to my mother for a quick kiss and hug before heading to the barn.

I'd learned the value of hard work early. The Kane family history was built on it. Early to bed and early to rise was just one of the adages I'd come to accept as life principles by the time I was old enough to comprehend. Along with "study to show thyself approved" from Second Timothy and "any job worth doing is worth doing right" from the Kane Protestant ethic, I was well versed in the virtues of the land by that spring of '65. My mother, a farm girl whose family lived one county over and who'd met my dad at a church soiree when she was sixteen, leaned on the teachings of the Good Book all her life and passed on to me the important coupling of earnest prayer and good work as soon as I could hold a dishcloth. Because I was a Kane I learned to love the feeling of body and spirit moving together in the work the Lord assigned, just as I learned that quietness was rooted in humility and that if the meek were to inherit the earth, I could guarantee myself a large tract through quiet industry, prayer and service. Granted, my father was a lot less intense about his spiritual devotion than my mother, him preferring laughter and fishing over hymns and service as expressions of his faith, but he'd never strayed far from his Christian roots.

It was my father who brought me the spirit of the land. He'd sink his furrowed fingers deep into it, roll its grit and promise around his palms, smell it and then rub it over the chest of his over-alls like he wanted it to seep through into his heart. It did — and it seeped into mine, too.

Very early some spring and summer mornings we'd pile sleep-ily into our fishing gear and head off in the old brown Dodge towards the distant Hockley Valley, whose small and ragged creeks were home to the most stubborn, wily and tasty trout in God's uni-verse. I'd lay with my head in his lap listening to the high-pitched whine of the tires in counterpoint to his soft humming of some Negro spiritual. He loved those songs. I can't begin to count the number of miles I traveled that way, swept up in the romance of motion and the frail pitch and sway of a hummed "Kumbaya" or "Swing Low, Sweet Chariot." The miles would pass quickly and we'd arrive in the valley about the same time as the sun — quiet, whole and shining. He'd lean against the hood of that old Dodge, head thrown back, eyes closed, slow deep breaths melding with the morning mist. And then, from his throat, a single, exhaled note that would shimmer across the silence of those mornings. *Yes,* that note would say. *Yes, yes, yes.*

He never had to explain it. Somehow, I just knew. As I stood there in the pure openness of my boyhood, my father's whispered note of earnest praise became the slender flicker of a tiny candle flame of faith I would nurture all my life. *Yes, yes.* That's all he ever had to say to teach me. As that note became absorbed in all that surrounded us those mornings and absorbed by something warm and pliant inside ourselves, I knew that my father was telling me, with that single note, that the spirit of the Lord still moved across the land. And as long as we were there, in openness, trust and belief, that the spirit was moving across and through and over and under every part of ourselves too. *Yes, yes.* He'd smile at me then, rough up my hair and hug me, and we would walk together in silence towards the creek, striding confidently, carefully, until our approach itself became another form of praise.

He taught me to approach the land like a hymn. Reverently, joyfully, gratefully.

So on those farm mornings, we'd stand together on the porch after breakfast and my father would gaze across those acres before we headed for the barn. He'd breathe deeply as though sponging up those pale morning ambers, grays, browns and blues that surrounded us, sealing them forever in a private chamber of his being. Then he'd look at me with eyes shining and I knew he'd just been to the valley again.

Those were the mornings of my boyhood. It never mattered to me then that I was physically different from the people I called my parents. What mattered to me then was that I felt like a Kane. Ezra and Martha Kane were my parents, and when I was ten my world was shielded, wrapped and protected by the overwhelming love and sense of belonging they planted in me. There were no Indians and there were no whitemen. There was only life. There was only Joshua Kane and there was only three hundred and twenty acres of farmland in southwestern Ontario. There was only faith and there was only devotion. There was only the motions of that soft, warm and pliant something inside of me that whispered a long, exhaled note of praise into the very heart of those mornings — *yes, yes, yes.*

Then came Johnny.

My life as a Kane was lit in the indigos, aquamarines and magentas of a home built on quiet faith and prayer. But Johnny changed all that. Where I had stood transfixed by the gloss on the surface of living, he called me forward from the pages of books, away from the blinders that faith can surreptitiously place upon your eyes and out into a world populated by those who live their lives in the shadow of necessary fictions. He introduced me to the fragments of falsehood that things like hate, anger, resentment and denial are built around. He introduced me to life's stygian underbelly, a visceral world you navigate by instinct. He introduced me to Indians and he introduced me to myself. I became a better man, a better preacher and a better Indian because of Johnny Gebhardt. I am still Joshua Kane and I still go out into mornings with the whiteman that I call my father, to fish and farm and pray. Only now we carry sweetgrass, sage and tobacco in a bundle alongside our Bibles. We pray in church and we pray in the sweat lodge. We bring ourselves to our God in the same manner we bring ourselves to our world — openly, honestly and without fear. Johnny made that possible.

This is a story about the light that shone throughout my friendship with Johnny Gebhardt. It's equal parts magic and reality because that, I've learned, is what life itself is all about. It's a story about boys becoming men and men becoming boys because that, too, I've learned, is what life itself is all about. It's about Johnny and me becoming Indians together, one because he wanted to, and the other because he had to. It's only now I understand that those parts are interchangeable. And if there is a lambency to it all, then it's the nebulous kind that lights our dreams, levitating us over footfalls and caverns, returning us to our lives with the gentle touch we find only upon awakening.

Part One

INVENTING BASEBALL

The telephone jangled urgently in the study. It was just before six. By the age of thirty-five I'd made a habit of a farmer's start to the day, and the idea that more cosmopolitan people's lives might kick themselves into gear that early always caught me off-guard. I moved quickly to answer before the ringing could disturb my wife and young son.

"Reverend Kane?" a weary male voice inquired.

"Yes, this is Joshua Kane."

"Good. Sorry to disturb you at this hour, Reverend. It must be, what, six a.m. where you are?"

"Yes. Well, just before. I was up. Who is this, please?"

"Oh. Yeah. Sorry," the man said, gearing down into a professional tone. "Name's Inspector David Nettles of the Calgary police, Reverend. You've got a friend name of Gebhardt? John Gebhardt?"

"Johnny? Yes. Is there a problem? Is he okay?"

"Well, he's alive, if that's what you mean. But we've definitely got a problem, Reverend. It seems your friend Gebhardt has taken it upon himself to solve the entire Indian problem in Canada. He's holed up in the Indian Affairs office out here with a dozen hostages, armed to the teeth and making demands. Says he wants a special sitting of the House of Commons to deal with this situation down in Oka, wants the army out of there and wants a guarantee that

none of those militants will be prosecuted once the conflict is settled. He also wants a special investigation through the UN and an
International Human Rights Tribunal to look at the Indian Third
World in Canada, as he calls it. Real fuckin' Rambo. Sorry about
the language, Reverend."

"That's okay."

"Well, he's a real peach, this guy. Long hair, braided, with an
eagle feather, war paint, beaded buckskin vest, moccasins, everything but scalps hanging from his belt. Hard to believe he's a whiteman. Says if the government won't come to the Indians, he'll bring
the Indians to the government. He's been faxing us on the Indian
Affairs machine. Faxing the press out here too. Signs all of them
Laughing Dog. Can you believe it? He's sending faxes faster than
arrows."

"What can I do, Inspector?" I asked, unsure of the role a minister in a small rural community might play in a drama like this.

"Well, we got him to the point where he says he's willing to
negotiate for the release of the hostages. But he'll only negotiate
through you, he says. Pretty close friend of yours, this Gebhardt, is
he, Reverend?"

"Yes, pretty close. Or at least we were. I haven't heard from
John since ..."

"Since when, Reverend?"

"Since a long time ago, Inspector. A long time. Are you sure I
can help here?"

"You're the only game in town, Reverend. Gebhardt's got the
doors and elevators wired with explosives, and he's huddled in an
office on the fourth floor with a couple of automatic rifles, grenades
and enough dynamite to take out half a city block. Oh, and he
remembered to bring groceries. Says unless you come and do the
talking for him, he'll start tossing bodies out the window. Yeah, you
can definitely help, Reverend."

The Johnny I remembered was not this crazed, armed reactionary. It was true we hadn't seen each other in years and even
though I'd received a letter every now and then, they had stopped
about eight years back. I knew he had traveled a lot, even joking

once about living like a member of a nomadic culture, and that he'd spent the bulk of his time at various ceremonies, rituals and gatherings. He'd even written me at length about the winter he'd spent alone in a teepee just to understand how it must have been. He'd made his own bow, fletched arrows with sinew, tanned his own buckskin, trapped and hunted, and carved a ceremonial pipe stem. After that winter the letters had stopped. Yet the sketch of the man Nettles described was, from what I remembered of John, not so difficult to imagine. Twelve years before, the last time we had seen each other, he'd called me to act as a character witness for him after he'd been arrested for participating in a road blockade to prevent logging on traditional Aboriginal land in British Columbia. Still, that had been minor civil disobedience, trespassing, verbal abuse, a long way from armed hostage-takings. But if he needed my help to get through the mess he'd created, I would be there for him.

"How do I get to you?" I asked.

"Well, you're gonna have to drive to the airfield at Walkerton. We'll have an Ontario Provincial Police plane fly you to Toronto where you'll switch to a regular flight to Calgary. There'll be a ticket waiting for you and you should be here by late this afternoon. Okay?"

"Yes. I'll need some time to make arrangements — my church, my family — but I can leave this morning."

"Great. I'll meet you at the airport when you land. I'm tall, gray hair, brown suit, wife says I'm getting the coach's profile."

"What?"

"You know, a little bit of the belly." Nettles laughed. "Will you be wearing your collar, or how will I recognize you, Reverend?"

"No, I don't wear a collar. Besides, Johnny's not a real big fan of the church. I'm, uh, tall, black hair, dark skin. I'll wear a blue suit," I explained.

"Make yourself sound almost like an Injun, Reverend," Nettles said with a laugh.

"I am an Indian, Inspector. Ojibway."

"Oh," he said quietly.

"I'll want to go right over to John as soon as I arrive," I said.

"Sure. We'll debrief you first, though. Standard stuff on how to deal with people in these situations, what kinds of things to say or not to say, what we can accommodate from here, background on the situation, our contact person, that sort of thing. Oh, and Reverend?"

"Yes?"

"You might want to put your friendship in your back pocket on this one."

"What do you mean?"

"Well, you and Gebhardt had some kind of fight, right?"

"Yes."

"Well, you might want to mull over why he'd only want you in this situation," Nettles explained. "I think that memory will be your biggest tool here."

"Yes. Yes, you're right. I'll think about that Inspector."

I sat down heavily in my desk chair. I had always been a pacifist. Even before I'd made the decision to follow the path of faith my parents had instilled in me, I'd shunned aggression. Mine was a humble, quiet heart. Armed revolts, hostage-takings and threatened killings were distant from any experience I'd had. In the back of my mind I wondered whether the fibers of a friendship would unravel in the face of such a crisis, or whether the Johnny I knew and the Johnny who was cradling an automatic weapon in an office in downtown Calgary would meld suddenly into someone I could recognize, reach out to and save.

All things considered, it had been a difficult year to be Aboriginal. No matter how far removed you might have been from actual goings-on — and as a small nondenominational pastor in a farming town called Paisley, I was about as far removed from things Aboriginal as possible — people still seemed to regard you as an agitator and now, more recently, as a Mohawk. All Indians were Mohawk in that dry, hot summer of 1990. Everywhere you went your brown face seemd to qualify you as one with an opinion, a solution or at least an explanation. The fact that some of us had none of these puzzled most people.

The Warriors, wearing camouflage outfits and bandannas as masks, had engaged in a wild shoot-out with the police when they had mounted an attack to dismantle barricades the Warriors and the Mohawk people had raised on a small road leading to a spiritual area known as the Pines. The Mohawks wanted to prevent a municipal golf course owned by the town of Oka from expanding onto land that they held as sacred. Oka was nestled against the boundaries of a Mohawk reserve called Kahnesetake, although the Mohawks referred to it as a Territory. One policeman had been killed in the dawn raid. The conflict had escalated, with pictures in the press and on television of masked, heavily armed Mohawks, white citizens rioting along bridges to Montreal that neighboring Mohawk communities had barricaded and stories of more and more Mohawk supporters streaming behind the barricades. The army had finally been called in to quell the situation. Nothing had been accomplished and it seemed, the morning of that telephone call, that the stalemate in Oka would linger forever. I sighed. Conflict was a wearying thing.

Shirley was shuffling around the kitchen when I emerged from my shower. She moved to sit at the dining-room table with her fingers curled around a coffee mug, a sleepy half smile on her face. In the sixteen years we'd been together, she'd always amazed me with her uncanny ability to know when I needed her most. We'd met in Bible College in Red Deer during our first year. Even then she'd known I needed her. A farm kid living and studying in the city for the first time, two thousand miles away from home, I was lonely, uncertain and withdrawn. She'd approached me on the third day of classes where I sat waiting in the most remote corner of the foyer, plopped herself down beside me, introduced herself, and then casually, gently and devotedly, reached inside me and opened me up. We shared our faith, we shared our awe and wonder at the simple beauty of natural things, our concern for people, good music, good books, baseball, and very quickly, silently, mysteriously, we fell in love. We graduated together and were married the summer we became ordained. Since then we'd shared churches and congregations and the birth of our son, Jonathan, who was now twelve. Shirley McCormack Kane. The only woman I had ever been with. The only one I ever wanted.

"I heard the phone. Is everything all right?" She eyed me over the rim of her coffee cup.

"No," I said, toweling my hair and sitting down across the table from her. "I have to leave this morning. There's an emergency I've been asked to help with."

I explained very slowly and deliberately what Nettles had told me. Her face remained calm, except for a small worry line above her eyes when I described the amount of weaponry Johnny had at his disposal and the fortifications he had arranged around himself. I expressed my concern for the hostages and my uncertainty over such an old and untended friendship holding up through the pressure of resolving the situation. When I finished she sat back in her chair, sipped her coffee and stared out the patio doors briefly before turning to me and nodding.

"There's no question of your going. But I'm worried about Johnny. How stable is he? How willing to compromise? Can you reach him? I share your concern about the strength of your friendship in this. It's been what, twelve years?" She reached out to take my hand.

"Yes. The year Jonathan was born," I said. "But Johnny's never tried to completely disengage himself from me. I've got that box of letters, after all. Even though it's been one-way contact all these years, he's always reappeared now and then in the mail. There's something still alive for him."

"And for you?" she asked quietly.

"There's something still alive for me too." I squeezed her hand lightly.

It had been one of the first stories I'd told her about my life, those nights when we'd disappear from campus and sit in Zak's Diner talking about our lives. She knew how much I loved him and how much I'd hurt when he'd walked away from me at the end of high school. And then twelve years ago I'd appeared in court for him. She had shared my jubilation over his reappearance, the fact that he needed me and trusted me enough to call upon me in a crisis. She also shared my agony over the result of that brief reunion.

"Then go, Joshua. Get in touch with that something that's still alive for you and use it, like Inspector Nettles said. Ask for the right words, for the strength and courage. Go and help those people. And help Johnny too," she said.

"And myself?"

"And yourself."

We packed quickly. I chose only enough to last me a few days since I couldn't see this lasting much longer. We would either settle it or it would end. There would be no extended negotiations. I knew Johnny well enough to know that he would want a resolution quickly. One way or the other. I decided against packing a Bible but I did include an old framed picture of the two of us taken the spring we met. Holding it and looking back across all those years raised a well of tears in my eyes and I brushed one hand slowly across the glass as though by that action I could touch the people we used to be one more time. Shirley beckoned from the bedroom doorway and I closed my valise and followed her into the hallway. Wordlessly, we crept to Jonathan's room. My son lay sprawled in a tangle of sheets and blankets, one arm thrown around his pillow, the other strewn along his side. My son. Named after my friend he'd never met, one who didn't know the honor he'd been given or how very much this sleeping boy reminded me of his namesake. Maybe now he would. I crept over and kissed Jonathan's forehead very gently and brushed my hand across his face before creeping out as silently as we'd entered.

Shirley disappeared into the study and returned carrying the old cigar box I kept Johnny's letters in. She smiled and handed it to me.

"You might want to go through these on the plane," she said and kissed me quickly.

"Yes. Thank you. Tell Jonathan not to worry, I'll be home soon. We've got that fishing trip with his grampa next weekend."

"I'll tell him. Joshua?"

"Yes?"

"I love you. Carry that with you too."

We walked slowly out to the garage, taking time to look around us at the yard and the neighborhood. It had been an agreement we'd made on one of our first trips to Zak's Diner. We would never allow ourselves to be anywhere without looking around and recognizing where we were. Window-dressing our memories was the way Shirley put it then, and it was something we did by second nature after all these years. We stood together looking up at a sky that was skimmed with frail, wispy clouds.

"Did I ever tell you about Johnny's magic trick?" I asked, still gazing upwards.

"No, I don't think you ever did. What was it?"

"The sky was filled with wispy little clouds like these. It was summer. August, I think, that first summer when they moved to Mildmay. We were floating down Otter Creek on inner tubes towards the dam behind the ruins of the old mill. Johnny pointed up at those clouds and said, 'I'm magic.' He picked out the smallest, wispiest cloud in the sky and told me to watch it carefully. Then he held both wrists up in front of his face and blew one quick breath against them. Whoosh! Then he closed his eyes, bent his head up towards that cloud and began rubbing his wrists together in small circles. I watched that little cloud as hard as I could and sure enough, it vanished in front of my eyes. We laughed like crazy. Said he'd been able to do that forever. He said he did it whenever he felt lonely, sad or afraid. I wonder if he still does that now."

"I'm sure he does," she said, softly.

"Yes. I hope so."

"Go with God, Joshua," she said.

I kissed her, stepped into the car and backed slowly out the driveway. As my home and family retreated behind me I realized how far I had traveled in this lifetime. We lived in Paisley, an hour's drive from the farm where I'd grown up, but it was far more than geographical distance I'd traveled. It was an emotional and spiritual journey that culminated right now in unquestioning obedience to unexpected callings. We knew, my wife and I, that these beckonings were divine in origin and our choice was never to answer or not to answer, but rather to decide how quickly we responded. We lived by the principles of faith, and as I turned that car towards the highway to Walkerton, my faith told me that this was a necessary step in the direction God had chosen for our lives. I could live with that. And as I settled into the seat for the start of this long journey, I began to think about Johnny Gebhardt making clouds disappear.

"Reminds me of the magic," he'd said.

"Magic?" I'd responded.

"Yeah. Magic. It comes in on the light," he explained. "It's everywhere. Only we can't see it because, well, because it's magic. Like the trees around us are growin' because of the light, but we can't see it happening. It's just there. Sometimes I just need to remember."

"How do you know it's magic?" I asked.

"Because it makes me feel better," he said quietly. "And only magic can do that. Sometimes, well, somtimes nothing can make me feel better. Except this. While I'm making those clouds disappear, I'm makin' other wishes too. You know, like wishin' my dad didn't drink so much, that we had more money and stuff. Watchin' those clouds disappear makes me believe that all my other wishes are comin' true too. Magic, you know. Try it!"

And so I had. We floated down that creek making clouds disappear and casting magic wishes against that high blue sky. Johnny and me. Oh, we knew it wasn't really magic, that it was just the wind. But something in us understood the need, the hunger, to believe that there's magic riding in on every particle of light. So we made those clouds disappear anyway and we surrendered ourselves to our friendship as easily as we surrendered to the current, drifting and bobbing, willing to travel wherever it would take us. Adrift forever in eddies of light.

I swept through that undulating farmland immersed in tranquil pools of memory. I remembered the boys we had been. Farmland such as this had been the backdrop for the friendship we'd forged. By the time I climbed aboard the OPP plane, I was ready for that long journey back inside the memories themselves, the box of letters beckoning me backwards and forwards at the same time.

I t had begun with the news that Ben Gebhardt was coming home after twenty years. He'd joined the army in 1945. After a hitch in Korea he'd disappeared entirely, except for occasional reappearances, the details of which his father, Harold, dispensed over the counter to everyone at his hardware store. Ben's life had become a random series of jobs and addresses in Toronto. By the time I was old enough to understand, Ben had been a tavern waiter, school custodian, used-car salesman and truck driver. When he failed to make even courtesy visits at Christmases and Thanksgivings, he achieved that status of all agricultural refugees who scrape the land from their heels and heart and hitch their wagons to the neon stars of the city. No one expected him to ever return.

We heard the news while my dad and I were on our bi-weekly trip to Harold's store. Actually, it was our bi-weekly trip for groceries, but Dad and I, along with the other men at loose ends while their wives shopped, gathered at Harold's for chatter, coffee and a peek at the farm equipment catalogues.

"It's the ticker, you know," Harold said, tapping his chest for emphasis. "Doc Niedermayer says all this gas I been having these last few years is some angina something something. Retire, he says."

"Retire?" Chester Shaus, our rabbit-farming neighbor, asked. "Retire to what? And what about the store?"

"Well," Harold said proudly, "retire to what I'm not sure. But the store's going to Ben."

"Ben? What does he know about hardware?" Karl Schumacher asked through the smoke of his meerschaum.

"Well, I don't rightly know, but he's my son, Karl, and I'd rather have it going to my own instead of some stranger or some big corporation that's only in it for the profits and not the community. Besides, Ben was raised around this store. It won't have washed completely off."

"When's he coming?" my dad inquired.

"Well, I spoke to him last week just after my talk with Doc and he seemed right anxious about it all. Said he had some things to settle in Toronto and he'd be here directly. They arrive next Friday."

"He's got family?" Lester Deiter asked.

"Wife and a son," Harold said quietly. "A wife and a son."

There are silences that run as straight and deep as fresh-plowed furrows. They alter our horizon and the landscape of our lives is tilted, askew and unfamiliar. This was one of them. Even I was old enough to understand that all of this was akin to catastrophe. Farmers know intuitively when the pitch and rhythm of things moves beyond the predictable and the usual. The security that comes from a familiarity raised and nurtured through the years was being removed with the retirement of a trusted friend and neighbor, and the idea that a man would not bring his family home to meet their own weighed as strangely in their hands as a stillborn calf. Everyone, now, had a stock in the success or failure of Ben Gebhardt, and his arrival was awaited with an expectancy tinged with caution.

"So we're all invited to Harold's place next Saturday for a welcoming," my dad explained to my mother on the drive back home.

"You know, Ezra, when Estelle died, Harold lost the biggest piece of his life. He seemed smaller after that. Now, he's getting some of that life back. He'll be a grandfather, a father and a father-in-law. Maybe Benjamin's return isn't so negative a thing as everyone's thinking right now. After all, the Lord gives us roles in our lives to fill our insides out, to make us more. To teach us how to live His way. This is a big gift for Harold right now and we *should* celebrate. I'll bake a cake," my mother said.

"You're right, of course," my father agreed. "I just find it a little tough to trust a man with my business when his family life's a little less than appropriate. Still, I should wait and see. No one really knows Ben Gebhardt. He may be a fine man."

"And be happy for Harold, Ezra. He hasn't had a family around him for six years. Be happy for him," she said and lay her hand on his shoulder. He gave her that wistful half smile he always used in tender moments and then winked at me in the rearview mirror.

The return of Ben Gebhardt became the chief topic of conversations that week. By the time the evening of the welcoming arrived, speculation around and about Ben and his family was rampant. We seldom got new folks in Mildmay. After a while the community begins to appear in your mind as whole and predictable as the shell of an egg. It has a feel and weight that's pleasing and familiar always, so that any hint of disruption or change becomes cause for concern. The imminent arrival of an expatriate towner like Ben was strange and generated more caution than low spring wheat quotations.

"Probably have to teach him tools and screws from A to Z," Mel Hohnstein said to my dad as they leaned against the railing of Harold's verandah that night. "The way I hear it, Ben's been pretty lucky to hold any kind of job for six months through the years."

"Well, it could be that Harold's right about the business being in his blood and all. He did grow up here and he was helping out in the store by the time he was ten," my dad said. "Family things are like that. From farming to selling cars — you pack it around with you when you've been raised in it. Coming back into it's a natural enough thing, I imagine."

"Easy for you to say," Helmut Hossfeld cut in, setting his tea cup down on the top step. "All you've ever known is that farm, Ezra. There's never been a returning for you. In your wife's way of saying, and bless her heart, you're no prodigal, Ezra."

"Well, that's true, Helmut, that's true. But you know, there were *two* sons in that prodigal story," my dad explained, leaning back and crossing his arms across his chest. "The one we hear about all the time is the one that went away. He left, he came back. That's the story as far as most of us know it. But there was the other son too."

A small crowd of men and women tied themselves in a loose knot around us and I wedged in closer to my dad and leaned my back against his legs to listen and watch our neighbors. People liked my dad. They liked to hear him think out loud like he was doing right then. Something in the easy way he had with his deepest thoughts drew people to him, and to me he's always been the epitome of the homespun philosopher, albeit without the straw between the teeth.

"And this other son was just as important to the story. He stayed. He was loyal to the farm, to the land, to the family. When his brother took his share of the family money and walked away, he was angry. Angry because, well, he saw that as a thumbing of the nose at his father, his family and the farm. So he stayed and his anger stayed too.

"When the prodigal blew his riches on wine, women and song, and came back with his tail between his legs, broke, hungry and dirty, his father threw a big celebration for him. A welcoming," he said and winked broadly at everyone. An embarrassed titter of laughter dribbled through the group around us.

"Why? Why? That's what the other son asked his father. And his father said that we should all celebrate when a lost one returns. Like shepherds do. Like farmers. Take care of them all, especially when they can't take care of themselves. Be here for them. Help them find their roots again.

"And the other son's ashamed. Ashamed because he knows, all of a sudden, that there's more than one way to be a prodigal. One's by leaving — like Ben — and the other one's by staying and not being true. By not being willing to take care of all of them, by judging and putting down, letting suspicion and hearsay keep you from celebrating the returnings when they happen.

"That about right, Mother?" he said, looking straight across the verandah at my mother, who'd appeared from the kitchen where she and a handful of other ladies were preparing the buffet.

"Yes," she said, smiling proudly. "That's about right. Now, all of you, come 'round back and meet your neighbors."

We moved together out onto the lawn and around the house in a raggle-taggled bunch like the herds we tended. The Gebhardts stood together outside the opened doors of their battered old '57 Mercury in the fight-or-flight position I recognized in the half-wild barn kittens we found each spring. A small orange U-Haul was hitched behind their car, and the back seat was piled high with blankets and boxes and a huge black Philco radio. A rusted orange Schwinn bicycle was tied on the top. Harold Gebhardt came down the porch steps as slowly and solemnly as Ben Gebhardt shook his hand once he reached him. The woman beside him smiled weakly at the process, and the thin-shouldered boy beside her swept his timid, blue-eyed gaze over all of us from beneath a mop of shaggy hair. They were dressed much like the rest of us, in the pressed and creased Sunday best sort of outfits we all try to appear comfortable in. Harold exhaled deeply and then clasped his bony arms around his son, whose face contorted at the sudden intimacy. Eventually he laid his hands limply on the old man's shoulders, patted distractedly a few times and then disengaged himself.

"My, uh, wife," he said to Harold, hooking his thumb towards her. "Ellen. Ellen this is ... my dad."

She came forward almost mincingly and extended a thin, pale hand that trembled slightly and earned her the sympathy of all the women in the background. "I'm glad to meet you. Finally," she said quietly and threw a worried glance at her husband. "This is our son. John. He's ten."

Harold bent down on one knee in front of him and tousled his hair. John Gebhardt stood there, straight shouldered, rigid. His hands were curled tightly at his side. He was as pale as his mother, fine boned and fragile looking.

Harold said softly, "Well, John Gebhardt, it's nice to meet you. I'm your grampa and these people behind me are friends of mine who came here just to meet *you*. Whaddaya think about that?"

The boy's eyes darted over all of us and he swallowed hard. "Fine, sir," he said quickly and looked at the ground.

"He's like that," Ben explained. "Don't talk much. Kind of a dreamer, you know?" He smiled weakly around at us.

"Well, we'll soon have him talking about those dreams, all right. Lots of good kids around this town to help him with that. In fact, one of them's here tonight. He's ten, too. Joshua? Come here, son." Harold waved me over with one hand while rubbing the boy's shoulder with the other.

My dad nudged me forward and winked encouragement. There was a flicker of surprise in John Gebhardt's eyes as I approached and then they settled back into a spot on the ground.

"John, this here is Joshua Kane. Him and his folks live about five miles out of town. Joshua, this is my *grandson*, John Gebhardt."

The hand that reached out to clasp mine was thin and meatless. Moist. Soft. Girlish, almost. My own were callused from forking and lifting, and the muscled forearms of the farmer were already bunching along the young lines of my arms. My grip surprised him. He looked up and the depth and clarity of his eyes shocked me. It was like falling through the sky. He stared at me hard, and for the briefest moment I felt the life force within his slender frame radiating outward in a roiling, churning wave, hard and insistent, like the feeling you get when you lay your hand upon the flank of a calving heifer. It startled me. And then it was gone. You could see it retreating. The energy folding in upon itself and moving backwards, down and in, leaving those crystal-clear eyes as languid, placid as troutless ponds.

"Hey, John," I said, shopping wildly for any bargain conversation. "Welcome. You'll like it here. It's nice. Town, I mean. Maybe you can come out to the farm sometimes. Wanna?"

"Corn," he said so quickly I almost missed it.

"What?"

"Corn," he repeated, still looking at the toe of his right foot, which was now doodling a small, loose circle. "You grow corn. Squash."

"Well, no. We grow cows mostly, chickens, a few pigs. My ma, she grows vegetables in the garden."

"No corn?"

"No. Well, yeah, some. A few acres, I mean. For the cows."

He looked at me puzzled, and then lowered his head again. I was lost for words. The adults were standing frozen like mannequins around the back stoop and only the faces of my parents were animated.

Harold looked at the two of us and smiled, patted me firmly on the back and pushed us both towards the house. "You boys head on in there and dig into some of that good food these ladies have brought for this shindig! Joshua, introduce John around to the other kids, will you?"

"Sure," I said. "Come on, John. Eats."

We threaded our way through the grownups and the kids scattered through them. Most just looked at us, but my mom and dad stepped forward to meet us.

"Well, well, so this is John Gebhardt. Hello there, John," my dad said and stretched out a big, worn hand to shake with him.

"This is my father. His name's Ezra," I said. "And this is my ma. Martha. This here's John Gebhardt."

"Hello, John," my mother said in her quiet way. "John's a strong name. We're really happy to have you with us. Welcome."

He performed the ritual perfunctorily, hands extended then retracted with the barest of contact with either of my folks. He simply offered a purse-lipped nod and pocketed his hands, shifting from foot to foot, while all of us searched for something more to say.

"Eats," he said finally.

"Yeah. Eats," I said, grinned at my parents and headed into the house. "Come on, John."

"Those were your parents?" he asked as we entered the house.

"Yeah. Nice, huh?"

"Yeah," he said. "Nice."

And that was that. John was introduced around to the rest of the kids and he was as tight-lipped and nervous as before. His parents seldom spoke at all, to each other or to anyone, and Harold made the rounds as the proud, gregarious host, as happy and comfortable as small-town shopkeepers generally are when surrounded by those they know, trust and count on. There was a world of difference between him and his son. Harold with the ruddy face of health and optimism, and Ben so sallow and tired looking that you wondered who was really the sick one. Mrs. Gebhardt remained as mousy and retiring as she was on her arrival, merely nodding in agreement through most of the evening and offering little or no return of chatter. We kids played hide-and-seek, and although I noticed that John was particularly adept at disappearing, there was nothing in his manner besides his silence and curt return of questions to mark him as any different from the rest of us.

The night passed in the flurry of childhood with nothing extra-ordinary to remember, no alteration to the rhythm of things. I guess the significant moments in life are like that. They come and they go in such random anonymity that their gravity and conse-quence are lost upon us. They're masked in simplicity, in the slouching, casual day-in, day-outedness of our lives, so that you greet them in an unfeigned openness. Because they're simply moments. Yet they lay on the highways and byways of our lives like stones, singing their histories, clamoring for the comfort of our attentions, the nurturing of our remembrances. And when we return to them, well traveled and wiser with years, cradle them patiently in our hearts and minds, feel the lives within them, then, then we realize how very much of the people we have become, lives within the stones we ignore.

You know the old joke about men crying when we come out of the vagina and then sixteen years later, crying because we want back into it? Well, I cried because I wanted back in right away. My ma said I cried all the time and I believe it's because I really didn't want to be here. Not with them anyway. You only ever saw their public faces, the eerie lit-tle social minuet they performed for propriety's sake. Her, all caked in the ghoulish makeup she used to hide the bruises, and him, sober out of the fear of being found out, all cranked on the morphine he scored from an old army buddy. He said it was for treatment of the Wound. What a joke. No one ever saw the Wound, of course. I never. But he talked about it all the time. He'd be drunk and stupid, telling tales about the virgins in Pu San or some such place, or the fist fight in camp the night before the assault on Hill 68, and he'd get all teary, saying it would have all been different except for the Wound. He'd have been a hero except for the Wound. He'd have held a civilian job except for the Wound. He needed to drink or needed a shot of morphine because of the pain of the Wound. After he died I learned that the Wound was caused by his being drummed

*out of the army for drunkenness and that he'd never been to Korea at all.
He was a desk jockey who filed the papers that sent guys there and
shipped them back. That's how he knew all the names of places and battles. He typed them all the time. He couldn't stand being a soldier without a war, so he made our lives one. Nice, huh? I was never a son. I was
a prisoner of war.*

*So, needless to say, I was glad to get out of Toronto. Not that com-
ing to a place called Mildmay was my idea of a good move, but any place
was going to be better than those sorry streets. And actually it's not the
streets themselves that I hated. It was the me that walked them. And my
life. I lived all my life learning how to shift gears. I'd be coming home from
school or the library (where I did my living) and I'd be feeling pretty good.
I'd just spent a few quality hours in a book and I'd be on fire with new
ideas, information or some story. I'd feel like a real kid, motoring in the
passing lane of life. Then I'd get to the door of wherever it was we were
living at the time. My hand would pause just as it was about to grab the
doorknob, like reaching for the stick shift. I'd scrunch up my eyes and
heave a deep breath before I opened that door. Downshifting into neutral
because I never knew whether I'd have to make a sudden getaway or if I
could park and idle for a while. He'd either be passed out, drunk and slob-
bering, drunk and ranting, slapping my mother, drunk and crying, hung-
over and sick or even, on occasion, sickeningly lovey-dovey and wanting
to hug me with his drinker's breath and tobacco stench. Wonderful. So I
guess part of me held out hope that a new town would change things,
change him, change us.*

*And my mother? Well, they say that love is blind but in her case it
was totally insensate. Her idea of protecting me was to tell me not to disturb him. Great. He's got a choke hold on me, feet off the floor, and she's
telling me not to disturb him. He's passed out in a puddle of puke on the
kitchen floor and it's "Don't disturb him." She's got another ice bag on
her face and "Don't disturb him." She was in love with his necessary fiction, the soldier he created for the world because he couldn't tell them
what a loser the real one was. Or maybe, in their first days, he showed
her a side of himself that I never saw, something that swam under all the
bullshit drunkenness that she alone could see, and maybe she held on
because she thought that it would break the surface one of those days and*

he'd be the man she needed. But I wish, just once, just once, she'd have stuck up for me the way she stuck up for him. I could never understand how you could love someone you always had to lie for. And me, hell, I would have even settled for that.

Yeah, I couldn't wait to get out of Toronto.

'll never forget Alvin Giles. Alvin Giles was principal of Mildmay-Carrick Public School all through the years I went there. Born and raised in Bruce County, he'd come as close to home as his job would get him once he'd finished teacher's college and a brief stint in the city system. He was one of the Paisley Gileses, and although his family weren't farmers, they were fourth-generation townies whose lives had so intertwined through marriage and friendship with our own that they might as well have been. Farming communities are like that. The land just reaches out past the concrete and grabs you. There's plenty of towners who are as capable a hand around threshing time as any farm people and you never see them grimace over the suck and pull of manure on their rubbers or complain about blisters on their hands from forking stooks.

Alvin Giles was one of those people. He was a local hockey hero in Paisley and was known, even then, for his hard work and fair play. When he came back as a teacher and a principal, it was like having an old friend back for most folks around Mildmay. Alvin was one of those teachers who fires your imagination and takes you into the heart of whatever they're teaching. His classes were like one long show-and-tell. And he cared. No one was considered stupid, slow or incapable around him. He knew farmers and he knew their children, and things were always couched in terms we could identify with. He was the kind of teacher you remember all your life. The kind who lives forever in certain words, concepts and activities you carry with you into the adult world. He made us all better students, more curious, creative and independent. But it was his teaching of life that makes him memorable for me. He had that peculiar kind of psychic sense that told him where his kids were at.

There were one hundred and forty-five students or thereabouts in that school all those years and Alvin Giles knew every one of them. Not just knew as a name on a roll call or a face in the hallway but *knew* like a brother would know. When there was sadness, sickness or worry in someone's family, he knew and would take the time to comfort us. He encouraged the poets, artists and athletes we showed ourselves to be as much as he encouraged the studious like me, the wallflowers and the indolent. Teaching wasn't a job for him, it was a way of life. Stern when he had to be, laughing and jovial most of the time, and always present those times when you needed him most. And I will never forget him for bringing John Gebhardt and me together.

When John arrived at Mildmay Public School, Alvin Giles was there to greet him. By the time he escorted him into Mrs. Thompson's Grade Five class just after the national anthem and the Lord's Prayer, John's fists had uncurled at his sides and his shoulders were up and confident.

"Class," Alvin said with a smile and a hand on John's shoulder. "I want you to welcome John Gebhardt. He and his family are here from Toronto and I know you'll all help him feel comfortable and welcome."

He introduced John to Mrs. Thompson, who shook his hand lightly and gazed at him intently over the top of her rhinestoned cat's-eye glasses, which she kept on a cord around her neck.

"Joshua Kane?" Alvin asked, searching for my face along the rows of desks. "Ah, there you are. Joshua, I would like you to be in charge of helping John get to know his way around. Is that okay with you?"

"Yeah. Sure. Hey, John, remember me?" I asked.

He looked at me with those big blue eyes and half grinned my way in recognition, nodded, looking up at Alvin Giles for direction.

"Good. You two will get along fine. Well, carry on then, Sarah," he said to Mrs. Thompson. "I'll see you children outside at recess. First day for baseball!"

Mrs. Thompson indicated an empty seat behind mine and John made his way down the row. Faces were turned towards him all over the classroom and he reddened deeply. As he passed he gave me that pure open stare and I felt opened up, known, recognized. It scared me just a little. I noticed Sue Crawford and Connie Shaus whispering and giggling to each other and arching their eyebrows. Ralphie, Gus and Lenny were staring hard at him and his strange appearance. He wore army fatigue pants, black high-top sneakers and a black T-shirt. Compared to the crewcuts, jeans and sneakers the rest of the boys wore, he was as much an anomaly as me.

My parents believed in clothes that were functional as opposed to fashionable, and I'd always appeared at school in chinos and white long-sleeved shirts for as long as I can remember. It was hard sometimes. Once when I'd come home in tears over the teasing, my mother had explained to me the virtue inherent in simple dress. She'd showed me pictures in the Bible of Jesus and the disciples in their simple robes. Food, shelter, family and tithes to the church were far more important ways to spend money than on material things like clothes, she'd said. My dad, of course, put it far more simply.

"Worldly things are fine, Joshua, they're really fine, and one of these days, if you want them, you can have all you want. But, son, no one ever pulled up to heaven with a U-Haul!"

So I sympathized with John Gebhardt.

Once the morning's lessons were under way I disappeared into them and recess arrived before I knew it. There was generally a big race for the schoolyard, but that morning there was even more hurry. Alvin Giles believed that young bodies shouldn't be exposed to activities beyond their capabilities, and so up to Grade Five we'd had to content ourselves with soccer, tag, red rover and assorted schoolyard games. We'd watched the older grades playing baseball and football and hungered for the day when we'd no longer be little kids. By the time I reached the tarmac, Ralphie Wendt had commandeered the equipment bag and was rapidly tossing gloves and balls around to his pals. John lingered behind with me and we watched as Ralphie and his cronies ran down the shallow hill to the playing field and began tossing balls around the smallest diamond of the three in the yard. Finally, Alvin Giles appeared with his coach's whistle and we followed him to the field along with a throng of girls.

Soon, to Ralphie's disgruntlement, we were arranged in two equal teams of boys and girls and our first attempt at the game of baseball was under way.

Sports and I had been only casual acquaintances until then. Living on a farm meant there wasn't a whole lot of free time for games. I'd gotten used to the idea of helping my dad with chores, and even though he would have allowed me to run around and be the child that I was, we both appreciated the time together keeping the farm going. I played in the hay mow whenever kids came around, building forts or leaping from the upper beams into big piles of loose hay, and I ran along beside the tractor lots, just for the joy of it, but organized games weren't part of my life. I was missing the excitement of this new event and I could tell that John was less than keen on the activity.

"Fun, eh?" I said, trying to open conversation while we were leaning on the backstop watching our team at bat.

"Fun? What's fun about this? I'd rather play lacrosse."

"Lacrosse?" I asked, my face screwed up in wonder.

"Yeah. Lacrosse. Indians played it all the time. Thought you'd know about it."

"No, never heard of it. What's it like?"

"Like hockey, only better."

"Well, I don't play hockey either. Here goes nothing!" I said and left to try my hand at batting.

Ralphie Wendt had been chosen for the team in the field and I heard him as soon as I stepped to the plate with the bat held awkwardly in my hands. I was used to Ralphie's snide manner in class but he'd always bothered me in the schoolyard. He was one of those kids who seem to always be a year or two ahead of his classmates physically and he was better at games than I was. He knew it too.

He also knew that he lived on the opposite side of the learning curve from me, so his schoolyard ribbings were his compensation.

"Hey, Kane," he yelled from his shortstop position. "Is Kane your name or what you need to help you run?"

Alvin Giles was pitching for both teams. He turned his head and advised Ralphie to keep it down. Then he explained to me what it was that I was supposed to do.

"You just swing at the ball, Joshua. Try to hit it. Don't worry about how hard. Just try to hit it. When you do you run to that first base over there." He pointed.

Sue Crawford was standing on that base after having connected fairly well, and I was sure I could do the same. I missed completely with my first swing and nearly spun completely around with the effort. Ralphie laughed. I settled in and swung again. This time I fell and the laughter came from everywhere. Even Alvin Giles had his glove in front of his face to conceal the smile. The third time I just tried to punch at the ball with the bat and the snap of the motion tore it out of my hands and it sailed away to land beside the startled principal.

"Strike three, strike three!" Ralphie was screaming. "You're out! You're out, Kane! You hit even worse than the girls!"

"Fun, eh?" John Gebhardt said to me as he passed me on his way to take his turn. He fared no better. His pale, thin arms looked no thicker than the bat, and although he never fell, he failed to make contact. Ralphie was in heaven.

"Hey, Kane," he screeched. "Looks like you guys can form your own team. You can call yourself ... the Spazzes!"

"Yeah. Real fun," John said as we headed out to our turn in the field. "Real fun."

After completely botching the catching process, I was hit in the chest with a ball and John waved weakly at any that came his way. Ralphie, of course, was loving every minute of it and by this time Lenny Weber, Victor Ringle and Teddy Hohnstein had joined his catcalling chorus. Fortunately, recess was only twenty minutes long. We could hear them snickering away behind us on our way up the hill.

"Hey, guys," Ralphie crowed. "We can even have more laughs at lunch hour. The Spazzes get to play for forty-five minutes!"

John's face was drawn into a tight-lipped glare. The rest of the morning passed in that slow, inexorable weight of childhood, when dread is the mood of the moment. We sailed through reading and science like a ship through the doldrums and when the lunch bell rang, John and I looked at each other with the resigned look of kenneled pets. Even town kids brought their lunches and we ate as a class with desks pulled together in small groups for cards, games and conversation. John and I sat together. Ralphie and the boys were wolfing down their sandwiches in gleeful anticipation, while Sue Crawford, Connie Shaus and Lorraine Deiter sat across from us gazing intently at John and giggling and whispering to each other. We looked at each other now and again and slowly chewed the sandwiches that, at least for me, had taken on the consistency of sawdust.

Sides were chosen, with Ralphie and Lenny as captains. John and I were picked last, more out of obligation than any keen desire for our presence on their rosters. We were both dispatched to the last rung of the batting order and to the deepest part of right field when our turns came. Alvin Giles patrolled the edge of the diamond, and even his proximity to things was small comfort to me that day.

For the first while it was smooth sailing. No balls came my way for the first two innings. John had the same good fortune. We simply shrugged at each other as we traded gloves at the end of each turn at bat. The slow trots into right field were filled with the desire for any and all balls to avoid my area. Looking away across the sweep of country over Otter Creek behind the school, I could see the new lush green of pastureland, edged in ragged browns of treeline, the silvery pencil nubs of silos and the gabled edges of barns and outbuildings. Right then I knew I would feel far more comfortable and capable among them than on that playing field.

But Victor Ringle laid into a pitch and the smack of contact woke me from my reverie. The ball landed twenty feet in front of me and began rolling speedily towards me. I ran in awkwardly and bent to pick it up. Somehow it missed my outstretched glove and rolled between my legs to the shrill cheer of Victor's teammates and the dirge-like moan of my own. I pumped my legs crazily to catch up with that rolling ball, which stopped, finally, against the fence at the edge of the Kuntzes' forty acres of alfalfa. I turned to throw but the ball landed fifteen feet in front of an exasperated Lenny Weber at centerfield. "Way to go, Spaz!" he snarled and heaved a hard rope of a throw into Gerhard Metzger at second base. I saw him shrug and shake his head sadly in Ralphie's direction. "Spaz!" was Ralphie's echoing cry.

When Allie Conroy dribbled out to the pitcher, John stepped up to the plate. From where I stood he looked as frail as wheat in a windstorm. The bat, an inconsistent thing, lay limply on his right shoulder. On three consecutive pitches he swung mightily, twisting his back into it and missing by miles. I could hear the hooting and the hollering from my teammates and see the frown of displeasure on Ralphie's face on the sidelines. "Spaz," I saw him mouth slowly, silently, right into John's face. For an instant, John paused with the bat in his hands and half turned towards the smirking bulk of Ralphie. But the moment passed and he moved away.

"Thought you were gonna hit him," I said as I gave him my glove.

"Mighta," he said curtly and jogged away.

I might have too after my debacle. Determined to avoid falling down or throwing the bat, I swung timidly at three pitches. Each time Ralphie hooted away from shortstop, alluding to my girlish demeanor, my rubber arms and how my mother could probably do a better job of baseball, army boots and all. I hated baseball.

"Jocks!" John said to me on our way into the school when the bell rang. "Can't stand 'em."

"Jocks?" I said.

He looked at me with his head cocked. "Yeah. Jocks. As in *jock*-strap? Athletes? Big dopey meat-head morons with muscles? Like *him*!" he said, hooking a thumb towards Ralphie, who was carrying the equipment bag over his shoulder like a hunter slinging a carcass. "They don't use that word around here?"

"Not that I ever heard. At least until now. But you're right. He is a big dopey meat-head moron with muscles!" I said villainously, enjoying my shared venture into spitefulness. We laughed.

"I hate baseball," John said. "It's dumb."

"Yeah. Kind of a waste of good farmland," I said and we laughed again.

"Hey, the girls have got the giggles!" Ralphie said, giving Lenny a nudge in the ribs. "Dress like retards, play like retards," he said with a hiss and disappeared into the school. Lenny looked over his shoulder at us with a look that was equal parts pity and relief. Then he shrugged and followed Ralphie into the building.

"Dipshits," John said, shaking his head.

"Huh?"

He laughed, and the blue eyes sparkled for the first time. "Kane," he said, punching me lightly on the shoulder, "we got a long way to go with you. A *lo-o-ong* way!"

I have always loved the spring. The farmer in me thrills to the knowledge that growth becomes possible again, that life returns in all its various forms, that my hand can guide and direct a portion of it, and the romantic in me picks that one spring out of the forty I've lived to nurture, re-enter and relive. I've become a seasonal prodigal, returning to it as full of expectation, comfort and release as my biblical namesake. Springtime will always be the birthplace of magic and light, though it wasn't at first that spring of '65. With the coming of baseball, school became a burden for the first time. Ralphie and the boys were relentless in their pursuit of a higher level of play and of ridicule. John Gebhardt and I were thrown together like prisoners. For that, I suppose, I owe a world of thanks to the smirking bulk of Ralphie Wendt. Still, my inability to come to terms with a seemingly simple game wore on me.

But frustration, like so many things in life, has an alter ego. Mine was the budding friendship I was discovering with John. We helped each other in lessons and I found that he shared a love of learning and a hunger for a deeper understanding of the things around him. He was quick and he was funny, and he hated Ralphie about as much as we both began to hate baseball.

"Josh," he whispered one lunch hour, leaning forward in his desk, "you can really tell that Ralphie belongs on a farm."

"Really?" I asked. "How?"

"Look at how he eats." Ralphie had this head-down, elbows-up feeding position. "He doesn't dine ... he grazes!"

I smirked and covered my mouth with my hand, horrified at the put-down as well as the pleasure I found in it.

"It's okay, Kane, it's okay," John said. "Yuk it up. It's good for you."

"No wonder he's good at baseball then," I blurted.

"Why's that?" Johnny asked.

"He's more at home in a field!" I said, wide-eyed with excitement.

He laughed. "Good one. Good one. There's hope for you yet, Josh."

We began to spend every moment of our school days together. Naturally, this drew the predictable response from Ralphie and his buddies about birds of a feather, wieners in the same package and shit sticking together. John bristled at the slurs but I shrugged them off, as I'd been taught to do.

"One of these days you're gonna run out of cheeks!" Johnny said to me.

I'd turn in my seat and catch him looking at me every now and again, but he'd always slide into that shy lopsided grin I came to know, look back at his books, out the window or across the room to the blackboard. We came together as easily as the confluence of streams, no turmoil, no roiling backwater, merely a curlicued blending, a sifting together of the textures of the countries between us, an elegant intertwining.

W e groaned.

"So the tournament will take place the third week of June, followed by the biggest picnic you can imagine, with presentations to the winners and those judged Most Valuable to their teams," Alvin Giles was saying. He'd succeeded in setting up a small base-ball tournament between our Grade Five class and the ones in Teeswater and Wingham. "This is a chance to show the kind of athletes we raise in Mildmay! Everyone will play, except those excused for medical reasons."

The rest of the class bubbled with excitement. Johnny and I looked at each other hopelessly. It was bad enough to be forced to play in phys-ed classes in front of our classmates, but now we were to be put on display for three whole communities. We'd taken to walking the perimeter of the schoolyard at recess and lunches, gabbing about anything and everything. The taunting had died down as our lack of interest grew, and we found ourselves looking forward to the privacy of our friendship rather than the acceptance of our peers. For me, baseball was extraneous effort I'd have sooner applied to my studies, and for John, it was neolithic goonery.

"Neo what?" I'd asked.

"Neolithic," he said, his eyes blazing the way they did when he was chasing down an idea. "Neolithic. The age when man invented simple tools and crude weapons. Like bats."

"When was that?"

"Long time ago. Maybe not so long in Ralphie's case."

"Neolithic. I like that word. Sounds soft and fuzzy."

"Soft and fuzzy? Kane! It was the Stone Age! The only thing soft and fuzzy about the Stone Age was our brains. That's why we were goons. Brutes. Louts. Barbarians!" he said, arms flapping up and down in excitement.

"Baseball players?" I asked timidly.

"Baseball players!" he echoed thunderously, one fist pumping at the air. "Yes! Baseball players!"

So the news of the tournament was traumatic. "We're gonna stink!" was Johnny's prediction. "We're gonna stink bad!"

That's why when our phone rang one Friday evening and a frantic Johnny was on the other end, it suprised me.

"Josh, I got it! I got it!" he was saying wildly.

"Got what?"

"The answer!"

"What answer?"

"To baseball!"

"You got the answer to baseball?"

"Yes! Yes! The answer to baseball! I got it *right here!*"

"What is it?"

"I can't tell you over the *phone!* You gotta see it to believe it! I mean, *really!* Wow!"

"Can you bring it to school?"

"Are you *kidding?* I'll pedal out to your place tomorrow and we'll go over it. Bring it to *school?* Josh, we can't share this with *anybody!*"

"Anybody?"

"Well, maybe your parents, because, well, we're kind of going to have to use your place to work this all out," he said, calmer, con-spiratorially. "But you can't tell them right away! We gotta refine some things first. Where are you, anyway?"

"Come straight out Highway 9. Can't miss it. It runs in front of your dad's store. Ride out until you come over this long sloping hill with an old baler sitting by the fence near the road. The next cross-road is ours. Turn left. You'll see our place at the top of the hill going west."

"Got it. Long hill, baler, house on the hill. I'll be there. And Josh?"

"Yeah?"

"This is all hush-hush. *Big* secret. Keep it under your hat."

"What do I tell my folks?"

"Don't tell 'em anything for now. Just say I'm coming to see your farm. Oh, yeah, got any paint?"

"Paint?"

"Yeah. Dig up some paint. See ya!"

"Who was that?" my dad asked over the top of his *Farmers' Almanac*. He read lots in the evenings while my mother knitted, quilted or did the small watercolor paintings she gave to friends and relatives.

"Johnny," I said, uncomfortable with the idea of keeping a secret from them.

"Oh. And how is John?" my mother asked from her chair at the window.

"He's good," I said. "He's coming to visit tomorrow. Is that okay?"

"That's great!" my dad said and winked at my mother. "What are you two going to do?"

"Probably look around the farm and stuff. You know."

"Sure. Has John ever been to a farm?" my mother asked, her hand busy with a stitch.

"I don't know. Probably not," I said, wanting out of this conversation more than anything in my life at that moment.

"Well, that's just fine. Will he stay for supper? Dad can drive him back into town in the evening."

"Don't know. I'll ask when he gets here. Probably. Do we have any paint?"

"What kind of paint, son?" my dad asked.

"Don't know. Any kind."

"There's some in the tool shed we used to redo the stalls last spring. It's whitewash, really. Why do you need paint?"

"Well ... I don't. At least, not really. Just asking. Where in the shed?"

"Top shelf. Sure seem interested in that paint for someone who doesn't *really* need it," he said and winked at my mother again, who smiled.

"Yeah, well, big day tomorrow. Think I'll turn in."

"Turn in? It's only eight o'clock. It's Friday," my mother said, arching her eyebrows in mock surprise.

"Yeah. Well, I'll read or something till I fall asleep. G'night," I said and moved to hug and kiss them before I headed up the stairs.

"Good night, son. Prayers, remember," my mother said.

"Good night, Joshua," my dad said, hugging me a little tighter and tousling my hair. "Painters need their rest, eh, son?"

"Yeah. Good night."

I wasn't that much more talkative the next morning and I caught my parents giving each other those "let's pretend we're not aware of anything" looks. I felt a little relieved about all of this, since I really didn't know what I was keeping secret from them. The morning passed slowly and my dad whistled while he worked, not pressing me for small talk and letting me know by his easy manner that wherever I was that morning was okay with him.

Johnny was sweaty and out of breath when he finally coasted up to our back verandah with a white plastic bag in his carrier basket and a lumpy canvas packsack on his back.

"Hey," he said, with a small wave.

"Hey."

"Long ride."

"Yeah. Is that *it*?" I asked, pointing to the plastic bag.

He glanced back at the house and then glared at me. "Josh! Keep it down, will you? Yes. Well, that and what I've got in my pack."

"The answer to baseball comes in parts?"

"All answers come in parts. That's what makes solving things so much fun. Only the smart ones can assemble the pieces. Like us!" He set the rusted Schwinn against the verandah railing. "Paint?"

"Yeah. In the shed."

"Good. But first, where can we be alone?"

"You're in the middle of three hundred and twenty acres. Take three steps and you're alone!"

"Oh, yeah," he said. "Kinda forgot about that. It's nice out here. Where can we go?"

"Let's go sit in the willow tree. I got a board nailed across big branches halfway up."

"Cool."

My mother appeared with a jug of lemonade and a plate of sandwiches. She beamed at John and set the plate and jug on the bench. "John. It's nice to have you here. How's your parents?"

"Good, ma'am. Thanks," he said quickly, lowering his gaze once he'd shaken her hand.

"You be sure and say hello for us and tell them we'll have to get together sometime soon and compare notes on the two of you characters," she said and disappeared into the house. "Joshua, don't forget to ask John about supper," she called back through the screen door.

"Okay, Mom. I will. Let's go!" I grabbed the plate and jug and led the way around the house.

Johnny swept his wide-eyed gaze all around. "Boy, I wish we had a farm. Sometimes I hate town. Hated Toronto, anyway."

"Big, huh?" I said, beginning to climb the ladder rungs I'd nailed to the trunk of the willow.

"Big and ugly and fast and dirty and too many people," he said, clambering up after me. "No trees like this. This is great!"

The willow sat in the middle of our yard. It was huge, with thick branches low to the ground that I'd discovered were great for climbing when I was about six. When the summer swung into high gear the leaves thickened on the branches and concealed you when you climbed it. It had become my tree fort a couple of summers before and I spent many a lazy afternoon in its shaded coolness, reading, or doing puzzles from a book. It was one of my favorite places, and it felt right taking my new friend up into it. My dad had been the only other human being allowed into its sanctum.

"So what is it?" I asked once we'd pulled the snacks up in a pail on a rope.

"Easy," he said. "Soon enough. Let's have a sandwich."

I slid the plate and jug his way, far too excited to eat. "Come on. Let's see!"

"Okay, okay. But you gotta be sworn to secrecy. At least for now."

"I can keep a secret. I never told my folks about what we're doing."

"That's only 'cause you didn't *know* what we were doing. Once you know it's harder. You gotta pledge."

"Pledge?"

"Yeah. Make a solemn oath," he said, gravely.

"Okay. I pledge."

"Not solemn enough," he said, chewing and digging into his pack. "It's gotta be official. Since this is your special place it's perfect. You Indians always did solemn things in special places."

"We did?"

"Yeah. Vision quests, sun dances, those sorts of things. Always in a special place. So this is kinda right up your alley, being Indian and all."

He produced a needle from a little packet of about a dozen. He licked it and then turned to me.

"Pledges gotta be done in blood. Blood's the most magical ingredient. So, I'm gonna prick your finger and prick mine at the same time and we're gonna rub our fingers together. We'll smear the blood around and promise each other to secrecy and loyalty. Blood brothers."

"Blood brothers?"

"Yeah. Indians do this all the time. I saw it on TV."

"We don't have a TV. Mom says books are better."

"Smart, your mom. But TV's good too sometimes. Ready?"

"I guess."

"Get serious. This is important."

"Okay," I said, trying hard to sound solemn and serious.

He took my finger and with the tip of his tongue pressed between his lips, he pricked me hard with the needle. I jerked back in pain and a little drop of blood appeared. Then, closing his eyes and grimacing, he pricked his own. He looked at me then with that wide-open gaze, took my hand in his and pressed our bleeding fingers together, mashing them around and smearing our blood around.

"Got a warrior name?" he whispered.

"No."

"Me neither. I'll give you one and you can give me one. Then we can pledge. Okay?"

"Sure. What's a warrior name?"

"You know ... like Crazy Horse or Sitting Bull. Something fierce like we have to be."

"Fierce. Hmm. Can it be anything?"

"I think so. As long as it's strong. Animal names are best."

"Animal names. Okay. How about ... Laughing Dog!"

"Laughing Dog? Laughing . . . *dog*? You wanna name me after a dog? What the heck is a laughing dog, anyway? Dogs don't laugh," he said, sounding rather disgusted.

"Well, our neighbors on the north side, the Dietzes, have this big collie dog. He never barks. But when strange people come into their yard he just sits there looking at them with his mouth open and his tongue waggling around. Like he's laughing. They get all comfortable figuring he's quiet. But as soon as they get out of their car, that dog's snarling and growling like a demon. Scares everybody. He did that to my mom one day. My mom says there's nothing scarier than a laughing dog."

"Hey, I like that! Cool. Laughing Dog."

"What's my name?" I asked.

He looked away through the branches for a moment, serious looking and deliberate. Finally, he nodded a few times and looked at me. "Your warrior name is ... Thunder Sky!"

"Thunder Sky? That's not an animal."

"No. But it's cool. And it's strong. Maybe not fierce but it's really strong."

"How?"

"What'd you say?"

"How?"

"And you told me your weren't really Indian!" he said and we laughed. "I picked Thunder Sky 'cause, well, thunder's really loud. Everyone listens. And I think one of these days everyone's gonna listen to you, Josh. Really."

"Wow," I said, humbled. "Thanks."

"Okay, let's pledge. Say like me, only use your warrior name. I, Laughing Dog, pledge to keep this and every secret of my blood brother and to always be loyal and good and kind. Except in battle 'cause that's different. Now you."

"OK," I said slowly, "I, Thunder Sky, pledge to keep this and every secret of my blood brother and to always be loyal and good and kind. Except in battle 'cause that's different."

We looked at each other, uncertain of what was next and lost in the importance of the moment. I had never had a brother and now, through this strange ritual, I was tied by the solemn oath of friendship to the heartbeat of my blood brother, John Gebhardt, Laughing Dog. I knew that I would do anything in my power to stay loyal and kind and good to him. He smiled, licked his finger clean and reached for another sandwich.

"Cool," he said. "Ready?"

"Ready? I've been ready since you phoned me!"

"Okay, then. Here it comes!"

He opened the plastic bag and placed two books face-down on the plank. In my mind he'd discovered a strange and wonderful device that maybe could alter gravity, or some magnetic force that attracted horsehide to wood, or a magical glove that caught anything. Mere books were a let-down.

"That's it? We're going to *read* about baseball?"

"That's exactly what we're going to do. Look," he said and turned the first book over. The title spread in huge red letters across the cover with the figure of a man swinging a bat at a ball. *Baseball in Words and Pictures*. "This is going to unlock all the doors. It tells everything about everything about baseball. Look."

We spent the next half hour or so paging slowly through that book, casually munching sandwiches, sloshing lemonade and lifting our eyebrows towards each other in emphasis at certain images. For the first time we saw diagrams of proper throwing technique, how to perform a hook slide, the correct positioning of feet for infielders, the dip and kneel required for blocking ground balls with the body, how to lean while running to scoop grounders, how to take a proper leadoff once you'd reached base, the best way to grip the bat, how to swing and the elements required to lay a bunt down along either foul line.

"Wow," I said finally. "Baseball's like a world."

"Yeah," he said. "And a world's gotta have rules. Science. As long as there's science to it, how dumb can it be?"

"There's math too. Look at all the measurements."

"Science and math. I figure, since we're good at both of them and Ralphie and Lenny and those guys are such clods, we study this book, practice this stuff, we can't help but be better than them. Am I right?"

It seemed right. Studying was second nature to us both and the practice part was just the discipline my parents had taught me. "Yeah. That's right. Study and practice. Let's do it!"

"Okay, but first. Look at this!"

He turned the second book over slowly, reverently almost. It had a pale green cover with a photo of a man swinging a bat. His swing had twisted him around so that his ankles were crossed and the bat came to rest far over his shoulder. It gave the impression of great power. The word *Boston* was splayed across the front of his gray jersey. The title read *The Science of Hitting, by Ted Williams*."

"Wow," I said. "The *Science* of Hitting."

"Yeah. And this guy was the best! He batted for a four hundred average when most guys fight to hit two fifty."

"What's that mean?"

"It means he hit the ball more often in the same amount of chances as everyone else. In here he says it's the hardest thing in the world to do. To hit a pitched baseball."

"Why?"

"Because you gotta hit one round thing with another round thing."

"It says science, Johnny."

"That's right. This book shows you everything about hitting. We study this and we're gonna be like Ted Williams."

And we disappeared into the diagrams and explanations of that book. The answer to baseball, apparently, was baseball itself. We looked into another world that afternoon. A world filled with wonder and possibility. A world as full of precise laws and rules as our own. Laws and rules that could be studied, mastered and conquered. We saw it as a world that could be navigated with those two books as our maps and charts, and a world that was far more than some simple game for simple minds. The mathematics and the science coupled with the resounding echoes of those schoolyard catcalls, were the enticement to try, and somewhere in our young boy minds was the belief that this game could make us more, lift us above and beyond the fields and concrete around our lives and on into the realm of magic. Science was reality, the explainable and the game itself, the magic that we hungered for.

"Wow," I said when we'd been through both books twice.

"Wow is right. Who'd have figured it was so complicated? I gotta try this stuff," Johnny said. "Oh, yeah. Here's a present."

He pulled a glove out of his pack. It was new and redolent with possibility like new gloves are. Sliding it onto my hand felt as natural as warm mitts in winter. *Wilson* was inked in big curly letters and the deep, shadowy pocket seemed to call out to flying objects like a siren to disoriented sailors. My first glove.

"Wow," I said again. "Thanks, Johnny. Where'd you get it?"

"My dad's store. There's a bunch of stuff in boxes in the basement and I found them. I got one too. And a couple balls," he said, slipping his new glove on.

"Wanna go try?" I asked rhetorically.

"Yeah. But where?" he asked. "I mean, I wanna look like I know what I'm doing before anyone sees us. You know?"

"Yeah, I know. No one ever goes behind the equipment shed. My dad sometimes but usually in the mornings. Let's go there."

"Okay. Josh?"

"Yeah?"

"Blood brothers, right?"

"Blood brothers," I said and we shook hands solemnly before climbing out of that tree and down into a world that seemed bigger somehow, more focused, brighter, backlit with possibility.

The paint, it turned out, was for outlining a strike zone on the wall of the shed. We got the general dimensions from the words and pictures in the book, and I stood close to the wall as

Johnny described a rough rectangle with the whitewash between the height of my knees and my chest. Then we scouted around the outbuildings for a piece of board, which we cut into a seventeen-inch length that we whitewashed as well. "The plate," Johnny said quietly. "We can use what's left as the pitcher's rubber." He'd brought a tape measure, and we measured out sixty feet, six inches from where we laid the plate and placed the pitcher's rubber down. Then we painted a similar rectangle on the wall of the shed on the opposite side of the new plate. "Lefties" was all Johnny said, and I nodded in agreement. By the time we'd finished we were splattered with whitewash, dusty and hot. But it all looked like the diagrams in the book. My dad had passed by a few times, whistling jauntily and pretending not to notice what we were carrying, where we were going or the paint that covered us.

That first afternoon we tossed the ball back and forth for about an hour and a half. Each time it prescribed a loose arc between us and we spent a lot of time chasing it down before returning the throw. The words-and-pictures book was laid in the shade of a chokecherry tree by the fence and we wandered over to it again and again to peruse the section on proper throwing technique. What seemed so natural on the page was much harder to realize once you'd gotten ready, thought about it and then tried to do it. Slowly through that ninety minutes, we traveled the distance between what the mind wanted and what the body could achieve. The throws became throws. Our catches were fumbling, awkward efforts, but by the end of that first afternoon we were both making adequate grabs at least half of the time. I knew that the look of grim determination that slowly transformed itself into joyful satisfaction on Johnny's face was mirrored in my own.

"Okay. The book says that the pitcher looks at where he's going to throw," Johnny said. "Then he steps in that direction. Right?" We were headed towards the house and the supper he'd agreed to readily when I'd mentioned it.

"Right. Pushing off with his back foot," I answered.

"And the throwing arm follows his weight forward over the line of the shoulder."

"Yes. Over-hand delivery. Using the shoulder, elbow and wrist. Stepping forward keeps it straight," I said.

"Right. You did good."

"Hey, you too."

"Tomorrow?" he asked.

"You bet. Do you think we should play at school on Monday? You know, get some practice?"

"Are you *crazy!*" he shouted, arms beginning that erratic flapping. "We don't play at school until the tournament. That gives us six weeks to tune up. Remember, you pledged."

"Wow. So all we do for six weeks is get ready? Every day like today?"

"Yeah. Training."

"Wow. Okay."

"But remember, Josh, you can't tell anyone. Not your parents, not anyone. For a while anyway."

"I got it. How long?"

"Till we're good."

"How long will that take?"

"After today? Not too long," he said. "Not too long at all."

Of all the farmer's rituals, the one I love the best is the washing up. The sweat and grit of the land mixed with the flowered aroma of the soap has always induced deep pangs of hunger in me. But it's the tactile facet of the ritual that charms me. Land and water, the stuff of life, coming together in a familiar rubbing of the hands and splashing of the face. I've always thought of it as the one human ceremony that joined us all, primordial to present, Bedouin to fisherman to farmer, linked forever by well-scrubbed hands and the common delight in a meal well taken. Scrubbing and rubbing the whitewash, dirt and perspiration from me that day was pure boyhood glee.

Johnny was coming out of the other bathroom off the kitchen by the time I got back downstairs. The afternoon in the sunshine had tanned him a little and he looked far healthier than the pale reed of a boy I'd first seen at his grandfather's. He grinned and held a finger up to his lips. I nodded, and we headed into the living room to await my mother's call to supper. Life without television leads people to a level of invention unseen in more electronically attuned homes. Cards, board games and hobbies were the television of the day back then, and although we had an Electrohome console with record player and radio, it was seldom used. My mother's gospel records and Mozart concertos and my dad's Floyd Cramer and Chet Atkins records were as close as we ever came to contemporary entertainment. "Cool," Johnny said and headed over to the unit as soon as we entered the room. He fiddled with the radio dials and for the next minute or two the room was filled with snippets of sound, until he finally heard what he wanted and eased up the volume.

"Curt Gowdy here on a day that's seen some dramatic ups and downs at Tiger Stadium. The visiting Boston Red Sox lead the Tigers by a run in the seventh, erasing a three-run deficit on the homer by Tony Conigliaro. Tony C.'s bat is in fine form this season after his sensational rookie year last year. Twenty-four balls cleared the fences for the Fenway faithful last year, and he's on his way to eclipse that mark this campaign."

"See, Josh, baseball's everywhere!" Johnny chortled. "We can even watch it on the TV at my place sometimes."

"Wow. I've never seen a real game before."

"Me neither, really. We never watch it at my place."

We settled into chairs to listen to the mellifluent voice that flowed from the radio and although we both had some trouble identifying the situations he was describing, we listened intently, eager to hear anything that might give us a hint, an edge, an advantage in this game we were discovering. When my mother entered carrying a small tray of cheese and crackers, Johnny leapt for the volume control, spun to greet my mother and smiled shyly all in one flash of motion.

"Hi!" he said, managing to sound casual.

My mother grinned and set the tray down on the coffee table. "Well, hello, John! What are you boys listening to?" she asked secretively.

"Oh, nothing really. Just stuff. Checking around, you know," Johnny said, looking hard at me and pumping his fist against his thigh.

"Yeah," I said, smiling. "Just stuff. How's supper?"

"It's ready. We're just waiting on your father to come in. Roast pork, beans, potatoes, beets and pie for dessert. Sound okay to you, John?"

"Oh, yes, ma'am. Great."

"Well, you boys enjoy the snacks and have fun with the radio," she said and returned to the kitchen.

Johnny sighed with relief. I was beginning to discover that secrets were a hard thing to maintain. We munched on the cheese and crackers and listened to Curt Gowdy call the rest of that game before my father came in, washed up and whistled his way into the kitchen. Tiger Stadium was in Detroit, which was only a day's drive away, but it was the sound of the Boston team, the Red Sox, with players named Carl Yastrzemski, Rico Petrocelli, Tony Horton and especially Tony Conigliaro that drew our hopes that day. Their names sounded like working men's names. The kind of men I was used to seeing around me. Callused, gritty, down-to-earth and diligent men with families like my own, battered cars, hearty appetites and a chair on a porch they eased into when their days closed in upon themselves like the blooms on a rosebush. My mother's call to supper broke our reverie, and we gave each other a firm thumbs-up and marched in to eat.

My mother bowed her head for grace. Johnny looked uncomfortable, though he politely followed suit. She finished her blessing and my father and I followed with a diminished "Amen" before we raised our heads and looked at each other. Looking at each other, recognizing our presence and our connection, was as much of a ritual as the offering of grace. Again, Johnny appeared discomfited, but he nodded his head at each of us and grinned shyly.

"Well," my dad said, "this is a fine spread, Mother. Joshua, please hand the meat to John and let's get at this feast! You boys must be hungry after all the painting you were doing."

Johnny and I looked wide-eyed at each other as he reached for the platter and I saw my parents trade a smirk.

"What were you painting, son?" my mother asked.

"Nothing, really. Just fooling around," I said, uncomfortable with the lie.

"Nothing really?" my dad said, voice rising. "There's some kind of work of art on the equipment shed and you say 'nothing really.' John?"

"Umm. Well, it's kind of a secret, sir," Johnny said, reaching out to secure the potato dish I was offering his way.

"Oh," my dad said. "Secrets. Well. There's good secrets and there's bad secrets, I suppose. Would this be one of the good secrets, John?"

"Yessir. It's a good secret, eh, Josh?"

"Yeah. It's a school project," I said. Johnny raised his eyes at my cleverness.

"Will we get to see this project when it's finished?" my mother asked.

"Yes, ma'am," Johnny said. "Everyone will get to see it."

"Well, that's good," my father said. "And when will that be?"

"Don't know. Maybe ... two weeks?" Johnny said, grimacing.

"That doesn't seem like too long to wait," my mother said.

"Two weeks. Hmm. Well, I guess I can rest my worries about my equipment shed for two weeks. You guys aren't going to move it or anything, are you?" he asked.

"Oh, no, sir," Johnny said. "It'll be right there when we're done."

"Good. Good. How's the folks, John?" he asked.

Johnny gulped down a mouthful of beans. He glanced around at us and I could sense his uneasiness with this turn of conversation. "Fine, sir. They're fine." He shoveled in a mouthful of potatoes.

"Your dad's never worked in the hardware business before, has he, John?" my mother asked quietly.

"No, ma'am."

"And your mom. What does she plan to do in Mildmay? Will she work?" she asked.

"No, ma'am. She doesn't work. I don't know what she'll do."

"We'll have to have them out here one of these days for a visit. We'd like that," my mother said, smiling at Johnny.

"They don't go out much, ma'am."

"Surely they'd come to meet your new friend's family?" she asked, surprised.

"No, ma'am. I kind of don't think so."

"Well, we'll work on that," she said, kindly.

"Your dad's not really a stranger to hardware, John," my dad said. "I remember when we were kids, he was always helping your grandfather out in the store after school. Nuts and bolts and things are in his blood. Just like Joshua here with farming. No matter what he does or where he goes in life, he's always going to have the farm and the land in his blood. He was born to it."

"I didn't think my dad was ever a kid."

"Pardon me, John?" my mother said.

"Nothing. Can I have some more beans, please," he said, with the energy withdrawing from his face like I'd seen at the welcoming. My parents looked over at him with concern and then at each other.

"Pass the beans, Joshua," my mother said.

"So what is it you like to do, John? Do you have hobbies? Sports? You don't happen to fish, do you?" my dad asked, with a wink at me.

"Fish? No, sir. I've never been fishing. I'd like to, though. Mostly I just read, sir."

"Well, reading's good," he said. "Joshua reads all the time too. What do you like to read about?"

"Indians, mostly, sir."

"Indians?"

"Yessir. I like 'em."

"You know that Joshua's an Indian, don't you, John?" my mother asked.

"Yes, ma'am. But I mean *real* Indians. You know, warriors and stuff."

"I think there's more to Indians than just being warriors, isn't there, John?" my dad asked.

"No, sir. I read about it. They were warriors."

"Joshua's not a warrior," my mother said.

"Yes, ma'am. That's what I mean. *Real* Indians."

The rest of that meal passed amiably with my parents chatting about the farm, the animals and the crops and Johnny and me eating as hungrily as boys can eat, grinning at each other now and then, happy with the secrets of baseball and blood brotherhood.

I had a sense that these secrets were leading me up and away from the nest of security I'd always found in the friendship with my parents and I teetered on the edge of flight, wings flexing slightly, eager for the adventure of the air.

My dad drove Johnny back to town at twilight. We strapped his bike to the roof and sat in the front seat together, and we grinned when my father started whistling a slow version of "Sally Gooden" while he drove. No one spoke, we just watched the road and the setting sun over the ripple of hills, the cows in the fields and the hawks swooping low over them. It was a comfortable silence. Now and then Johnny would turn his head and we'd exchange a grin, joined forever by our mingled blood and our solemn pledge. Such are the bonds of Indians and of boys.

We pulled up in front of Old Man Givens's place. The Gebhardts had moved into it after turning down Harold's offer to live with him. Old Man Givens was about ninety-five when he'd passed away the year before. He'd known everything and anything about everybody. He'd watched generations of boys become men and girls become women, friendships formed and ended, marriages, funerals, farm foreclosures and Mildmay itself move from shabby hamlet to bustling agricultural center for the county. Farmers liked Mildmay. Walkerton with its three thousand people was like a city in our scope of things and Mildmay was, and is, the unofficial center of Bruce County.

Old Man Givens had watched it all evolve, and the days when he was well enough to make the journey to Harold's store were days rich with storytelling and laughter. His wrinkled, bony fingers pointed out individuals, and the crowd huddled around the coffee station listened intently while he recounted embarrassing escapades of their younger days. His passing left us shallower somehow. I remember him for the smell of snuff and old houses and the lollipops he always seemed to have for any kids lurking around the store those days. I was glad that Johnny was living in his house.

We were pulling the ropes that secured the bike when Ben Gebhardt appeared on the porch. He was reeling slightly and he leaned on the porch column.

"John! Is that you, you little bastard? Get in here!" he growled.

"Evening, Ben. Everything okay?" my dad asked, handing the bike down to Johnny.

Ben Gebhardt squinted through the haze of twilight. "Who's that?"

"It's Ezra Kane, Ben. I've just driven John back from visiting us."

"Ezra? Well, thank you very much, Ezra Kane," he said theatrically, with a sweep of his arm. "God'll love ya for that. Now send the little prick in here and we can get to bed!"

"You gonna be okay, John?" my dad asked, putting a hand on Johnny's shoulder.

"Yessir. He's always like this. Good night, sir. Josh," Johnny said and started to trot the bike towards the porch.

"Good night," I said.

"Coulda phoned, ya little prick!" Ben said as Johnny passed him on his way into the house.

"Good night, Ben," my father called, and Ben Gebhardt offered a lazy flick of the hand as he followed Johnny into the dark house. A single light burned in an upstairs window and I saw a flicker there and then Mrs. Gebhardt's gaunt face peering out at us. She held the gaze for a moment and then she was gone. The door slammed and we looked at each other before climbing back into the car.

"What a grouch!" I said when we'd reached the edge of town.

"He was drunk, son."

"Drunk?"

"Yes. People get kind of ugly sometimes when they've had too much to drink."

"Like beer, you mean?"

"Yes, like beer. Other kinds of alcohol too."

"You and grampa have beer at threshing."

"That's true. But there's a difference between having a beer or two and drinking too much."

"What's that?"

"Well, too much means you don't care much what you say, who you say it to or even how you say it."

Like Johnny's dad?"

"Yes. Like Johnny's dad."

"Will he be okay?"

"Johnny?"

"No, his dad. He looked kind of sick."

"I'm sure he'll be fine, son. I'm sure he'll be fine," he said and reached over to rub my shoulder.

We drove the rest of the way in silence. The kind of silence that good friends share when they're busy with their thoughts. I don't know where my dad was in his thoughts that night, but I know that I was in the branches of the willow tree, feeling the prick of pin on flesh and the weight of the words we'd spoken. Laughing Dog and Thunder Sky. Blood brothers. Guardians of a secret and of each other. Friends. As our headlights pierced the night and framed the highway ahead of us, I offered a silent prayer of thanks to the God of the universe for bringing me Johnny Gebhardt. I lay my head down upon my father's lap as he drove and the hum of the tires eased me into sleep. I felt him pick me up, cradle me in his arms and carry me into the house and even though I could have made it on my own, I surrendered myself to the brawn of his arms, the warmth of his shirt, the gentle nuzzle of his lips on my cheek and the whispered words, "I love you, son," that I whispered over and over to myself as I drifted into sleep in the downy comfort of my bed, my new baseball glove tucked beneath my pillow. Such are the bonds of Indians and of boys.

I could have killed you when you came out with Laughing Dog that day. I mean, really. I wanted a warrior name to beat all warrior names. Something on a grander scale than Laughing Dog, though now, after all this time, I have to tell you that it fits me. Laughing Dog. Canus Satiricus. I've become far too cynical for the Lightning Hawk, Mountain Bear or Wolverine that I imagined myself to be. Funny, eh? I think we all dream sometimes of names other than out own. Like maybe if we live another name we could maybe live another life. That's what I thought back then. That if I could have a fearless, independent name, then I could be fearless and independent too. That's what I thought I wanted. Needed. But no, you come out with Laughing Dog after the Dietzes' mangy collie. I hated that dog. Not because he was such a bad pooch. Just on principle.

But you know the funny thing? Whenever I go back there in my mind, I always remember the night more than I remember the day. You and your dad dropping me off at the house and my dad coming out to the porch all sloshed and angry. I hated that son-of-a-bitch right then. Not that his drunkenness or his anger was foreign to me. I'd been through that inning lots. But that night man, I was filled with light for the first time. Light, Josh. Your parents, that day, the way I felt around you and the way we both latched onto the idea of the game. And secrets. When you live the way my mom and I had to live, you get used to having secrets. You just can't share them with anybody. Not even each other, even though it's the same life. They become evil somehow. Like you're trapped by them but at the same time, you know that letting them out will trap you even more.

Too bad. Kids and secrets should be indivisible. The world of kids is filled with a lot more magic and mystery than the world of adults, and you pretty much have to have secrets so their grown-up sense of reality can't wash away the magic. Sharing your secrets is all part of the kinship in being a kid. And suddenly, I had a secret and someone to share it with. Someone to trust. Everything was filled with light and I was too. It was like the feeling you get coming out of a long tunnel in the road. It's so bleak and dark and chilled in there, you think it's a permanent condition. Then the light hits your eyes so suddenly you blink. You think you're going blind because the intensity of things is too much and it takes forever for your mind and your eyes to register color, shade and texture. Dazzled. You get dazzled by the light. You Christians call it rapture, I think. Us warriors call it getting vision. Either way, it's the world and Creation opening up its inner life to you, spooking you some by its radiance.

That's what I felt that day. Spooked but hopeful. Hope was a precious commodity in our house, so I clung to the little I had like the proverbial reed. And then him. Of all the things I never had and all the things he took away, I hate him most for taking away the light that day. When I walked away from you and your dad and into that house, I felt like I was walking back into the tunnel. The world, my world, closing in on me with all its shabbiness, dinginess and darkness. I quit crying over that bastard sometime in Toronto but I cried that night. For me. My mom. For the light. Funny. That's what I remember most about that day. Crying. It felt good.

Keeping secrets demands routine. Johnny and I began practicing baseball every chance we could get and that demanded a strict regimen of movement. For me it meant that my schedule of school, study and chores remained the same while I fit baseball into the corners of my life. Johnny, who had far more free time, began coming out every evening after school with his bike crammed onto the schoolbus. We'd chat with my mother for a few polite minutes and then head to my room with peanut butter sandwiches to leaf through the baseball magazines and cards we were collecting on the sly.

We analyzed everything. The players in the magazines were critiqued for their proper or improper body alignment. The statis-

tics on the cards were computed and the players rated for their effi-
ciency or lack thereof. Science and math. We were becoming eloquent in our unraveling of hidden meaning, motion and
application. We knew from the Ted Williams book, for instance,
that more bat speed meant more power. Using the hips generated
more speed and follow through. We knew that everyone has a
sweet spot, a place in their strike zone where the most power could
be directed into the ball, and that higher batting averages could be
had for learning your high and low contact zones. We knew that
leverage was everything in throwing and hitting. Leverage was
achieved by using the body correctly, and we practiced in front of
my mirror for hours, going through our throwing motions, our hitting motions with the thumb of our bottom hand clasped in the fist
of our top hand, watching each other, critiquing, cajoling and
encouraging. We knew that better baseball was better fundamentals and we drilled each other on correct thinking about techniques.

Soon we had favorite players in our swelling collection of bub-
ble-gum cards. Mine were all Red Sox — Conigliaro, Petrocelli and
Yastrzemski. Johnny, who shared my sentiments about Yaz and
Tony C., also cheered on Maury Wills, Orlando Cepeda and Al
Kaline. Good-natured arguments about our choices erupted often,
especially when we assumed their identities during our batting
pantomimes.

"Petrocelli's at the plate. Bottom of the ninth in Fenway. Two
on, the game tied. Here's the pitch!" I'd say.

"He's out!"

"Out? He hits a single!"

"Come on, Josh! His average is too low. He'd strike out."

"Yeah, and Kaline would homer?"

"Yeah."

"Just like that?"

"Just like that."

"Johnny?"

"Yeah?"

"You dream too much."

"I dream too much? You just had Petrocelli make a big hit and

I dream too much!"

Once supper was finished we'd race each other to the equipment shed. My parents didn't press us for details. They respected our secret and waited for it to be revealed. Of course, we both knew that they knew, that their knowledge of our secret was their secret too, but we respected each other too much to ever let on. We went through our charades casually, and those mealtimes were rife with chatter and gossip and laughter. Johnny became like one of the family, and if he didn't want to speak about his own, we allowed him his reticence. We talked of tests and schoolwork while my parents shared farm business and stories of their childhoods. Johnny and I laughed at their reminiscences. Our world of science and math precluded things like horses and buggies, butter churns and hand-milking. We traded winks a lot during those conversations.

Johnny had come up with the idea of using an India rubber ball. One of us would stand on the pitcher's rubber and practice throwing into the strike zone, while the other lined up beside him and ran in to retrieve the rebounds, or grounders as they were called. We switched after every twenty-five pitches, and it wasn't long before we were hitting the strike zone every time and scooping the grounders routinely, either on the run or kneeling down to block their progress with our bodies like in the diagrams in the words-and-pictures book. Our arms grew strong and our legs fluid with accustomed motion. After two weeks we measured out the distance to second base and began to throw from there. The fielder's responsibility was to fire the ball to second base as soon as he gathered in the grounder.

Those evenings were filled with the solid whack of the India rubber ball on the equipment-shed wall, the scrape of running feet on earth and the grunts of satisfaction for a play well made. We were proud of our command of the fundamentals of fielding and throwing, and the challenge soon shifted to achieving a higher average of successful strikes and scooped grounders. We stopped at one hundred each time for easier computation.

"Your fielding's slipping, Josh. You're down to an .850 average."

"I am not. I'm .900."

"Last night, yeah. Over*all* you're .850."

"Over*all*?" I asked.

"Yeah. Over*all*."

"You know what that means, then?" I asked.

"You're gonna work harder?" Johnny replied.

"No," I said. "It means I'm not wearing overalls anymore!"

By week three, we'd invented a strategy for flyballs. We hadn't yet figured out how to get ourselves a bat so invention was the name of the game. One of us would stand at the pitcher's rubber and heave the ball high against the gabled eaves of the shed. The other would close his eyes and flick them open as soon as he heard the whack of ball on wood, locate the ball in the air and run to catch it. At first it was frustrating. It was a demanding skill. But eventually, with determination, we bagan to master it. Our gloves grew softer and our instincts grew sharper. We were making running catches effortlessly and our throws had force, velocity and pinpoint accuracy. The science and math of things was making it all possible.

"It makes an arc as it flies," Johnny said.

"Yep."

"All we need to do is learn how to follow that arc."

"Yep. And be there when it lands."

"Right. And it will land in our *glove*," I said.

"Just like Kaline."

"Yaz."

"Kaline."

"Yaz."

"Dreamer," he said.

"Ditz."

Those first three weeks flew by. On weekends we practiced longer. If it rained we practiced in front of the mirror, listened to the game on the radio, compared notes on players or read one of the baseball books Johnny was uncovering all the time at the Mildmay library. Our lives became richer with the images and sounds of the game. Durocher, Yawkey, Jackie Robinson, Shoeless Joe, Pee Wee Reese, The Say Hey Kid, Dizzy, Satchel Paige and Juan Marichal became etched into our consciousness. We began to eat, sleep, think and dream baseball. Johnny said using regulation-size balls and distances was the best way for us to prepare for the tournament. According to his view, learning to control the rules and motions of the smaller ball and the bigger distances meant using the larger softballs would be a cinch. It made sense to me. I'd learned all about the benefits of smaller and faster over larger and slower from chasing chickens and herding cows. It was far easier to herd cows.

School demanded even more routine. The schoolyard games went on every day but we resisted the temptation to test our newfound skills in competition. We settled for watching warily on our walks around the edge of the field. Alvin Giles was disappointed with our lack of participation, but he'd been around boys long enough to know that not everyone liked the rough and tumble of sport. Johnny and I were at the top end of the class academically, so neither he nor Mrs. Thompson encouraged us to join in if we were not so inclined. For their part, Ralphie and the boys let us be. We were called sissies and whiners. Johnny and I just grinned. We knew from our cursory scannings that Ralphie and company were operating at a lower level of fundamentals than we were and that their chances of catching us scholastically were next to impossible. Sue Crawford was making eyes at Johnny all the time now and that seemed to rile Ralphie, who'd had designs on Sue's attentions since Grade Three. Johnny relished that, too.

As the tournament crept closer, it became obvious that all three communities were eager for the day. Teeswater and Wingham were keen rivals of any Mildmay team. Naturally, the sporting excitement spread to the families. Gatherings of any sort were a challenge to the ladies, who went out of their way to provide a galaxy of foodstuff. Already, baking was under way and plans made for culinary contributions while the men talked of things like a horseshoe tournament, an afternoon away from the farm and whose kid was the best at ball. They always referred to it as *ball*, which drove Johnny and me crazy. It was *base*ball. Not softball, not slow pitch, but *base*ball. Pure and simple.

We laughed now when a good catch was made and shouted praise for a hard, accurate throw. The more we disappeared into the effort of the game, the more the numbers and the analysis disappeared too. We kept the cards and the books, but we read them and shared them in different ways. Now the careful scrutiny for form and function was being replaced by a reverential awe at the pictures of Ted Williams, Lou Gehrig and Cy Young. We quit trying to copy their stances and tried instead to articulate their spirit in our play. Play. The game was becoming a game in our hearts and minds and we abandoned ourselves to it utterly.

Science and math were being replaced by something far grander in scope and magnitude. Each time we arrived behind that equipment shed became like an arrival at a shrine. Our feet hit the soil of that playing area and it was like stepping into our true selves. Together. Baseball became the root of our friendship and it manifested itself in the grunts and groans, sweat and smiles of the challenge of playing a simple game at a high level. Each level of technique and experiment brought us closer. Every element of grace our ten-year-old bodies were able to bring to our play transferred itself by osmosis to the fiber of our friendship.

Finally, unable to keep her knowledge of the secret any longer, my mother said one night as we prepared to dash from the table, "Okay. Just what is it you two have been up to all this time? What are you doing out there?"

And I will never forget the words Johnny used.

"We're inventing baseball."

I lived in a family whose lives flowed forward like the supple line of hills beyond our farm. There were no distances to be traveled, no geographies charted or destinations planned beyond the faith that we would all gather together in a common place when the journey of living was over. Kane family tradition, steeped in a rich Protestant farmer history, meant only that compliance to the will of God, obedience to His commandments and working demonstrations of those precepts in our daily lives were all the plan and plotting that were needed. "Becoming" was a process dictated only by the anonymous hand of loving kindness that connected everything.

There were no arguments and there was no control other than the nurturing guidance my parents provided me. I was encouraged to look in books besides the Bible for the ways of the world beyond the borders of our small farm, and the only silly question that existed for me then was the one that went away unasked.

My parents knew the ways of that outside world and unlike more fundamentalist believers, encouraged me to encounter it, experience and learn from it. They were there like sentinels, watching over me, providing me with answers as they were needed and sheltering me only with the knowledge that my home and my God were my safety, my refuge and my source of strength. I can't remember a time when I didn't want to be there. Stepping into my life each morning of my childhood was like stepping into an old and favorite pair of slippers, finding them loose and comfortable. Slipping out of that life each evening was like the dimming of a lamp, gradual and easy with no sudden rise of shadow.

"Josh?"

Yeah?"

"Do you think I could come and stay with you guys?"

"Stay with us?"

"Yeah. Not always. Just sometimes."

"When?"

"I don't know. Just sometimes."

"I guess. I'll ask, okay?"

"Hey, thanks, Josh."

I was the only one surprised by Johnny's question. My parents reacted almost as though they'd been expecting it. My dad lay down his fork slowly and deliberately and my mother straightened slowly in her chair like they always did when there was a decision to be made about the farm or money. I looked at them and waited. My dad rested his forearms on the table and looked at me with an expression that was as close to sadness as I could remember seeing on his face. My mother sighed softly and cradled her hands in her lap.

"We can't do that, son. I'm sorry," he said.

"We'd like to, Joshua. We'd really like to. We love John and we want to help him ... But we can't. Not right now," my mother said.

"He doesn't want help," I said. "He just wants to stay with us sometimes."

"In his own way, son, Johnny's asking us to help him," my father said.

"Help him with what?"

"With his life, son," my mother said and reached over to pat my hand. "Johnny's not having a very happy life at home."

"How come?"

"Well, do you remember when we drove him home the first time? The way his dad was?" my father asked.

"You said he was drunk."

"That's right. Do you remember what I told you about people who drink too much?"

"Yeah. You said sometimes they don't care what they say, how they say it or who they say it to."

He smiled. "That's right, son. Well, Ben Gebhardt doesn't care a lot of the time. It's not so bad a thing to drink in your home, that's a person's choice. But Ben drinks everywhere."

"Everywhere?"

"Yes. Even at the store. People have been talking about how he smells like liquor most of the time and how forgetful he is about things."

"Gordon Shaus needed a big crescent wrench to adjust the auger in his granary," my mother explained. "He told Mr. Gebhardt what he needed and why and told him it was important that he have it quickly. Mr. Gebhardt said he'd order it and never did. He forgot."

My dad said, "I drove into town one day for wood screws. Ben was dropping them all over the floor trying to get them out of the tray because his hands were shaking so much. He needed a drink, son."

"When someone drinks all the time they get so that they need it all the time," my mother said. "Their body needs it. When their body doesn't get it, or get enough, they start to shake. They get sick."

"Mr. Gebhardt's sick?"

"Yes, Joshua," my mother said softly.

"Should he go to the hospital?"

"Well, maybe, son." My father looked at me affectionately. "But Ben's sick in a different way." He looked at my mother.

"Remember King David?" she said.

"Yeah."

"Remember how in one of the Psalms David cries out to the Lord?"

"Yeah. His heart is heavy, you said. Mr. Gebhardt's heart is heavy?"

"Yes. He's sad inside. That's why he drinks," she explained.

"But what made him sad inside?"

"No one knows that but Mr. Gebhardt himself," my mother said.

"Can't we help him?"

"Son, the only way we can help Ben and his family is to stay out of things right now," my dad said. "That's why we can't help John by letting him stay with us. Even sometimes. See, Ben's got to get to the point where he can't stand himself drinking. Until he does that, nothing anyone else can do will help him."

"And letting Johnny stay with us wouldn't be helping him?"

"That's right," my mother said. "But for now we can be John's friends and support him and show him our love. But we can't interfere with family business, even though we'd like to. But Mr. Gebhardt can't recover if we step in and interfere."

"What's recover?"

She smiled. "It's what everyone who gets a heavy heart needs to do. You know when our calves are born and they slide out of their mother's belly all covered in wet, gooey slime?"

"Yeah."

"Well, when we're born we're covered in that too. Every baby is. It's what God sends babies into the world with to protect them before their mothers can take over. But we're covered in other things too."

"Like what?"

"Well, when God gives us life He brings us out into the world covered in His love. And His love is made up of things like kindness, gentleness, honesty, forgiveness, humility and respect, loyalty and love itself. We're all born covered in those things, right, Ezra?"

"Yes, Mother. That's how we're born, son. All of us. But then, Joshua, we start to move around in our lives and sometimes, well, life is hard. Sometimes it's so hard that those things we're born with get rubbed off. That protective coating gets removed somehow and we get heavy-hearted. Some people don't know how to deal with their heavy hearts and they drink. When they do the alcohol removes the last part of that covering. It gets washed off."

"But God never forgets us. Even if we forget Him," my mother explained. "He knows how much we need that covering to protect us and He allows us to hurt. When we hurt enough and we turn to Him for help, He allows us to begin to *re*-cover ourselves in His love, with all of those things we come covered in. But we have to *want* to. No one can make us and no one can tell us. We have to want it."

"So sometimes God lets us get sick?" I asked.

"Yes," she said.

"And then He lets us make ourselves better? To re-cover ourselves?"

"With His help, yes."

"Right in our home."

"Right in our home," she echoed.

"I like that. God's kind of like Doc Niedermayer."

"How's that, son?" my dad asked.

"Well ... He's still willing to make house calls."

They laughed.

Baseball had become more than a game and more than a trial, because we had come to love it. It had become a part of who we were, part of our smell, our laughter, how we looked at things, the way we felt when we held it, and something that always made us bigger somehow. Inventing baseball, he had said. I guess all of us invent the things we love. Losing ourselves so completely in the nuance and gesture of things and people that it's like they never existed before — like *we* never existed before. Almost as if they had slid from the ether whole and complete. Like they entered the world and walked straight towards us, embraced us, enfolded us, gave us breath. That's what invention is, I guess — the discovery at the end that it's ourselves we've created. Love too. We become more through love and invention. Johnny and I invented baseball behind the equipment shed and we grew to love it just as we grew to love each other. Every running catch, every pin-point throw, every scooped grounder became another entrance we made together. Each day we saw and felt and experienced the game more and more, and along the way we saw and felt and experienced each other more, too.

"Josh?"

"Yeah?"

"You ever wanna be someone else?"

"Someone else?"

"Yeah. Like you feel like your skin's too tight or something and you just wanna walk around in someone else's for a while?"

"No. Why? You?" I asked.

"Yeah. Most of the time," he said quietly.

"Why?"

"I dunno. My dad, I guess. He makes me wanna be *anyone* else."

"Because he drinks?"

"Yeah. Because of that. Other stuff too, though."

"What other stuff?" I probed gently.

"Like his arms."

"His arms?"

"Yeah. I don't know how they feel. Only his hands. I only know how his hands feel."

"How's that?"

"Tough. Tough and cold and hard. And ... empty."

"Sorry."

"Me too. Josh?"

"Yeah?"

"How does it feel to be held?"

"Well, it feels kinda warm and safe and good."

"I believe that."

"Johnny?"

"Yeah?"

"You think maybe the difference between a good hitter and a poor one's how much they been held?"

"Yeah. The good one's haven't been. So they're pissed off enough to hit with power!"

With two weeks to go before the tournament, Johnny and I could throw from the outfield and hit each other's strike zone. We were good. Together we'd traveled the distance between ineptness and proficiency. Now we could charge a rolling grounder, scoop it and throw in one easy sweeping motion. Casually, almost, we'd throw up a gloved hand to snare the ball. We began to play with the nonchalant confidence that marks the beginning of second nature. But there was more. Despite all the hours of pantomime in front of my mirror, we still hadn't actually hit a ball. We knew the science of it all. We understood the singular physics that surrounds the process of hitting a baseball, but we hadn't actually *done* it. Neither of us could figure out how we were going to get our hands on a bat, and Johnny had even gone to the trouble of cutting a broom handle to a thirty-two-inch length so we could practice with that. It snapped after three whacks.

We were tossing the ball back and forth one evening considering the possibilities when my parents suddenly appeared around the corner of the shed. In her hands my mother carried a shiny new wooden bat with a big red label. "Louisville Slugger," it said. My dad carried a flattened glove that looked prehistoric. They were both grinning.

"How's the inventin' going?" my dad asked casually.

"Fine, sir," Johnny said, eyes as glued to the bat and glove as mine.

"Well, good," my mother said. "We thought we might be able to help."

"That's right. Every inventor needs assistants and we're here to assist," my dad said.

My mother held the bat out to Johnny. He looked at it hard and gulped. Wide-eyed, he turned and looked at me as if asking for help. I was far too surprised to even begin to know what to do or say, so I just stared right back at him. The silence between the four of us lay as flat, broad and rich as the sweep of land behind us.

"I think you might need this, John," my mother said after a moment and smiled.

"Yes, ma'am," he said. "Thank you."

My dad laughed heartily. He slipped the battered old glove on his hand and whacked it with his free hand a couple of times to loosen what was supposed to be a pocket. "Haven't used this thing for a hundred years. I used to be pretty good. Figured maybe you could use a fielder. Whaddaya say?"

Johnny and I stared at each other again. Unable to speak, Johnny reached out and took the bat from my mother's hands and handed her his glove.

"I used to be a pretty fair hand at pitching a few years back, you know," she said. "Why don't you two inventors step up to that plate and we'll see if I can't strike you out!"

For the rest of that evening the four of us played baseball

behind the equipment shed. My mother pitched underhand, lobbing the ball towards us as we swung. That's it. Mostly we just swung, unable to transfer the science and the physics into contact. My dad stood patiently by the rail fence cheering us on from our outfield. "Batter batter batter batter batter!" he'd say and whack his glove with each swing and a miss. Time after time we'd take our stance — mine copied from a photo of Tony C. and Johnny's a strange hybrid of all his heroes — wait for the pitch to sail in, swing, miss and start it all over again.

Once or twice we'd make contact and the ball would sail out over the pitcher's mound towards the lanky form of my father, who'd run and retrieve it, bounding after it like a spring colt, heavy steel-toed work boots slamming into the ground. We hunched over the plate each time, the bat clenched in our fists, heads down, eyes straining for the first glimpse of the ball my mother released. Each time we sought the satisfaction we knew could be born from a skill acquired, mastered, controlled and celebrated. Each time we swung with resolution, grit and love. Each time we'd have to start again, tapping the wooden plate with the bat, settling into our stance and waiting.

My parents played with something close to glee. It never mattered to them that we couldn't hit, that our skills in this area were severely limited or that we were largely silent, intent on our game. What seemed to matter was the being there, that feeling of being part and parcel of this new world that Johnny and I were entering, our friendship and the game. They loved every minute of it. By the time the sun went down and it was too dark to see the ball, we were all laughing and joking with each other. The game had swept all of us up into a collective joyful heap.

"Where'd you get that old thing, anyway?" Johnny asked my dad as we drove him home.

"The glove?"

"Yeah. It's funny looking."

"Well, John, strange as it may seem, I was once a young whipper-snapper, too. Long time ago, but I was just like you two.

I loved baseball. Played it all the time. That glove was a present from Joshua's grandfather, my dad. He couldn't understand why a farmer could want to be running off every night to play a game. But he let me do it. He let me because he loved me and he knew it made me happy. Just like you two. I always had to borrow a glove to play. We didn't have the money for extras. But I came down to breakfast one day and there it was, sitting where my plate should be. He just sat eating his oatmeal and reading his paper like there was nothing strange going on. He was like that. Never made a fuss over anything. On the outside anyway. But I know he was churning with happiness on the inside. So I sat down, picked it up, put it on and ate my cereal through the biggest, thickest lump anyone ever had in their throat. I loved him then. Loved him as much as I ever did, maybe more.

"That night he came to see me play. Mildmay was playing Wingham and I was the left fielder. Pretty good game but not much hitting. We were up by a run going into the ninth inning. Wingham put a couple men on base with two out and their best hitter was at the plate. Everyone was tense. Mildmay has always hated to lose to Wingham. Anyway, he connected with a shot that sailed out into my field. It looked like it might go over the fence but I chased it down anyway. As I got closer and closer to the fence it seemed like the world slowed down to slow motion and all I could think about was my father and the glove I was wearing on my hand. Well, I wanted that ball more than I wanted anything in the world. I ran a step faster and then at the very last moment I leapt into the air and came down with it right at the fence! What a feeling. Everyone cheered, of course, and we won, but the best moment for me came right at the last. Everyone had been making a big fuss over me and my catch and I finally got away from them. My dad was right there, waiting. He was looking at me with a world of pride and love in his eyes and I handed him that ball. He stood there looking at it for a long time and we never said anything. We didn't have to, I guess. He just put his hand over my shoulder and we walked to the truck and drove home. He kept that ball on his dresser right up until the day he died. I made sure we put that old ball in the casket with him. He would have wanted to keep it.

"So that's where I got that funny-looking thing, John, and I guess that's why Joshua's mother and I decided to get you guys the bat. Because if this game makes you guys happy, we want to be part of it. When you're happy, we're happy."

As the highway spun away beneath us we were each lost in our thoughts. I'd never known until then that my dad and I shared any passions beyond fishing, faith and farming. Thinking of him playing the same game with the same zeal and verve as I was bringing to it was magical. We were tied together so seamlessly. That night I discovered for the first time that loving is a learning process. The geographies of our lives demand it. Just when you start to believe that you know all the territory, the sweep of a life, you're surprised by a sudden scarp of habit, of history or belief. And that's the magic of it all. You're always being given someone new and the pull of it is tractive, strong and relentless. That night I knew for dead, absolute certain how much I loved my father.

Where Johnny was I don't know. He stared straight ahead and never said a word. I can only imagine. His world was so different from mine. Ben Gebhardt lived his life like a covert operation and Johnny bore the detritus of that on his shoulders like an unkept promise — cumbersome and cool to the touch. The comparison between my father and family and his own must have seemed titanic that night, and I believe that's what he was thinking.

My dad could have been anywhere between the back forty and Cooperstown. But we shared our silence as respectfully as friends can, and when we pulled up in front of Old Man Givens's place and Johnny clambered from the car, I knew that any distance that may have existed between us was now shrunken, diminished and spare. He grinned, waved and walked his bike slowly to the porch, where he turned, waved and disappeared into the darkness of the house.

"My friend," I whispered.

Every night for those last two weeks the four of us gathered behind the equipment shed for batting practice. Soon, both Johnny and I were connecting solidly and regularly. My dad moved beyond the rail fence and stood in the alfalfa field and my mother moved back a step or two for her lobbed pitches. Johnny and I compared notes endlessly as we hit. We knew that we needed to stay motionless in the batter's box, that any degree of motion hindered the necessary transfer of energy into our swing. We knew we had to find the optimum height for our elbows in order to snap our hands out fast. We knew our hips were essential to our swing. We knew all of it, and once again the particular magic of baseball transformed the science into joy. As our swings leveled out and we began to hit with power and precision, we cheered and my parents cheered too. We were hitters. I was a natural line-driver and Johnny was a belter, a pure and wonderful machine that could uncoil itself effortlessly and punch holes in the sky with a baseball. Time after time my dad raced backwards as Johnny's bat arched another long flyball deep into our alfalfa field. Each time he looked at me with blue eyes blazing and I had that odd sensation again of falling through the sky.

"Just like Ted Williams," he said. "I told you, didn't I?"

"Yeah. You did."

"Now I know what the answer to baseball is."

"What's that?" I asked.

"Love."

"Love?"

"Yeah. You gotta love it," Johnny said.

"No science?"

"No."

"No math?"

"No."

"You just gotta love it?"

"You just gotta love it."

"Johnny?"

"Yeah?"

"I think you're gettin' it," I said.

"Dreamer."

"Ditz."

⊚

They sent me to camp one summer when I was eight. They were always sending me somewhere. I got dropped off more than junk mail. But that summer they actually did me a favor. I got to this camp, not knowing what to expect or even why to expect it. It had this hokey name. Camp Mi Ma Ho. Can you believe it? I'll never forget it. It was perched on the shore of this little lake in the Muskokas and had all these cute little A-frame cabins that were supposed to look like teepees. Keeping it all in theme, you know? Anyway, they had a program that was designed to introduce us all to the ways of the Indian. Their idea of the ways of the Indian was canoeing, fire starting and storytelling around the fire. We also got our faces painted, put on dyed turkey feathers, waved small wood-and-rubber tomahawks and danced around the fire to some taped powwow music. It was all very sickening. I stuck to myself and read mostly. After a week the counselors knew that I was a hard sell and pretty much left me alone.

They had this little library in the main cabin. Hardy Boys, Nancy Drew, Treasure Island, Peter Pan, the usual stuff for kids. But they also had a book called Indians. That's all, just Indians. I opened that book and I was gone.

Sometimes in life you never know that you're searching for something until that something reaches out and grabs you. Well, I'd been needing some thing for as long as I could remember. My life had more holes in it than a right-wing argument. Anyway, this book was magical. Today I'd call it bullshit, but for a city kid who really needed to be something, it was the key to the door. There were stories in there about the Indians helping the pilgrims survive and the first Thanksgiving, about them being brave and loyal guides for the fur traders, warriors, vision seekers, hunters, fishermen, and there were pictures that showed the romance of everything. Suddenly, all I wanted to be was an Indian. A warrior. When you grow up like I did, all your dreams involve being the opposite of the way you are and the warrior thing was directly opposite from me and my life. I *devoured that book. After Camp Mi Ma Ho I knew what I wanted to be. What I had to be.*

Once school started again I dug around the library and read everything they had on Indians. Back then no one had anything close to being relevant or true but I didn't care. All I was after was input. Ignorance is such bliss, eh?

Soon I was walking around singing, "My paddle's clean and bright, flashing with silver, swift as the wild goose flies, dip, dip and swing, dip, dip and swing," reciting the ever-popular "By the Shores of Gitche Gumee" and believing that Hank Williams's song "Kawliga" and that sappy song "Running Bear" by whoever were really paeans to the culture, for God's sake. Paeans. Jesus. And movies? I watched every single movie on TV that had anything to do with Indians. I didn't know whether I wanted to be an Apache, Commanche, Cherokee, Sioux or Cheyenne, but I knew I wanted to be a warrior.

Try growing up without a history. I never even knew I had a grandfather until we took over the store in Mildmay. My father, as you know, wasn't real big on details. So sometime around eight-and-a-half I became an Indian. I never told anybody. How do you tell somebody that you've just become someone else? I just kept it to myself and worked at being a warrior. When I met you I couldn't believe it. I mean, who thinks they're going to meet a real Indian in the middle of the farm belt? When I discovered that you had no knowledge of yourself as an Indian it confused me. I knew more about who you were supposed to be than you did. Even though my information pool was shallower than Otter Creek in midsummer, I still knew more. That's when I started to lose it — the moment I figured, at ten years old, that I knew more about being an Indian than the Indians.

Tournament day blew in bright and clear and hot. It was one of those windless, cloudless summer days when you stand on the land and you can actually feel it changing beneath your feet and all around you. Growth. Life. Farming. Ordinarily I would have loved a morning like that, but this day was different from any I'd experienced. I moved through the routine of chores like a zombie. My father grinned and let me be. By the time we were ready to load the car with food, extra clothes and lawn chairs, I was as nervous as I can ever recall being. The idea of taking the game we'd learned behind the equipment shed and playing in front of people from three towns and three schools was suddenly terrifying. I knew we were ready, that we'd honed the fundamental skills to a high level and that we could think our way through any game situation, but we'd never really *played* the game. I had no idea what it was like to be a part of a team aside from our small quartet behind the shed.

"Nervous, son?" my father asked once we'd pulled out of the driveway and headed down the hill towards Highway 9.

"Yeah," I answered in a small voice.

"Well, that's good," he said. "Shows that you're not overconfident or cocky. You'll play better."

"I will?"

"Oh, yes. You'll see better, think clearer, and when the time comes to make a play, you'll be ready. Once you do something and get into the game, you won't be nervous any more."

"I hope so."

We were picking up Johnny on our way through town since neither of his parents was going. He was waiting on the porch steps, looking as spooked by things as I was.

"Hey," he said as he sat beside me, smiling weakly.

"Hey," I said.

"John, you're looking well today," my mother said, turning in her seat to look at us.

"Thank you, ma'am," he said. "Sure wish I felt well."

"Nervous?" my father asked.

"As a cat on a hot tin roof," he answered.

They laughed. I missed the humor in this entirely and could only sit and grin vacantly. Johnny punched me lightly on the shoulder. I punched him back.

"Man on second, none out. What do you do?" he asked in a hush.

"I make contact," I answered automatically, "try to move him up. Long flyball or a single. Either one."

"Cool."

"What would you do?"

"Knock the hell out of it!"

My father laughed. He looked at us through the rearview mirror and his eyes were alive with an excitement I'd only seen when either of us had landed a good-sized trout. "I'm prepared to offer you guys some incentive," he said.

"Some what?" we answered in chorus.

"Incentive. It's like encouragement, only better," he said.

"Like what?" Johnny asked.

"Well, I think any run batted in is worth a dollar. A base hit is fifty cents and a home run is worth at least two dollars. A ball caught is a quarter. How's that?"

"Ezra!" my mother said, aghast at this sudden philanthropy. My mother had always figured that money, like salvation, was never guaranteed and not to be needlessly squandered.

"Oh, Mother," my father said, "it's okay. The boys have worked hard enough these last weeks that they deserve the chance to earn something for it. I'm not giving cash away. They have to earn it."

"By playing?" she asked.

"Sure. But by playing fair, well and hard. Where's the shame in that?"

"It seems to me that playing fair and well and hard should be its own reward."

"Yes. That's true and I'm sure it will be. But I think this deserves special consideration. You know how hard they've worked."

"Yes."

"They never let their schoolwork slip and Joshua never once let up on his chores."

"Yes."

"Well?"

"Well, I suppose. This once."

"Great! Hear that, fellas?"

"Yeah!" We were jubilant at the idea of earning some spending money.

"How's the farm doing, sir?" Johnny asked suddenly.

"It's doing well, John. Why?"

"Because ... you're gonna be awful poor by the end of today!"

The parking lot at the Mildmay fair grounds was filled. There were two buses from Wingham and Teeswater and everywhere small clumps of players were throwing balls back and forth. We noticed that both schools had uniform jerseys with numbers and matching caps. Johnny and I exchanged glum looks. People were moving between vehicles and the picnic area and the two baseball diamonds. There seemed to be a lot of visiting going on between friends and relatives who hadn't seen each other in a while and the whole scene looked as convivial and open as fall fair days.

Alvin Giles smiled when he saw the four of us approaching. "Ezra. Martha. Boys," he said, saluting casually with his index finger. "Glad you could make it."

"Hello, Alvin," my mother said. "What a great day you got for this!"

"That's true. It should be fun."

"We've brought two excellent players for you, Alvin," my father said.

Alvin Giles looked at Johnny and me, eyed the gloves in our hands almost warily, squinted in concentration and then smiled. "Well, that's good. Boys, I thought you weren't interested in baseball."

"We weren't. Not at first. Now we wanna play," Johnny answered.

"Well, good. The team's over by the first diamond. We've got jerseys for everyone, and caps. So if you hurry over there you can get suited up. We play Wingham in twenty minutes!"

Ralphie Wendt was handing out jerseys to the late arrivals and he looked at us in disgust. Behind him Lenny Weber and Victor Ringle looked on in surprise. Sue Crawford and a circle of girls huddled closer together and whispered.

"Spazzes? The spazzes showed up? What next, retards?" Ralphie smirked at Lenny and Victor.

"And look. They got gloves," Lenny said.

"We need jerseys," Johnny said firmly to Ralphie.

"Yeah, sure," Ralphie said. "We probably got a zero and a double zero here somewhere!"

"Anything's fine," Johnny said quietly.

"Anything's fine," Victor Ringle mimicked with a whine.

"Okay. But listen, Spaz," Ralphie said. "We're only lettin' you play 'cause we gotta. Nobody wants you here. Just try to stay outta the way, 'kay?"

"Yeah. Sure. Now can we have jerseys?" Johnny asked calmly.

"Here." Ralphie tossed us each a jersey. They were white, with maroon pinstripes and Mildmay scrawled across the chest in curly letters. "Spaz One, right field. Spaz Two, oh, shit, well, second base."

As we walked away to change and warm up we traded looks.

"Which one are you? Spaz One or Spaz Two?" I asked.

"I think I'd rather be Spaz Two," Johnny said with a grin. "Second base is busier."

"Okay. Spaz One is me," I said heartily.

We changed into our jerseys and began tossing a ball back and forth lightly. Alvin Giles and the Wingham principal appeared and got ready to start the first game. We understood that we would play each team twice and the two winning teams after four games would play for the championship. Each game would be five innings. After a brief huddle around home plate, Alvin Giles blew his coach's whistle and signaled us all towards our bench.

"Okay, team, we're home team so we're in the field first this game. It's five innings with one point each if it's tied. No extra innings. So let's get out there and show these slouches how we play ball in Mildmay! Ralphie, have you got everyone in position?"

"Yup." He looked glumly at Johnny and me.

"Good. Let's go, team!" Alvin Giles said and clapped his hands.

Johnny and I trotted out onto the field. We stopped at second base and looked at each other. In the bleachers we could see my parents gazing at us and when they waved, we waved back weakly.

"Ready?" he asked.

"Guess. You?"

"Guess," he replied.

"Scared?"

"Yeah."

"Me too."

"Good."

"Good?"

"Yeah. I wouldn't wanna be the only one."

Ralphie jogged over from his shortstop position. He looked beefy and out of place in his tight jersey, and his ears stuck out from the sides of his cap like cauliflowers. "You Spazzes wanna visit or play ball? Come on. Get with it!"

I ran out to right field with my stomach churning and a familiar wish that all balls avoid my area. I reached deep right field just as the first Wingham batter stepped up to the plate. Finally, after all this time, Johnny and I were playing baseball. The bleachers were full. Loose children raced around the perimeter followed by bounding dogs and from somewhere behind them, a radio played a country song. It was a fair-like atmosphere, and I understood, finally, how baseball felt. It was a game and an event and I loved it. Sue Crawford was pitching, and as she delivered her first lobbed pitch I felt a fluttering in my stomach like the first motions of a newborn chick. There was a pause that seemed like an eternity as the ball arced towards the plate and for me it was filled with images of every minute behind that equipment shed. I swallowed hard.

The solid whump of ball meeting bat shook me from my reverie. I looked up just in time to see Johnny race to his left for a ground ball, scoop it and throw hard to Teddy Hohnstein at first base. It was a bullet. Poor Teddy could only hold up his glove in self-defense, grimacing with his eyes closed, face turned away. The ball stuck in his glove from sheer velocity. The crowd in the bleachers cheered and clapped and Ralphie Wendt gaped. Johnny pounded the pocket of his glove and bent forward for the next batter. Victor Ringle shook his head rapidly in left field while Lenny Weber stood there in center staring blankly at Johnny's back. My dad gave me a thumbs-up from the bleachers.

The next batter lifted a high foul ball beyond first base. All the practice with the India rubber ball paid off as I moved with the crack of the bat, eyes glued to the flight of the ball as I ran forward. Time slowed to a crawl and I could hear myself breathing deeply as I got closer and closer to the ball that was now dropping rapidly. Silence. For the briefest of moments I existed in the world alone except for that ball. I lowered my hands to my knees, pocket up, and caught it on the dead run. The world jumped back into focus and I looked up to see my mother and father standing and clapping in the bleachers, Alvin Giles scratching his head at the bench and Johnny leaping up and down behind second base, waving his arms in joy. Ralphie Wendt paced back and forth at shortstop, shaking his head.

"That's a quarter, Josh! That's a quarter!" Johnny yelled, and my dad gave me another thumbs-up.

When the next girl dribbled a grounder to Ralphie and he threw her out, I trotted in towards our bench with a huge smile pasted to my face. Johnny met me halfway and we looked at each other, eyes shining, and nodded. That's all. Just a nod. There was no need for words. We went out on our first three batters, Ralphie swinging mightily but futilely at strike three and Johnny and me smirking with enjoyment as we grabbed our gloves and headed for the field.

"Who's the spaz now?" Johnny whispered and grinned.

We were buried so deep in the batting order that we didn't get to the plate until the third inning. By then we'd both made catches, Johnny on a routine pop-up and me, an over-the-shoulder grab of a line drive that I almost missed. It felt good, and by the third inning our teammates were calling us by name and cheering us on. But we wanted to hit. Teddy Hohnstein blooped a wounded duck of a single with one out and it was my turn.

Johnny stared at me wide-eyed as I took a few practice swings and headed for the plate. "Ted Williams," he said, and I nodded. My hands shook slightly and I had to wipe the sweat from them on my pants before I settled in to hit. The first pitch was outside and I let it go. The second was at my knees so I let it go too.

"Joshua!" my father yelled.

"Good one, son, good one!" my mother added.

"Come on, Spaz!" said Ralphie.

The third pitch was a thing of beauty. It arced in slowly and crossed the plate about waist high. As I stepped into it I felt like I was Tony C. himself, a perfect combination of grace and power. The thud of contact rang right up through my elbows and settled in the back of my shoulders as the ball rocketed off my bat and screamed into the gap between the center and left fielder. By the time Wingham could recover I was on third, Teddy Hohnstein had scored and we were up by one run. Johnny grinned from the on-deck area and stepped up to the plate. He didn't wait. On the first pitch he uncoiled, lunging out at the pitch and lifting a long, deep flyball that the left fielder simply stood and watched as it orbited over his head. There was a long beat of silence from the crowd before they began to cheer and yell and stamp their feet over what must have seemed an impossible hit for such a skinny kid. Ralphie Wendt glared as Johnny loped around the bases. Alvin Giles stared and stared, and Sue Crawford smiled as Johnny crossed the plate.

"Way to go," I said as I slapped his palm.

"Routine," he said.

"I think you're up about three dollars."

"Try for ten?"

"Try for ten."

We won that first game. I smacked a solid double in the fifth and Johnny followed me with a triple to the opposite field. Both times the crowd, and especially my parents, were jubilant. Johnny just grinned and punched my shoulder while Ralphie's face was screwed up with curiosity and something perilously close to admiration. The rest of the team was as happy as the crowd, although I know there wasn't a single one of them that wasn't amazed at the transformation they were seeing. For his part, Alvin Giles had a little half smile pasted to his face and thumped us warmly on the back.

We existed now, far beyond the science and math of the game. We'd entered the magic that is baseball and never were there two more reverential pilgrims than Johnny Gebhardt and I.

Game two was a blowout. Johnny hit two home runs and a triple and I was on base all three times with doubles. In the field our gloves became the final resting place for anything that came our way. Games three and four went much the same, with Johnny's bat doing most of the damage. By the time we went into the final game against Teeswater we were heroes.

It was wild. Each team scored runs almost at will. By the time we sailed into the final inning we were tied sixteen to sixteen. We were the home team for that game, so we had last bat. Teeswater went out one, two, three on grounders to Johnny and Ralphie and a flyball that Victor Ringle snared while falling down.

"Now's our chance, team," Alvin Giles told us while we fidgeted at our bench. "Just relax, have fun. And remember, we still get a point for a tie. So just have fun up there. Joshua, you're leading off."

As I took my practice swings Johnny walked up to me. "Hey," he said.

"Hey."

"We can get this over fast, you know."

"Yeah."

"Yeah. Just hit a homer."

"Me?"

"Yeah, you. You can do it."

"Never have before."

"Well, now's the time. When you go up there just think ... warrior."

"Warrior?"

"Yeah. That's what you are."

"I am?"

"Yeah." He laughed. "You are. You're an Indian. You're a warrior."

"I guess."

"Guess nothing! It's what you were born to be. You're a *warrior!*"

"Okay."

"Okay!"

I walked towards the plate. Everyone was milling about on the sidelines; Ralphie Wendt looked at me and showed his crossed fingers. Alvin Giles leaned against the fence and tapped his thigh with a lightly closed fist, while Sue Crawford and her friends sat on the bench with their legs bouncing up and down in anticipation. Warrior. It was what I'd been born to be, he said. Farmer. That's what I really believed I was born to be.

I began thinking of my father and the story he'd told about his glove, my grandfather and the game he'd played as a boy. I thought about my mother and the quiet ways she'd instilled in me, the peace I felt because of it and the smooth cool of her hands on my brow. I thought about mornings on our back porch, watching the sweep of the land like it was a living thing and the curious sensation that you could actually see it breathe sometimes when the light was right and your soul was filled with gratitude. I thought about Johnny and the weeks we'd spent behind the equipment shed inventing this game, about the willow tree and the answer to baseball.

Love, he'd told me. You have to love it. I loved the game right then. Loved it as simply and completely as young boys can. As I gazed up at my parents one more time and then over at Johnny standing at our bench, I knew I could step up to that plate as a warrior. Only it would be as a spiritual warrior because it was all I knew, a spiritual warrior leaning on the common love of common people, and right then, as I stepped into the batter's box, I wanted that ball more than I wanted anything in the entire world.

I swung so hard at the first pitch that I almost lost my balance spinning around. Strike one. I gulped hard and settled myself. I felt the thud of contact on the next pitch and watched the ball sail foul on the third base side. Strike two. And then, time slowed. I could hear my breathing. I watched the mouths of my teammates shouting encouragement and heard nothing. The clapping hands of the crowd, the yelling, were all lost in the vacuum I'd moved into.

I heard the scrunch of the dirt as I twisted my feet for traction, and then the soft rustle of my jersey as I lifted the bat. My breath. Deep and slow and long. The ball as it was lobbed looked as big and full as a watermelon, and as I stepped into it, the distant blue hills loomed right behind it. I swung into it with a rotation of the hips and an extension of the arms that was pure Ted Williams. Only when I saw the ball rocket over the head of the left fielder did time slide back into its proper meter. As I rounded first and saw the Teeswater player scrambling to retrieve the rolling ball I knew it was over.

The crowd erupted and Johnny was leaping up and down and all around at the bench as I rounded second and began sprinting for all I was worth. I beat the throw to home plate by five feet. Johnny was all over me, hugging and thumping and yelling. My teammates lined up respectfully to shake my hand, and in the stands I caught a quick glimpse of my father standing and clapping and whistling through his teeth. I walked over to claim the ball from the Teeswater catcher, who stood staring at it in his glove. "Thanks," I said and walked away.

We whooped and hollered for a while at the bench. Ralphie shook my hand, followed by Victor Ringle, Lenny Weber and Teddy Hohnstein.

"Way to go, Spaz," Ralphie said and smiled.

"Thanks." I smiled back.

"Game, Josh," Lenny said. Teddy just grinned shyly and walked away.

"Did you think warrior?" Johnny asked when everyone had dribbled away.

We seemed bigger right then, taller, stronger, heavier. We were more than skinny kids now. We'd become bigger through our friendship and the love of a game we'd spent a long time inventing for ourselves. "Yeah," I said. "Yeah, I thought warrior."

"Knew it!" Johnny said and punched my shoulder.

My parents were standing by the backstop, my father with one long brown arm draped over my mother's shoulders. I felt, for the first time in my life, like a man. I held the ball in my hand and it was a comfortable weight.

"You guys made me broke today," my dad said.

"And you made me proud," my mother added.

Johnny had fallen in behind me, and the four of us stood by the backstop while the last of the crowd filtered away towards the picnic area. We were a team. More than our schoolmates and more than any team I've been a part of since. I held the ball out to my father. He took it without a word. We stared at each other, and on his face was a look I will remember forever. He turned that ball around and around in his palm, looked at my mother, at Johnny and then back at me, nodded, sighed deeply and pulled me into a deep hug that ended with a solid whack on the back. My mother looked at me in the same silence while Johnny stared at me with that pure open gaze.

"Way to go, Spaz," he said quietly.

⊚

As the small OPP plane whisked us high over the farmlands north of Toronto, I gazed out the window and down at the shadows spilled around the base of hills. They reminded me of home. I found myself walking the soft brown hills of Bruce County sometimes as though they were my life, casually, reverently almost, the pitch and wallow of the topography a mute comfort to feet grown accustomed to different soil and different land. Growing up. I'd learned through the years that all of us grow up and out of the land of our births. At least, the lucky ones do. It graces our feet with permanence, its grit and promise tattooed indelibly on our heels, salvation and geography intermingled like blood, making returnings as vital as memory.

Prowling those rolling heights and hogbacks is like stepping back into myself. I used to watch those hills from my window. I remember how they reacted to every change in light, every nuance of weather, and every mood and emotion of my boyhood. I used to believe they sang to me then, sang me sweet songs of growth and life, of breezes rife with whisperings of distant lands and peoples, of an earth rich and bountiful, and songs of minor gods who inhabit the places only the wind can reach. They sing me different songs today. Songs in a lower register, inaudible almost. Songs of sorrows and purple moods, of changes, of loss, and of a boyhood whose vastness evades me because sometimes it seems that the more we move into our adulthood, the more we move away from things like magic, adventure and hills that sing. Still, I would come. I would come to listen for the ancient voice of those hills. I would come for the reconnection to the belief that the land is a feeling, a dance we learn, a song. I would come and gaze away towards the west, towards three hundred and twenty acres that once was my entire world. A farm that spawned crops, love and a friendship framed forever by a game invented by the very spirit of our boyhood.

We didn't win the Most Valuable Player award. That went to Connie Shaus for a capable job at third base. When it was announced at the barbecue that evening, Johnny and I were shocked at first but we laughed about it later. Alvin Giles and his farmer's sense of fair play, we figured, deemed her efforts more valuable than our own simply because she had to try harder. Our level of play was second nature. An instinct and reflex born behind the equipment shed had elevated us beyond a childhood approach to the game. That and a deep desire to silence the catcalls and put-downs of our peers. But we knew. We knew we'd succeeded for ourselves and we walked away from the tournament that day being most valuable to ourselves and each other. My mother and father beamed all evening. We knew, Johnny and I, that we had a pair of fans who would always be eager to applaud our efforts.

He never spoke much about the absence of his parents. I guess when you grow up like Johnny did, absences become a familiar part of daily living, something you learn to negotiate your way through like tying your own shoes. Now and then he'd mention something of his life, something cryptic, infused with bitterness and sorrow, and the energy would retreat from his eyes, their blue becoming the melancholic blue you hear in slow jazz ballads or see between the rolling clouds that come before the thunders. When we dropped him off that night the Gebhardt house was dark again. He'd never learned the comfort that comes from a lighted walk and rooms aglow with welcome. Never felt the warmth of anticipation for the lives awaiting your step at the door. No, Ben Gebhardt's days ended early with the sodden haze of drink, while his wife, loyal to a fault, would collapse with him seeking the solace of dreams, where life was romantic, gentle and easy and her man was still the fair-haired boy with laughter in his eyes.

I tried to imagine how it must have felt to him back then, entering their dark world alone, creeping through that house using silence as a defense against the railing of his alcoholic father, reading his way into sleep and the security of his own frail dreams. I never could. But in my prayers each night I offered a simple entreaty to God for the safety and well-being of my friend and perhaps, too, for a gift of light in his darkness.

We moved into that first summer of our friendship effortlessly. School ended. We made our polite good-byes to the new friends that baseball provided us, closed our desks and wandered out into the fields and steams of Bruce County. I worked alongside my father as usual and Johnny joined us as often as he could, generally showing up around noon on the old Schwinn, pumping his thin legs like crazy topping the Conroys' hill and waving as he turned up the gravel road towards our house. He wasn't much of a hand for chores but he tried. Like most folks unfamiliar with farms, he'd mince his way across the barnyard with careful placings of the feet as though cowpies were land mines. My father would wave us off early those afternoons, so we'd head for the willow tree to read, or jump on our bikes for a swim in Otter Creek or wander through three hundred and twenty acres exploring the small woods and creating adventures.

We still played baseball behind the shed. As those endless summer evenings stretched before us, we would run, hit and throw with exuberant abandon. He'd call to me from home plate as we practiced base running, "Come on, Kane, it's the bottom of the ninth and we need you home!" I think I ran faster then, spurred on by the love of baseball, friendship and the idea of home.

He told me about magic. About how it exists all around us, infusing everything with its life-giving energies. "No abracadabra, Josh," he said, "just magic. All around us. Always."

So we looked for magic that summer. We found it in the wood duck chicks we watched feather and grow and fly, in the way the light diffused and colored on its way through the depths of our diving hole on Otter Creek, in the feel of a cow's teats when you milk by hand and in the taste of the wind redolent with rain. Inventing baseball was only the beginning. We learned that it's possible to invent the world. All you ever need are eyes open to magic and mystery, ears attuned to the sublime and the marvelous, a heart desiring of more and a spirit gilded with an expectant joy.

"Like Indians," he said.

Laughing Dog and Thunder Sky. If I missed the importance of the ritual, I understood the power of the bond. For me it never required blood itself, the prick of flesh or elaborate solemnity. It was a heartsong, a concerto of notes and rests, swells and pauses in the meter of friendship. Our pledge had already been effected in the blending of our lives, in a shared response and a common purpose. Had our blood never mingled, the bond would still have been the same — unspoken, unritualized, but real. I understood this in its Christian context more than I did through Johnny's Indian methods. Brothers in the blood. A promise nonrefundable, inextinguishable, eternal.

And as I prepared to land at the Toronto airport that day I thought of myself prowling those hills, watching the sky and becoming aware that I know certain things. I know there is a dance going on all around us all the time — a cosmic dance directed and choreographed by the patient hand of an anonymous God — and that we are partners in that dance. I know that magic exists. I know

that the boys we were and the men we became are inextricably tied
to that magic working in our lives. I know that love is the most
powerful force in the universe. I know that hills can sing and that
a trick of the light can make them breathe in the distance. I know
that light is the promise of the Lord through the darkness. And I
know that one day when the light of my life grows dim and fades,
I will be encouraged by the voice of a reed-thin boy who could
punch holes in the sky with a baseball, yelling at me from heaven,
"Come on, Kane, it's the bottom of the ninth and we need you
home!"

Part Two

THE MAZE

had a three-hour wait for my connecting flight to Calgary. The scurry of the airport was irritating after my reverie and I felt compelled to flag a taxi so I could be alone with my thoughts.

"Where to, bub?" the cabbie asked.

"Oh, I don't know. Anywhere. Take me to the Parkdale area, I guess."

"Sure thing. You a tourist?" he asked, eyeing me in the rearview mirror.

"No. Well, yes. Sort of."

"Thought maybe. Parkdale really ain't much of what you might call a tourist mecca. Sure you wouldn't rather see the CN Tower? SkyDome? Yonge Street?"

"No," I said. "Parkdale's fine."

Johnny had mentioned Parkdale once and I felt a need just then to have some physical connection to his life, however vague it might be. I wanted to see the schools he might have attended, doorways he may have walked through, parks he might have sat and read in, the streets he walked. There is, I believe, a part of all of us, born in our wounding, that wants to believe that there are answers to be found in the hollow faces of the buildings and places our loved ones once inhabited. We arrive expectant as pilgrims, believing that something real will emanate from those surroundings and touch us with the fabric of the life we seek to reclaim. We want to walk across the territories they navigated, carrying a need like longing across the floorboards, gardens and pavement, our desperation making it holy ground, awaiting the consolations of a reticent earth. It never happens, of course, because they are only buildings, streets and cities, and they speak only of the anonymous passage of time with no voice to soothe our melancholy. Still, we are pilgrims.

We moved through the hodgepodge of the city. Neighborhoods melted into neighborhoods and there were no lines to distinguish one from the other. I wondered how children grew up here, their sense of land and sky limited to irregular patches of green and blue caught between the sprawl of concrete, their sense of time escalated to the pitch of the city. There was something of Johnny in all of it. This was the first world he saw. This interplay of lives, constant and unyielding, was his first taste of community. The random familiarity with which those lives passed through and around each other became his first sense of security. He'd arrived in Mildmay educated in the proper use of distance, aloofness and a forced politeness. The city was a maze he'd learned to travel well and safely, and as I thought of that I remembered another maze he'd proven proficient at.

We were thirteen, just about to enter Grade Eight and our final year of elementary school. We'd taken to playing in the hay mow on rainy afternoons. We played daring games of tag along the beams, leaping across the yawning chasm between our feet and the floorboards, or performed Tarzan swings from ropes secured to the upper rafters, sailing across the wide expanse of the barn with a yell and then letting go to fly into a pile of straw at the far end, totally alive and bursting with adrenaline. And then, one afternoon, bored with the regular games, we invented the Maze. We took turns building tunnels through the stacks of hay bales. Long, elaborate tunnels complete with dead-ends, double switches, drop-offs and elevations. The point was to erect a tunnel system so elaborate that the Spelunker, as we dubbed the one who would crawl through the system, would be forced to push up the bale overhead and admit defeat. At the end of the tunnel was a loosely fitted bale that fell away with a light push.

Crawling through those switchbacks and dead-ends in the heat, humidity, dust and darkness, pushing on the unmoving bales at their ends, was a challenge. Chaff stuck to the skin and reduced the eyes to itching, seeping vessels, knees were scratched, and the one above could follow the Spelunker's progress by his rooting, snuffling and hacking. But a challenge was a challenge and neither of us had ever surrendered to the parching swelter of those caverns and exploded through the baled ceiling to gasp in relief for fresh air. Every rain-soaked afternoon found us in that hay mow erecting more complicated, harrowing versions of the Maze for each other. I know that I sketched tunnel systems on paper in preparation for the next set of expeditions and I'm sure, given the complex nature of his tunnels, that Johnny did the same.

One day he looked at me with eyes sparkling as the rain fell in sheets, slapping hard against the ground like a thousand horses were cantering past. "Give me an hour, then come out to the barn," he said and pulled on his slicker.

When I got to the hay mow Johnny was sitting on a bale that sat above a dark opening. The black slot seemed to glower at me, and for the first time in all the times we'd played the Maze, I felt a chill along my spine. Grinning, he gestured broadly towards the opening. "It's all yours, Mr. Spelunker. Good luck!"

Now the thing about the Maze was that the moment you entered the murky depths of the tunnels, the world you knew disappeared completely. As the architect dropped the bale over that opening, silence and darkness filled the universe. Combined with the sense of isolation was the discomfort and the disorientation you felt worming your way through that hay mow. There was no east or west, nor was there an up or a down. It was life in the absence of light — spooky, eerie and infinitely exhilarating. The reward of pushing against that loose bale at the end of it all and seeing the architect's beaming face framed against a world of light, color and sound was magical. We never minded that we defeated each other's dastardly designs. Rather, we celebrated each other's aplomb and courage. The Maze was just another test of fortitude, another passage in the journey to manhood, and we reveled in our blood brother's ability to navigate the darkness and difficulty.

But entering Johnny's tunnel that afternoon, I felt apprehensive. I took one last gulp of fresh air and disappeared into it, the darkness folding around me like a sarcophagus.

At first the going was easy. The tunnel swept forward in a straight line for what I guessed was about twenty feet. Then a sudden cut to the right was followed by an immediate cut left. A zigzagging series of switchbacks had me disoriented in no time. When I fell into a drop-off and my breath was knocked out of me, I felt fear, deep tremulous fear for the first time in my life. The sweat seeped into the corners of my eyes while the heat plastered the hair to my scalp. My palms and my kneecaps itched crazily. My lungs felt clogged and wizened from the chaff and dust. Still, I prowled onward. Each time I discovered a dead-end I lowered my head in frustration, squirmed through a turn-around and crawled on. Dead-end after dead-end, switchback after switchback, drop-off after drop-off, I meandered my way through the darkness. I was coughing, wheezing and now and then felt the pressure of Johnny's footfalls against the sides of that tunnel. It wasn't a comforting pressure.

I lost track of time.

When you spend enough time peering through darkness your eyes begin to play tricks on you. They start to tell you that you can see shapes in the nothingness. That there are spinning, wheeling, cavorting pinwheels of energy in front of your face with definite shape and texture. Minuscule cyclones of movement. Darkness alive. The pitch blackness becomes your enemy, fear and alienation gnaw at your spirit, and your heart, a driven thing, pounds madly against your ribs. The farther I crawled, the more the fear mounted. I wanted out. I wanted to be anywhere except in that tunnel. I wanted light, air and color and I wanted coolness on my brow.

The darkness grew thicker as the hay scraped against my forearms and legs like coarse sandpaper. I wheezed. Finally, after heaving my shoulders against the end of a shaft of tunnel and finding no release, I could handle no more. With a groan I pushed against the ceiling and was flooded with a welcome rush of air and light. I collapsed against the edges of the tunnel, heaving deep wet dollops of air into my lungs and trying to focus on Johnny's sneakered feet in front of me. The world drifted slowly into focus.

"Man, you were in there forever!" he said. "Are you okay?"

I nodded. I lay there with my head lolled against the hay bales, shivering, mouth agape and eyes wandering along each beam and rafter of that barn.

"Tough maze," I said finally, weakly.

"The toughest," he said.

"Couldn't beat it."

"Yeah, but Josh, you were in there for way over an hour!"

"Yeah?"

"Yeah."

"That's warrior stuff, man! Warrior stuff!"

"Don't feel much like a warrior right now."

"You will, Josh. You will."

"Promise?"

"Promise."

"Johnny?"

"Yeah?"

"I was scared."

"Really?"

"Terrified. Can warriors be scared?"

"I guess."

"Good. 'Cause I sure was. Tough maze."

"Not as tough as you, Josh."

"Thanks, Johnny. Thanks."

We never designed another maze. Our lives moved forward into the jet-propelled world of teenagers and we became lost in the new look and sound of the world. That summer passed in the high heat and sunshine that makes for thick fields and crowded hay mows. As we heaved and piled bales that summer and watched the hay mow grow higher and higher towards the rafters, a part of us vanished. We'd met and challenged fear in that barn and we'd discovered that it was the Minotaur that inhabited our creations. We'd tasted its bitter breath in the chaff and dust and saw its face in those pinwheels of energy spinning away in the darkness. Together we learned that the successful navigation of life and living demands the presence of fear. Johnny sprouted courage and bravado in those tunnels. I developed a deeper and more profound faith, the interplay of darkness and light becoming a metaphor for a life built on the premise of salvation and grace. As we moved out of the adolescence and into our youth, we took the lessons of the Maze with us as we plied our way into a newer teenage world, a cosmography that would challenge us wholly.

I never told you about Timmy Parks. I never told anybody. Maybe because some people are so special and their presence in your life so valuable that when they leave it you think it's impossible to describe them fully, so you leave their names and their lives unspoken forever. Like you can preserve them and their memory more honorably by your silence. Some Indian tribes are like that. It's considered disrespectful to speak of the dead. Like it defiles their spirit, and I guess in a way it does. I mean, who can really define a life except the one who lived it? We're only ever given hints of the motions beneath the flesh and bone we see every day. You know, like I could tell you how a warm spring rain makes me feel when I catch it on my tongue and you might have an idea, might relate to the sensation and the reaction, but only I know how it really feels to me, how it flicks all those little lights on inside my belly and makes my world come alive. Only I will ever know how it electrifies my spirit, makes me feel like more, like I'm bigger for it. When you speak of the departed you speak only of hints and indications, and as broad as some of those might be, only the dead can speak rightly of the dead.

     I never spoke much about Toronto. Some things you'd just rather forget and that first period of my life is one of the erasable parts. My dad was always on the move from one job to another. He'd get into some shit or the other, yell at somebody because he was hung-over or be drunk on the job and screw something up and we'd be on the road to welfare again while he scouted around for another position. My mom and I got used to never having much. Even when he worked we were lucky if he even made it home on pay nights. Yet he'd never let my mother work. Too proud in that old school way that says the man has to be the bread-and-butter winner. Or maybe he was just too scared that she'd find some backbone by making her way in the world and wake up to the realization that he wasn't an anchor so much as a burden. All her life she never fought back against any of it. She took the slaps, the empty bed at night, the lack of any kind of real security, the death of any dreams she might have had as a young girl, everything.

Instead, she defended him, lied for him, covered up. And suffered. I've hated cowards ever since. She even drank with him for a while. That was charming, coming home to two drunk parents instead of just one. Luckily, she didn't have the constitution for it and she quit. No one could keep up with my father. People would say "Let's go out for a couple" and they'd be thinking a couple of beers and my father would be thinking a couple of weeks. Anyway, we got used to living on next to nothing and moving around from flea-bag house to flea-bag house. A city the size of Toronto is perfect for men like my father. You can live as anonymously as you need to, pull the hustle and bustle around you like a cloak and lose yourself in the traffic jam of lives. I must have gone to eight different schools by the time I hit Mildmay.

Timmy Parks was my first real friend. Until I met him I lived in books. Long John Silver ranting away could always drown out Ben Gebhardt ranting away and I learned to disappear into fiction very early. I never took the time to try and make friends. When you get used to the idea that nothing's going to last and that permanent is just a word on a Magic Marker, you get used to the idea that alone is more practical, that the pain of leaving can be avoided by never arriving in the first place. So I lived and read and dreamed alone. I didn't believe there was a single human being who could match the people I was discovering in books. Until I met Timmy Parks.

He was a daredevil. One of those kids with perpetual scratches and cuts and bruises from all the climbing, tunneling, falling, tumbling and exploring. Timmy was always the first one to try anything. The tree that

*couldn't be climbed, the fencetop that couldn't be walked, the space
between rooftops that couldn't be jumped, all of these belonged to Timmy
Parks. He was a swashbuckler, scamp and rogue and the first person that
I met before you who lived their life heart first.*

*Timmy adopted me. Why, I'll never know. One day he just walked up
to me where I was reading on the front steps and started talking. He talked
about adventures, about night-time raids on the winos in the hobo jun-
gle by the railroad tracks, about jumping bikes over the drainage ditch
behind the industrial park, about getting the dog at the scrap yard to
chase him and a myriad of big-city derring-do I'd never considered either
fun or possible. Soon, I was tagging along with him and the rest of his
gang. We were out every day and night carousing and playing, creating
adventures out of the heaps, piles and confusions of the city. He challenged me constantly. He talked me into leaping, climbing, crawling,
hanging, rolling and running. He talked me into life. I still read my books,
but I was beginning to see that adventures could be lived, that magic was
invention and fun was possible even in the dreariest of circumstances.*

*Timmy Parks was the first one of us to ever dive from the high div-
ing board at the Parkdale pool. That board must have been a good ten
feet off the water but when you're eight years old, ten feet might as well
be a thousand. We went there every day that summer to see if one of us
could work up the courage to go off that board. Anyone who ever did
would merely sit on the edge and drop off like a stone. But Timmy Parks
dove. One day he climbed up, heaved a big breath into his lungs, ran the
length of it, hopped up and sprang off that board into a soaring head-first
dive to the gasps of those of us perched safely on the edge of the pool. He
surfaced, grinning, and swam back to do it all over again. One by one we
made the same climb but no one was able to screw up enough courage to
make the same dive. Finally, one day, Timmy looked at me with eyes shining and said, "Your turn, John. You can do it!"*

*The climb up that ladder was the longest and hardest thing I'd ever
done. I was shaking when I reached the top and looked out over the pool,
the park and a section of city. The eyes of our gang were on me as I stood
there with Timmy pumping a fist at me in encouragement. You can never
plan the big things in your life. You can never tell yourself that this one
thing will be bigger than anything else that's gone before or that this one*

act will open doors in yourself and in the world you'd never anticipated. And it's a good thing, because you'd probably talk yourself right out of trying the very things that set you up for the rest of your life. I just stood on the board that afternoon for what seemed like forever, afraid but alive. Alive, Josh. There I was, facing danger and risk of my own choosing for the very first time and feeling the swell of courage rising in my chest. I knew I was going to do it before I did it. As I ran the length of the board and sprang off into a big, clumsy swan dive, it felt like I was running to meet myself. Like I was leaping past the two-dimensional adventure I'd found in characters and books and soaring into the three-dimensional adventure of living. It was magic.

I surfaced to the applause of my new friends and the beaming face of Timmy Parks. "Cool," was all he said as we raced each other to the ladder to climb and do it all over again. For the rest of that summer we dove from that high board. We learned jack-knives, swans, gainers and flips. Every time I felt queasy, Timmy would be there to show me how courage could get you through. He planted that warrior seed in my heart. Timmy Parks was the first warrior I ever met. He was totally alive, totally fearless, and somehow he made it easier for me to live the life I'd been given to live. I was able to shrug off the drab nature of my house and home, the railings of my father, the sickness, the puke, the lack of any Norman Rockwell renderings of family. Timmy Parks made me brave.

Of course, my dad got drunk, lost another job, and we moved across the city again and I had to say good-bye. That was in the early fall. I snuck back across town one day around the beginning of December. I remember that the whole place was festooned with Christmas lights and trappings. I wanted to spend an afternoon running the streets with my old companions, but when I got there I learned that Timmy was dead. He and his family had been killed in a car-crash. The lights and festive paraphernalia were incongruous on that trip back across town. It was the first ache I ever really allowed myself to feel. I never cried though. Not out of bullshit bravery or anything like that. No, I never cried for him because there was nothing to cry for. Something in me understood that Timmy Parks really lived. Lived. He never once backed down from life or its challenge, never once allowed himself to feel smaller in the face of anything, never failed to risk. We're perched forever on the diving board. That's

*what he taught me. We can either sit there and get diminished by fear,
slink down the ladder to the safety of the ground or we can soar off into
that big, wide empty and feel the rush that comes with courage. Become
more.*

*We carry something of the people that affect us within us forever, and
I carry the heart of Timmy Parks within me. Life's a high board, Josh, and
there's only two choices — back down or soar into space. Warriors soar.*

T his is Parkdale, chum," the cabbie was saying. "Any place in
particular you wanted to see?"

"Yes. Drop me off by a school," I answered.

He eyeballed me in the rearview mirror as though memorizing
my features. "Yeah. Sure, pal. Schools. You got it."

He wheeled arrogantly through the streets while I watched the
houses flow by, searching for a break in the uniformity. I imagined
Johnny walking out of one of these houses and turning up the street
towards his school. If school, books and lessons were the security
blanket he'd pulled around himself back then, I needed to see one.
It didn't really matter whether it was Johnny's old school or not, I
just wanted to soak up the atmosphere.

It was summer and there were children everywhere on the
streets. I found myself searching among them for a face like
Johnny's until I realized that the faces of the lonely, disenfranchised
and afraid are everywhere. Their faces passed in clumps of browns,
blacks and white. There didn't seem to be a whole lot of movement
between the races. The color lines were drawn indelibly everywhere,
even in the playgrounds. Latino youths played soccer together,
while a group of black kids hustled through a basketball game at the
opposite end of the same park. Beyond the fence two teams of white
children played slow-pitch baseball, yelling and laughing.

We pulled up in front of an older high school. The glass and
brick facade had a strangely recognizable quality you could find in

a school practically anywhere you traveled. Our high school in Walkerton looked almost like this Parkdale Collegiate Institute. Walkerton Secondary School, 1968, the year Denny McLain won thirty-one games for the Detroit Tigers, my father won first prize for our favorite heifer at the Mildmay Fall Fair, and I became an Indian. The first pair of events was greeted with unbridled exultancy and the latter was fraught with wonder at the hard kernel of meanness that exists in human hearts. I paid the driver and began to walk.

There's a hushed atmosphere to empty schools. It's almost as though the walls want to collapse upon themselves in loneliness for the clamor of voices, running feet, slamming doors, laughter and the stentorian trill of exasperated teachers. As I walked around the school that afternoon I remembered my own high-school years — how Johnny and I had grown through all the changes that happened to us.

When we'd walked into the halls of Walkerton Secondary, we entered with the expectation of adventure. Walkerton drew students from Paisley, Pinkerton, Kinloss, Formosa and all farms in between. There were roughly three hundred and fifty students there. We saw high school as a passageway into a world filled with the excitement of books, a place where dreams became tangible, a step closer to our manhood and the adult world. We were able to select courses for the first time, so I stuck pretty close to the academic bone while Johnny filled his options with music, art and drama. When the timetables were mailed out we were happy to see we would share three classes — phys ed, math and biology. That first morning a handful of our old Mildmay classmates was making the bus trip with us, and I felt comfortable and secure in that familiarity as the bus rolled up Highway 9.

Our lockers were just past a short hallway with wide ledges along the windows. When we passed through on the first morning we discovered that the ledges were a favorite gathering place for seniors before and after classes. There were about twenty boys and girls gathered there that morning. Awkward with people I hadn't met, I lowered my eyes as I passed. Johnny was beside me, along with Lenny Weber and Connie Shaus. I remember thinking, as the hubbub in the short hallway died down as we entered, how strange it was that silence was something you could hear.

"Holy shit! Is that an Injun?"

"Damn. You know, I believe it is. How'd he get here?"

"Musta escaped the reservation."

"Or jail."

"Circle the wagons! Circle the wagons!"

"Hey, Injun. Gottum heap big squaw in wigwam?"

"Look at him. He is a heap big squaw!"

The chorus degenerated into a hand-over-the-mouth war whoop as we passed. I made the mistake of looking up with a half grin in an attempt to deflect the teasing. Johnny stepped in a little closer as the laughter grew louder, more insistent.

"Hey, look. The Injun's got a handler."

"That's not a handler, that's his *trainer*."

"Can Injuns be trained?"

"Nah. Don't need to be. They shit outside by instinct!"

Johnny gave me a hard look and picked up the pace. By the time we got to the end of the hallway, the crowd along the ledges was listing all the known euphemisms for Indian, laughing and clapping at their favorites. Johnny's face was red and his lips were pinched tight together as we stepped into the main hallway near our lockers. Connie and Lenny stared straight ahead.

Johnny was staring at me wide-eyed. "You're just gonna take that?" he asked quietly.

"Take what?"

"Take *what*? Josh! They slammed you."

"Oh, that. They were just joking." Yet there had been a note underneath it all that rang with an unfamiliar urgency, an unsettling pitch I'd never heard before.

"Some joke. You like being called a squaw hopper?"

"I don't even know what that is. Besides, it doesn't matter."

"Doesn't *matter*? It doesn't *matter* that you have to spend five years listening to people put you down? Come on, Josh!"

"Johnny, they're just giving me a hard time because I'm new. Everyone gets a rough time when they're a niner."

"No, Josh. *I'm* a niner. You're an *Injun*."

"Big deal. It'll pass."

"Being Indian will pass?"

"Yeah. To them," I said.

"You're crazy."

"Yeah. I'm a crazy Injun. How's that?"

"Just watch yourself, okay? I'll see you at lunch."

The words and their edge had unsettled me. When I'd raised my eyes to the kids on the window ledge I'd seen something in their faces I couldn't name, a look vaguely familiar.

One early spring a wild cat had crossed the fields to invade our barn. They did that now and then, appearing shortly after the birth of a litter, killing the helpless kittens before their eyes had even opened, as if removing a challenge to their territory. My dad and I had taken the .22 and staked out a spot in the stable to wait for the cat. It had slunk out of the shadows and sat motionless on a beam, staring. Even as my father had raised the barrel of the gun towards its head, the cat had stared. As the seconds stretched unbearably towards eternity it had looked straight ahead at us, a look in its eyes that moved between defiance, recognition and a colder, darker emotion, one without edges or limits. When the shot rang out, it simply collapsed in a heap on the beam. I always wondered why it hadn't made an effort to flee. Instead it had sat there, that colder, darker emotion driving it to stay steadfast in the face of its own destruction.

I couldn't shake the image of that barn cat and as I entered my home-room class, I thought I saw it on the faces of some of the students. Ralphie Wendt grinned at me in recognition. We'd become almost friends in the final three years at Mildmay, joined by the bonds of sport and competition. He'd grown stocky and thick with the muscle of his father, and he admired the verve I'd begun to show in sports. Along with Ralphie were Victor Ringle, Teddy Hohnstein, Vera Dietz and Nancy Hossfeld. Their proximity helped ease the lost feeling I had in my belly just then. I nodded their way, heading towards an empty desk near the middle of the room.

"Can't sit there," said a red-haired boy with huge buck teeth.

I shrugged and headed to another desk closer to the back. As I approached, a tall blond in coveralls and sneakers slid over and sat in it with his hands on the desktop, fingers interlocked. He stared straight ahead, saying nothing. When I turned to the desk he'd just vacated, he slid back across in front of me and took the seat again.

"Mine," he said.

We repeated this little dance a few time. The silence in the room was thick as I stood there trying to believe it was all just some initiation ritual.

"You can't have both," I said.

He stood up suddenly. He was four inches taller than me, heavier, with a chiseled, rough-hewn look about him. He stared at me and I was reminded again of the cat in the barn.

"I can have whatever I want. Wanna try and take it? *Injun.*"

As I stepped away I saw Ralphie, eyes down, shaking his head sadly. The blond gave an exaggerated thumbs-up to the buck-toothed redhead and snickered. I took a seat at the back of the room, but as I sat the students around me rose silently and crossed the room to take other seats. Oppressive silence stretched all around us until our home-room teacher, Mr. Tooke, entered and began calling the role. The redhead's name was Allen Begg, the blond boy was Chris Hollingshead. When I responded to my name with a polite "Present, sir," they both turned and stared at me.

"What?" I said.

"Kane?" the redhead said. Your name is *Kane*?"

"Yeah. Why?"

"Nothin'," Chris said. "We just figured it'd be ... Shits in the Woods or something like that." Chris Hollingshead gushed to a roll of laughter across the room.

Mr. Tooke explained the daily procedures of home room, but I barely heard any of it. When we were sent out to find our way to the first class of the day, I walked the hallway alone. Ralphie, Victor and Teddy scurried down the hall as quickly as mice in flight. I felt, for the first time, a thick melancholic ache like homesickness, the kind you get on rainy afternoons a thousand miles away from those you love.

I ran the gauntlet again at lunch time. As we passed to and from our lockers, the crowd along the window ledges cat-called, whistled and whined words like wagon burner, spear chucker, squaw hopper, savage and itchy-bum. I held my head down, hoping to pass by invisibly. When we cleared the area and the hooting and hollering died down behind us, John laughed.

"Rednecks. I thought I left rednecks behind in Toronto. I don't believe it."

"What's a redneck?" I asked, grateful for a friend to talk to.

"*They* are," he said, hooking a thumb back over his shoulder. "A redneck is someone who hates anyone or anything that's different than them. They're stupid."

"I don't think they hate me. They don't even know me."

"They don't have to *know* you. They just have to see you're different."

"Different?"

"Yeah. You're Indian, they're white."

"So?"

"*So*? That's all they need."

"Why?"

"I don't know. I told you ... they're stupid."

"Maybe if I just talk to them."

"Yeah, right. Didn't you hear all that? Think they wanna talk to you? They'd just shit on you all over again. Worse, even."

"Because they think I'm an Indian?"

"Because you *are* an Indian."

"But I'm not! You know that."

"You are, Josh, you are. You're gonna have to face that. In your house, on the farm, with your parents, in Mildmay, maybe you think you're not, but you are. Out *here* you *are*!"

The afternoon had phys ed, biology and math, so Johnny and I stuck together for the rest of that day. Now and then, we'd pass clumps of students slouched against lockers or sitting in the hallways, and the silence would descend until we walked by. Johnny would stare ahead of us, tight-lipped and quiet, but I looked right at them. I looked to see if there were traces of that barn cat in their eyes or perhaps, even, a break in the iciness, a mute sign of welcome, or just a simple neutrality. I became aware that mine was the only brown face in the entire school.

I realized that even in Mildmay Public School the case had been the same. I just hadn't noticed it because I'd always been a part of a small, insulated world. Any differences had simply melded into the general background — I was accepted as the farmer and the Kane I believed myself to be. This new reception was like one of those bitter winter days when the wind cuts through the warmest of clothing, settling into the bones like a weight. I stood in the hallways of Walkerton Secondary School that day feeling as obvious and alone as a fencepost in a field of snow.

You lacked vision, that's all. If Indians and Christians have any common ground, it's visions. Your tradition has the burning bush, Ezekiel's wheel, the fiery chariot that comes down to take Elijah to heaven. Indians have the white buffalo, Black Elk's vision and the intimate kind that come from a vision quest. The difference is that Indians promote the seeing of visions while the church wants to keep it a part of the Bible. If you'd grown up in an Indian environment, you'd have known about vision, maybe even had one by the time you were fourteen. Vision gives you a sense of yourself, a sense of the universe and your place in it, your direction, your focus, your role. Instead, you walked into Walkerton with rural blinders on. I spent my first ten years in Toronto where I saw what the world was really like. Sure, the laid-back atmosphere of a place like Mildmay can help you get over that, maybe even forget some of it, but the world slaps you in the face sometimes and you wake up. You got slapped hard for the first time that fall. But you didn't need to.

I love your parents, Josh. If mine had been a fraction as devoted as *yours, maybe things would have been different for me. But once you step into the adult world and realize you have to react to everything one way or another, then you start to realize that devotion has a price. The price is vulnerability. You walk into the world used to protection and shelter, the idea that you're always going to have that cocoon around you. No one's ever explained to you that there are spiteful, hateful, mean and vicious people out there. No one's ever told you that the world, for the most part, categorizes on a skin-first basis; all your niceties, all your manners, all your faith and belief, all your spiritual spit and polish doesn't add up to a hill of beans in their eyes. You're just an Indian, a nigger, a chink, a rag-head, a nip or a Paki.*

But the people that have learned all along how it feels to live within that skin, all the things their skin encloses, all the truths, the strengths, the uniqueness, the histories, philosophies, those are the people who can transcend the judgments. They have a vision of themselves and their people. Your parents, Josh, never let you find a vision of yourself that was real. They were so devoted to you, so set on the principle of teaching you the good Christian way, the Kane way, they never allowed you to find the Indian in you. They never allowed you the knowledge of the world as it really is, the way it can slice into you like it did that first day in Walkerton. They let you walk into a hostile environment unarmed. You walked in there without a vision of yourself or a vision of the world. All you had was love, faith and belief. Now that's good for most things but without vision and action based on that vision, love, faith and belief are just butter in the hot skillet of living.

You were unarmed. You didn't even know what a redneck was. You didn't have one thing to fall back on when the name-calling and the hatred came up in your face. You didn't have any cultural pride, any heritage, any tradition, any knowledge of Indian things at all except for the hokey shit we got in textbooks. Pocahontas and the First Thanksgiving hardly qualify as ammunition. And that's dangerous. How the hell is a person supposed to defend their self when they don't know what that self is, what it represents or how it's sustained, defined and perpetuated?

That's how assimilation starts, Josh. They take everything away and never allow you access to the real information about yourself or your people, your history, your heritage, your spiritual legacy, your language.

When the attack starts you're so removed from yourself, a part of you starts to believe it all. Pretty soon you're willing to do anything to fit in, to appear to be a part of instead of apart from, to shut the shouting off so you can live with some semblance of peace. The more you adopt the outside ways, the more you disappear because there's nothing left to chain you to yourself, your real self. You'd do anything to shut off the shouting, but by the time it dies down around you, the price tag appears and you realize that it's going to take forever for the yelling to go down inside yourself.

How do I know all this? Look at my life. I was never given a history or a heritage either. I guess the truth is that you don't have to be an Indian to be disinherited. The only difference between you and me is that I was white and never had to enter a room skin first.

I have always loved photographs. The way they bring time and place and emotion into your hands like an offering. The way they capture the essence of their living subjects, making them alive again in intimate recollections, the little things you put aside as minor until you see them again. The way the hair may have tufted atop the curl of ear, or the tiny wrinkles on a young girl's brow, the half-worried look like yearning around the eyes, or the way the mouth behaved in unrestrained jubilance. They sit in the shallow cup of your palm pulsing with history, the hushed notes of a life, a scale, measured, exact and timeless. I have always looked a photographs as though I could reinhabit the places they showed, like I could re-enter my life at certain junctures and recall the thought that passed through my brain at the moment the shutter closed, or that I could be present at the moments of my history that existed before I did, step into the anonymous lives of people like my grandparents and feel the veined and furrowed backs of hands I have always admired but never known.

I sat in the living room the evening of that first day at

Walkerton Secondary thumbing through the Kane family album like I'd done countless times before. I saw the passage of generational time in the photos of great-grandparents, grandparents, uncles, aunts and cousins, the great spawn of Kane family history. I saw the ruddy, weathered look of farmers, their wives and children. I saw the carbon-copy features passed on unmistakably down the line of years. I saw the faces, the skin, the color, white — until mine. Suddenly sepia.

The darkening like an eclipse across the face of a planet.

As I leafed through fourteen years I saw myself for the first time as a grafting on the family tree. My father reading *The Farmers' Almanac* in his chair beside the radio and my mother, lips moving slightly, perusing Catherine Marshall's *A Man Called Peter* beside the window seemed to me as pale and luminous as we imagine ghosts to be, their whiteness stark and startling. I stared at the flesh of my arm, back up at them, down to my skin again and back up at them, the contrast mesmerizing, suddenly compelling, the word *Indian* and the word *Kane* voicing themselves in whispers with each shift of focus.

"What are you looking at, son?" my mother asked.

"The family tree," I answered quickly, quietly.

"Finding anything?" my father asked.

"Branches," I said. "Just branches."

Allen Begg and Chris Hollingshead started the trouble. They were townies from Walkerton who'd never associated much with farmers. Chris's father ran a small mechanic shop, fixing small engines and doing odd welding work, and the Begg family had run the local laundromat and Sunoco station for years. Their families were third-generation Walkerton people, and for Allen and Chris the town was their undisputed territory, something claimed by virtue of the years they'd crawled, strolled, cycled and run through its streets, shortcuts and pathways. Because both sets of parents had to work full time to make ends meet, they were used to a lack of supervision and the freedom to make their own decisions. By the time they reached Walkerton Secondary School they were rebels and were used to proving it. They'd grown up lean and tough from schoolyard fights and tussles after hockey games. Allen and Chris were a pair of alley cats on the prowl, stalking their territory, eyes keen for prey.

Every day in home room they huddled together whenever I'd walk in, snickering and pointing and making faces. Chris, the biggest of the two, would purposely stand in my way, glaring down the four inches in height that he had on me, fists on his hips, smirking. When I'd back away or step around him, they'd both imitate the sound of a chicken, to the laughter of our classmates. In the hallways they'd follow me, trying to trip me or knock the books out of my hands. I was fortunate that they were both enrolled in technical shops and I shared only home room and phys ed with them. Still, facing their derision first thing each morning was an ordeal, and having to play against them in the competitive atmosphere of gym class was the breeding ground for trouble.

Johnny and I had grown a few inches and put on about fifteen pounds each. Neither of us was very big but as we'd grown out of the bony adolescent phase, we'd become coordinated and lithe in our movements. Our baseball game was running at a higher level and we found most sports easy. The glee and abandon we'd discovered in baseball allowed us to relish other sports too. We were fast, strong from the farm work and energetic in our play. We'd become athletes.

At the start of the second week of high school we trooped into the gymnasium with Mr. Hughes to begin learning football. Johnny and I both favored black high-top sneakers, loose white T-shirts and baggy gym shorts for the freedom of movement. At that time everyone was wearing white Adidas running shoes and T-shirts emblazoned with cartoon characters or college crests and tighter, sleeker, colored gym shorts. Chris and Allen jumped right on us the first day.

"Hey, look. Welfare checks mustn'ta come in yet!" Allen said, buck teeth gaping.

"Yeah. Are those shorts or some kinda loin cloth?" Chris added to yowls of laughter from the class.

"Not this shit again," Johnny murmured.

"Check the sneakers! Geek shoes. Bet you'd rather have yer moccasins, eh, Injun?" Allen whined.

"Hey, Al," Chris said, elbowing his partner in the ribs and glaring at me. "Better keep your eyes on the football."

"Why?" Allen asked.

"Because. I think the Injun figures it's a turkey. He might try to eat it!"

"Nah. He'll never catch it. How could he eat it?"

"Easy. He'll sneak up on it. Injuns are always sneaking up on things."

"I know what you mean. I have a bad case of Indian underwear right now."

"What the hell is Indian underwear?"

"You know, the kind that keeps creeping up on you!"

Mr. Hughes whistled us into a circle and began explaining the proper motions for throwing a spiral. He tossed a few light passes to Ralphie, who was trying out for a lineman's position on the school team. The passes settled into his big hands easily. After having us all line up and mime throwing for a few minutes, Mr. Hughes dumped a large bag of footballs in front of us. Then he asked us to get in groups of four to begin passing back and forth. Johnny and I headed towards Lenny and Ralphie, but Chris stepped in front of us.

"Hey, fellas. Wanna be in our group?" he asked, glaring down at us.

"Not particularly," Johnny said, looking right up into the tall boy's face.

"Why? Scared? Or are you afraid we throw too hard?" Allen asked.

"Neither," Johnny said.

"Well, then? Come on," Chris said, motioning us into a square.

"Don't talk much, that Injun," he said to Allen as we headed to our spots.

Johnny and I exchanged glances as Chris tossed a soft pass diagonally into Allen's hands. Allen promptly threw it back to him, and they played a private game of toss-and-catch while Johnny and I stood there watching, restless and embarrassed. They kept it up, ignoring us entirely and laughing, congratulating each other loudly on their passes and catches.

"Hey! We're here too," Johnny said loudly.

"What?" Allen said, feigning surprise.

"You guys wanna play? Oh, my goodness, Al, how could we be so rude? Let's let the geeks play with us," Chris said and whipped a hard, fast pass at Johnny's chest. The ball was a blur, a straight bullet of a spiral. Johnny caught it lightly, fingers spread like a baseball glove, letting his hands slip back slightly to cushion the ball's impact. Then he turned the ball over a few times and tossed a soft, easy spiral to me. He looked at Chris and grinned.

"Nice toss," he said lightly. "Wobbly, but nice."

Chris reddened. All the throwing we'd done with a baseball had strengthened the muscles needed to throw a football. Even though the motion was different, our arms were used to throwing. When I unleashed a blur of a spiral myself, it went right through Allen's hands and caromed off his chest with a solid thud. We heard cackles of laughter from across the gym as Allen reddened and limped away to retrieve the ball. I felt a sudden sense of revenge that a part of me cherished. Johnny looked at me and grinned mischievously.

The drill became just that — we began to drill the ball at each other diagonally across our square. Chris threw at me and I threw at him, while Johnny and Allen squared off against each other. For all his height, Chris couldn't match the speed and weight I was able to generate on each throw. Meanwhile, poor Allen was staggered time and time again by Johnny's line-drive spirals. We could hear the resounding splat of leather on skin and bone as the townies struggled to hold onto our passes. For our part, we simply applied science to the game, cushioning each catch with a slight relaxing of the fingers and arms. We looked surprisingly casual compared to the disarray of Chris and Allen. Their arms grew tired quickly, but ours were just getting nicely warmed up when Mr. Hughes whistled the drill to a close.

He instructed us on two pass routes. For a Y-out you ran ten yards straight up from the passer and then angled to the right five yards where the passer hit you with the ball. For a button-hook you again ran straight up from the passer, stopped, and turned abruptly to face him as the ball arrived in your hands. It looked simple enough and we were eager to try it. Chris and Allen were red in the face after our first drill and somewhat more silent than they had been at the start of the class. We moved outside to the football field and began the drill.

Never ones to slouch in games, Johnny fired a hard pass right into my hands on my first Y-out. As he moved out to run the same pattern, Allen wobbled a throw over his head. It looked uncatchable but Johnny leapt high into the air, grabbing the ball down with one hand and squeezing it to his chest with the other. Chris ran a gawky pattern, and I hit him in the shoulder with a bullet. He grabbed the wounded shoulder with his other hand, grimacing. Again the drill deteriorated into a test of wills and stamina. No one took it easy on anyone else, although Johnny and I both threw harder when we passed to the townies. We caught everything that was thrown our way. Allen and Chris were bruised from balls that bounced off wrists, forearms, shoulders, chests and foreheads, but they stubbornly refused to let on that Johnny and I were getting the best of them and we silently appreciated that. All of us were covered in sweat when Mr. Hughes whistled us in for the end of the class.

"Well done, boys," he said. "Kane and Gebhardt, you guys might consider trying out for the Wolverines. We could use a couple of good players. You need to beef up, though."

Chris and Allen glared at us. They never said a word while we showered and changed, disappearing before the rest of the class. Johnny and I basked in the accolades of our peers and agreed to show a few of them how we managed to get such tight spirals all the time. It seemed again that sports would melt the barriers away and I felt myself relaxing, believing that it was all going to pass. Chris and Allen were silent the next day in home room, but I began to notice them huddling with the seniors along the window ledge when we passed by. I believed that they were finally letting up, trying to score points with the seniors instead of putting pressure on me.

In the second gym class of the week, Mr. Hughes whistled us in to divide us into teams of six for flag football. Johnny and I somehow made the same team and lined up across from a smug and volatile-looking duo of Allen Begg and Chris Hollingshead.

The whole point of flag football is to score touchdowns. It's primarily a passing game: once the receiver catches the ball and begins running, the defense attempts to ground the ball by tearing off one of two cloth strips, or flags, attached to a belt around the receiver's waist. Play continues from the point where the defense drops the flag. The game is designed for little or no physical contact. Which is why it surprised everyone when Chris flattened me at the line of scrimmage with a two-handed straight arm to the chest just as the ball was snapped. It was a hard shot. I felt the air rush out of my lungs and as I hit the ground, I saw twinkles of light in front of my eyes. The world spun sickeningly, slowly beneath me. I could hear Allen's wild cackle and then Chris's face spun into focus above me. He was leering at me and laughing.

"Josh! Josh! Are you okay?" Johnny was shaking me by the shoulders and peering into my eyes.

Mr. Hughes dropped into focus beside him. He cupped my head lightly with one big hand and brushed my forehead with the other. "Kane? Joshua? Are you okay?" he asked, looking relieved when I nodded limply and struggled weakly to get up. "Wait just a minute, lad. Take it easy for a second. What happened here?" he asked, looking around at the circle of faces above me.

No one said a word. Johnny looked at me, nodded slowly and then turned a slit-eyed gaze at Allen and Chris, who stood there with smug smiles on their faces. They looked back at him and then down at me. Chris shrugged his shoulders innocently and Allen offered an exaggerated expression of surprise, shrugged as well and moved away. The rest of the class shifted uneasily from foot to foot as Mr. Hughes peered at them one by one, awaiting an answer. When he didn't get one, he helped me slowly to my feet, checked me one last time and called us into a circle.

"Okay. Now I don't know what happened here but it better not happen again. We're here to have fun. Any more incidents like this and the people responsible will answer to me. No contact, grab the flags, play fair. Kane? You okay?"

I was leaning on Johnny's shoulder while my head cleared. I nodded. Mr. Hughes looked at me hard for a moment, then tossed the football to me and motioned us to carry on with our game. As we split into our groups, Allen spit at my feet and grinned at me impishly.

"Tough game, eh, Injun?" he said and spat again, narrowly missing my sneaker.

"Stay away from my area, Chief! Next time you'll stay down!" Chris said, fist in front of his chest.

Johnny looked at them both with a steely glare. As we gathered around him for a huddle, he looked at me and winked. "You go quarterback, Josh. Hit me ten yards out coming across in front. Then watch!" he said.

The ball was snapped and I stepped back four steps to pass. I saw Johnny make a ninety-degree cut ten yards upfield and speed parallel to me with Allen in hot pursuit. I hit him with a feathery little pass at his waist and as he dropped his hands to gather it in, he stopped abruptly, jamming his feet down hard and leaning backwards slightly. Allen barreled right into him at full speed and the collision sent Johnny sprawling forward while Allen folded limp as a wet rag to the ground. Chris ran up and shoved Johnny roughly.

"What the hell was that?" he demanded, red in the face.

"First down," Johnny said calmly, flipping me the football.

We gathered for a huddle as Chris bent over to help Allen to his feet and help him back into the defensive zone. The faces of our teammates were agog in admiration for the effects of Johnny's play. He looked at me and grinned, wiping a little sweat off his brow. "Now, let's embarrass 'em with speed! Josh, go out five yards, fake a button-hook, then take off straight up the sideline. I'll hit you with a bomb!" he said and clapped his hands in enthusiasm.

With the snap of the ball I drove hard straight at Chris, who back-pedaled furiously, sneering into my face all the while. At five yards I planted my feet hard, turned a perfect button-hook and as Chris tried to step in front of me, I whirled and took off as fast as I could up the sideline. He swore loudly trying to catch me but I was too far ahead and too fast. Johnny's high bomb of a pass settled into my arms like a butterfly about thirty yards out and I scored easily with Chris lurching along behind me. He leaned over with his hands on his knees, panting for breath and swearing between gasps. I trotted past, aglow with the satisfaction of scoring and the sweet taste of revenge. I dropped the ball wordlessly at Chris's feet. Our teammates celebrated loudly, tousling my hair and slapping Johnny on the back. When I looked back, Allen and Chris were watching us, whispering back and forth.

On their first play from scrimmage Allen and Chris's team ran a Y-out for a twelve-yard gain. Then a shovel pass to a receiver coming from the backfield late got them ten more yards and they were threatening to score. We prepared ourselves grimly for the third play, determined to shut them down. At the snap of the ball Allen came right at me like I'd done to Chris. I back-pedaled, keeping my eyes on his chest so I could read the direction of the turn I was expecting any second. As Allen turned to button-hook in front of me, I planted my feet at the exact same second. I didn't see Chris steamrolling across the field and he hit me with full force. I flew through the air and my right shoulder plowed into the ground. Groggily, I got up just in time to see Johnny punch Chris hard in the jaw. The taller boy crumpled. Mr. Hughes's whistle was tooting madly from somewhere down field as Johnny clobbered Allen, who was trying to get past him towards me. The redhead fell to one knee, holding the side of his head in both hands and grimacing. Our teammates swarmed around Johnny to keep him from inflicting further damage on the two townies, and he struggled mightily against them before Mr. Hughes arrived to settle things down.

"All right, all right!" he said, wading into the middle of the melee. "Who started this?"

"The fuckin' Injun!" Chris screamed, pointing wildly at me and trying to claw his way past his own team. "He's dirty. He cheats."

"Gebhardt. What about it?" Mr. Hughes asked, staring hard at Johnny.

"He doesn't cheat," Johnny said.

I wobbled over to the crowd.

"Kane? You got anything to say about this? Who hit you, son?"

I looked at Johnny. He just stared at me with that wide-open gaze and I knew exactly what it was I had to say. "It was an accident. I wasn't watching where I was going. I didn't see who ran into me."

Mr. Hughes surveyed us all. He shook his head sadly. "Okay, that's it, then. Everybody into the showers. And no funny business in there. I mean it!"

Silently we paraded into the gym and on into the change rooms. Johnny draped an arm over my shoulders and squeezed lightly. At the door Allen and Chris stepped past us, glaring over their shoulders. Not a word was said all the time we showered and changed. Finally, as he was reaching down to tie up his shoes, Chris looked over at us on the other side of the room.

"This isn't over, *Injun!*" he spat.

"Long way from over," Allen added.

"Why don't you guys just leave it alone?" Johnny said. "He's not bugging you."

"What are you, his baby-sitter?" Allen said. "Gotta do his fightin' for him? What is he, chicken? You chicken, *Injun*? Huh?"

"No," I said quietly.

"*No*," Allen mimicked. "Fuckin' redskin!"

Johnny stood up. "Hey. You guys wanna do it one more time? Right here?" He looked back and forth at both of them.

"We ain't got no beef with you, Gebhardt," Chris said. "I'm willing to forget the cheap shot you gave me out there 'cause I think you're okay. It's the Injun we wanna get."

"Too bad," Johnny said. "You wanna get him, you're gonna have to get me too."

"Why doesn't he talk? Is he stupid?" Allen whined.

"No, I'm not stupid," I said.

"If you think not rattin' us out to Hughes is gonna make us grateful or make us forget," Chris said, "you're wrong, Kane. We don't want you here. Nobody does. You're a fuckin' Injun. You belong on a reserve, not here."

"Just watch your back, Injun," Allen said.

"He doesn't have to," Johnny said, firmly. "I'll be watching it for him."

"Then that's where *you're* stupid," Chris said before heading out the door.

I climbed aboard the bus that afternoon and slumped into the seat beside Johnny.

"You okay?" he asked.

"Yeah. Sore but okay."

"Nice move on the touchdown."

"Thanks. Nice pass."

"What are you gonna do?"

"About what?"

"About *what*? Are you *nuts*? Hollingshead and Begg are gunning for you and you ask me about *what*?"

"Oh, that. I'm going to do nothing."

"You can't do *nothing*."

"Why not?"

"Because you have to fight."

"Why?"

"Because you're a warrior."

"You always say that. Warrior this and warrior that. Like because I'm Indian I'm automatically a warrior. Well, I won't fight. I'm just going to do nothing and when they see it's not bothering me, they'll let it go."

"So it's not bothering you?"

"Well, yeah, it's bothering me. But it'll pass."

"Bullshit. They're gonna pound you out one of these days."

"Why?"

"*Why*? Because they hate you."

"I don't hate them."

"Well, you should. You like all those names? The lipstick on the locker? The notes? You like all that?"

"No. But it doesn't mean I have to fight."

"What does it mean, then?"

"It means I have to forgive them."

"*Forgive* them? Is that what your folks say?"

"They don't know."

"What?" Johnny gaped.

"They don't know. I haven't told them."

"Why not?"

"Because it would just bother them for no reason. Look, in a week this will all be over. Everyone will get interested in something else and they'll forget about me. I won't upset my parents over something that doesn't add up to much in the first place."

"Being hated doesn't add up to much?"

"Not to me."

"Bullshit."

"Johnny!"

"You're full of shit, Josh. You've been learning from my old man."

"What's that supposed to mean?"

"It means you're behaving just like he does. You walk around letting on that whatever's really eating away at you isn't really eating away at you. That everything's okay. That *you're* okay. But you're not."

"I'm not like him."

"Sure you are. Neither of you wants to fight. Him because he's too drunk and you because you think God's gonna swoop down and save you, change everything for you, make it okay. Well, it ain't gonna happen."

"How do you know?"

"Because God's a warrior too. He wants to see you fight for your answers."

"Yeah. I agree."

"Well?"

"Well what?" I said.

"Why don't you fight?"

"Because that's not the kind of fighting God wants me to do. He wants me to fight with kindness and understanding. He wants me to fight with love."

"Then I'd better keep watching your back."

From my earliest days when my parents and I would kneel by my bed together and I would clasp my little hands against my chest, bow my head and whisper the "Now I lay me down" prayer of childhood, prayer has always been a soft and gentle place. Throughout my life it has been my refuge and my strength. I never once doubted that the Lord harbored my soul those nights or that I would not die before I woke. I eased into dreams secure in the knowledge that angels hovered over me and that I would awake again to the resplendent light of love of God and parents.

As I got older and my parents schooled me on the nature of prayer, I began gaining comfort from sincere prayers for the well-being of others and for the world. I knew intuitively that prayers of thanks at the end of a day for all its blessings, both the seen and the unseen, guaranteed me peaceful slumber. A grateful man is a contented man, my father would say, a sentiment echoed in my mother's assertion that salvation was born in an attitude of grati-tude. I learned that I should never pray selfishly unless the things I asked for would ultimately benefit others. I also learned that courage came from offering prayers for those that hurt you — your enemies and revilers. Faith, my mother would say, grew from the courage to pray for others before yourself and for the courage to pray for strength and direction instead of answers. Contrary to Johnny's belief that I expected God to swoop down and change everything, I believed that he would strengthen me and that the answers would come when I was ready. So each of those nights, alone in my room, I prayed for strength and I prayed for the health and well-being of everyone at that school who mistreated me.

These days I know that faith is an acronym. It spells out Finding An Insight That Heals. I know that having the courage to pray for the strength to do God's will in troubling situations — instead of for its immediate resolution or removal — results, eventually, in the dawning of an insight that heals the situation. An insight far removed from what the mind or desire might tell you is right and appropriate. But in the privacy of my room those nights, I knew only that the answer would come in God's time and not mine and that prayer was the source of the comfort and strength that allowed me to walk back into those hallways each morning with a measure of dignity.

"I was speaking to Pastor Chuck about you the other day, Joshua," my father said one morning in the middle of the second week of high school.

"About what?" I asked.

"Well, Mother and I think it's time you started communicant classes."

"That's right, son," my mother said, setting aside her Bible. "You're old enough to become a confirmed member of the church and to take Communion with us."

"Really? When?" I asked.

"Tomorrow night. We'll drive you in to the church and hang around for late-night shopping until you're through," my father said.

"How long are the classes?"

"About an hour or so. For six weeks," my mother said. "You could take Communion on Thanksgiving Sunday."

Johnny called later that night and I told him my news. For all I knew the Gebhardts had never been churchgoing people and I took great pains to explain the concepts of Communion, confirmation and church. I told him about the responsibilities involved in being a good church member and what I believed it could mean to my life. Things like being connected to a community of people who shared the same beliefs, traditions, ceremonies, rituals and outlook. (My father, of course, put it more eloquently. When two believers get together, he'd say, whether it's under a tree or in the middle of a corn field, and they share their belief and faith, or they simply share themselves openly and honestly, open their hearts to each other, then the shade of that tree or the sweep of that field becomes their church.) I explained what I knew of the Presbyterian church, its organization, history and message. I also told him about my prayers at night and how this opportunity seemed like a partial answer.

"So, it might not exactly solve my problems at school, but it could lead to the answer," I said.

"And you believe that?" he asked.

"I do," I said firmly.

"Well, good for you. Me, I think you should just deck Chris Hollingshead."

"But that won't solve anything," I said.

"It'll shut him up! It'll make him back off! It'll at least make people know that you won't be pushed around!"

"But will it, Johnny?"

"Yeah, it will. Trust me."

"I do trust you."

"Then fight, Josh. Fight!"

"I can't."

"Why?"

"Because. I just can't."

"Because that's what your *church* says?"

"Yeah. Well, no. It's what *I* say."

"You wanna know something, Josh?"

"What?"

"You just told me that when you sign up as a member of the church, that you're gonna have a whole community that shares your beliefs, ceremonies, rituals and stuff, right?"

"Yeah."

"Well, you already got that."

"I do? Where?"

"Inside you! The *Indian* inside you! All you gotta do is hook up to that and you have all the stuff the church says you need. You're an Indian, Josh. You're a warrior."

"The way you talk, all Indians do is fight."

"Yeah, well, at least it's doing something about it."

"You think I'm chicken, Johnny?"

"Chicken? No, Josh. I just think you gotta start being who you are."

"I'm Joshua Kane."

"You're Joshua Kane, warrior. You're Thunder Sky, remember?"

"I remember. But, Johnny, you gave me that name. And ... and ... you said that one day people would really listen to me. So maybe this is one of those times they'll listen to me."

"Maybe. But maybe they'll listen to you cry, Josh."

"Do warriors cry, Johnny?"

"No. Everybody knows that Indians don't cry."

"Then I guess I'll never be an Indian.

"You already are. And you already have a tribe."

"I do?"

"Yeah. Me. Look, Josh, I don't like church. I only went there maybe two times in all my life but I don't like it. I don't really believe in God and stuff. I think that if there really was a God He'd have given me a whole better deal than I've got. So, we're different. I think you gotta start being an Indian but you don't see that. I think you gotta be a warrior and fight. But you won't. Why, I do not know, but you won't. You wanna start these classes because you believe they'll lead you to an answer. I don't think so. I think the answer is to knock the shit out of Hollingshead and Begg. So, we're *really* different. But you know what?"

"What?"

"I'm your blood brother and I'm right behind you, Josh. Even though I don't agree with you, I'm right behind you."

"Thanks, Johnny."

"No problem. It's a warrior thing."

"It's a Christian thing, too."

"Sure, Josh. Sure."

P astor Chuck was a good man. He'd started his theological training at a small Bible college in Alberta when he was just out of high school. He incorporated the ebullient, hand-clapping effervescence of small gospel churches into his services and had been one of the first ministers to introduce popular inspirational readings into his services. We'd hear selections from Hugh Prather, Anne Morrow Lindbergh, Kahlil Gibran and even *The Velveteen Rabbit* once, as prologues to sermons. He wore jeans and sandals under his robes and spent a great deal of time and energy encouraging the young people of the congregation to participate in services. Under his guidance the junior choir had swelled and sang spiritual lyrics to the tunes of hits of the day accompanied by electric guitars, piano, bass and drums. Many times there was a short skit presented by the St. Giles' Players he'd started. He organized hikes along the Bruce Trail, sing-alongs, camp outs, volleyball games, fishing trips and bake sales. St. Giles came alive under his direction, transforming the word *church* in the minds of the entire congregation.

His real name was Reverend Charles Hendrickson, but his manner reflected a farmer more than it reflected a doctoral degree in theology. He preferred Pastor to Reverend, even as far as requesting that the Elders of the church call him Chuck or Pastor Chuck, which of course spread to the entire membership. He spoke of God as a friend, someone he talked to and shared with every day of his life, someone he turned to in the face of sorrow, desperation or simple human longing. When he came to visit us, as he often did, making the rounds of his rural congregation, our house seemed even brighter than normal. He joke, laughed, teased, talked of crops and weather, crafts and readings and always had time to spend alone with me, talking and gossiping like old pals. I liked him and I trusted him.

There were four of us young people who gathered in the basement classroom to begin confirmation classes that fall. We were all about the same age, two boys and two girls, but the others had the advantage of being town kids who'd spent a great deal of time with Pastor Chuck in either the choir or the Young People's church group.

Pastor Chuck arrived wearing jeans and a faded sweatshirt. He shook our hands, welcoming each of us warmly.

"Well," he said heartily and paused to look at us. "You're here. I'm really glad to see each of you. Three of you know each other pretty well, and Joshua will be a new friend to the rest of you. I'm sure you'll all have a chance to talk a lot in these next six weeks. Welcome, everybody."

He went on to explain what membership in a church meant to him. He talked about his life as a young boy in Eastern Ontario and how his parents had to work very hard to keep the family going. So hard that Sunday was always just another day of working and never set aside for family or God. He spoke of his brothers and him having to go out to work alongside their bricklayer father when he was only twelve. The only life lesson he learned from that experience was that life was hard and you had to work hard to survive.

He spoke of school and how in those days reciting the Lord's Prayer right after the national anthem was standard practice, but the words had always seemed so empty to him, just another exercise they had to do each day. Because he had to work at such a young age, he never had the chance to play with his classmates. He and his brothers moved around their city and their school as outsiders, unaccepted and belittled. Loneliness was a feeling he got used to very young, he said, and by the time he was fifteen he'd come to accept it as a condition of living. Then, his father died. The family was swept into turmoil, not knowing how they'd survive on his mother's small seamstress's salary, or how they'd afford the funeral costs. The boys prepared to drop out of school and work their father's business. Then, he said, the first of many miracles happened in his life. A group of people from the church down the street arrived the afternoon following his father's death. They brought hampers of food, clothing, a promise from the congregation to offset the funeral costs, offers of part-time jobs for each of the boys, a better-paying job for their mother in the office of the church. And, most important, they brought the light of Christian example into his world.

He became a regular at that church, Knox Presbyterian. Every time he walked into it, he said, there were hands stretched out in welcome. There was a peace that flowed from every board, stone and nail, and in the singing, in the depths of those old, staid Presbyterian hymns those Sunday mornings, it seemed the loneliness he'd lived with so long was swept away on those undulating refrains. When he was sixteen he took confirmation classes and became a member of the church.

And his life changed.

He became active in the youth groups, joined the choir, read the text in services and attended every function the church held. Through all of it he was led by the example of those who'd been there during his family's need. They showed him what it meant to be a Christian, how it took the walking of the walk, he said, not the talking of the talk. If his Bible didn't have pictures, he told us, it was because all the illustrations he ever needed were sitting around him every Sunday morning. They led him to a belief, faith and dependence on the hand of a loving God to guide and nurture him. They were all the pastor he'd ever needed, he said. Now that he was a minister himself, he said, he realized that membership in the church and the feeling of belonging, rightness and wholeness that came with it was the catalyst that led him to a fulfilled life.

I felt honored by this open sharing of his life and I felt a bond with him growing inside me. He finished the first session by outlining our course of study, encouraging us to read our Bibles, pray and be good to each other and ourselves. Then we draped our arms around each other's shoulders and he led us in a prayer asking for our protection, shelter and guidance until our next class.

He stood by the door as we paraded out; I made sure to be the last in line. As I shook his hand he smiled broadly at me.

"Well, Joshua, what do you think?" he asked.

"I think I like it," I said, waiting as he locked the church door behind us.

"Good. I hope you find as much here as I did when I was a teenager."

"I know what you meant," I said.

"About what, Joshua?"

"About the loneliness. I felt alone lots."

"Really?"

"Yeah. It's hard to have friends when you're on the farm. You're always so busy and it's kind of far between homes, you know."

"I understand. Do you have friends, Joshua?"

"Yeah. One, anyway. Johnny Gebhardt."

"Gebhardt? We don't have them in our congregation, do we?"

"No, sir. They live in Mildmay and they don't go to church."

"Oh. And he's a good friend, this Johnny?"

"Oh, yes, sir. He's the best. But, Pastor Chuck ... I was wondering about something."

"Yes, Joshua?"

"Well, it's kind of about ... belonging."

"Belonging to the church?"

"No, sir. Just ... belonging. You know that I'm adopted and that my real mother was an Indian?"

"Yes, I knew that."

"Well, my friend Johnny says that makes me an Indian. But I've lived with *this* mother and father all my life and ... well, that makes me a Kane, doesn't it? I mean, I was born an Indian but I've never lived as one. I've always lived as a Kane. But Johnny says that I have to start being an Indian — a warrior — because that's what I was born to be. But I believe that God wanted me to be a

Kane, otherwise he wouldn't have brought me to this family. Besides, I don't know anything about being Indian ... but I know how to be a Kane."

"And how do you go about being a Kane, Joshua?"

"I just do what my parents taught me to do. Be good to people, pray, work hard, study. That sort of stuff."

"And do you like being a Kane? Doing that sort of stuff?"

"Yeah! But Johnny says I gotta have a tribe, people who share the same ceremonies, rituals, beliefs and stuff. That's where I'll learn to be who I am, he says."

"Your friend Johnny's right about needing people, people who share the way we look at the world, the way we react to it. In that sense you've already got a tribe, Joshua."

"Sure, in the church. But what about my Indian part? How do I learn to deal with that? Do I pretend I don't know where I came from? Go on being the only brown one in my family and in my school, ignoring it?"

"Joshua, God created you. He sent you into this world to become the best person that you can become. And in order to help you do that, He gave you the power of choice, the ability to make choices about who you become. You can either use that power alone and find your way the best you can, or you can use the other power He gave you. The power of prayer. You can use that and ask for help to make the right choices, guidance, Joshua. I don't know what He has in mind for you, so I can't tell you how to deal with this question, what choices to make. All I can do is tell you that He'll provide answers. Just trust and pray, Joshua, and things will get clearer. Trust and pray."

"Will I become an Indian?"

"I don't know. But you *will* become who you were meant to be."

He squeezed my shoulder affectionately before I headed towards the parking lot where my parents sat waiting in the old Dodge. As I moved between the church and my family that night, I knew intuitively that it would be the journey I would make always, a path I would travel by memory long after my sight had faded, a straight line that ran from heart to home to family.

The first indication that things were changing was that my home-room class didn't automatically fall into silence when I entered the next morning. Allen and Chris stared innocently towards the front of the room when I passed and walked silently out the door behind me when we were dismissed to our first class. When I passed through the crowd of ledge-sitters that day, both of them were part of the group, but the catcalls and name-calling were absent. Johnny and I exchanged surprised looks, and relief surged through me. The nature of prayer was working its course, and I offered a silent prayer of gratitude for the reprieve.

That day the banners went up inviting everyone to the Freshman Welcoming Dance the next Friday. There was going to be a buffet, a brief introduction of all the club leaders and sports teams, welcoming speeches by the class president and the administration, followed by a big dance with door prizes and a dance contest. Johnny and I had never been to a dance before, so we were unsure of what to expect. With the apparent withdrawal of hostilities around me I figured it would be a fun thing to be part of and I encouraged Johnny to show up as well. He mumbled something about two left feet, buck-toothed girls in sweaters and jocks in suits. I grinned and told him it would be good for him.

When gym class passed with no confrontation, just an awkward silence from Allen and Chris, we were both relieved. We left school that day in high spirits, the chatter on the bus centering on nothing but the dance. It would be our first high-school event, a benchmark in our passage from elementary school kids to teenagers, and everyone was eager for it. My parents welcomed news of the dance as a good thing and we talked about the clubs with great enthusiasm. The weekend passed in a whirl of hay baling and I was in a good mood for the first time in what seemed like an eternity.

We were sitting in the cafeteria with Ralphie, Lenny and some Walkerton kids Monday morning when Mary Ellen Reid and a group of her friends approached our table. Mary Ellen was a Walkerton girl whose father ran the local Credit Union and was the publisher of the *Walkerton Times*. The Reids were one of the richest families in the whole of Bruce County, solid church members and staunch supporters of any community initiative. Mary Ellen was easily one of the prettiest girls in school. She was quick to laugh, intelligent, lithe and popular. Johnny had even expressed an interest in her during our first week when we discovered we all shared the same biology class. As they approached our table we all fell shyly silent.

"Hi, Joshua," Mary Ellen said cheerily, as we all stared.

"Hi, Mary Ellen," I replied, gulping as Johnny elbowed me solidly in the ribs.

She plopped down in the chair across from me. "Are you coming to the dance on Friday?"

"Well ... uh ... yeah. I thought I'd go," I said.

"Good. I was wondering about something." She looked down at her feet.

"What's that?" I asked, fascinated to have her undivided attention.

"Well ... I was wondering if you're taking anyone."

"Uh, no. Well, me and Johnny are going."

She laughed. "Not like that, silly. I mean, do you have a date?"

"A *date*? No," I said, more surprised than ever.

"Well ... me neither," she said coyly.

"Are you asking if I would take you?" I asked, looking down the table at the amazed looks on the faces of my friends.

"If you asked me I'd go with you."

"Well ... uh ... okay."

"Okay. Can you pick me up at seven-thirty?"

"Yeah. Sure. Okay. Seven-thirty. Sure."

"Great. I'm really looking forward to it, Joshua," she said, touching my hand slightly as she rose and departed with her friends.

The silence at our table was deafening.

"I don't believe it. I just don't believe it," Ralphie Wendt said, shaking his head in disbelief. "Mary Ellen Reid and Joshua Kane. It can't be happening."

"Man," Johnny said. "I don't know what kind of magic you got, Josh, but hand a little around to the rest of us guys, eh?"

"Mary Ellen Reid asked *you* to take her to the dance?" my father asked at the supper table. "Wow."

"I didn't even think she knew I existed," I said through a mouthful of potatoes.

"Well, the Reids are a good family," my mother said. "Mark Reid is a good upstanding church member and Ellen Reid has been a pillar of the community as long as I can remember. I think it's a good thing."

"She's cute, eh, son?" my father said and winked.

"Yeah. Really," I said and grinned.

"Betcha the guys are all pretty jealous, eh? What's Johnny think?" he asked.

"Everyone's as surprised as I am and Johnny, well, he can't figure it out at all."

"What's to figure?" he asked.

It seemed the perfect time to let them in on the way the school year had been going. To let them know the hurt I'd experienced and the confusion that had settled in my brain about Indians and family and color and hate. But I didn't. I believed that the passing of the ordeal meant that it could all remain my secret. That it was better that way.

"Ah, you know," I said quickly, "I'm a farm kid, she's a townie. Not much in common."

"Well, you never know. Obviously she's seen something she likes in you, Joshua. You're a fine boy. She's lucky to have you as a classmate." My mother patted my hand.

"So you'll get all gussied up and dance up a storm, I suppose?" my father asked, stretching his legs out from under his chair, clasping his hands behind his head.

"Dance? Geez. I don't know how to dance!" I stammered.

They laughed.

"Well, young sir," my mother said, rising from her chair and taking me by the hand. "There's no time like now to start learning!"

She walked me into the living room. Then, as my father floundered through the records for one we could dance to, she showed me how to hold her, the placement of the hands, their proper weight, and the gentleman's distance. When a bouncy country waltz began to fill the room, she led me through my first faltering steps. We moved awkwardly around the room, until gradually I began to follow her lead and the one-two-three, one-two-three rhythm settled into my brain and feet and we were dancing. As my father clapped time, whistling encouragement, the sun settled into the lap of the west, while my mother and I danced and danced and danced. She looked into my eyes and smiled, nodding. As the strains of that music died away, and she stepped slowly away from me and curtsied, I was filled again with the love of family, God and life. I couldn't wait for Friday.

God within. My father explained to me once that our word *enthusiasm* comes from the Greek word *theos*, or God. *En*-theos meant God within, and the *ism* meant it was something that was acted on, displayed or lived. So, enthusiasm was living like you carried God within yourself, each day becoming a source of light, a celebration, a cause for great joy. It made perfect sense to me. The dawning of our days is the dawning of life, and to greet those days with joy, verve and aplomb is the stuff of life itself.

Despite what I faced that first week of high school, I still awoke with the unshakable belief that the God within me would lead me to resolution. That's another tricky word. *Resolve.* It's another faith word, really. If you believe and trust, then you believe and trust that God has already *solved* your problem, that He has a solution mapped out for you. Your responsibility then becomes to walk the path you're directed to walk and to use the tools of your faith to simply *re-solve* the problem. It was another seed of faith that my parents had planted in me, one I couldn't define at fourteen but that lived within me nonetheless.

The week leading up to the Welcoming Dance passed in a blur. I awoke each day full of excitement and enthusiasm. The talk in the hallways and on the buses was of nothing else. I relished the idea of appearing as an equal before the school body, the catcalls and whispers drowned in murmurs of appreciation, welcome and regard. This, of course, was hinged to the thoughts of waltzing Mary Ellen Reid through the evening, thoughts that were strangely enticing, affecting my body and senses with a warmth I'd never experienced. In my mind's eye I saw us, together beneath a swirl of party lights, moving delicately over each note like stepping stones, the rhythm buoyant and the eyes of our classmates glistening in the aura of our connection as they encircled us, swept up in the magic of romance, music and our untethered youthfulness.

I fumbled my way through the Friday-evening meal wordless and clumsy, merely grinning foolishly at my parents who tittered merrily at my nervousness.

Upstairs I scrubbed and lathered almost to the point of pain. I combed and recombed my hair, settled on a dab of Brylcreem and clipped my nails, and as I crossed the hallway to my room to begin dressing, I stopped before the mirror at the head of the stairs to check myself. I saw a slim, muscled young man with clear eyes, healthy skin and close-cropped hair. I saw Joshua Kane.

As I traced the line of my cheekbones with my fingertips and trailed them slowly over the ridge of my chin, down my throat to my chest and abdomen, I saw myself clearly as the spawn of my parents. But this was not my father's chin. These were not my mother's eyes. This angular scarp of cheekbone and broadened nose had not come from the joining of their chromosomes nor had the black pitch of my hair resulted from the critical mix of my father's brown hair and my mother's red. No, I was a singular creation in their midst, and if I was not their biological son, the young man staring back at me from the mirror had been incubated, formed, fed, nurtured and grown from the spontaneous mechanics of love that moved and directed them. A love germinated, tended and tilled in the arable soil of Creation. I was their son. Love had made me that. I was Joshua Kane. They had created me, that much I would never deny. The Indian in the mirror existed somewhere beneath all that, an unknown, present only in skin.

I dressed quickly. I'd worked arduously the night before, putting an impeccable gloss on my shoes, and I'd learned how to press a shirt and pants by the time I was twelve. My standard fashion statement was white shirt, black pants and shoes. A paisley tie was all the worldliness I allowed myself. As I walked into the kitchen where my parents waited, I felt dapper, a dandy on the loose.

They stood there in the doorway smiling at me. At first I thought there was something wrong with the way I looked and gave myself a hasty once-over. My mother kissed me on the cheek and handed me a beautiful white and pink corsage in a clear plastic container.

"For the lady," she said.

"And this," my father said and brought a bundle out from behind his back, "is for the gentleman. Try it on."

It was a black tuxedo jacket. It fit perfectly. I ran to the downstairs bathroom to look in the mirror and they followed close behind me. It was the first dress jacket I'd ever worn. It felt secure, comfortable and familiar. I loved it.

"It used to be your grandfather's," my mother explained. "When he was younger. I dug it out of the attic and took it in while you were at school. It fits you well."

"We wanted this night to be one you'd remember forever, Joshua. A boy's first date is a mighty big event and we wanted to help make it special. You look terrific, son," my father said.

"Your grandfather would have been proud of you," my mother said.

"Thank you," I whispered. "Thank you." The jacket felt like my grandfather's arms around my shoulders.

I clutched the corsage and fingered the fabric of my jacket all the way into town. No one spoke much, my parents allowing me the privacy of my thoughts and feelings, and me, uncertain of what to say or whether anything that came out would even make any sense. My nervousness had been replaced by a quiet happiness. I settled into the seat of the car, watching the fields turning slowly into smaller acreages, backyards and billboards before we finally spun past the Welcome to Walkerton sign.

When we pulled up in front of the Reids' house, I was shocked. It was a three-story red-brick palace with a wide verandah supported by thick white columns. The windows were huge and bordered with curlicues of stained glass. The front door was extra-wide, appearing to be one large piece of burnished oak with discreet brass fittings. The lights blazing within showed high ceilings and natural woodwork. As we got out of the car my dad gave a long whistle and my mother rearranged her hat. My nervousness returned in a rush.

Mark Reid answered the door. He was a large man bristling with the energy that comes from a lifetime spent making important decisions for other people. He boomed out a greeting and swept us into the living room, where Mrs. Reid and Mary Ellen waited on the sofa. They rose as we entered. Mrs. Reid was a wealthier version of my mother with her restrained suit of clothes and clasped hands. Mary Ellen absolutely shimmered in a long-sleeved yellow gown. Her hair was swept up from her face while the slight touch of makeup she'd applied only enhanced the soft glow of her skin. As our parents exchanged pleasantries we stared wordlessly at each other.

"And who knows, maybe it's time we sent a local to Ottawa. Lord knows, the farmers could use a neighbor on the Hill, couldn't they?" Mr. Reid was saying as I surfaced from my reverie.

"Yes, that's true," my father said shyly, never comfortable with political discussions.

"Well, let me tell you," Mrs. Reid said abruptly, "we were never so happy to hear that our Mary Ellen would be escorted by a boy from a solid churchgoing family like yourselves. These Walkerton youths are so callow and disrespectful."

"Thank you," my mother answered. "We're pleased, too."

I presented the corsage to Mary Ellen, who accepted it as graciously as someone used to ceremony. She smiled as I fumbled, trying to pin it to her gown, until my mother came to my rescue. We all laughed, and as I looked into Mary Ellen's eyes I felt something small and birdlike move around somewhere in the vicinity of my heart. Finally, pleasantries finished, we were in the car and on our way.

Mary Ellen and my parents chatted animatedly about school and her plans for university. She kept one hand perched delicately on my leg all the way and the slight pressure felt heavy with intimations beyond my understanding. Now and then we'd glance at each other and she would crinkle the edges of her eyes, squeezing my leg lightly. I felt dizzy with excitement.

When we pulled up to the school I was glad to see Johnny prowling back and forth at the top of the steps. He was wearing a brown houndstooth jacket that was at least two sizes too big, a blue shirt with a skinny black tie, blue jeans and sneakers. As we said good-bye to my parents I felt a pang of regret, that unsettling kind you feel entering new territory for the first time.

"Man, I thought you'd never get here," Johnny said. "You guys look like page eighty-eight."

"What's that supposed to mean?" Mary Ellen asked, suspiciously.

"Page eighty-eight, Sears Catalogue. That's a compliment," Johnny replied.

She smiled. "I've never heard it put that way before. Thank you."

We headed into the school and Mary Ellen again laid her gloved hand on my arm. Johnny's eyebrows shot up and he mouthed a slow "ooh-la-la" at me behind her back, shaking one hand for emphasis.

The gym was packed. Party lights criss-crossed the room in low-slung arches and a huge Walkerton Wolverines banner was strung across one end of the room. A line of tables with placards denoting the various clubs attracted a large crowd. A bright orange Welcome Freshmen sign hung above the stage, and just inside the main doors a buffet table laden with sandwiches and salads stretched along the wall. As we walked through the doors we heard a long wolf whistle and a sea of faces turned to watch. Mary Ellen gave a small smile of satisfaction and nodded in the direction of a few friends. Johnny and I cringed a little at the sudden attention while we followed along beside her. We were headed towards Ralphie Wendt and Connie Shaus by the front of the stage when Mary Ellen gave a sharp tug on my sleeve.

"Joshua, I'm going to see a couple friends at the drama table, okay? I'll catch up to you later."

"Yeah, sure," I said, uncertain of the right protocol. "That's great. See you later."

As she approached the crowd a space opened up in front of her. Friends streamed over from everywhere to greet her and marvel at her outfit. Johnny and I watched her departure and then joined our Mildmay friends at the front of the room. All of us were somewhat humbled by the display. We gawked at all the people, light and motion until the sound system gave a sudden squawk and Principal Holmes began to speak. Spike, as he was dubbed in the hallways, droned on and on, followed by another dull speech by the class president, Neil Metzger. Finally, the curtain was drawn back on the stage to reveal a five-piece music combo who swung into a rambunctious pop song that had couples on the dance floor immediately.

Our little group moved together between the club tables, stopping to load up at the buffet table. We seemed to be lost in the crowd and no one paid any particular attention to us. Johnny signed up for the Drama Club and Ralphie penned his name on the growing list for hockey while Connie and I looked on. Clubs were a luxury neither of us would likely be able to afford since we both helped out on our farms. When we reached the end of the row of tables, we returned to the edge of the dance floor to watch.

Mary Ellen was jitterbugging wildly with Allen Begg, laughing while her friends, mostly seniors from the window ledge, stood in a group clapping and hooting encouragement. She was an entirely different person from the demure girl I'd arrived with. My three friends looked at me inquisitively but I just shrugged. As the music changed, Chris swept up Mary Ellen as she tried to leave the floor and she allowed herself to be propelled back into motion. Allen caught my eye from across the floor, grinning and nudging the boy next to him. They snickered into their hands. Song after song, Mary Ellen danced with her group.

"You should go over and ask her to dance, Kane," Ralphie said after about an hour.

"Yes, Joshua," Connie said angrily. "I think it's really rude what she's doing. Go over and ask for a dance. Townies. No offense, Ralphie, Johnny."

"None taken," Johnny said. "She's right, Josh. Mary Ellen's nothing like us. We wouldn't do what she's done. I say, if she wants to hang with Neanderthals like Begg and Hollingshead and the rest of those rednecks, screw her!"

As I was mulling it over the song ended. We watched Mary Ellen and her group head out the back door of the gym and to the football field. I felt a lump rise in my throat as I watched her disappear. It felt suddenly like the entire room knew I'd been dumped. I wanted to slink away home. The laughter on the faces of everyone around me seemed directed at me, my humiliation a public thing. Still, the part of me that was willing to grant the benefit of the doubt overrode everything else, and I told Johnny that I would confront Mary Ellen.

"Are you nuts? Or are you just a glutton for punishment? She dumped you! She embarrassed you in front of everybody. She's making like you don't even exist and you *still* want to talk to her? You're crazy!"

"I guess I just need to hear it from her, that's all," I said.

"It's your life."

"Might as well do it now," I said. "It's quieter out back."

"What about Hollingshead and Begg?"

"It'll be okay. They haven't said or done a thing since the football game. I'll be fine."

"Want me to come along?"

"Nah. I won't be long."

"Okay. But, Josh?"

"Yeah?"

"Keep your head up, okay?"

"I will."

I made my way through the crowd to the back door, noticing vaguely that people were aware of my movement. When I stepped out back, the cool evening air refreshed me and gave me hope. A small group of students stood smoking by the picnic tables and beyond them I heard the laughter of another group behind the bleachers. As I moved closer I recognized Mary Ellen by the shine of her gown against the darkness. I saw her and her friends passing a bottle back and forth. She was in the middle of taking a gulp from it when I walked up to them.

"Hey, looky looky," Chris Hollingshead said. "Mr. Dressup's here."

"Hey, hey, it's the farm guy. John Deere, isn't it?" another voice said.

"Nah, it ain't John Deere. It's Running Deer," Allen said sharply, stepping to the front of the group.

"Joshua, what do you want?" Mary Ellen asked, worry in her voice.

"Well, I, uh ... you know ... I, uh ... " I stammered.

"Yeah, well, like, uh, but, *geez!*" one of the seniors mimicked. "Speak English, Injun! You can do that, can't you?"

"No," Allen Begg said. "No speakum. Injun dumb."

"Look," I said, "I just wanted to know if I could have a dance later. If not, then maybe I'll just leave early."

"Hey, who invited this Injun to our party anyway?" a girl slurred loudly.

"It was Reid. It's her good deed for the month. Take an Injun dancin'," someone answered.

"Why? She think this was a B.Y.O.B. party?" the girl asked.

"Whaddaya mean, B.Y.O.B.?"

"You know ... Bring Your Own *Buck!*"

There was raucous laughter all around.

"Hey, that reminds me," a tall guy said, putting an arm around Mary Ellen's waist and pulling her towards him. "What does a faggot Injun do on Saturday night?"

"We don't know, Hollingshead," Allen Begg replied. "What *does* a faggot Injun do on Saturday night?"

"Not much," said the boy, who I realized immediately was Chris's older brother. "He just heads downtown to blow a couple *bucks!*"

Everyone in the group laughed long and loudly and there was much slapping of palms and back-thumping. Mary Ellen stared at me blankly, offering neither support nor ridicule. I turned to leave.

"Hey, wait a minute, wait a minute," the older Hollingshead said. "The Injun came here to ask for a dance. We should give him a dance!"

"Yeah, but I think he needs a drink first!" Chris said. "Firewater, Injun? Wantum firewater? Make you feelum horny? Do-um good dance with white woman?"

Allen advanced toward me. "Fuck that! No faggot Injun's dancing with one of our women. He's gonna show us a real Injun dance! Ain'tcha, Injun?"

"No, you guys," Mary Ellen said sharply. "You said you were only going to scare him! That's enough! Please!"

"Oooh. I believe Reid's got a crush on Little Beaver here," the older Hollingshead said, stepping quickly behind me. "Thinking of maybe getting a little beaver, Little Beaver? Think again, you fuckin' wagon burner!"

Hands grabbed me and I was thrown to the ground, arms pinning my shoulders and knees. Someone grabbed my head roughly and pinned it back with their palm against my forehead. As I opened my mouth to protest, the thick burn of alcohol ripped a trench down my throat. I gagged. As my mouth opened, more of the fiery liquid was poured in and I heard laughing and swearing all around me. I heard Mary Ellen crying, begging them to stop. My eyes burned with tears from the booze and the fear in my belly. More was poured, and just as the vomit was rising in me, I was yanked to my feet and shoved from behind. I reeled dizzily and as things spun into focus I saw Mary Ellen in front of me. I reached out to her for support but instead fell heavily against her and then to the ground. I grasped at her to halt my fall and one sleeve of her gown tore away in my hand.

"Hoo hoo! Little Beaver's almost got the white woman undressed! Anybody know the Indian Love Call?"

"Yeah, it's — Hey, you awake!"

They hollered. I was having trouble making sense of anything. Hands grabbed me again and spun me around in circles. As I reeled around fighting for balance I was punched in the face. A fantail of light exploded behind my eyes. I stumbled backwards and was punched again. I tasted the spongy warmth of blood and the bite of bile rising in my throat. Again and again I was punched and kicked, in the face, on the shoulders, in the belly, in the thighs.

"Dance, Injun! You wanted a fuckin' dance? Dance! *Woo woo woo woo woo!*" I fell deeper into a roiling pit of darkness. I barely recognized a scream and the smash of a bottle. I fell heavily to the ground and as I opened one eye I saw bodies hurtling around. The world began to spin and I closed my eyes. There was the sound of fists landing, swearing and then, as I collapsed into a warm bed of white light, feet running hard in many directions, shouting and a girl sobbing. Soon, firm hands reached under my head and a cool palm was laid on my brow. I groaned, let my head slide downward into a white light, downward and downward.

My parent's faced slid into my awareness like cattle in fog. I began to climb higher and higher on the same white light I had descended on and as I did, I became aware of noises. The bleep, bleep, bleep of a monitor, the soft squish of rubber soles

across linoleum, the clinks and rattles of metal, the rustle of whisperings arranged themselves slowly. I became aware of the thick-
ness of my body — my face, joints and belly distended and sore.
There was a dull throb that started in my temples and pulsated
along the length of my upper body, nestling finally in paroxysms of
pain in my legs. Gradually, I surfaced.

The harsh glare of fluorescent lighting stabbed my eyes and I
narrowed them to slits to peer up at my parents, who spun in a lazy
circle around me. I closed my eyes. When I screwed up the courage
to open them again, the world had steadied itself on its axis. I looked
at my mother and father. His face was set grimly, and there were
tears on her face as she reached out to lay a hand on my forehead.

"Good to have you back, son. We were worried there for a
minute or two," my father said thinly.

"Are you in pain, Joshua?" my mother asked, searching my
eyes.

"Some," I mumbled.

"Doc Niedermayer's examined you," my father said. "You
might have a slight concussion. You took a pretty good beating
around the face but there's nothing broken. Time and rest, he
says."

"What happened?" I asked thickly.

My mother said, "We're not sure. There are two stories."

"Two?"

"Yes, son," my father said, leaning closer. "Three or four town
kids and Mary Ellen are saying that you were drinking behind the
school. When they came out for some fresh air you attacked Mary
Ellen, ripped her dress trying to get her to go behind the bleachers
with you. The boys tried to restrain you but you started swinging.
The bigger Hollingshead boy admits to beating you up in defense
of Mary Ellen and the rest of the kids."

"But John says you went out to talk with Mary Ellen," my
mother added. "He and Ralphie found you being beaten by four of
the boys."

"There was a fight. John and Ralph put a pretty good thumping on them from what I hear," my father said, with a weak grin.

"Johnny's okay?" I whispered.

"Well, yes and no. Yes, he's okay physically but he's been arrested," my father said.

"Arrested!"

"Yes, son," my mother said. "He's been charged with assault, and assault causing bodily harm. He broke a bottle over Chris Hollingshead's skull and beat Allen Begg severely before he was stopped. Mr. Holmes and Mr. Hughes had to wrestle him off."

"Johnny's in jail?"

"At least until we get this all sorted out," my father said.

I tried to concentrate, to get a handle on how all this could have occurred, but the whiskey and the beating had taken their toll and I slipped down into sleep very quickly. When I awoke it was late morning. My mouth tasted sour, while my head and body thrummed with pain. The sounds of the hospital were hushed. My mother was asleep in a corner chair with my father's overcoat pulled around her shoulders.

I could see myself crossing the darkened playing field and approaching the bleachers. In my ears the sounds of the dance behind me were gradually replaced by the rowdy banter of the group in the darkness — swearing, and throaty laughter. I saw Mary Ellen's face. Worried. Scared, even. And then the spinning. The lights. The heavy blows to my body. The smell of the ground, the booze, my fear. I groaned, and immediately felt my mother's hand on my brow. The tears came, thick and heavy, pushed by sobs rising from deep within me. I cried deep racking sobs while my mother lay her head gingerly across my chest and offered me the comfort of her presence.

I cried until my chest ached more with the effort of sobbing than from the bruises, until I felt a space open up within me, a release, a hollow that was filled quickly with the warmth of my mother, her tears on my face and neck. I swallowed hard and opened my eyes. My father stood in the doorway, dressed in his barn clothes and clutching a small pile of books and the tiny blue transistor radio we used in the stable, tears flowing down his face too. He set the items on the bedside table, then put a hand on my mother's back and one on my shoulder, looking down at the two of us. We stayed that way for a long, long time.

[spiral symbol]

f I could rearrange that whole evening I'd have never let you walk out that door alone. It was stupid. I knew Hollingshead and Begg were up to something. The way Reid dumped you that night should have tipped me off. No way they were going to settle for making you look bad in front of everybody. I knew that but I also knew you needed to at least try to get an answer, some kind of explanation, because you were never one to believe that people are cruel and cold and hard without reason. You'd never seen that. I had to let you go. Why, if I knew it was a bad move? I guess because even then, Josh, I was kind of living through you. Some part of me wanted you to walk out there, confront the assholes and get an answer, wanted you to prove to me that the world and its people, even the kids, aren't a collective slag heap, that the refined ones like you can still get through to them. To us. Maybe if you had succeeded that night, come back understanding that some people are unknowable, our lives would have been different. I would have been different.

After about ten minutes I knew I had to go out there. We heard the racket as we stepped out the back door. The closer we got to the bleachers, the more I felt something rising in me, until I saw you being kicked and punched.

I don't remember anything about the fight. It was like I blacked out in anger. You don't see red like they say. You see black. Makes sense to me. Black is the absence of color, of light. When you slip into that kind of anger, there is no color. No red of anger, no blue of sorrow, yellow of happiness, pink of peace. It's like the black holes astronomers describe. Something that had the chance to shine so brightly suddenly collapses in upon itself and becomes so compacted, so dense that it won't even allow light to escape. Blackness. That's what I was swinging and kicking through that night, all the accumulated blackness. I was swinging at my father. I was kicking at every sick drunken night I had had to live through.

Punching at every midnight move, every laughing, scowling face in every new school I ever walked into, at every lousy, flea-bitten flop we had to call home, every name he ever called me, every slap, push, pinch, every mop I had to squeeze the puke out of and every piss-filled vodka bottle he left lying under the couch. I swung at all of it. And I swung at my mother for not being brave enough to get us out. The blackness won that fight, Josh. Not me.

I had never experienced such anger. Oh, sure, I'd had my moods as all kids do — the self-righteous petulance over chores, mild resentments — but never anything approaching a malignant anger. When I walked out of the hospital three days later I could feel it roiling and churning inside me. At home, as I looked into my bedroom mirror at my blackened eyes and purplish torso, it grew thicker, churlish and weighty. I needed an explanation. I needed to make sense of all that had happened, to take this tangle of emotion and circumstance and set it into an order that I could understand. My best friend was in jail, I was a pariah in my own school — the brunt of a hatred I neither deserved nor understood — and no one had ever explained to me that the world could operate this way. I began to understand the heft and scope of vengeance, just as I began to understand, for the first time, that sin is a desire we can carry so easily within us.

My parents spoke in soothing tones, made all the right gestures and took great care to see that I was comfortable, but even their doting upset me. My parents took my reticence as concern for Johnny, who had been moved to the Galt School for Boys while he awaited his trial. They allowed me my distance and I used it to walk the fields.

I returned to the house and we sat for supper in silence except for the blessing. I kept my head down as I ate, seething. I felt that if I spoke, everything would erupt from within me and I would go

mad with the effort. But unable to restrain myself any longer, I laid
my knife and fork down alongside my plate, moved my chair back
from the table and looked up with tears streaming down my face. I
shook as I told them everything about those first two weeks, allowing my voice its stridency, its pain, confusion and vitriol. When I
reached the part about the beating I began slamming one hand
down on the table, rattling dishes, spilling milk and water and
crumbling the worried faces of my parents.

"Why?" I cried. "I didn't do anything! Nothing! They hate me!
They *hate me*!"

"I don't know, Joshua," my mother said, softly.

I stood abruptly, my chair clattering to the floor. "You don't
know? You sent me out there! You sent me to that school! You sent
me to get yelled at, screamed at, put down! You sent me to get beat
up! You *sent* me!"

"Joshua," my father said firmly, evenly. "Sit down."

I stared at him hard. The first time in my life I ever gave him a
look that wasn't respectful, admiring, kind. The first time in my life
he was ever the focus of anger. I clenched my fists in front of me
and looked at him, his peaceful manner suddenly distasteful. The
tears at the corners of my mouth were hot and acrid and I felt
laughter building in my belly, a demonic laughter, frightening, fas-
cinating, energizing.

"No!" I half screamed. "*You* sit down! All my life — Joshua, sit
and listen. Joshua, sit and listen, here's how the world works,
Joshua, *you just sit and listen,* this is how God wants you to be,
Joshua, here's what you believe, Joshua, *you just sit and listen*! Well,
where was God when this was happening to me? Why didn't *He*
just sit and listen? Why didn't He listen to me?"

My father rose easily and stepped forward slowly to lay a hand
on my quaking shoulder. "Easy, son," he said.

"No!" I swiped his hand away. "No! No more *easy, son*! They
beat me!"

"I know, son, I know. But you have to look past that. Look at
how you can help them," he said.

"Help them! I'll help them. Me and Johnny, we'll help them!" I said through clenched teeth. "We'll help *them* feel how I feel . We'll beat *them* up. We'll kick them. We'll slap them. We'll laugh at them!"

"No, Joshua," my mother said. "That will only make things worse. Johnny's in enough trouble now and you don't need any more either. Fighting won't solve anything." She reached out towards me, but pulled back and lay her hand on the table.

"Oh, yes, it will. Oh, *yes*, it will! They call me a savage, a wild Indian, an animal? Well, maybe I should act like one. Maybe I should be a warrior like Johnny says and give it right back to them. That's what warriors do, you know. They fight!"

"John's wrong, son," my father said. "There's more to being an Indian than just being a warrior."

"What do you know?" I said, pointing a finger at his face. "What do you know about being Indian? All my life you never said one thing, one thing to let me know what I was supposed to be. One thing to tell me how I was supposed to behave — what people expected of me, what they thought of me. You never told me anything. You never told me that they could hate me, that they wouldn't want me, that they'd beat me. You just let me believe that I was Joshua Kane and that everything would be all right. Well it's not all right! I'm an *Indian*! I'm not a Kane, I'm an *Indian*! And I don't even know what the means ..."

"You're Joshua Kane. You always have been. You always will be," he said, reaching out to me slowly with both arms.

"Bullshit," I cursed, slapping his arms away. "That's bullshit. I wasn't *always* Joshua Kane. My mother was Indian. I'm Indian. You know that, I know that, God knows that. The whole fuckin' world knows that! But you ... you wanna believe that takin' me away from my mother doesn't make me Indian any more. The growing up with you makes me like you — makes me *white*, makes me a Kane. Well, I'm not white, I'm not a Kane. I don't know what I am."

"You're my son and ... I love you."

The laugh erupted finally, derisive, insane. "Love me? You love me? Well, why didn't you *protect* me! Why didn't you tell me they would hate me? Why didn't you tell me what to do? What to say? Why did you let me walk out there without knowing?"

I righted my chair and sat down heavily. I collapsed forward, my head settling on my crossed arms. The laugh robbed me of my energy and I felt drained of everything but a sudden sadness, deep and all-encompassing. I cried. Long wailing cries like thin screams, taut and brittle. When my sobs quieted we sat around the table, silent, wounded — a family confronting itself, its pains and failings, its future clouded, awaiting the hand of an absent God to guide it. We had entered a country without words. I looked at the people I had called my parents all my life and felt the coiling snake of anger slither across my belly once again. I needed away. I mumbled "Excuse me" and headed out the door. My parents sat in their chairs as silent and immobile as abandoned idols.

I walked the fields until the moon rose above the outbuildings. The anger roiling in my belly made me ashamed. When I entered the house my parents were sitting in the living room as silently as I had left them. We merely nodded at each other as I passed on my way to my room. I don't know how long I lay awake in my bed that night, thoughts cascading over thoughts and images pouring through images, but I vaguely heard the creak of the floor as they went to bed themselves. There were no murmurs and chuckles that I would normally hear now and again, just the rustle of bedclothes and the silence they pulled over themselves like a comforter. Sleep, when it came, was deep and dreamless.

I slept late the next morning. The crunch of tires on the graveled driveway woke me and I crept downstairs to find a scribbled note on the table saying they'd return by lunch time. I felt grateful for their absence. I stayed in my room all morning, aching with bruises and an unaccustomed heaviness. I did not move from my

bed, shifting from shallow, fitful sleep into thick, purple wakeful-
ness. They missed lunch, and by the time I heard them return, it
was late in the afternoon. The whistle of the tea kettle and the
scrape of chairs told me they were seated at the table, and I walked
slowly downstairs to face them. They greeted me with half smiles.
I hitched my chair up to the table, my eyes brimming with tears.

I'm sorry," I said, shakily.

"No, Joshua. We're sorry," my mother said, smoothing my hair
and wiping the corners of my eyes with a finger.

"Why are you sorry? It was me. I was horrible."

"No, you were right. We should have helped you understand.
We should have helped you know yourself. Your Indian self, not
just the self you became with us," she said quietly.

"That's right, son. You have nothing to apologize for. It's us,"
my father said. "We went to speak with Pastor Chuck. We didn't
know what else to do. We had no way of understanding what it
was you were going through. We had no way of knowing how to
go about helping you. We never once thought that we needed to
offer you other things."

"You are both an Indian and a Kane, Joshua," my mother said.
"We were wrong not to teach you or help you to learn how to be
both instead of just one. We were selfish thinking we could recreate you. God created you to be an Indian as well as our son, and
we got so busy teaching you as our son that we neglected to help
you learn to discover yourself as an Indian. And that's wrong.

"But, son, we couldn't tell you what the world was like — what
people are like, what to expect from them, how to *be*. Because then
you would have gone out into it with our perceptions, our fears,
our views, and that's wrong. That's what the parents of the kids
who beat you passed on to them. It would be just as wrong of us
to send you out into the world carrying our beliefs and attitudes,
even if they are Christian. You have to find out things on your own,
make up your own mind, reach your own conclusions. We just
have to be here to guide you, to help you choose."

"Yes, son," my father continued. "Even if the world hurts you
sometimes, we have to let you feel that. Even if it's confusing and

scary, you have to feel that too. If we protected you from that, we'd be wrong again. But you have to come to us when you feel all those things and tell us so we can help you see your way through them. Go through them together, learn from them together, so you won't lose yourself in the process."

"Either of your selves," my mother said.

"I should have told you," I said quietly.

"Told us what, son?" she asked.

"About school. About the teasing, the hassles. How confused it made me. How scared. But I thought it would stop. I thought it would go away. And I didn't want to trouble you with nothing."

"Something that troubles you is never nothing, son," my father said. "It's something. Yes, you should have told us, but that's behind us now. What we need to do now is move forward."

"To what?" I asked.

"To finding a way to teach you about your Indian self. To teach us. And to finding a way to forgive those kids," he said.

"Forgive them? You need to forgive them too?"

"Certainly. Do you think you were the only one who wanted to sail into town and beat the dickens out of a few people?" he asked, eyebrows raised.

"You wanted to do that?" I asked, incredulous.

"Oh, yes. When I saw you lying in that bed in the hospital all bruised and battered, I wanted to find those kids and beat them to within an inch of their lives. Their parents too. *Especially* the parents."

"But you're a Christian."

"So? Christians get angry too, Joshua. Anger's something we all have. The trick is to learn how to control it rather than have it control you."

"Remember Jesus in the temple?" my mother began in the earnest, pious tone she used when she spoke of biblical things. "He erupted in anger at the buyers and the sellers. He allowed Himself to feel the rage, allowed Himself to let it out. If our Lord can be human enough to be angry, then we certainly ought to be."

"You're not mad because I swore, because I pushed your hands away?" I asked.

"Well," my father said, "we could have done without the cussing, but the important thing is that you let out how you felt. And it's okay. It's okay that you were angry with us. It's okay to feel vengeance, to want to hit back. It's okay to be angry because you don't know how to react to things in life. Anger's never right or wrong, son. How you *act* out of anger is, though. That's the sin."

"Did Johnny sin?" I asked, looking back and forth at the two of them. They exchanged a long look, one that spoke volumes in a second or two, and I knew in that instance how incredibly close and connected my parents were to each other, how devoted they were to me. It was my father who spoke.

"Well, son, we should all try to be free of anger. But that doesn't mean we shouldn't have it or feel sinful because we do. It's a part of us, something the good Lord gave us to help us deal with ourselves and others. So being free of it means understanding why we have it. Being free of it means controlling *it* instead of *it* controlling us. That's freedom. Do you follow, son?"

I thought about it. I said, slowly, "Johnny didn't know why he was angry. He just blew up. He didn't control it, it controlled him."

"Yes. So, I'd say that John was wrong but I don't think he sinned. Mother?" my father said.

"Yes. You sin when you've been taught what's right and what's wrong and you choose to behave wrongly. I don't think John's parents have ever taught him that. He only knew to fight. To hurt back. But that doesn't make him a sinner, Joshua, it makes him ignorant."

"Johnny's not ignorant," I blurted.

"I don't mean ignorant as in rude and wicked, I mean ignorant because he doesn't *know*. There's a difference," she said.

"Those town kids are ignorant, then, huh?"

They smiled.

"Yes, son. They're ignorant," my father said and squeezed my shoulder gently.

"So I should try and help them know? Help them know that Indians aren't dirty, stupid savages? That *I'm* not?"

"Yes," they said together, quietly.

"I know why I had the anger then," I said.

"Why is that, son?" my father asked.

"Because of ignorance. Theirs and mine. They're ignorant of who I am and so am I. We all only see one part of me. They only see the Indian and I only see the Kane. They hate the part they can see and I hate the part I can't see. Wow."

"And we'll help you see that part of you, son. I don't know how just yet but we'll help you see it. I promise," my father said.

"Joshua?" my mother said.

"Yes?"

"Do you know why we chose your name?"

"No, Mother, I don't."

"Well, your father and I spent a lot of time thinking about your name before we signed the adoption papers. We wanted it to be special. We sat at this table and we wrote down all kinds of names and we couldn't find one that we really, *really* liked. Then, one Sunday, Pastor's sermon used the story of Joshua bringing down the walls of Jericho with his horn. And on the way back in the car that day we decided we wanted to name you Joshua — after a great warrior."

My mouth fell open.

"A great *spiritual* warrior," she continued. "Someone who was never afraid to call on God's help to help in all his battles. The walls of Jericho that Joshua destroyed are the walls of ignorance — the walls of people who don't know God's way. They're big and mighty walls, but Joshua brought them down with one blast of his horn. His horn is a metaphor for God's teachings. When we heard that story that day, we knew your name should be Joshua because something told us you would use God's teachings one day to bring down walls of ignorance. Maybe this is that time." She reached out to hug me to her.

"Wow," I said quietly. "I've got two warrior names."

"How's that, son?" my father asked.

"Nothing," I said. "It's kind of a secret."

"Oh," they said and smiled.

As I lay in bed that night I thought about the two warrior names I had been given. It could be no coincidence that they both reflected the same message. I knew how to live as Joshua, but learning how to live as Thunder Sky was going to take a great effort, and although I didn't know that night where or how to start, I did know that the answer would come, that the two halves of my being would come together. I thought about Johnny and our blood brother pact to be loyal, good and kind, how the promises of childhood travel with us through the years, metamorphosing, galvanizing themselves to withstand the pressures of age, maturity, the world. I thought about my parents, how we shared that same pact, unstated but lived nonetheless. I thought about loyalty, goodness and kindness and how they felt better than the hard ingots of anger they replaced. I thought about warriors.

As sleep folded itself around me that night, I prayed for the strength to be a spiritual warrior. I drifted into dreams of Johnny and me dancing around on the crumbled walls of a great city, its bricks and facades strewn around our feet, its cornices and columns shattered, our exultant cries shimmering across the great song of the universe like a grace note — the muted vibrato of a great trumpet.

I didn't mind Galt. It wasn't real different from home. They called it a training school, but hell, I'd been trained that way all my life. All the adults ignored you until you made it absolutely necessary for them to recognize you. People yelled and screamed at each other even though no one really knew each other. You ate together but no one talked. You were never sure from one day to the next who was going to be around and who wasn't. So adjusting wasn't exactly one of the great theatrical stretches of all time. I actually liked it. I didn't have to worry about getting slapped and pushed around by some drunken boob and the lights stayed on after seven o'clock every night. Guys would be crying in their cots at night because they wanted to be home. I'd have to smother my face in my pillow to keep from laughing — home was my prison and Galt was a day at the beach.

There was this Indian guy there named Staatz. Real big, muscular, long haired and mean — a real take-no-shit warrior. Staatz hated white people. He'd been there since he was fourteen and he was seventeen then, so he'd done quite a bit of time. Normally, he wouldn't have had anything to do with some skinny white kid like me but he heard I was in there for assaulting four guys and when he found out it was an Indian I was standing up for, it was like he adopted me. We'd sit on his cot for hours talking.

Staatz was from a big family and all of his brothers were in the Movement. The Indian Movement. He'd grown up hearing them talk about working for it and he knew everything. That's why he hated white people so much. He told me about broken treaties, about reserves with no running water, no electricity, about Indian agents, about not being able to go to high school or university, about kids being taken away from their families and given to white people, about drunks and addicts and suicides, murders and all the shit stuff that comes from having your people kept under.

I was amazed. This was a vision of Indians I wasn't prepared for. Until then I'd believed that everything was sweat lodges and sunsets, the whole romantic noble savage stuff. Staatz told me about smallpox on blankets, about whole tribes being thrown into slavery and how they committed suicide rather than live as slaves, about women and children dying under the thunder of cavalry guns, about having ceremonies and rituals outlawed, about graves being robbed, religious artifacts stolen, about the Indian Act and how they had to ask permission to do almost everything we take for granted. He told me about Indians being the real explorers of the country, not just dumb brown lackeys in canoes. About the Iroquois Confederacy and how it was a model for the US Constitution, about council fires, how Indians had such respect and honor for this land that Indian soldiers would volunteer to fight for it, even though they weren't allowed to vote in it.

He talked about the black civil rights movement. Indians were Canada's niggers, he said. They suffered the same indignities, and they needed to find a common front to gather on to fight the same fight the blacks had fought and won. He talked about the Movement members taking over Alcatraz prison, claiming it as sovereign territory, and the impassioned declaration they sent out to the media and the government. He told me that direct warrior action was the only answer to the problem. It wasn't an Indian problem, Staatz said, it was a white problem. He said that confrontation was the only way to be heard.

I got angry at all the stuff he told me. Angry at the unfairness of it all. Angry at the short-sightedness, at the unnecessary death of cultures, angry at the fact that I was one of the race of people who'd made it all happen. Most of all, I got angry over the sudden demise of my romantic vision, my innocence crushed like all those teepees and wigwams. Staatz was going to be a warrior. He told me that a warrior fought for his people. Fought to get them out from under. Fought to protect them. He told me I was a warrior for protecting you. And that's when I knew, Josh. That's when I knew that somehow the cosmic signals had gotten crossed and I was born with the heart and soul of an Indian imprisoned in a white man's body. That's when the seed was planted. The seed that would sprout and grow into the warrior consciousness that was my destiny. The only thing I needed to fulfill.

Power in the hands of the humble is a subtle thing. It's no less effective a force as power controlled by the vainglorious and strident but it remains understated, discreet, building slowly, inexorably, gathering its force, its thrust, its integrity, until it lifts off suddenly, beautifully, like a bird across water. I learned that when I walked back into school next week. No one spoke much on the bus, so I had time to consider how I wanted to handle the entrance. That was my first inkling of newfound power — that I could choose my reaction. I walked to my locker quickly, eyes up and straight ahead. Both Allen Begg and Chris Hollingshead were recuperating from Johnny's beating and had not returned to school yet, but the rest of the crowd from the field that night was grouped along the window ledges as usual. Conversation stopped abruptly when I moved along that hallway. Chris's brother, both his eyes blackened, stepped in front of Mary Ellen, who simply turned and looked out the window while I passed.

All through the first day, I remained reticent. At lunch time, as I sat with my Mildmay friends in the cafeteria, I noticed that I was not the uncomfortable one. The uneasiness settled into the camp of seniors who watched me guardedly from a distance. Mary Ellen did not acknowledge my presence in any way, and as painful as that was, I appreciated her distance. Up to that point I still had no clear idea of what I was going to do. But as the day progressed and the faces of those involved betrayed their discomfort, I began to realize the power that was in my hands. My truth remained unspoken. Their story of my drunken lust was the only one that had surfaced. Since I had neither spoken to the police, the school administration nor their parents, they were firmly ensnared in their lie. With Johnny's preliminary hearing set for the next Monday, my silence was an unbearable weight on all of them. When I was summoned to the principal's office, I knew the power that I held.

Mr. Holmes wanted my side of things. As he expressed the options open to the administration, like expulsion for Johnny, the others or myself, formal charges or transfer to Hanover High, I realized the scope of my power. It would be their word against mine, and the onus would be on me to prove my case. That was my hole card. I told Mr. Holmes I would wait to speak at Johnny's preliminary and he reluctantly allowed me that right. When I returned to my locker to gather my books, Chris's brother, whose name I had learned was Steve, and the other boy involved, Kevin Carmichael, were waiting.

"So, what did you say to Spike, Injun?" Steve challenged.

"Yeah, did you finger us?" Kevin asked.

I slowly twirled the combination on my lock, smiling.

"Come on, out with it," Steve badgered. "Did you rat us out? You goin' to the cops?"

I grabbed my homework and jacket and turned slowly towards them. Mary Ellen and the seniors appeared from around the corner, waiting in the background. When I looked at her she lowered her eyes. Steve and Kevin stood waiting. Looking them both square in the eyes, I spoke, quietly and firmly.

"I didn't say anything."

"Yeah, right," Kevin said. "You expect us to believe that?"

"Yes," I said. "It's been four days and I haven't said anything to anyone." I slipped on my jacket.

"You ain't charging us?" Steve said.

"Charging you with what?"

They looked at each other, confused by my answer.

"You know, assault?" Kevin said, drawing a strong elbow in the ribs from Steve.

I grinned. "Assault? Did you say assault? Should I charge you with assault? Why? *Did* you assault me?" I said it as non-threateningly as I could.

"Look, we just want to know what to expect, that's all. We don't want no big scene here. Just let us know what to expect," Steve said.

"Well, you should expect the truth. I'll see you at the preliminary," I said, moving down the hallway.

"So you didn't say anything?" Steve called after me.

"No," I said over my shoulder, catching Mary Ellen's gaze. She didn't lower her eyes this time, but looked straight at me unwaveringly, questioningly. When I nodded at her she offered a half grin that disappeared as quickly as it came.

And that was that. The rest of the week passed uneventfully. I sensed my silence was the center of everyone's attention, but there were neither reprisals nor threats. Allen and Chris returned to classes. Neither of them spoke to me, settling for sidelong glances instead. My parents left me alone to consider my direction. By the time the weekend was over and we were preparing for the drive to Walkerton for Johnny's court appearance, I was ready. When we arrived at the courthouse I asked for permission to see Johnny. I was escorted to a small visiting room.

He was sitting at a table, arms folded across the top, and he grinned when I entered. "Hey," he said.

"Hey."

"You okay?"

"Yeah. Sore, stiff, but I'm okay. You?"

"Ah, you know. I been whacked before."

"What's it like at Galt?" I asked.

"It's okay."

"Your parents go to see you?"

"Are you kidding? They probably won't even be in court."

"What are you going to do?"

"In court? Plead guilty, I guess. I did attack them."

"For a reason."

"Yeah. For a reason. Are you gonna tell what happened?"

"Yes."

"Are you gonna charge them?"

"No."

"No! They kicked the shit out of you! I'm in jail? They treated you like dirt!" He was standing, waving his arms excitedly. "What are you gonna do, just take it?"

"What would you do?" I asked quietly.

"No question — I'd charge them. I'd send *them* to Galt. I'd get revenge."

"I already got it."

"Yeah? How?"

"By not saying anything."

"You're crazy."

"Maybe. Maybe not. See, I haven't said a thing about anything. And it's driving them crazy! They know that I know the truth but I'm not saying anything. They're wondering why. All the time they're wondering why, they're asking themselves what happened. What would they do if they were me? They're facing the truth."

"That doesn't do you any good. Not unless they own up to it."

"They have owned up to it — to themselves. See, if I had charged them, they'd deny everything, right?"

"Right."

"They'd be angry, threatened and they'd deny it all. They'd find some way to convince themselves that their story was the truth. But because I didn't, there are big questions in their minds — questions that are making them look at the real truth. Maybe if they see the truth on their own, they can change. Maybe not all of them. Maybe just one, but that's enough."

"Yeah, but maybe not."

"Maybe not."

"You're willing to risk letting them off the hook hoping they'll start feeling guilty?"

"They're already guilty."

"I say charge them. Make them suffer. They made you suffer," he said, pointing a finger at me.

"You know what my dad says?"

"No. What?"

"He says there's an addendum to the saying 'Know the truth and the truth shall set you free.'"

"What's an addendum?"

"You know, an add-on. Know the truth and the truth shall set you free ... but first, it'll make you miserable."

We laughed.

"So they're miserable, right?" Johnny said, grinning at me and sitting down again.

"Yeah. That's what my revenge is. And I'm not the one who's going to come out with the truth today," I said confidently.

"Yeah? Well, who is?"

"I don't know. But someone is."

"I hope so. Galt's okay but I wouldn't wanna live there."

"You won't. I promise."

"Okay. But if it looks like it's not going to happen, you better speak up and defend me."

"If it comes to that, I will."

"Josh?"

"Yeah?"

"I think you're crazy. Really crazy. I think you believing that the hand of God is going to move through that courtroom today is crazy. I think you believing that any of those kids out there have any kind of conscience is crazy. I think not taking revenge is crazy. But crazy or not, I'm with you. Always."

"Thanks, Johnny."

"Josh?" he said again, quietly.

"Yeah?"

"Nothin'," he said and looked at me for a long moment with those crystal-clear eyes before hugging me, then punching me lightly on the shoulder.

The hallway outside the courtroom was packed. Mr. Holmes and Mr. Hughes were talking with a group of adults I took to be the parents of those involved in the beating. Contrary to Johnny's belief, Mr. and Mrs. Gebhardt were there, along with old Harold, talking in hushed tones with my parents. Pastor Chuck was just arriving with a handful of people from the church, and a large contingent of Mildmay friends and neighbors stood around the benches chatting and eyeballing everyone else. Mary Ellen and her parents entered behind Pastor Chuck and headed straight towards my family.

Mr. Reid looked at me with a steely-eyed squint and Mrs. Reid simply stared at me, shaking her head slowly. Mary Ellen looked away.

"Ezra. Martha. I'm sorry that we all have to be here," Mr. Reid said. "I'm sorry we didn't know your boy better before we allowed him to escort our daughter. It's too bad you didn't do a better job of raising him. I expect more from farm folk."

My father regarded Mark Reid with as hard a look as I've ever seen him give. My mother moved a step closer to the both of us and laid one hand on my father's elbow.

"I'm sorry too, Mark," my father said. "I'm sorry you don't know my son. That you don't know us."

"Ezra, I want you to know that I'm considering charges of

assault against Joshua. He ripped my girl's dress, he demeaned her and who knows what else might have happened if Mary Ellen's friends hadn't stepped in and stopped him. Once this Gebhardt boy gets sent to trial today, I'll speak with my attorneys."

"That's entirely your decision, Mark," my dad replied. "But Joshua didn't assault your girl. I think you know that. I think she knows that."

"I don't know anything except what I've been told. And, quite frankly, Ezra, that's enough for me." Mark Reid began to steer his family away.

"That's too bad. But you need to hear the other side of the story," my dad said.

Mark Reid turned to face my father again. "And what side of the story is that?"

"My son's," my father said firmly.

"Well, what about your son's, Ezra? He hasn't said anything yet. I'll give you credit for that. The boy may be a lecher but at least he won't compound it by being a liar, too." Mr. Reid strode off brusquely with his wife and daughter in tow.

Pastor Chuck had approached as the exchange progressed and he stood with a hand on my shoulder and the other on my father's. My dad introduced him to Mr. and Mrs. Gebhardt, who'd been silent throughout the confrontation. They smiled weakly at him and remained silent. Before he could speak to us we heard the bailiff announcing that court would be sitting in two minutes, so we all began our move towards the doors. I noticed the town kids entering from the front where they'd been having a cigarette, and they all glared at me. I stared back, openly, unchallenging. When I took my seat alongside my parents, Mary Ellen turned her head and looked at me. I returned the look, and she offered me the same half grin I'd seen in the hallway a few days earlier.

Just before the door to the judge's chambers opened, a line of students filed in quietly, formally, and stood along the walls. Ralphie was there, along with Connie Shaus and a dozen or so other Grade Nines. Neil Metzger, the class president, stood calmly at the end of the center aisle. The judge entered and raised his eyebrows in surprise at the packed courtroom. Johnny was brought in. He too was wide-eyed at the turnout.

Neil strode down the aisle and approached Johnny's attorney. They discussed something briefly, agitatedly, and then Neil retired to stand at the front of the center aisle beside a nervous-looking Ralphie Wendt, who had also moved to the front. He looked at me, his Adam's apple bobbing in his throat like a seal in rough seas. I'd never seen fear on Ralphie's face before, and it startled me.

Johnny's attorney cleared his throat and said, "Your Honor, it has just come to my attention that the court could be saved considerable time this morning by hearing from two individuals who were also involved in the altercation that brings us here. I believe testimony from Ralph Wendt and Neil Metzger can resolve this issue without further cost or impediment."

Judge Hallett asked the prosecutor if he had any objection to hearing from the students. When no objection was raised, Ralphie moved to the front between the lawyers' tables.

"My name is Ralph Wendt," he began shakily, looking around quickly and gulping. "I'm ... a friend of Joshua Kane and Johnny Gebhardt. We've been to school together since we were kids. At least me'n Joshua have been. I've known Johnny for about four years now."

"And why are you here, Ralph?" Judge Hallett asked, leaning back in his chair and folding his hands on the bench in front of him.

"Well, I'm here because I was there that night and I saw what happened. I fought just as hard as Johnny. All you need to do is look at the raccoon eyes on Hollingshead to figure that out," he said to a burst of laughter from around the room.

The judge banged his gavel for quiet. He said, "This may not yet be a formal proceeding, but I will have no uproar in my courtroom! Any further display and I'll have it cleared. Go on, Ralph."

"I wasn't gonna say nothing. I figured if I did I'd get in trouble too. But Josh and Johnny have always been good to me. I was a jerk when we first met but they treated me right, you know. These guys have been on Joshua's case ever since he walked into school this year. I'm in his home room. I seen it. I heard all the names and the swearing that he's had to put up. Not just from these guys but from a lot of people. I never did nothing to try'n help him or make them stop and now I'm real sorry about that. I didn't wanna be left out, you know. I figured if I stood up for Joshua I'd be off the hockey team, off the football team. I wanted to fit in, you know. Not be on the outside? I was stupid."

"Okay, I appreciate that, Ralph, but what do you have to tell us about this incident specifically?" Judge Hallett said.

"Specifically? Well, Joshua wasn't drinking. He was with us all night. Me, Johnny, Connie. Mary Ellen dumped him right in front of everybody and left to hang out with Hollingshead and Begg and their friends."

"Hollingshead and Begg? The victims, you mean?" the judge asked.

"Well, yeah," Ralphie said, looking at me nervously. "Anyway, he went out to talk to her about it. After about five minutes me'n Johnny got worried on accounta Chris and Al had been trying to fight him all year. So we followed him out. When we got out the back door we heard a lotta shouting and laughing and Mary Ellen screaming at someone to stop. We ran over to the bleachers where everything was happening and Joshua was being punched and kicked by four of them. We ran over and started to pull them off and the fight broke out. No one figured Johnny was that tough. I sure didn't."

"What happened exactly, Ralph?" Judge Hallett asked.

"I remember yanking Chris Hollingshead backwards before Johnny cranked Allen Begg a real good one on the side of the head and knocked him down. Chris tried to nail Johnny with the bottle that was lying on the ground where he landed, but Johnny ducked and the bottle broke against the bleachers. Johnny punched and kicked Chris and he fell on some of the broken glass. That's how he got cut so bad."

"John Gebhardt never struck him with the bottle?" the judge asked.

"No sir. He didn't have to," Ralphie said to another, lower titter of laughter across the room.

The judge glowered at the crowd until they fell into silence.

"I squared off against Steve and Kevin. They're big but they
can't fight for beans. And Allen, well, he's just plain mean. Johnny
kept knocking him down but he kept getting back up so Johnny
would knock him down again. He's mean but he can't fight either.
At least, not good enough to take Johnny."

Allen Begg stared at the floor.

"So what they said, about Joshua being drunk and all, well,
that's bullshit. They started it right from day one at school. And
that night, it was four against one. If we hadn't gone out when we
did, Joshua would probably still be in the hospital," Ralphie said.

"Why didn't you say anything before this, Ralph?" Judge Hallett
asked.

Ralphie took his time answering. "Like I said, I was scared. I
didn't want to be on the wrong side. I thought this was an Indian
and white guy thing and, well, I'm white. I thought I had to stick
with the white guys. If I defended Joshua I thought everyone would
go against me. Already people are callin' us who hang around with
him Injun lovers. But it's not about that. It's about what's right. It's
about friendship. It's about rememberin' when people been good to
you and these two spazzes have always been good to me. Even
when I was bein' a jerk back in public school, they treated me right.
And I guess I'd rather have Joshua and Johnny for friends than
these creeps!" he said, pointing at the four Walkerton kids. "Least
they have enough balls to fight fair!"

"Anything else, Ralph?" the judge asked.

"Just that I'm sorry. I shoulda been braver. I shoulda stuck with
my friends. I shoulda stood up for Josh when all this started." He
looked at me with shiny eyes and I nodded. He grinned.

"Thank you, Ralph. Next."

Ralphie went to stand beside Connie, who slipped an arm
around his shoulder. He hung his head and looked at the floor, one
big meaty fist rubbing the corner of his eye. Neil Metzger strode to

the front of the room and introduced himself as class president of Walkerton Secondary School.

"A bunch of us got together, Your Honor, and decided to offer our testimony if the court needs it. There's a bunch of us that know all about the trouble that's been going on in our school since the start of the year. We should never have allowed it to go on as long as it did. Maybe we were just scared like Ralph was or maybe we just didn't care enough. But we know we were wrong. Especially now," he said.

"There are a number of us who knew about the plan to lure Joshua to the dance. We knew that Mary Ellen was supposed to get him there and then the guys were going to do a number on him, but we didn't try to stop it even though we knew about it. I've got a list of names of people who are willing to come forward and testify to that. We were wrong, Your Honor. We were all wrong.

"We should have been braver. We know that now. But I guess we were all like Ralph, here. We didn't want to cross any lines because we were afraid we'd be all alone on the other side. Being a teenager is all about not being alone, or different. But I guess we learned it's about being honest too. Even if it's tough. We're sorry it went as far as it did," he said and handed his list of names to the prosecutor.

The courtroom was abuzz. When I looked at Johnny, he was staring straight back at me, shaking his head with an absolute look of wonder on his face. I grinned and shrugged, casting my eyes up to the ceiling and beyond. He grinned back, circling one finger around and around one ear. Judge Hallett banged for order.

"Well, I wish all preliminary cases were this easy to adjudicate. Would there happen to be anyone else who would like to say a thing or two?" he said wryly.

Everyone fell into silence when Mary Ellen Reid stood and walked to the front of the room. Her shoulders were shaking slightly and her step was hesitant. When she got to the front of the room she looked at me briefly. When I nodded encouragement, she gulped nervously and faced the judge's bench.

"I'm Mary Ellen Reid, sir," she said quietly.

"Yes?" Judge Hallett said.

"It wasn't supposed to happen like this. It wasn't! I thought it was just a big joke. I thought everyone knew that. I didn't know that people actually *hated* Joshua! These are my friends. I grew up with them. We make fun of people, sure — like people with pimples, homely people and the ones who dress funny — but we don't *hate* them. At least *I* don't. I don't hate anyone. When they asked me to get Joshua to the dance, I thought it was just so they could scare him and get a laugh out of him being there. No one was supposed to get hurt. It was just supposed to be fun. Like the name calling we did. I said those things too, sir, but I didn't *mean* it! I didn't think anyone did. It was just funny. When they started beating him up it scared me. I didn't know they could be like that. He only ripped my dress because he was falling down. And it wasn't him who was drinking — it was us. We were the drunk ones."

"I'll ask you the same question I asked Ralph, Mary Ellen. Why didn't you say something sooner?" Judge Hallett leaned forward in his chair and stared straight at her.

She swallowed nervously. "Because I was afraid. Because I've known these people all my life. I thought I owed them some kind of loyalty. I was afraid I'd be alone, unpopular, an outcast. I was afraid that I'd be on the wrong side of the line, like Neil said. But it's not about lines. I know that now. It's about what's right. What happened to Joshua and Johnny wasn't right. *We* weren't right. If anyone deserves a beating, it's us for thinking we were so much better. And it's me for not seeing that the people I called my friends could be wrong. That if I didn't say anything I was wrong too. I'm sorry. Dad. Mom. I'm sorry. Johnny, Joshua, I'm sorry. And I apologize to the court too, Your Honor."

The courtroom was abuzz again and I saw Mr. and Mrs. Reid join hands, their faces solemn. Judge Hallett leaned back in his chair, removed his glasses and rubbed the bridge of his nose with a thumb and forefinger.

"In light of these developments I'll see both counsel in my

chambers. Court will recess for fifteen minutes," he said.

As the crowd filtered into the hallway I turned to see the Reids standing beside their daughter. Mark Reid whispered into Mary Ellen's ear while Mrs. Reid stood stock still, the picture of propriety and composure. The noise in the hallway was tremendous. Neil approached my family with Mr. Holmes directly behind him.

"Joshua, I'm sorry we didn't help you earlier. I guess none of us really realized how nasty things were getting. But I hope we helped today," he said earnestly.

"You did," I said. "And I guess no one really knew how tough things were going to be."

"I've been an educator for thirty some years now, Mr. Kane," Mr. Holmes was saying to my father. "I've never seen anything like this. I mean, you read about it happening in big-city schools, the US, you know, but you never think it could happen in your school, in your home. I hope you and your family will accept my apologies on behalf of my school."

"Yes," my father answered quietly.

We spent the recess talking with as many people as could squeeze through to reach us. When the bailiff shouted to reconvene, I spied the Hollingshead boys and their cronies standing sheepishly behind a circle of their parents, with a wall of students preventing the flight they so obviously wanted to make. They were ushered into the courtroom with little ceremony. Johnny sat alone at the front of the room, ramrod straight, staring at the judge's bench.

"Well, this has certainly been a different scenario than I expected," Judge Hallett said, rustling papers into place in front of him. "I want to thank Ralph Wendt, Neil Metzger and Mary Ellen Reid for coming forward. I don't feel it's necessary for the students who have volunteered to testify to do so at this time. In light of the presentations we have heard today, I do not feel this court requires any further action on this matter. Charges against John Gebhardt are dismissed. It is the court's belief that he acted in defense of his friend and although his reaction was extreme, it was not unwarranted. But I wonder if Joshua Kane would stand."

Caught by surprise, I sat there until my father lifted my elbow slightly and I stood nervously. The judge looked at me briefly, then continued.

"Joshua, you have been, by all accounts, the victim in this case, along with your friend John, who has had to spend time confined unnecessarily. You have the right to press charges against the individuals who assaulted you as well as for the harassment you received prior to the incident. I would, in fact, encourage you to do this. If you wish to have them charged, we can take care of that immediately. Is that what you want to do now, Joshua?"

The room was silent. I gazed around, catching Mary Ellen's eye, then the blank faces of my tormentors and finally Pastor Chuck, who crinkled up the corners of his eyes and nodded encouragement. I looked at my parents, who watched me carefully, and over at Johnny, who held me in that pure, open gaze. Revenge was mine if I would have it.

"I only want one thing, sir," I said.

"And what would that be, Joshua?" Judge Hallett asked.

"I want an apology from everyone that was involved, both to me and to Johnny."

"Very well," Judge Hallett said, banging his gavel a time or two. "Apologies are certainly due. At the very least. You're an honorable boy, Joshua. I admire that greatly. Court dismissed."

We were immediately surrounded. I fought through the throng and worked my way to where Johnny stood. He grinned broadly at me.

"You knew," he said.

"Kinda. But not really," I said.

"Man, when I saw all those kids, I thought — they're all here to hang me. And Ralphie! Holy! Who'da figured? And Mary Ellen? Wow! I wouldn't have believed it."

"So ... you wanna get outta here or are you starting to like this jailbird stuff?"

"Well, I thought I'd hang around and see if they give me a new suit and a couple bucks, but no, let's get lost!"

But Mr. and Mrs. Gebhardt were standing right there. They stared at us blankly. There was a quiver in Ben Gebhardt's hand as he reached for his son, and Mrs. Gebhardt swallowed and dabbed at her eyes with the corner of a hanky. Johnny stood stiffly, unmoving. The three of them stood there, merely staring at each other, Johnny and his father shuffling from foot to foot.

"Let's go home, son," Ben Gebhardt said in a gravelly voice.

Johnny looked at him hard. "No, you go ahead. I'm gonna stick with Josh. I'll see you later."

The Gebhardt's nodded solemnly. They took a few steps and Mrs. Gebhardt stopped and looked anxiously back at her son, mouth moving as if searching to remember how words were formed. Her hands fluttered to her cheeks, her waist, and then she clutched them in front of her chest before staring nervously at Johnny again, nodding and turning to begin walking after Ben, who was already halfway up the aisle.

"Yeah," he said quietly. "Me too."

"What?"

"Nothin'. Let's go."

We walked into the hallway. The crowd had formed a huge semicircle in the foyer with the four boys and Mary Ellen standing in front of them all. Mr. Holmes, Mr. Reid and Neil Metzger stood directly behind them as solemn as judges themselves. Johnny and I traded glances and walked slowly towards the gathering.

"Boys, I believe you have something to say to Joshua and John," Mr. Holmes said firmly.

The four boys looked at each other and finally Chris Hollingshead stepped forward. "Look ... I'm, uh, I'm sorry. I was wrong," he said shakily and added, "You're all right, Kane. You're all right."

"For an Injun?" I asked, with a grin.

He looked at me. "For anything," he said.

One by one the others stepped forward, offering terse apologies and handshakes. None of them made eye contact when they spoke and they left, one by one, wading through the crowd quickly until there were just Johnny, Mary Ellen and me in front of the crowd. She looked at us and then at her father.

"Johnny. I'm sorry. It shouldn't have happened. I hope ... we can be friends," she said reaching out to shake his hand. Johnny looked at her, unmoving, and then very slowly took her hand and shook it firmly, solemnly.

"Joshua," she said. "I'm really, really sorry. You've been brave and kind, forgiving and understanding through all of this. I'm sorry I didn't see that in you before."

"I'm sorry too," I said. "You think we might have a dance sometime? I practiced."

She looked at me with tears building in her eyes. "You're amazing," she said. "Yes. Sometime, yes, I'd love to have a dance with you."

I watched her leave with her parents, who'd been silent throughout everything. I thought then, that everything would be all right, that we, all of us — Johnny, me, Mary Ellen and the boys — had passed an enormous benchmark in our histories, a first great hurdle in our passage to maturity.

@

Threshing came and went, the Mildmay Fall Fair saw my father claim top prize for Sarah, a recalcitrant heifer, I joined the school cross-country running team, Johnny began working for his father after school and weekends and my mother set a record for the most preserves jarred by one person in history. By the time Thanksgiving rolled around, life had settled into a comfortable pattern again. School was an exhilarating place. The antagonism of those first weeks did not resurface. In fact, Chris Hollingshead and I became the anchor of the cross-country team, generally finishing one-two for Walkerton in every competition. We became teammates and, very slowly, casual friends. Our little circle, which included Johnny, Ralphie, Connie and a member of my confirmation class, Karl Tabinger, studied together in spare periods, went for pizza, bowled Friday nights and talked on the phone long into the evenings. They all came to see me become a member of the church that Thanksgiving Sunday.

I understood why they called them confirmation classes. Everything I'd learned in six weeks of classes had only confirmed what I already knew. The church was a living body of the people who gathered under its beams and arches, and its strength came from a shared faith and belief in the benevolence of a God who asked only that we enter this world learning to treat each other well. True worship of this God was reflected in how well we lived rather than in how well we prayed, sang or attended. And this God, a living God, was present in all things, unseen and eternal. I eagerly awaited the Sunday when I would step forward in front of our congregation and proclaim, by celebration of my first Communion, that I believed in that living body, that tribe of God as Pastor Chuck put it, and wanted to live my life by its precepts and teachings.

My parents planned a party with Pastor Chuck, my confirmation class, Johnny and the rest of my friends and their parents at our farm following the service. There would be a big open-pit barbecue, a sing-along around a bonfire and even, perhaps, a baseball game. By the time we piled into the car Sunday morning, I was filled with a joy and expectation that was indescribable. I had put my faith in the God of this church; He had answered with a resolution that I could not have planned, an outcome that was better than anything I could have imagined or hoped for. This joining was my commitment to always seek that guidance, to always come in earnest, humble prayer, asking for strength, inspiration and motivation to live according to His will. It was my first act, my first choice, as a mature, free-thinking person.

The service was beautiful. The four of us who were being confirmed that morning selected the hymns and text. After I'd shared the metaphor of the walls of Jericho being the walls of ignorance, everyone agreed to use it as the text, and our hymn selection was exuberant. I chose Pastor Chuck's rewritten version of "Blowin' in the Wind" and the others asked for "Just a Closer Walk with Thee," "Onward, Christian Soldiers" and, quite naturally, "Joshua Fought the Battle of Jericho." The church music combo replaced the organ and the St. Giles' Players performed a skit about John the Baptist. Pastor Chuck's sermon focused on the difficulties involved in battling the thick, mighty walls of ignorance and misunderstanding and how the horn of God, His teachings and principles in action, can bring those walls down. We were welcomed as new members of the church as the rite of Communion was solemnly performed. As I chewed the bread and tasted the wine that morning, I felt lifted up, buoyant and suspended, and I realized that for me, being saved, as our more evangelical brethren call it, was beyond mere rescue. No, saved was not so much a verb as a noun. Saved. Something cherished and wonderful, gathered lovingly, protected, kept whole and shining, a singular treasure. I cried as I looked at the faces of my parents, and they cried too.

I don't know how much Johnny understood of either the service or my commitment, but he stood with us, silent and reserved, arching his eyebrows now and then at an enthusiastic response to song, a line of text or the vigor and flourish with which Pastor Chuck brought the message to us. I caught his eye as I stood at the front of the church that morning prior to Communion. He was staring at me, offering a clenched-fist salute in front of his chest. I was glad he was there.

Back at the farm, we had the barbecue ready in no time, with corn roasting over the fire, hamburgers, hot dogs, a few salads, three or four homemade pies and marshmallows for later. Pastor Chuck offered grace and we ate, the whole lot of us strewn across the verandah on chairs, on the steps and railings. When we'd finished, Johnny hiked a thumb over his shoulder. We excused ourselves, stopped to pick up our gloves and a ball from the garage and slipped away behind the equipment shed. The paint had faded from the strike zone, and our old wooden slat of a home plate had long since disappeared, although it still looked like the same place. We quietly thumped the pockets of our gloves, staring around an area that once was like a shrine to us.

"Ever wonder what would have happened if I hadn't found those books in the library, Josh?"

"Yeah, sometimes," I said. I looked at the sky. "I guess we would have found another way to get by."

"But I found them."

"Yeah. You found them."

"Think it was coincidence? Luck?" Johnny asked.

"My dad says coincidence is just God working anonymously. Our lives are just His unsigned portraits."

"Your dad said that?"

"Yeah. Well, the first part. I said the last part."

"That's pretty good."

"The last part?"

"Nah. The first part!" He punched my shoulder, laughing.

We stood there until I finally flipped him the ball. He caught it, turned it slowly over a few times in the pocket of his glove and asked quietly, "You think we meet people the same way we find books? The right ones when we need them? Even if we don't know we need them at the time?"

"Yeah, I guess we do," I said.

"Me too. Ever wonder why we met?"

"No," I said, smiling at him. "No, I never did."

"Why not?"

"I guess because it never felt like I had to. Why'd you ask?"

"I don't know. I've been trying to figure a lot out lately. Why you're here, why I'm here, why we're *all* here. Remember when I asked you if you ever wanted to be someone else?"

"Yeah. You still wanna be someone else, Johnny?"

"I don't know. I wouldn't mind finding out who this self is first, really. I kinda got a confession to make."

He looked at me with that pure, wide-open gaze and I could sense, right then, the wounds he walked with. I wanted to hug him to me, letting him know that everything would be all right, that we were still Laughing Dog and Thunder Sky, that we always would be despite the choices and changes we'd lived through.

"Remember the Maze? The last one?" he asked.

"Yeah. That was the toughest maze ever."

"Know why it was so tough?"

"No."

"Because there was no end."

"What?"

"There was no end. I didn't build one. It all just doubled back on itself."

I was shocked at the meanness in the idea.

"I wanted to see how long you'd stay in there wandering around through the heat and the dust and the darkness before you finally gave up."

"Were you gonna pull me out eventually?"

"Yeah. Yeah, I was pretty close to doing that when you pushed out yourself."

"So why are you telling me this now?"

He sighed and looked away across the fields, absently turning the ball in the pocket of his glove. When he spoke it was in the quietest voice I had ever heard him use.

"I guess because I see you solving your own maze right now. Your life, you know? Like, you didn't know where the end was in all of that school shit but you kept on trying to find it. Because you believed that there *was* an end, just like the maze in the hay mow. You stayed in there a long time because you believed I'd built in an end to it all, that you'd tumble out into the light eventually. And when it finally got to be too much, you decided to get out. You *decided*. Just like the decision you made when you couldn't find your way out of the school thing. You didn't know where the end was but you decided to get out. Only when you pushed out of the maze at school you pushed out into your faith. And that was the end for you. You solved the maze."

We were both quiet for a long moment. Me, while I considered what he'd just told me, and Johnny, I believe, to allow himself to feel what was roiling in his chest.

"Life is like a maze, Josh. You wander through all the switchbacks and drop-offs believing there's light and air somewhere. That someone's designed an end to it all. Except I don't think there's an end to mine. I just keep on tunneling around in the darkness, pushing on bales. I wish I had your faith. I wish I could stand up and say *enough*. But you know what I'm afraid of?"

"No, Johnny. What are you afraid of?" I asked softly.

"I'm afraid that when I push out, there isn't gonna be any air or light. That there isn't gonna be anybody there to help me learn how to breathe again. That all I'm gonna find is another maze."

"I'm gonna be there to help you, Johnny."

"You sure?"

"Yeah, I'm sure."

"I'm proud of you, Josh."

"You are?"

"Yeah. I'm proud because you hang in there and don't get ruined by any of it. You're a warrior."

"Thanks, Johnny."

"No problem. Think you can still handle my curve ball?"

"I didn't know you had a curve ball."

"You didn't?"

"Nah. The only thing you ever threw that broke was a cow chip!"

And we fell into the game we invented. When the rest of our crew rounded the corner of the shed, they found us laughing, teasing and running like boys, the men we'd briefly exposed tucked away again in the shelter of our youth like nestlings. We played a scrub game for an hour or so and then wandered back to pile wood for the bonfire. As the evening arched slowly into the deep pocket of night, we sang, laughed, ate, drank and talked. The line of people walking towards their cars was a satisfied line, deep in the tranquil fullness of feast and merriment. As we watched the last taillights flick out like fireflies in the distance, our house, our farm and our hearts were still. The four of us stood out beneath a canopy of stars, staring away across the great bowl of the universe, immersed in the ancient light of a billion distant suns. So many possible worlds. Amazed.

Part Three

BURY MY HEART

As I flew over the undulating conversation of Ontario and then the eloquent hush of prairie, I thought about how very much our lives are like the land. The lives of the wounded are scant, stark and remorseless — the barrens, almost. While the lives of the saved are lush, arable and gratifying — a heartland. The wouded are nomads, moving like ghosts, incorporeal, ethereal, leaving no sign on the territories they cross. And the saved, well, the saved are enlightened émigrés, permanent homesteaders, edifices scrawled like joyous graffiti across their homelands. The saved in their plenty dream of travel, and the wounded in their barrens carry dreams of permanence. Johnny and I had not changed. It's just that he had always wandered alone in the vacuous maze of the wilderness and I had taken the guided tour.

Circling the Calgary airport I said a humble prayer for guidance and strength for the struggle before me.

Nettles was waiting when I emerged from the arrivals area. His brown suit was immaculate, crisp. From his voice and manner on the phone I'd expected a rumpled fedora, checked suitcoat, whiskey breath and tobacco-stained fingers. Instead, the hand that reached out to shake mine was manicured, steady and strong. The eyes were steel gray, clear, with a hint of humor at their corners.

His trimmed silver hair gave him an elegant, refined look incongruous with the voice that greeted me.

"Reverend. Good to see ya!" he said, laying a hand on my shoulder and gently guiding me towards the escalator. "The missus said I should offer to put you up with us instead of having you flop in a hotel. How's that?"

"That's fine. I prefer to stay with families," I replied.

"Travel a lot do you, Reverend?" he asked.

"Not generally, no. Conferences sometimes."

"Me neither. Planes? Keep 'em. Me, I figger God wanted us to fly he'da give us wings *before* we become angels, you know? Oh. Hey, Reverend, no offense, eh?"

I grinned. "None taken, Inspector."

"Good. Missus says, me, I gotta learn to engage the brain before my mouth pulls out into traffic sometimes. Habit, you know." He pointed to my small carry-on. "That all you brought?"

"Yeah. I don't think I'll be here that long."

"Why's that, Reverend?"

"Johnny always liked a fast solution. I don't expect he's changed much," I said quickly.

"I don't know. He's been pretty methodical. Don't exactly come across as a snip-snap kinda guy, you know," Nettles said.

His car was a new maroon Crown Victoria. It was as immaculate as his suit except for the food wrappers crumpled beneath the pedals. He kicked them back under his seat as he settled. A statue of the Virgin was glued to the dash and a strand of rosary beads hung from the rearview mirror. Nettles grinned sheepishly.

"The missus. Good Catholic girl. Her waya tryin' to get me converted. Me, a convert's the kick followin' a touchdown, you know?" he said, wheeling sharply out of the parking lot and onto the highway.

Nettles reached down to plug a cassette tape into the player and fiddled with the volume as the sounds of thrashing guitars filled the car. He drummed his fingers out of time against the steering wheel.

"Jason and the Scorchers," he said, hooking a thumb at the tape player. "Figure it's gotta be country might as well be wild. Kid gave it to me a few years ago. I like it. Better'n all the twangy slop they play on the radio. You a country lover, are you, Reverend?"

"Music? Yes. Gospel mostly."

"Oh, yeah, gospel's good. Hard to write a good drinkin', wife cheatin' gospel tune, though, eh, Reverend?" Nettles said, winking.

I laughed. "You know what happens when you play a country song backwards, of course."

Nettles looked at me with raised eyebrows and a silly grin. "Yeah, yeah, yeah. You get the wife back, the truck back, the dog back! Huh! You're okay, Reverend, you're okay. Listen. We need to go over a lot of stuff before we get you to the scene. Me, I figured you'd feel more relaxed if we worked at home 'steada the office. 'Sides, the missus is real excited about me havin' to spend time with a man of the cloth and wants to meet you as soon as she can. Wants you to get to work on my conversion, I guess."

"That's fine," I said.

"Gebhardt knows you're comin'. We told him as soon as you confirmed. He's gonna cool out till he talks with you. Promised not to do nothin' rash as long so we didn't. So we're okay for now. Mornin's soon enough to get you out there, I figure."

"A fresh start," I said.

"Yeah. Kinda gotta have all your faculties workin' when you get there."

I nodded. Nettles drove like he talked, randomly sashaying in and out of traffic, aiming rather than steering. We swept through the streets quickly and by the time we pulled up in front of a coral brick split-level, I was ready for the relative safety of a plane again. He reached into the back seat to retrieve my valise.

"The homestead," was all he said.

The door swung open as we walked up the sidewalk and a small, pretty red-haired woman stepped into the doorway. She smiled. Nettles took the last steps quickly and swept her up in an enthusiastic hug, twirling her around. She patted down her curls before smiling at me again.

"Honey, Reverend Kane. Reverend Kane, my wife, Vicky," he said, standing with his arm around her waist.

"Pleased to meet you, Reverend Kane," Vicky Nettles said so primly I almost expected a curtsey.

"Please, will everyone just call me Joshua? My parents called me Joshua long before anyone called me Reverend."

"Well, Joshua," she said merrily, "welcome. Once you're settled in the guest room we can have dinner. It's ready."

"Thank you. That would be very welcome."

Vicky led me to the guest room while her husband left to "get out of the monkey suit." It was a small room, cheerily decorated in soft blues and pinks. A small crucifix hung above the headboard.

"We're Catholic," she said quickly.

"That's terrific," I said, lightly. "A hundred religions, one God."

She smiled. "Yes," she said. "Come down when you're ready."

I settled myself on the bed once she'd left. It felt good to be in the company of a family, to feel the warmth that spelled out home, even if it was someone else's. I meditated briefly, then wandered downstairs to find the dining room.

They were standing around the table when I entered. The Nettles had three children, two boys and a girl, all in their middle teens. I was introduced to Henry, the oldest, Sharon and then Samuel, the youngest. They all shook my hand solemnly, politely and silently. We sat down to a traditional roast beef dinner complete with mashed potatoes, gravy, corn, salad, buns and pumpkin pie.

I was asked to offer a blessing, which I did gladly. I was happy to see that the Nettles were as respectful of ceremony as they were lax with propriety. Hands reached out instantly as the amen faded and the clink and clatter of plates being scraped and filled was a joyous cacophony.

"You gotta have a boarding house reach if you're gonna get anything at this table, Joshua. Help yourself. Can't reach, just yell. Someone will toss it to ya!" Nettles said. He was wearing faded jeans now with a ragged sweatshirt that read "I Got Crabs at Fisherman's Wharf." He pointed and waved while he talked and ate, pulling all of them easily into the flow of his words. Their chatter was enthusiastic, animated with a great deal of laughter and encouragement from each other over school projects, team sports and hobbies. Vicky Nettles was demure, matriarchal almost, the perfect foil for her husband's garrulous conviviality. She smiled at me as I watched her family and I sensed her deep and abiding pride in all of them. The meal passed quickly. When Nettles and I took our coffee to the downstairs den I was totally refreshed and invigorated.

In the den were shelves of books, family pictures, trophies, overstuffed armchairs, a fireplace, an antique table that held a marble chess board and a set of medieval pewter chess men. The books were largely classics, eclectic and well used. Nettles fiddled at the stereo until the sounds of a Baroque concerto filled the room elegantly.

"Bach," he said, easing into an armchair, lacing his fingers behind his head, "Brandenburg. Sappy but soothing, you know."

"It's a nice room. Very comfortable, very homey," I replied, settling into the opposite chair.

"Yeah," he said with a hearty sigh. "The wife set it up as my space. First it was gonna be an office but hell — oops, sorry, Reverend — I spend all day in an office. Who needs one at home, you know? I come here to relax, listen to tunes, read, try'n figure out this chess thing. You play, Joshua?"

"No," I said. "Far too militaristic for me."

"Too bad. You'd probably be a good player. Thought you might give me some pointers. Vicky, she says the chess and the books are good for me. She's been trying to refine me since day one. The suits and all. Me, I always been a desert boots and Levi's kinda guy, you know. Cuss too much, drink a bit, watch Stallone movies, that kinda thing. But I love her. So I read the books. But chess? Forget it. Checkers? Now there's a game! Want a game, Joshua?"

"Sure. I'd like that."

"Don't tell Vicky, but that's all the boys 'n me use the chess board for!" he said, reaching up to the top of the bookcase for a yellow box. "It's an ammo box. She never touches 'em. Last place she'd look!"

We settled ourselves around the antique table and Nettles replaced the pewter chess set with the checkers. He took the first move.

"So, you think about you 'n Gebhardt, Joshua? Your friendship?" he asked while I considered my move.

"Yes," I said quietly. "It's a lot to think about. We go back a long way."

"You remember anything that might help? Good move."

"Thanks. I don't know exactly. The Johnny I knew and the one you describe are two different people. I knew an angry man at the last but I didn't know a violent one."

"Well, I can tell you this. He's an articulate son-of-a-bitch. Oops. Damn! Shit! I mean ... Aw hell, Joshua, you don't mind a little cussin', do ya?"

I laughed. "No. I was raised with farm kids, David. I could probably give you a few lessons!"

"Probably! Good. Anyway, he walks into the building cool as can be, nobody notices anything. Walks up to the commissionaires' desk on the mezzanine, asks them if he can leave his knapsack with them while he goes to his appointment. Commissionaire figures he's a little weird lookin' but he's well spoken and polite so he figures, what the hell. He gets directions for Indian Affairs, goes into the Reserves and Trusts section on the fourth floor, asks to speak to somebody and sits calmly in reception for about ten minutes. Receptionist liked him. When he's called to go in he excuses himself, saying he needs to go to the bathroom first. Comes back carrying a duffelbag. Receptionist figures that's a little strange but thinks nothin' more of it. Your move, Joshua."

I looked down at the board and moved a man perfunctorily.

"Oooh!" Nettles said deliciously and pounced over two of my men. "Been a while, has it, Reverend? Anyway, he walks into the office of this James Mueller. Sits. Sets the duffelbag at his feet. Introduces himself. He chats up Mueller for about two minutes. Mueller likes him. Then, while he's talkin', all calm still, a real no-fuss, no-muss kinda guy, you know, he takes a sniper's rifle outta the duffelbag which he assembles in front of Mueller. Loads it. Sets it down on Mueller's desk and tells him he's got four bombs planted in different places on the floor. Four's some kind of special number to you natives, is it Joshua?"

"It is," I said.

"Figured. Four's been poppin' up regular all through this. Fourth floor. Mueller's office is four-forty-four. Gebhardt releases four hostages. He takes over the place at four p.m. Fourth day of the fourth week. Closes off all incoming phone lines except for line four. Not really a rocket scientist kinda guess about significance, right? Anyway, he shows Mueller what he tells him is a remote detonator. Tells Mueller there's a knapsack full of dynamite behind the commissionaires' desk and that he should phone building security and tell them to evacuate. Then he pulls out a pair of grenades and lays them on the desk. By now Mueller's convinced he's for real. He makes the call.

"Then Gebhardt moves him out through the offices in that section where he gathers up sixteen people and herds them into the boardroom where there's a fridge, hot plate, microwave and a view of the hallway and the cliffs across the river. Knows his stuff. Knows we coulda put snipers on the building so he chose a room that faces the river. Harder shot, you know. Security evacuates, they call us, we respond, he calls us. Tells us the elevators are rigged, his location, what he's packin' for weapons, short list of demands and a promise to release four people as a show of good faith. Staff tell us he's genuine, about the weapons they seen, we get worried. He ties up twelve people, walks four downstairs. He's got the detonator in one hand, .45 auto in the other, small pack on his back. He locks all the doors, leaves a block of dynamite taped across the handles on remote detonators and lets the hostages out the last door. They tell us he's armed to the teeth, calm but threatening nonetheless. We get a fax telling us the phone line for communications. We talked to some of the hostages to assure us they were okay. They tell us he's all war painted up and dead serious. One of our guys takes a look at the explosives on the door, says it's hard to tell for sure but it looks like the real thing. We decide not to risk entering the building. That's when he tells us he'll only deal with you or he starts shooting people. We call you, you're here, it's showtime. And it's also your move again."

I moved. Nettles chuckled and took three of my men. I didn't care. The situation he depicted was volatile and the Johnny he described was a calculating, thorough and desperate man, a dangerous combination. I knew Johnny well enough, I believed, to know that he would have thought out and examined his plan from every angle, that the science of this particular game would be airtight, perfect.

"He sent you faxes?" I asked, finally.

"Yeah. Well written. Tight, punchy. Mostly political but not a lot of radical rhetoric. He's a sharp bastard, this Gebhardt. King me, Reverend."

I crowned his man as Nettles rubbed his hands together with boyhood glee. Any other time and I would have enjoyed this game. "What about his demands? Are they things you can deal with?"

"Well, we've been on the phone to national Indian groups. They say they don't know him, don't know about his actions, his plans. They're calling it a nutcase reaction. Legitimate? Maybe if he was Indian. White guy doin' it? Nice touch but no way, they say. The demands? Same thing. Callin' for the House of Commons to reconvene over the Oka situation is reactionary horseshit, never happen, they know it, we know it. Gebhardt? He don't know it. The UN thing? Some kinda tribunal to examine the Indian condition? Big deal, they say. A little press, no real action, no solution. They'd take it but it's mostly show. So we got some sway there. The army thing? Forget it. No way they can pull out and let the Warriors in Oka off the hook. Just tryin' to keep that from explodin' into open warfare's a trick in itself without this. So I don't know. We're city cops, Reverend, we can't promise much. Maybe we can swing an MP into the works but that's about it. Shit, the feds ain't even makin' a sound over Oka and there's a few hundred lives involved there. No prime minister, no minister of Indian Affairs, no nothin'. So it looks doubtful."

"Do I tell him that?" I asked.

"My gut tells me yeah, you gotta. My brain tells me no, play it out, get the people home safe, get the son-of-a-bitch in custody. That's what we want. People safe, bad guy locked up. You gotta want the same thing."

"Like I don't?"

Nettles looked at me for a long moment, then leaned across the table and looked directly at me. "I don't know, Joshua. Which side of the fence are you on?"

"What do you mean?"

"I mean, you're Indian. I gotta tell you that took a lot of us by surprise. We figured church guy, white guy, right? No offense, Joshua, but that puts you in tough, too."

"How so?"

"Well, you got a stake in this thing, bein' Indian and all, don't you?"

"We all have a stake in this, David," I said firmly. "Bein' people and all."

"Touché. Still, politics is politics. I hadda ask, you know. We gotta know if you're pro-Indian or pro-white."

"I'm pro-peace, David. I'm pro-life. I'm pro-harmony. The last time I checked I don't think they rang up as exactly specifically Aboriginal attitudes. Or specifically white."

"Yeah, yeah, okay. Look, I'm sorry. I don't wanna ruffle any feathers but we gotta know goin' in where you stand on this thing. We gotta know whether you're pullin' for the nation or pullin' for solution. That's all."

I looked at him steadily. I didn't think he believed that I arrived carrying an Indian agenda into this situation. Instead, I believed he was being a policeman and asking, for him, a very hard question and I respected that. "I'm pulling for life, David. Johnny's. Those people's. And mine," I said, with a level look.

"Why yours?" he asked.

"Why not mine? I'll be in there too."

"In there? You think we're gonna let you go *in there*?"

"Yes. How else do you want me to negotiate?"

"On the phone, of course. Where you'll be safe."

"I'll be safe with Johnny. Besides, he wouldn't settle for a phone-line negotiation."

"Why not?"

"Because it's not the Indian thing to do," I said simply.

"I gotta clear it. You sure he won't work it any other way?"

"No way — not in a million years. We meet in council, face-to-face, smoke a pipe and talk."

"You're not serious."

"Completely."

"And you're workin' for resolution? No deep-seated angst for the whiteman? No anger towards Gebhardt? No residue from whatever fight you 'n him had?"

"What makes you think there was a fight?"

"You told me he was a really good friend. You also told me you hadn't seen him in a long time. Me, I got good friends, Joshua. We see each other regular. Good friends don't speak for years tells me maybe they ain't such good friends anymore."

"There's no residue, David. Unless you count sorrow."

"And Gebhardt?"

"He asked for me. That tells me he trusts me with his future."

"Or it gives him a good excuse to get you into his sights. You're a reverend, Reverend, how *could* you refuse to be here? Maybe that's what he wanted. A chance to take you out with him? You remember what this fight was about."

"I remember."

"And?"

"And what?"

"And ... are you gonna tell me?"

Our game lay before us, forgotten. I remembered. I remembered everything. "It's a long story, David."

"I got all night."

"Okay. Maybe I need to hear it again too."

"Could be you do, Joshua. Could be you do," Nettles said, settling back into his chair.

"I need to get something before I start. It's in my room."

"I'll fetch us a pot of coffee and some snacks while you're gone."

As I stopped in the guest room to get the box of letters, I thought about the place in my memory I was about to revisit fully for the first time in a long while. We step across the line that is etched in the sand of our histories unexpectedly and realize that it will always be the looking-back place, the line we toe to scan the territory that was our childhood, the frontier of our maturity. As I went downstairs to rejoin Nettles I was already toeing the line.

Pastor Chuck came up with the solution. Throughout the winter and spring, after Sunday services I'd wait around while Pastor Chuck closed up the church and he would drive me home, where we'd have lunch with my parents. Standing in the hushed nave of St. Giles all those mornings I was always struck by the quiet dignity and power of the building. It was like standing on the land — a pure, resonant thrum of power everywhere. That's really where the church became security for me, those long moments alone with my thoughts while Pastor Chuck attended to the chancel and secured the rest of the church. We'd chat amiably on the drive to the farm about school, that Sunday's text, life and farming. Pastor Chuck became a brother figure to me.

Things at school had settled down so much that I could almost convince myself that the turbulent start had never happened. I moved through the hallways, confident and secure. The challenge of high school was my catalyst and I responded with high averages and inventive themes for projects. When I mentioned this to Pastor Chuck one Sunday in May he responded with concern.

"You're not forgetting about it, are you, Joshua? You're not getting so comfortable in the absence of conflict that you're allowing yourself to believe the conflict never happened, are you?" he asked, looking sideways at me as he drove.

"No. Well, I don't spend a lot of time going over it, if that's what you mean. But things remind me of it all the time."

"And what do you do when things remind you of it?"

"Nothing. I just let them pass."

"Don't you think the reason you're being reminded is because you're supposed to take some action?'

"What action?"

"I don't know, Joshua. I do know that just because things are different now doesn't mean you don't have to resolve them. You found out that in the eyes of the world, you're an Indian. You've still got to come to terms with that part of your identity. Just sitting back and enjoying the peace doesn't guarantee that it will always be peaceful. It's a big world. You're getting old enough to think about the day you move out into it. Someday, somewhere, you're going to be presented with that conflict again and you need to have a way of responding positively to it."

"I am. I mean, I forgave all of those people," I said earnestly.

He smiled. "Yes. That's good. But a forgiving nature isn't going to spare you agony. Identity is a tricky thing. We think we know who we are but the world has a strange way of asking us how well we *really* know ourselves."

"What do you mean?"

"Well, look at me. If someone asked me to describe myself I would say that I'm a thirty-four-year-old Presbyterian minister who believes in a kind, loving and nurturing God. I think that explains it all. My work speaks for itself. In the eyes of the world I am what I believe I am. Right?"

"Yeah. So?"

"So, suppose someone comes along one day and says, 'Pastor, how come you're not married?' Innocent enough question, and the answer could be really simple. Like, I haven't met the right person yet. And I could probably get along with that answer. I could convince myself that it's the truth because it comes out so easily, without any edges. It's true *enough* to be believable. You follow?"

"Yeah."

"But all of a sudden I start looking at that question. I ask myself, Why *aren't I* married? Other pastors are married, have families, why not me? I live with that question, realizing that it's because I'm scared. I'm afraid that no one will find me attractive enough, smart enough, rich enough, funny enough to want to be with me. I'm a minister and women will think I'm boring, no fun. So I don't try. It's safer not to. To the outside world and to myself, I'm a confident, approachable, friendly man of faith. Everyone believes that — even me. But because of that one marriage-related question, I find out that I'm in conflict inside. I'm scared, I'm feeling inadequate, I'm lonely, and the man I think I know so well is gone, replaced by the scared, and lonely, one. Conflict. No identity. All from one innocent question."

"So what do you do?"

"Exactly. What do I do? I resolve the conflict. I don't allow myself to wander through my life believing there's nothing wrong because everything looks good on the surface."

"How do you do that?"

"I don't know yet, Joshua. I'm still working on it. I'm thinking of asking Rebecca Norton out to a movie, actually."

"You mean that's true? It wasn't just an example? You really feel that way?"

He smiled again, staring ahead at the road before he answered. "Yes, it's true. And as intimidating as asking her out is for me, I have to do it. I have to face the scared, inadequate self I discovered. Otherwise, I'll have to face the same conflict somewhere down the line, maybe when I'm eighty and alone. By then it will be too late to change. Joshua, you have to face yourself too."

"I don't know where to start," I said seriously.

"Sure you do."

"I do?"

"Think about it. What's the first thing you do when you have a problem?"

"Pray?"

"Yes, asking for guidance. Guidance and the strength, motivation and inspiration to handle whatever you're facing."

"I can do that."

"I know. And I'll pray too. Who knows where the answer's going to come from? I don't."

"Me neither. But I do know one thing," I said.

"And what's that?"

"Rebecca Norton thinks you're hot."

"Oh, she does, does she? And how do you know this?" Pastor Chuck said, laughing but looking a little relieved.

"I've got ears. I heard her talking in the choir room one Sunday. She'd go out with you like that!" I said, snapping my fingers.

"Well. See? Now I'm going to have more confidence. Now I'll actually take the chance and ask her. Hot, you say?"

"Hot," I said and we laughed.

He did go on the date. About a month later he showed up early one Saturday morning. My father and I were working on the old tractor when he appeared around the corner of the garage whistling, holding one of my mother's fresh strawberry tarts in one hand. He was wearing khaki shorts, sandals, sunglasses and a wild-looking Hawaiian shirt. My dad and I grinned when we saw him.

"Why, Pastor, if I didn't know better I'd say your wardrobe's getting a little on the playboy side of things," my father said, wiping the grease from his hand so he could shake Pastor Chuck's hand.

"Well, Ezra, I don't know about playboy exactly but I have been feeling somewhat younger lately," Pastor Chuck said, winking at me.

"Must be the heat," I said.

We laughed. I'd shared our conversation about Rebecca and identity with my parents. Pastor Chuck spent a few minutes inspecting the work we were doing on the old Cockshutt and making polite conversation about the farm before moving on to his real reason for visiting.

"Truth is, Ezra, Joshua, I have an answer to this identity question. I know someone who can help us."

My father and I exchanged surprised looks. We'd been to the library in Walkerton and pored through the card catalogue for books about Indians — Ojibways in particular — without too much success. I was reading *Flint and Feather* by Pauline Johnson and while the poems were nice I wasn't getting a whole lot of answers from them. The same could be said of the Grey Owl books I'd finished recently — I knew more about beavers than I did about Indians.

"Who is this person?" my father inquired.

"I'll get to that, Ezra, I'll get to that. But let me tell you what's happened. I think you'll appreciate it," he said, motioning us over to the shade of the garage where we sprawled loosely on the grass. "Turns out Rebecca has an uncle who's a teacher. We went over to her folks' for dinner one night and he was there. We got to talking about the interesting places our work had taken us and he told us about the five years he spent on the Cape Croker Indian Reserve near Owen Sound.

"Well, he met an older woman there — a medicine woman. She knew all the herbal cures of the Ojibway people, led many ceremonies and taught the language. Through their acquaintance he gained an insight into her people he could never have attained through either books or his job. Said he was fascinated by the depth of genuine spirituality that exists in the traditional way. So naturally I explained that I had a member of my congregation who really needed exposure to that kind of awareness and he promised to contact this woman. She phoned me last night and she's eager to meet you, Joshua."

We looked at each other like conspirators. We all understood how this had evolved, but still, it didn't diminish the awe we felt at the unfurling of the plan. There was no question in my mind that I would meet this woman, that our acquaintance would be a vital link in my growth or that this development would lead me to other things.

Pastor Chuck continued to explain that Jacqueline Kakeeway was in her early sixties and was a grandmother about twelve times over. She'd been raised in the church but returned to her traditional ways when she was a young woman. She'd dedicated her life to teaching the young people of her reserve the traditional ways of the

Ojibway because she'd seen the difficulties they faced coping with the non-Indian world. She wanted to give them the support of a strong cultural identity when they moved out to face that world. Pastor Chuck had tentatively arranged for my parents and me to travel with him to Cape Croker for a visit the next weekend.

My father shook his head slowly before he spoke. "Seems to me it's like farming. You can't learn it from a book. You need to live with the soil, the weather and the stock. You need to experience it — see a calf being born, feel the wheat when it's waist high, smell the way the land smells in every season and feel the big push inside your heart that comes when a crop is in the barn. Then you know how to react to it all. How to make it grow. Fella learns farmin' from a book is only half a farmer. He knows how to make things grow in his head and maybe on the land but he doesn't know how to make 'em grow inside himself. It's the same with Indians. You can't learn to be one from a book. We'll go. Of course we'll go."

I missed the Kodak moments, the trippy little Polaroids that document the lives of normal people. I've been to other people's houses and gone through the ritual of thumbing back the years, seeing all the Grampa Earls, the Auntie Mays, the Cousin Its and Frankie What's-His-Names, the accountant from Dauphin who dated sister until he tried to assess her assets in the back of the Rialto. You know, the flotsam and jetsam that people cling to like lifeguard rings. Details. Cunningly simple little details that don't add up to much unless you lived them. I grew up without details. And to tell the truth it's not the absence of the photo album so much as it is the lack of Kodak moments. I always wondered how that felt. The little pop inside when a moment is forever.

I never felt that until we invented baseball. Once I was on my own again I never pressed the shutter. Sometimes I feel like one of those little old men who live in shabby hotel rooms, spending their days swilling cheap wine, telling impossible stories of what a wonderful life they've had.

But when you take a careful look you can only find one photograph on their walls. One faded, crinkled little photograph of someone, or someplace, that once existed for them. One three-by-five piece of life that quit being memory a long time ago and now just exists as an addictive kind of pain they can't live without. That's how I feel sometimes.

You spent so much time and effort trying to come to terms with your identity. You're lucky that you could find a history and a heritage. I never could. There're not a lot of photographs depicting the rise of white trash, their ceremonies and their rituals. And that's what we were, white trash. We weren't supposed to be but my father created us in his image. He walked away from everything. From family, from tradition, from history, from community. Everything.

That's what white trash is — a motley collection existing without the life-enhancing benefits of background. No cultural, historical anchor. No rich emotional homeland. Nomads willing to settle anywhere the grass looks greener or else latching on to some scrabbly semblance of order and squatting there, hoping boards and bricks can heal them, flesh them out, give them detail. Life without detail is life without edges, borders, perspective. I hated it. I heard an elder say one time that in order to know where you're going, you need to know where you've been. History. I never had one. My father kept it all to himself. His story. That's all I had. Not history, just his story. He mongrelized us, lessened us, defined us by his bleary-eyed vision of the world. Great. Try growing up with a bloodshot sense of yourself.

Did you know that the Gebhardts are descendants of the Teutonic Knights? I found this out a few years after I split from Mildmay. I met this guy named Gebhardt in Seattle and he told me. Seems the Teutonic Knights were a religious order formed in the Holy Land during the Third Crusade. They were noblemen. Me, from a lineage of noblemen. By the time I found that out it was too late. By then I wanted to be anything but a whiteman, a Gebhardt. My father could have given me that — could have told me where we came from, the type of history we carried in our veins — and I would have had something to latch on to. Some semblance of roots. But he didn't. Or maybe he just couldn't. Anyway, I learned how to live without an anchor. No Kodak moments, no homeland, no history.

Small wonder I've lived my life ducking through towns and friend-

*ships, leaving marks like Zorro. I've tried on more people than your aver-
age hooker, hoping against hope that something will adhere to me, that I
can get past the explosion of light that happens when lives and bodies
collide and live in the glow of home and history. But I never pressed the
shutter. I always believed that the self I was searching for was just beyond
that near horizon, in the next situation, the next opportunity, the next person. After a while you start to realize that for people like me, going back
and moving on are the same thing. Zorro, in his mask, has dreams of
permanence.*

From Walkerton you slip through Elmwood, Scone and Hep-
worth, traveling the pebbled artery of Highway 6 through
Wiarton before you ease out of the azure arms of the Bruce
Peninsula and into the unfettered shimmer of Georgian Bay. You
move out from an agricultural world and spiral slowly into the
riparian world of the Cape Croker Ojibway, a world bordered by an
impossible blue rolling northeasterly towards Parry Sound and farther, northwesterly, to the antediluvian promise of Manitoulin. We
made that journey for the first time on a cloudless, windless summer day. As we wound our way through diverse topographies I had
no sense of homecoming, no wild gush of emotion, no tremulous
anxiety or psychic recall, merely a heightened sense of expectation
like the kind scholars must get easing into a tome for the first time,
the answers beckoning, palpable almost. No, it was not the prodigal relief of the refugee I felt but rather the hushed awe of the
explorer.

Pastor Chuck sat in the front seat directing my father to the
band office where, he said, it was necessary to announce ourselves
and our destination. My mother and I sat in the back looking
around wordlessly. Only when I stepped out of the car to enter the
band office did I feel discomfort. Suddenly, my parents and Pastor
Chuck were the remarkable ones, pale in a world gone suddenly

brown, and for the first time I melded into a background of faces. It was discomfiting and alien. I felt as if I'd lost the proper use of my body, not knowing how to stand or walk. I opted for staring at the ground while Pastor Chuck spoke to someone about our visit. I raised my eyes and saw a small crowd of Ojibway people staring at us curiously. When I reached for my mother's hand they followed it with their eyes. I was glad to leave.

Jacqueline Kakeeway's house sat at the edge of a marshy area. A narrow trail wound its way through the rushes to a dock where a small knot of children threw stones into the water. I sat in the car a moment or two longer than my parents and Pastor Chuck, who stood patiently waiting for me. A wiry, tail-wagging dog appeared from beneath the front stoop and its obvious benevolence coaxed me into stepping out to join them.

"It's okay, Joshua. We're with you," my mother said. She placed a protective hand on my back as we followed Pastor Chuck to the screened door. He knocked loudly.

The woman who answered was tall and thin, with luminous obsidian eyes above two knots of cheekbone. Her skin was wrinkled and her white hair hung in two thick braids down her chest. Smiling, she opened the door wide in welcome. She wore a simple cotton-print dress and moccasins. A rust-colored shawl spread over her shoulders highlighted an intricate bone and leather choker at her throat. Pastor Chuck introduced himself and my parents, who stepped forward shyly to greet her. As he began to introduce me, the old lady hushed him with a raised palm and stepped towards me slowly.

"You're Joshua," she said simply.

"Yes, ma'am," I croaked.

"I know why you're here," she said, shaking my hand solemnly.

"You do?" I asked, surprised at the firmness of her grip.

"Oh, yes. You're about the right age," she said and smiled.

"Right age for what, ma'am?"

"For the world to start tappin' on your shoulder. Tryin' to get your attention. Askin' who you are. Tapped kinda hard, eh?"

"Kinda," I said, liking her and feeling better.

"Yes. It's like that sometimes, that world. Come. There's tea," she said, leading the way into a warm-looking kitchen where she directed us to chairs around a solid, rough-hewn wooden table. We all gazed around the room. It had the air of an old country kitchen, replete with canisters, a rack of pots along one wall, bright tea towels, dried flowers in a wide-mouthed vase on the window sill and children's art taped and tacked everywhere. It was a family place.

As we drank the thick black tea and nibbled on bannock bread the adults chatted the way adults do. Finally, Pastor Chuck cleared his throat and told Jacqueline about the kind of life my parents and I shared, the circumstances of my introduction to high school, and the beating. All through his explanation her glance moved between my mother, my father and me, those deep glistening eyes probing, giving the impression that they saw everything. She nodded a lot, tsk-tsking as Pastor Chuck described events at school, and sat back in her chair smiling quietly when he described the Christian upbringing I'd had and my decision to join the church. When he finished, she poured more tea all around, helped herself to a piece of the bannock spread with a thick coating of lard.

"Tell me about this boy, Martha," she said. "Tell me about how he came to you. About how it feels to be his mother."

My mother set her tea cup primly on the table and sat a little straighter in her chair. She told the story I had heard so often about her inability to conceive, my adoption, how she felt when she held me for the first time, and the joy and gratitude she felt towards God for bringing her a child. She talked about watching me grow, and feeling like a part of her was blossoming and filling out as I did, about the world of our farm and the lessons inherent in that world being so vital for children to understand. Lessons about caring and nurturing, learning that all parts of the world are connected and pulsing with a common life and energy that required my respect and honor, kindness and stewardship, love and commitment. She talked of directing me towards teachings and disciplines but allowing the choosing to be my own, about my choices and the happiness they'd brought her, about my nature and the pride she held for me. I felt a reaffirmation of the love I had for her rise within me.

Jacqueline nodded slowly, appreciatively. "And you Daddy?" she said. "What do you know about this boy?"

Grinning, my father sat back in his chair, folded his arms across his chest and stared up at the ceiling, rocking slightly. "What do I know about this boy?" he asked rhetorically, and then launched into a litany that lasted a good ten minutes. He spoke of his knowledge in the beginning that I was a gift from the God he knew, and that his role was to help me grow into whatever and whoever God would have me be. He knew my gentleness, my kindness, my loyalty, and the deep and abiding joy I felt for the land and my openness to its lessons. He knew that I believed in and trusted a benevolent and nurturing God. He knew my confusions, my doubts and the subtle signs I gave when I moved through either one of them. He knew if I dreamed as he watched me sleep, my tiredness by the slight, almost nonexistent droop of my left eyelid, my happiness by the lift of my shoulders and the way my eyes smiled an instant before my face creased in laughter. He knew that the longest trek I would ever make in this world was the one between my head and my heart and that already, I was an experienced traveler on that road. He knew the bond that existed between us was one that went beyond mere blood and kinship, race and religion. It was a spiritual union tempered by life itself.

"And there's one more thing I know," he said, looking squarely at Jacqueline. "I failed him," he said, quietly.

"Ahhh," she said.

"I failed him because I neglected to remember that he was born an Indian, an Ojibway. That God, in His mercy, created my son, sent him out into this world, an Indian," my father continued. "I spent all my time trying to make him something he's not. I tried to teach him *our* history, Kane history, and I tried to teach him *our* values, *our* philosophy, *our* belief system, forgetting that he was born to none of that. He's not a whiteman. He never will be. I can line the edges of his being with all the good things I can, but the core of him will always be Indian. He's got to learn what that is. How to live that. And I never gave him the chance until now. I tried to create him in my image and that's wrong. Only God can do that," he said, ending with a look at Pastor Chuck.

"I think we all learned something about that," Pastor Chuck said with great dignity.

Jacqueline did not speak for the longest time. She sat there sipping her tea, looking at an invisible point of space somewhere between the table and the wall. When she set her tea cup down, hitched her chair a little closer to the table and spoke, it was gently and softly.

"See these braids here. They're old and white now, but one time they were black. They changed. Everyone who sees them now sees them as white, forgetting that they started out black. But me, I always see them the same. Not white, not black, they just are. Because someone taught me one time, a long time ago, what they're supposed to mean. You see Indians on TV and in movies all the time and they all got braids. Pretty soon people start to believe that Indians always got braids. If you're Indian you gotta have braids. Even us we start to believe that. So lots of us wear our hair in braids because we think we're supposed to. And that's all we know so it's all we pass on to others.

"But braids are there for a reason. See, the old people, way back, were looking for a way to teach their people to remember how they were supposed to live. They wanted a symbol. Nothing fancy, just an everyday symbol to help them remember. Well one day, an elder was sitting in the tall grass thinking about this problem. She watched a group of people walking by and saw how they flattened the grass. She came by that same place a few days later and she saw that the grass had stood back up again even though it had been flattened a few days before. She thought, 'That grass is sure humble. It allows people to pass, surrenders to it and then stands back up again.' Humble and strong, you see?

"Well, pretty soon she starts to see that that's how people are supposed to be — humble and strong. So she takes a bunch of that sweet-smelling grass and starts to braid it. As she braids it she thinks about three things that people gotta remember if they want to live a good way. She thinks about humility, respect and kindness. She thinks about faith, honesty and love. She keeps on thinking about these things and praying. When she's finished she ties a small knot at the end of the braid of sweet-smelling grass, like an amen, kinda. For four days she keeps the braid by her bed. She looks at it when she goes to sleep and looks at it again as soon as she gets up. Every time she sees it she's reminded of three things she needs to live her life in a good way. She remembers how she prayed as she braided it and how she focused on each of those qualities as she prayed. Well, pretty soon she sees how strong a symbol that braided grass is. She starts to pray with it and she finds out that when she burns it while she prays, the smoke is sweet smelling too, comforting and kind. Pretty soon she starts teaching her people how to burn it, what it represents. Soon, the teaching of the grass is everywhere.

"But it wasn't enough. People would go hunting or on a journey, and not having the grass around to remind them, they would forget the principles they needed to live their lives in a good way. One day she's standing on a big rock bluff with the wind blowing her long black hair around. It touches her face and she thinks how much it feels like long, soft grass. She sits down and begins to braid her hair like she braided the grass. She thinks of three principles as she braids, just like when she did the grass. First one side, then the other. When she's done she realizes she has two strong symbols right on her head. So she taught her people to braid their hair while thinking of three spiritual principles they needed to live their lives in a good way. Every time they passed each other they would see braids and be reminded of how they were supposed to live their lives.

"Also, they got to spend a portion of their days considering those principles, those teachings, as they braided. And that's not such a bad way to spend a portion of your day, is it, Pastor Chuck?" she said, smiling at all of us.

"No," Pastor Chuck said with a grin. "Not such a bad way at all."

"So, no matter how white these old braids get, I'm always going to respect them for what they stand for, not for what color they are, how thick or how long. Even if I went bald all of a sudden and they fell off, or if I cut them off out of respect for the passing of a loved one, I will always remember the teaching. Always. Bein' Indian, Ojibway, is about learning the teachings and putting them into practice in your life. It's not about how you look, where you live, who you live with. It's about what you carry inside, not what you show to the world. It's an inside truth. When you have it within you, you can go anywhere, do anything — you will always be an Indian, an Ojibway.

"You people done well with this boy. You know him. You respect him. And you're willing to come here to help him find out about himself and his people. That tells me you love him very much. You love him enough to give him a choice of worlds. You don't fail when you offer choice — only when you don't. This is the only place he can learn to choose. You got to wander around with your own, learning to see parts of yourself in them. When you can do that, then you can learn to see parts of *them* in *you*.

"Joshua?" she asked suddenly. She smiled at me.

"Do you want to come here for a weekend every now and then to learn about us? Where you came from, maybe some of the language, ceremony, stuff like that?"

I thought about the teasing and how it felt to have no recourse. How it felt to be hated for being something and someone I had no knowledge of. How lonely it felt to be like a fencepost in a field of snow. How right all of this felt. How the word *Kane* and the word *Indian* had always seemed to exist in juxtaposition despite the dormant knowledge that I was both.

"Yes."

"Good," Jacqueline said. "And Ezra and Martha, you're welcome to join us any time. Pastor, same thing."

Jacqueline told us that she didn't have an agenda. She wanted me to come up and be around my people on a regular basis, and the teaching would come as it was supposed to. When we'd finished she took us on a tour of the reserve. We met her grandchildren, sons and daughters and a handful of community members.

"You know, I think I'm gonna like this Indian stuff," I said to no one in particular.

Gradually, the edges of my world folded together as strangely, as exotically as an origami bird. Throughout the summer of 1969 I spent every second weekend prowling around Cape Croker with Jacqueline and her family. We burned the sweet-smelling grass she'd talked about each morning and prayed long prayers for guidance, protection and blessings for those around and about us. Indian prayers weren't substantially different from Christian prayers, and the smell of the sweetgrass was soothing, centering and healing. Jacqueline would sing a prayer song with her hand drum each morning, soft and low in Ojibway, one verse, it seemed, to each of the four directions. I found myself close to tears each time I heard that ancient language spilling out across the land accompanied by the heartbeat rhythm of the drum. She explained that the drum was the heartbeat of the people — its sound reminded all of us of the heartbeat we first heard in the darkness of our mother's belly. I understood my sorrow then, for a mother I had never known, and when I told her this, Jacqueline held me in her warm brown arms, cooing softly in my ear some Ojibway phrase of comfort while stroking my hair.

We spent most of our time on the land. Either Jacqueline or one of her children or grandchildren would take me fishing, snaring rabbits, picking berries or simply walking. The land, she said, was the greatest teacher of all. The land taught purity, harmony, balance and sacrifice, if you learned to really look at it. She would tell me stories of Nanabush, the trickster, the great teacher of the Ojibway, and take time to explain how there were different levels in each story. Every time you revisited a story you would discover more and more teachings. Like the parables, I later told my parents.

She spoke of the power of the four directions and the teachings you could find there — teachings that led you in a circular pattern of growth to an elegant, aged wisdom. Each of those directions focused on one aspect of a whole person — heart, mind, body and soul. Traveling, studying and applying the teachings of each of those directions was essential to becoming a good human being.

The limited idea of Indians I'd had coming into that first summer was replaced by the burgeoning knowledge that the Ojibway experience was as infinite as human possibility itself. You learned the foundational beliefs, the essential teachings, held them in your heart and carried them into every waking activity of your life. You became an Ojibway in everything you did. Just like being Christian, I explained to my parents, who listened raptly to everything I brought home to them. I came to regard those weekends not so much as a reconnection but as a natural unfolding of the wings of an exotic paper bird, its shape and movement mysteriously ordained by circumstance, kismet. The guiding hand of God hadn't lessened through exposure to my culture and heritage, but became enhanced, expanded and more intensely glorified within me.

Johnny stayed busy in the store that summer. His father began taking more and more to the front-room sofa, sick and unable to make the effort of keeping up appearances. Johnny and his mother were forced to pick up the pieces. Mrs. Gebhardt, under Harold's guidance, showed an innate ability to manage finances. While she cleaned up the ordering and accounting, Johnny learned the hardware business alongside his grandfather. Harold insisted that Johnny draw a salary, and over the phone those evenings Johnny talked about the books he could now buy and the weekend trips he could take to visit his friend Staatz in Galt. He didn't tell me much about Staatz except that he was learning a lot from him and being guided to certain books that were opening up his mind to things. He listened attentively to everything I said about my trips to Cape Croker. When school started again we fell into our usual routine of lunches and spare classes together and huddled conversations on the bus.

The first indication I had that things were changing was a phone call in late November that year.

"Hey, Josh," Johnny said excitedly. "What do you think about Trudeau and his White Paper?"

"White Paper?" I asked in my best straight-man delivery, certain that this had to be a joke.

"You know. The White Paper on Indian Policy," he pressed.

In 1968 the Trudeau government had come out with what they termed a "comprehensive plan" to deal with the Indians. Although there had been a lot written in the papers about it, I'd largely ignored it. There'd been a huge swell of protest from Indian groups across the country and it had never made it into law. For me, the realities of being Indian were the weekends I spent on Cape Croker. Politics was a distant reality. "I don't know, Johnny," I said.

"You don't know?"

"Yeah, I don't know."

"Josh! They wanna assimilate everybody!"

"Assimilate?"

"Jesus, Josh! *A-ssi-mi-late,*" he said. "You know. Make white."

"What are you talking about?'

"I'm talking about the government saying that Indians are supposed to be nothing special. They wanna take away the reserves, the treaties, everything, and make them all *Canadians*! Can you believe it?"

"Johnny, I *am* Canadian."

"No, you're not! You're Ojibway!"

"It's still Canadian."

"Bullshit. If they figured you were Canadian how come they didn't let you vote until 1960?"

"I don't vote, I'm fifteen."

"Not *you*. I mean you, the Indians."

"Oh. I'm all the Indians now?"

"No, of course not. I'm just referring to your political consciousness. You have one, don't you?"

"Yeah, I guess."

"You guess?"

"Yeah. What exactly is a political consciousness, anyway?"

"Jesus! Aren't you learning anything on the Rez?"

"The what?"

"The Rez. The *Rez*-ervation? You know? The place you go to learn how to be an Indian?"

"Oh, that Rez. No. They don't talk about it."

"How can they not talk about the death of their people? How can they not talk about the government trying to pretend that it doesn't have to live up to its agreements? What do you talk about up there?" he shouted into the phone, and I could almost see his arms waving in irritation.

"Well, we talk about a lot of things. We talk about legends, stories, about the things the grandfathers and grandmothers taught. We talk about the land, the things it teaches. That sort of stuff."

"That's it?"

"There's more?"

"Hell, yes, there's more!"

"Like what?"

"Like broken treaties. Like smallpox-infested blankets. Like banning ceremonies. Like no education past high school. Like welfare, chronic unemployment, like it being against the law for Indians to organize politically until a few years ago, like having to live under a paternalistic policy like the Indian Act, like Indians dying faster and younger than the national average. Like lots, Josh!" he shouted.

"Well, none of that ever comes up," I said quietly.

"Damn. You're *Ojibway*! Don't you know that the guys who started the Movement were Ojibway?"

"The what?"

"The *Movement*! AIM? The American Indian Movement?"

"Never heard of it."

"Jesus, Josh! AIM is where it's at! Didn't you hear about the way they took over Alcatraz? The protest camp they're planning at Mount Rushmore? About the Little Red Schoolhouse in Minneapolis? About all the education programs they're running to teach their people the true history of North America instead of the bullshit one the government's been teaching and preaching in schools and books? Man, AIM's the future, Josh!"

"How do you know all this?'

"How do I know? I know because I *read*, Josh. I read things like *Black Elk Speaks*, *A Century of Dishonor*, *The Long Death*, *Akwesasne Note*, *The New Indians*. You ever read any of those, Josh?"

"I never even heard of them," I said, embarrassed.

"Well, now you have. Maybe you should read them. You'll learn that there's more to history than what we get in school. Maybe you'll learn that there's more to being a righteous warrior than fishing, hunting and telling stories. Maybe you'll learn that you got responsibilities as a warrior. That there's a price to be paid for the survival of the people," he said, almost bitterly.

"A price to be paid? What are you talking about?"

"Security, man. The needs of the many over the needs of the one. Today is a good day to die. The spirit of Crazy Horse. That's what I mean."

"What's a crazy horse?"

"Only the greatest warrior the people had! Leader of the Dog Soldiers, helped kick Custer's ass at Little Big Horn. They don't tell you about Crazy Horse and all the warriors up there?"

"No."

"Man. What kind of Indians they got up there, anyway?"

"Ojibways."

"Not my kind of Ojibways," he said and hung up.

We grow into ourselves suddenly. One day you awake to find that your feet are too large for your legs. There are sprouts of hair in new places, and the soft swell of muscle in your arms, legs and back seem to say that you could run, lift, play and endure forever. Your eyes become sensitive to light, color, texture and the bright porcelain nature of girls. Your voice leaves its home in your throat and resides somewhere lower in your physiology, a deeper, more primal place that both excites and confuses you. You find yourself in front of the mirror for hours, staring steadily at the face you thought you'd recognize always, lost in the angular cut of jaw and temple, the sudden cliffs of cheekbone that replace the cool roundnesses of boyhood.

As you begin to move across this new expanse of territory you experience a strange push and pull. A part of you wants to step back into the lush familiarity of childhood as much as another part wants to circumnavigate this bold new world — explore and chart its depths and nether reaches. Life being what it is, of course, means the explorer always wins out. Oh, you'll step back across that line from time to time as life requires but it will always be as an itinerant traveler, a nomad who comes to gather memory in his arms like kindling, tinder for the fires that burn long into the hollow of solitary nights on the stark plains of memory.

We grew into ourselves in the first part of the new decade. I was as tall as my father, throwing hay bales up into the same wagons I'd ridden on scant summers before, while Johnny too was thicker, wider suddenly. Grades Ten and Eleven passed in a blur and when our worlds stopped whirring as school began in the fall of 1972 we were seniors, seventeen. I drove myself to Cape Croker now. Johnny had bought himself a '67 Mustang with his earnings from the hardware store, which was prospering unbelievably by then. He picked me up for school, speeding down Highway 9 rocking to the music of the Rolling Stones and Jimi Hendrix.

Johnny had grown his hair out into a long ponytail and he wore the standard Seventies uniform of jeans, desert boots, T-shirt and jean jacket. He was muscular, and his long hair and arresting blue eyes along with the cherry-red convertible made him a sought-after guy with the females of the senior class. He shrugged it off, paying no heed to the attention he was getting in the hallways. I still favored black cotton dress pants, white shirts and ties. While this didn't exactly place me at the top of the most-eligible-bachelor list, I had been dating Mary Ellen Reid since late in our Grade Eleven year, something Johnny couldn't figure out at all.

"Man, I just can't see it," he said one day, the wind whipping his hair around as he drove. "Mary Ellen absolutely trashed you back in Nine. Now she's like the foxiest piece in school, you're the same drab-dressing, peace-preaching, Bible-thumping nerd you've always been, and you're the hottest couple in school. What gives?"

I laughed. "People change, Johnny. Mary Ellen joined the church a year after I did. She says that whole episode back in Grade Nine really opened her eyes to what's necessary in this world. I guess you and I were a pretty strong example of what real friendship is about and she started to look for a God of her own after that. We have a lot in common now. And besides, drab-dressing, peace-preaching, Bible-thumping nerds need love too!"

"Great. Most of us pray to get a girl and you get a girl to pray!" he said with a wicked little grin.

"What about you? I never see you with girls."

"Yeah, well. I see a few now and then. Nothing serious. We go out, we touch, we feel, I give them what they want and we go our separate ways. Casual, you know? Nothin' permanent. No strings, no promises, no broken hearts."

"You're a playboy!"

He laughed. "Not really. I just don't want to get tied into anything."

"They let you be that loose?"

"Loose? It's not being loose, Josh. It's being honest. I'm not a stick around forever kind of guy. They know that, I know that, no one gets hurt."

On the surface he hadn't really changed. We followed the baseball standings as closely as ever. He'd become a staunch advocate of the National League while I remained a loyal American Leaguer. He had a New York Mets decal on his back bumper and a Tom Seaver autographed baseball fastened to the dashboard. He'd ordered me an aerial photo of Fenway Park and a Red Sox banner, which I hung proudly over my bed. Farm work and his duties at the

store took up much of our time after school but we found opportu-
nities for jaunts to the Harriston drive-in, hanging out at the
Walkerton A&W, working out in the school weight room and late-
night games of catch with a Day-Glo orange softball Johnny'd
spray-painted. Still, protracted silences plagued us. We would find
ourselves mired in them and could only clamber out by going our
separate ways, reconnecting later.

Where he went when he was alone I never knew, but I spent
many solitary hours studying college calendars, travel brochures
and my growing collection of Indian paraphernalia. I had my own
hand drum now — a present from Jacqueline's eldest son — a pair
of eagle feathers from Jacqueline for learning as much as I had,
some carvings, artwork, sweetgrass we'd picked and braided,
rocks, a vibrantly colored blanket I'd been given at the annual powwow and a beaded deerskin pouch Jacqueline said I would fill one
day with medicines. Each article said something about the self that
had lain dormant, undiscovered for fifteen years. I knew now that
being Indian was, as Jacqueline had said, an inside truth.

We were eating supper about two weeks before Thanksgiving
when Jacqueline called. She said I was old enough and knowledge-
able enough to partake in a spiritual ceremony and invited me to
come on the Thanksgiving weekend for a special sweat lodge she
was leading. She had told me about the sweat lodge ceremony but
I had never seen or entered one.

"You gotta fast the four days before, my boy," she said. "Sweat
lodge is for purifying yourself and fasting helps. You fast and pray
for the four days before. When you come you bring some tobacco,
maybe some colored cloth."

"What's all that stuff for, son?" my mother asked when I
explained things.

"I don't know yet. But I'll do it," I said.

"And the sweat lodge ceremony is for purifying yourself?' she
asked.

"Yes. Jacqueline says it's the most respected of all Ojibway rituals. It symbolizes a return to the innocence we're born with. The

lodge is built in the shape of a womb and we crawl into it humbly, on our hands and knees. We pray and sing while we're inside using the four elements of life — fire, water, air and earth — to center ourselves. We sit in darkness symbolizing ignorance. The light we emerge into when we crawl out of the lodge at the end of the ceremony represents the gift of awareness, faith and enlightenment. It gets real hot and we sweat out impurities. Physical, mental and spiritual ones, too. The heat reminds us of adversity, and enduring four rounds of prayer and songs teaches us that faith and belief will get us through adversity. It's a vital thing, really," I explained, hoping I was getting the essence of it all.

"Not bad for a heathen ritual, eh, Mother?" my father said, clapping me on the back.

"It sounds like a wonderful experience," she said. "We should all get to be Indians once in a while."

When I told Johnny about it he was silent for a long time. We were slurping shakes at the A&W after school and he stared out the window with his straw in his mouth. "The Sioux call it *inipi*. Did you know that?" he asked.

"No. I guess there's an Ojibway word for it too, but I don't know it," I replied.

"Never asked?" he said sharply.

"No," I said, surprised.

"Hmmph. I'da asked. So your parents are okay with this? They don't figure it's too pagan for a nice Christian boy?" he said, staring out the window again.

"They're okay. Ma was so impressed she even said everyone should get to be an Indian. They're behind me all the way on this."

"They know what it's about?"

"Yeah. I told them."

"You told them? Don't you know that you gotta be initiated?" he said harshly. "Prepared. Like you were. Learning the basics first, the understanding. If just anybody could do a sweat everybody'd be doing it. That's how the whiteman's been able to steal ceremonies. Because loudmouths spill the beans about everything. Indians gotta protect their ceremonies and rituals, keep them secret, not just share them with any Tom, Dick or Harry who asks!"

"My folks aren't any Tom, Dick or Harry."

"Still."

"Still nothing. I wouldn't be learning about any of this if it weren't for their support. And besides, Jacqueline says we're supposed to share our beliefs with others because you never know who might be lost and need help to find their way to the Creator."

"She must mean others as in other *Indians*."

"No, others as in anybody."

"Can't see that. You ever hear the story about the thousand-eyed worm? See, there was this Cherokee elder a long time ago, before anybody ever knew about white people. He dreams one night that he's sitting on a high rocky place looking towards the east. As he looks he sees a long shiny line lighting up the eastern horizon. It's all glittery and shining like a thousand eyes and as he watches it, he sees it moving, getting closer and closer, wiggling across the land like a huge worm. He wakes up and can't figure out what this dream means but he tells the people about it anyway. For years and years the people keep telling themselves about the thousand-eyed worm that the elder saw, with its thousand glittering eyes. No one ever figured out what it meant until one night a bunch of Cherokee are standing on a high rocky ridge and they see the lights from cities and towns on the eastern seaboard winking and glittering away in the distance just like —"

"Like a thousand-eyed worm!"

"Yeah. Like a thousand-eyed worm. The elder saw the arrival of the whiteman years before they got here. He saw the way they'd worm their way across the land, their cities and towns lighting up the sky like a thousand glittery eyes and the mouths underneath those eyes gobbling everything up, destroying everything. That's what he saw."

"So what's the point?" I asked.

"The point, Josh, is that we never knew what it meant before but now we do. We have to protect ourselves from the worm before it gobbles up everything. Especially ceremonies," he said bitterly.

"We?"

"Yeah," he said. "We, the warriors. Or at least, those brave enough to be warriors.

"**A**nd at that time you didn't know where he was getting any of this, did you?" Nettles was asking. "You didn't know where the Indian angle was comin' from. Seems like pretty heady stuff for some small-town kid to know," he said, pouring us another cup of coffee.

"I know now, of course. It was from the books, and from Staatz. But then? Then, I guess, I wanted to believe we were still the kids we were when we met. No one likes to think that growing up means you have to grow out of the friendships that made childhood special."

"That's what you felt? Like the friendship was maxing out, as my kids would say? Kaput? Finito?"

"Intuitively. I knew that we were on separate journeys. I was already feeling the emotional nudges which became a calling to the church, and Johnny, well, Johnny was feeling a lot of everything like he always did. A lot of unspoken things. I don't think I believed our friendship was *over*, per se, but I felt that it had moved to different ground. Evolving. Changing. Like us. That's one of the things that Jacqueline was able to cement into my spiritual foundation back then."

"What's that, Reverend?"

"That relationships never *end*, they just *change*," I said quietly, feeling tears building behind my eyes. "We're in a constant position of relationship with everything. Jacqueline taught me that when the Creator gave life to the universe, he did so with one breath. One breath — the breath of life. Everything carries within it the breath of life from the Creator. Animate and inanimate are all born of the same breath. Because of that, we're all related, we're all spiritual kin. Nothing ever breaks that kinship. Our lives and circumstances may change but our state of relationship never does. We're always in relationship, so once you've put footprints across someone's life, they're always there. You can be legally divorced from someone, emotionally estranged from friends and family, or someone may die. No matter what, though, you're still in relationship because they don't end, they just change."

"That's deep," Nettles said, nodding.

"Yeah. It's deep."

"So you went to the sweat, obviously. What happened then?"

"For us? Johnny and me?"

"Yeah."

"At first, nothing. He worked at the store and I worked on the farm."

"Real country mouse, city mouse kinda thing."

"Yes," I said, grinning.

"But something happened. Something bigger than the petty little nit-picking he was doing."

I closed my eyes. I could still see us skimming over the curves and stretches of Highway 9 in that cherry-red convertible, his long hair whipping in the wind. I'd be drumming clumsily, hopelessly, on the dashboard while we sang along to the Kinks' "Lola" or an a cappella "Midnight Special." Nothing in the world could have convinced me that it wouldn't be that way forever, that the edges of my life would hold and we would be framed, all of us, in a circle of light, expandable, resilient and eternal.

*I*n the time before man, the Creator called a great meeting of the Animal People. In those days the Animal People could speak with one mind and they shared the earth and its riches without conflict. There was harmony and there was peace. No one knew what the purpose of the meeting was. Speculation was rampant as the animals gathered in a clearing at the foot of a great mountain. When they had all arrived and were settled, the Creator spoke.

"I am going to send a strange new creature to live among you," the Creator said. "He is to be called Man and he will be your brother.

"This new creature will be born without fur or feathers on his body. He will walk on two legs and speak a strange language. And he will need your help. You will be his teachers and you will show him how to live rightly in the world. Because he will not be like you. He will not be born knowing who and what he is. He will need to search for that, and you will be his guides.

"Man will come into the world bearing a marvelous gift. He will have the ability to dream. And because of this ability to dream he will create many wonderful things. He will populate every corner of the world. But his inventions will take him away from you, keep him separate, and he will lose his way. So I am going to give Man a second marvelous gift. I am going to give him the gift of Knowledge and of Truth.

"But I want him to have to search for it. Because if he found it too easily he would take it for granted. So I need your help. No one knows the world better than you, and I need to know where to hide this gift. Where to place it so Man must search long and hard for Knowledge and Truth. Some place where it will not be an easy search."

The Animal People were surprised and honored by the Creator's request. They were thrilled to hear of the arrival of a new creature, a new brother, and they were anxious to be his teachers and to help the Creator find a place to hide the gift of Knowledge and of Truth.

"Give it to me, My Creator," said Buffalo, "and I will put it on my hump and carry it to the very middle of the great plains and bury it there."

"That's a very good idea, My Brother," the Creator said, "but it is destined that he shall visit every place on earth and he would find it there too easily and take it for granted."

"Then give it to me," said Otter, "and I will carry it in my mouth and place it at the bottom of the deepest ocean."

"Another good idea," the Creator said, "but with his ability to dream, Man will invent a wonderful machine that will take him even to the depths of the ocean and he will find it too easily and take it for granted."

"Then I will take it," said Eagle, "and I will carry it in my talons and place it on the very face of the moon."

"No," said the Creator, "that is an excellent idea too, but part of Man's destiny will see him reach even to the moon and he would find it there too easily and take it for granted."

One by one the Animal People came forward and offered suggestions on where the Creator could hide the gift of Knowledge and of Truth. One by one the suggestions were turned down. It began to look like they could never find a suitable place. Finally, a small voice called from the very back of their circle. All eyes turned to see a tiny mole, a tiny, half-blind mole asking to speak. Now, the mole was a very respected member of the Animal People. The mole lived within the earth and so was always in contact with Mother Earth. Because of this the mole possessed great wisdom. And because he had lost the use of his eyes the mole had developed true spiritual insight. So despite his size the mole was respected as a great warrior.

"I know where to hide it," Mole said, "I know where to place this great gift of Knowledge and of Truth."

"Where then, My Brother?" the Creator asked. "Where should I hide this gift?"

"Put it inside them," Mole said with great dignity. "Put it inside them. For then only the bravest and purest of heart will have the courage and the insight to look there."

And that is where the Creator placed the gift of Knowledge and of Truth. Inside us.

Some stories, I guess, we hear too late.

There's a moment during a sweat lodge ceremony when everything becomes clear. You've fasted for four days. Your stomach is slack. You feel light-headed. You strip naked, offering tobacco to the grandfathers and grandmothers watching from the spirit world as you walk clockwise around the fire. Already, you have tied prayer cloths to the trunks of trees surrounding the lodge, asking for guidance, direction and strength. Now, you crawl on hands and knees through the doorway of the lodge, entering again in an east-to-west direction, the direction the sun travels, the direction light moves, the direction of enlightenment, understanding and wisdom. Finding your place, you crouch or sit, staring at the fire pit in the middle of the lodge. One by one, glowing rocks are handed through the door by the lodge helper outside. The elder arranges them in the pit with a pair of deer antlers, splashing them as they arrive with water from a pail containing sage, sweetgrass and cedar. The aroma is pungent.

As more and more rocks arrive the heat builds. Finally, after thirteen rocks are placed, blessed with water and smudging herbs, the flap is closed over the doorway and the skin of the lodge is drawn tightly over a world that is suddenly reduced to heat and smoke and darkness. Darkness. Impermeable but for the eerie glow of rocks. The elder passes around rattles, beating sticks. They arrive in your hands with a nudge out of the darkness, the sudden movement unnerving. A prayer song is sung. Water is splashed on the rocks and you feel the first waves of wild heat sear themselves into the space around you. Another prayer song begins. More water is splashed on the rocks. Heat. The mordant smoke of smudge and a feeling of dislocation that sends the first wriggles of fear through your slackened viscera.

You've been told to pray in your own way and you find yourself reciting every prayer you ever learned, mumbling fast, furious as a zealot, the darkness, heat and sweat flowing down your body, propelling you into the incantations, taking you out of the bosom of the concrete world and into the realm of the spiritual. You feel elevated somehow, and as the elder tells you how to pray, to ask for health, happiness and prosperity for everyone and everything in your life, you direct yourself out of your being and feel the tangible release from the oppressive, sweltering darkness.

After what seems like an eternity, the flap is thrown open and light pours in on waves of cool air. You bathe in the relief. Four times you do this. Each time the doorway is opened the opportunity exists to leave the lodge without shame, but you stay. Thirteen more rocks are added each time, building the heat within the skin of the lodge unbelievably. As they are splashed with water you sweat and pray. Your body feels loosened, unencumbered. Your mind is cleared of obstructive thought. Your spirit moves within you, limber and lithe as a child. There is a rattle in your hands and you shake it to the rhythm of the prayer song that surrounds you, envelopes you in praise. You raise your face towards the curved dome of the lodge, eyes closed and jubilant, sweat streaming down your countenance. Nothing exists in the world except for earth, air, fire and water, your emotions, your spirit and the feeling of connectedness to all of it. You sink your fingers deep into the earth, smudge it over your chest, arms and face. You splash yourself with water and it electrifies you. The fire cauterizes the wounds of the world you carried in and you realize that healing is as much an ordeal as learning to live with faith. You need to learn to struggle through the darkness. That is the moment of clarity.

When the flap is thrown open for the last time, light pouring into your world and your skin steaming in the flush of cool air, you crawl back out into the world energized. You're abristle with life. You're grateful for the awareness of your place in the world, your sudden overriding humility, the knowledge that we are born into a world of light. We are always reborn when we emerge from the darkness of our doubt and fear to stand again in the face of Creation, wondrous, wide-eyed and whole.

I emerged from my first sweat lodge ceremony with that insight. When I shared it with Jacqueline she smiled and gave me permission to return to her lodge anytime. I did. Every month that winter, spring and early summer leading up to my graduating year of high school I returned to the lodge. My parents helped me pre-pare each time and we talked about the remarkable parallels between the faith I was raised in and the faith of my people. I began to see that faith — the unassailable belief that we are all under the guidance of a nurturing and creative God — is the foundation stone of all cultures, whoever that God might turn out to be.

I began to see that for me, Joshua Kane, living and expressing that faith was as essential as breathing. The Christian ethics and practices I was raised with were enhanced by my exposure to the ethics and practices of my heritage. The reverse was also true. I no longer felt like I stood in the middle of a bridge between two cultures but rather that I had a foot firmly planted in each. *I was the bridge*. My racial and cultural displacement hadn't assimilated me; I had assimilated it. And somewhere within me the spark of gratitude I'd felt all my life towards my God, my Creator, began to kindle and stoke itself. I began to sense that my calling, my gift, was learning to share and teach this bridging, this delicate joining of ways and means, this spiritual pilgrimage few are aware is necessary and even fewer respond to.

I also spent more time with Pastor Chuck talking about faith and belief, discussing the difference between being spiritual and being religious. We talked about the nature of prayer and its various manifestations around the world. We examined the things Jacqueline was giving me — the practical, vital spirituality that was inherent in everything. He encouraged me, praising me for the conclusions I was drawing and my growing theological acuity. By the time the summer of 1973 drew to a close I was becoming certain of the direction I would take.

On the last weekend of summer vacation I drove my parents and Pastor Chuck to Cape Croker. We sat at Jacqueline's table as we did that first weekend, nibbling bannock and drinking tea.

"I think I know what it is that I want to do," I said quietly, and they all looked at me steadily. "I believe that God put me here to learn how to live in two worlds — the Ojibway and the non-Ojibway. He brought me to my parents when I was a little baby because he knew that I needed what they had to give me. Then he led me here, to this reserve and to these people, because he knew that I needed what they had to give me too."

They all listened attentively. As I spoke that afternoon I experienced a feeling that I would come to recognize later as *conviction*. It underlay everything I shared that day as elegantly as polished stone.

"I really believe that I was supposed to have the benefit of two sets of teachings all along. Each of them has led me to a belief and

a trust in a loving, kind and nurturing God — a Creator, a Great
Spirit, Kitchee Manitou — just as each of them has led me to knowing myself.

"I'm the bones and blood and skin of my people. I know that
now. But I'm also the heart and mind and soul of my parents *and*
my people. I know that too. So, I think I want to do something that
will honor both of them. Right now, I'm really not sure what that is
but I've been getting an urge, I guess you could call it. I think I want
to go to Bible school or something and learn more about God,
maybe even preach someday.

"When the time is right and I learn enough, I would like to
come back here. Being here has helped me see that I carry the
sweat lodge, the pipe, the church and the Bible within me — I'm a
combination of all of them. But there's still a lot I don't understand,
and I know I gotta get an education, so I kinda think Bible school
or something is a pretty good idea."

As I heard myself speak the things that I had been becoming
slowly aware of as true for myself, I realized that, for the first time,
I was listening to my *self*. I was, after all, a singular creation, and
as I looked around at Jacqueline, my parents and Pastor Chuck, I
realized too that the only one missing from that small circle of
influence was Johnny Gebhardt. I promised myself to talk to him as
soon as I returned.

Jacqueline spoke first.

"No one can tell you that what you should do, my boy. Those
who love you can only give you what you need to help you make
that choice. You just told us what you believe and not what you
know. This is a good thing. Believing is feeling. Feeling is the basis
of the spiritual. One of these days, like you say, you *will* know when
it's time for you to come back here — to bring what you learned to
help people. Only you will know that time. So, go to your school
and see what it is that they can teach you. Go to ceremonies, see
what they can teach you too. Whenever you speak about those
things, speak what you believe, not what you know. Tell what you
felt. That's the only way to tell them. You'll be a good teacher, my
boy, because you're a good student." She hugged me deeply.

"Thank you," I whispered into her neck.

"Joshua," my mother said shakily. "When we brought you here I was very, very afraid. I was afraid you would decide that this was where you belonged and that you would want to leave us. I was afraid you would find out that you could only believe as an Ojibway believes. I thought you would resent us for keeping you away from your self all these years and that you'd find more of a home here than we could provide. But it all just brought us closer, made us more of a family. Gave me a vision of things I never had before. I am so proud of you and your decision." And she collapsed into my arms.

"I always figured denomination was the size of a bill anyway," Pastor Chuck said and thumped me on the back. "Believing's believing. That's what counts. You'd make a fine minister, Joshua. You obviously know how to speak, and with a name like Joshua, how could you lose?"

My father stood back and watched it all with eyes afire. When I looked at him he held my gaze for a long time, unblinking, pure and honest. The messages that passed between us in those moments never had to be articulated.

Johnny had never been to Hockley Valley. He'd heard my dad and me talk rapturously about it through the years, and he'd come along a few times when we'd ventured out to the Maitland River, the Saugeen or the tiny unnamed stream outside Tara that was home to ferocious river pike, but he'd never been to our version of an angler's paradise. Until that autumn it had always been my father's place — inviolable, sacrosanct. One of those locales you hold reverently in the warm chalice of memory, a place you want to believe you can return to always, a portal to your filigreed past. It seemed the perfect place for a disclosure of my intentions and my faith, and I invited Johnny to come with me one weekend in September.

Johnny was an adequate if heavy-handed bait-and-spin fisher-man but he'd never been introduced to the delicacy of fly fishing. As I expected, he welcomed the idea of learning how to work a fly rod. There was just enough science involved to attract him.

"Hey, great," he said over the phone. "We've got a Fenwick something downstairs that somebody ordered a few years ago but never picked up. Good-looking rod, and there's a Hardy Lightweight reel with it, a few spools of line, leaders and a box of flies."

I laughed. It was just like Johnny to stumble across a ready-made, top-of-the-line beginner's outfit. My eight-foot Fenwick rod and Hardy reel were as old as I was by then and still more than adequate for my elevated skill.

"And I'll check at the library for a good book on technique. I can practice on the lawn!" he said.

He showed up at school with *The Fly Fishing Companion* and a battered copy of *The Compleat Angler*. In our spare periods he talked about the hatching cycle of insects, how to fish the head of a pool, reading fast water for the best trout lies, and his proficiency with the roll cast, even if grass was hardly a substitute for placing a fly on water, and the relative difficulty in pulling off a good double haul. He was the old Johnny — on fire with science and technique and rampant in his enthusiasm. By the time we were ready to leave for our Saturday-morning rendezvous with the Hockley rainbows, he was filled with fly fishing lore and trivia.

"Hey, Josh," he asked over the phone the night before we left, "since it's fall I figure we should use a Muddler Minnow in the morning and a pale dun closer to sunset. Whaddaya figure?"

I laughed. "I think I'll use a black gnat in the morning and a pale dun at night."

"You think we should wet fly?" Johnny asked.

"Why?"

"Well, because it's the closest we can get to nymphing."

"Nymphing?"

"Yeah. I'd really like to try a Woolly Bugger."

"A what?" I asked.

"A Woolly Bugger. You've been fly fishing all your life and you don't know what a Woolly Bugger is?" he said gleefully.

"I *know* what a Woolly Bugger is, okay?"

"What is it, then?"

"It's a relatively accurate description of Principal Holmes!"

We decided at the last minute to travel in his Mustang since it had the better radio and an eight-track tape player. We roared out of Mildmay with a clatter of gravel and the Band's *Music from Big Pink*. It was around four-thirty in the morning as we sped down Highway 9 slurping coffee from our thermoses and gulping donuts from a sack Johnny brought. He was dressed in an oversized fishing vest and a floppy-brimmed hat adorned with a few dozen flies. A red-checked shirt, jeans and knee-high rubber boots gave him the look of a model in a pipe tobacco ad. He drove and drummed on the wheel and chattered endlessly about Izaak Walton, Lee Wulff and the spawning patterns of the brook trout. It was a far cry from the idyllic jaunts to the valley with my father but I loved it anyway.

We arrived in the splendor of a September morning, the sky a myriad of shade and lightness with mist rising over the gurgle and chuckle of the stream lending a mystical aura.

"Wow," was all he said.

Yes.

We did everything as silently as possible. Johnny eased the trunk open and we cautiously assembled our rods, threaded the line through the guides and tied on leaders and flies carefully, ceremoniously. Johnny tied a blood knot like a pro. When he clipped the line as close as possible to the shank of the hook with fingernail clippers, I knew he'd studied the craft intently. Step by step, we approached the banks of the stream like prowlers, parting wordlessly in opposite directions. I could see his breath in the air from where I stood. I watched as his false casts described a narrow loop behind him, the line arcing out over the water almost perfectly. I wasn't surprised.

I worked the stream for a good hour and a half, landing four rainbows, two of which I kept to cook for a late-morning breakfast.

As always, the stream provided great sport. The absence of any hooting from Johnny told me that for all his casting proficiency he still hadn't been able to land a fish. I only hoped the pacific nature of the sport had satisfied him. He was tying on a new fly when I walked over.

"No luck with the gnat?" I asked.

"Nah, nothing like that," he said dismally.

"It's okay, you know. My first couple times I had to settle for learning the intricacies of casting and presentation before I actually landed a fish."

"Josh."

"It takes practice."

"Josh. All I've been *doing* is landing fish. I'm changing flies hoping they'll leave me alone so I can *practice* the intricacies!" he pointed to three big rainbows beside his vest on the grass. "I let seven go, for Christ's sake!"

That really didn't surprise me either.

And there is nothing in the world that tastes like trout, freshly caught, fried in butter and served in the open air. I'd packed tomatoes, potato cakes, onions, mushrooms and half a carton of apple juice along with the extra-large thermos of coffee. We ate hunkered down on our haunches, our rods leaned against a nearby tree, and watched the morning break around us. Neither of us spoke. Me, humbled by the grace of morning and Johnny, perhaps, by the pervasive stillness of things. We drank the last of the coffee, the steaming plastic mugs as warm in our hands as our friendship then, a comfortable thing.

"Too bright to fish," he observed.

"Yeah. I figure we could either sleep a while or there's a trail up the creek a ways that winds through the hills. My dad and I walked it a few times over the years. Takes about three hours. There's a cliff over a small ravine about halfway. We carved our names in the rock when I was about nine."

"Okay. I'll throw some snacks in a pack."

"Cool."

The Hockley Valley is lush and rich. Verdant. In the early

autumn the display of colors is spellbinding. Interwoven through the dazzle are pastoral stretches of tilled land and abrupt rustic vistas. Here, a cobwebbed cabin reduced to crumble by the disdain of time. There, a sleepy farm anchored against a wooded hillside like a gnome's cottage. We surprised a porcupine meandering his way along the trail and the look of utter surprise as he raised his snout in alarm was comical. The skreel of a swooping hawk, the whisper of the wind through the branches and the muted crunch of our feet against the roots and detritus of the forest floor punctuated the morning air like canticles. We were joined, Johnny and I, by an unspoken reverence for the omniscient hymnodist who'd composed it all. In such times language can surprise you with its irrelevance.

I led him down the fifteen feet of cliff to the narrow ledge where my dad and I had stood to etch our names awkwardly into the rock. They were there, smudged some by the invisible hands of wind and air but legible still. *Ezra and Joshua Kane, June, 1964.* He smiled wistfully, handing me a small chunk of granite with a scalloped edge. Grinning, I brushed clear a small area, and gripping the rock deep in the cup of my palm I etched the letters of my name once again into the stoic face of the cliff. *Thunder Sky.* He followed suit, and *Laughing Dog* appeared alongside, with *09/15/73* beside it.

And thus we become eternal.

We climbed back up and sat with our feet dangling over the edge of the cliff, looking down into the ravine.

"Brought me here for a reason, didn't you?" he said quietly, offering me that pure, open blue-eyed gaze. "I mean, even I recognize finalities, Josh. Fishing. This place. It's like you're trying to write a poem, man."

"Sometimes I don't want to grow up, Johnny."

He nodded. "Yeah. It's a bummer. Here we are almost high-school *grad-you-eights,*" he slurred in a country bumpkin vernacular.

I laughed. "Doesn't seem like it. I saw Alvin Giles the other day and I could look right into his eyes. Wasn't all that long ago all I could see was his belt loops."

"Yeah, I know. I went over to the old school one night last week. Ran the base paths on the diamond we first played on.

Remember how it seemed like a huge distance from first to second? I ran it in about five strides. Funny, eh? Time and distance? How they shrink each other? Ever wonder what would have happened if we hadn't met or even if we hadda met and didn't like each other?"

"Nah. We were supposed to meet, Johnny," I said with certainty.

"Yeah. I guess. So why are we here?"

"I gotta tell you what I've decided. About my life. What I'm gonna do. Where I'm gonna go."

"You know all that?"

"Yeah. The first part, anyway. I'm going to Bible college in Red Deer, Alberta, and Pastor Chuck and I are checking out a church for me to get ordained in if I want to preach when I'm finished. I'm leaving right after graduation. What do you think?" I asked, eager for his feedback.

"What do I *think*?" he said, his eyes burning and his voice rising. "Haven't you learned anything all this time you've been spending on the Rez? Haven't they taught you anything about reality?"

I put my hands on the rock to steady myself. "Johnny, all I've been learning up there has been about reality. That's how I know this decision is the right one."

"According to your mother, your father, your esteemed church leader," he spat. "What about your elder? What does she think about all this?"

"She thinks it's good. And no, it's not according to them. It's according to me."

He glared at me. "Well, then, you *really* wanna know what I think?"

"Yeah."

"I *think* you're a fucking *apple*," he said, standing abruptly. "You don't even know what that is, do you?"

"No. What is it?"

"I figured you'd latch right onto it. Your church being so heavy with the metaphors and all. Think about it, Josh. An apple? It's red on the outside and white on the inside. What does that tell you?"

"You think I'm bullshit."

"You've been bullshit from day one. All this Jacqueline told me this and Jacqueline told me that. All this now I know where I came from shit you been spewing for the last two years. You haven't got a clue where you came from. If you did you wouldn't be heading into an institution that's been *killing your people for years!*"

"What are you talking about? The church has always been there to help people."

"Yeah, right. You ever heard of residential schools? You ever heard about outlawing spiritual practices? How can you outlaw what's spiritual, Josh? Ever heard of any of that?"

"No."

"No," he mimicked, with a whine. "Your problem is you're still stuck in the romantic idea of what it means to be an Indian."

"And you're a realist?"

"Yeah. I'm a fuckin' realist. You've still got the blinders on, Josh. You're still a cultural bumpkin, man. You haven't learned anything."

"And you have?"

"Yeah, I have."

"From where?"

"I'll tell you where. From *real* Indians, Josh. Real Indians. The ones who are doing something about all the shit that's come down in five hundred years. The ones who recognize it as shit. The ones who don't wanna swim around in it any more. I'm learning from *warriors*. And from books. You ever read *Bury My Heart at Wounded Knee*? You ever heard of Wounded Knee?"

"No."

"Figured. Well, *Bury My Heart* tells the truth, pal. The *truth*. It talks about brutality, murder, rape, theft, kidnapping, brainwashing, misappropriation and denunciation. The real principles this country was founded on, Josh, not the *one nation sea to sea* horseshit the textbooks give us. *Bury My Heart* is about real history. It's about the real nature of the whiteman."

"Johnny, you're a whiteman."

"Fuck you."

"What?"

"I said *fuck you*! You're the fuckin' whiteman, Josh!" he shouted, jamming me in the chest with his finger.

"I'm an Ojibway," I said firmly.

"Then why don't you fuckin' act like it? Why don't you learn about your own religion? Your own spirituality? Your own ceremonies? It's not like you don't have a choice here. You're a man. You're a warrior."

"That's right."

"What?"

"You're right. I am a warrior. Don't you see what I'm trying to say here? I'm going because it's what I *believe*, what I *choose* to believe. I choose. It's not Pastor Chuck, it's not my mother or my father, not Jacqueline, not you, not the honor of the people. It's *me*. I was created to be *me*. Everything that's happened to me in my life has been the grace of God helping me become who I was created to be. Sure, Jacqueline has helped me. Sure, I've been to the sweat lodge, smoked the pipe in ceremony, made offerings. Sure, I'm learning the Anishanabek way. But you know what? You know what the very bottom line of that way is, Johnny? The bottom line you won't find in any books?"

I looked away across the wide sweep of land. What I was about to share was something I'd never expressed to anyone. It had all existed until that precise moment as fragments, shards of emotion, thoughts and awarenesses, the scree and talus of a Brobdingnagian scarp of faith that was the backbone of my life. I thought carefully. It was essential to say it right. For him. For me. When I faced him again he'd lost the whiteness of anger, although it remained, grave, pensive, on guard.

"The most fundamental human right in the universe," I said measuredly, "is the right to know who you are — Indian, white, black, yellow. We all come into life bearing the right to know who we are. No one has the right to keep you from the constant process of discovering yourself. No one knows when we're born what the Creator has in mind for us. Crazy Horse's mother didn't know who she had crawling around the floor of her teepee. Sitting Bull's mother didn't know. Louis Riel's mother didn't know. My mother didn't know. Neither of them.

"When my parents adopted me and began teaching me their ethics, beliefs and ideals, they were helping to shape me, helping me to *become*. But when they didn't recognize that I needed my Indian sense of myself as well as theirs, they were actually denying me that human right. As much as they loved me and sought to protect and nurture me, they were denying my God-given right to know who I was. When they recognized that, they allowed me to search for that Indian self, despite fearing that I'd leave them, despite the fear that I'd resent them and walk away, despite the fear that I'd come to deny all they taught me. They allowed me that fundamental human right. They offered me choice," I continued as he gazed levelly at me.

"And that's the other part of the bottom line. Choice. The most precious gift you can offer another human being is the power of choice. That's what our parents are supposed to do. Teach us that we have choice in everything. To choose good from bad, right from wrong, strong from weak, and to help us learn how to make good choices. Friends are supposed to do that too. Lovers. Wives. Husbands. Because we're all teachers, Johnny. All of us. When we ask someone to think as we think, to act as we act, to react as we react, we're not teachers any more — we're wardens. Choice is the mortar that allows you to build on the foundation of that human right. It's how you become who you were created to be. God, the Creator, Allah, whoever, lets us choose too. We can choose to follow His way or we can choose not to. We can even choose *who* our God is going to be.

"All I know, Johnny, is what I've been given. I don't know your books, what they hold, what they teach. I only know my life and what I feel. And I might be wrong. I might get through school and into a church and find out I'm dead wrong, that I was supposed to go left when I went right, that I was supposed to be somebody else. But you know what?" I asked, smiling at him.

"What?" he asked.

"It's okay to be wrong. It's okay to take the power of choice and pick the wrong path. Because that's the other way you learn who you are. You just have to be brave enough to pick another path. Right now, right or wrong, I'm choosing to go where I feel I need to go. *For me.* Being Ojibway? Being Indian? It's the truth you carry inside you. The truth you carry anywhere, through anything. Once you've got it it's yours forever. Even in Bible college."

He looked at me for a long time, staring without malice, without anger. Just a cool look that spoke nothing of his inner workings. When he sat down again, dangling his feet over the edge, I thought he'd come back to himself, back to the Johnny who was my friend, my fellow dreamer. My blood brother.

"You know what's amazing? What's really fucking amazing about the pretty little speech, about your fucking rampant idealism, about the cutesy way you wrap the ideological around the inane, the Ojibway around the whiteman?" he said bitterly. "That you sound like you believe it. Like you expect *me* to believe it."

"I do believe it," I said.

"Horseshit! They want you to believe it," he replied, sneering at me.

"They?"

"Yeah, *they.* They, the whiteman. They want you to take it all hook, line and sinker. What is it Christ is supposed to have said — I will make you fishers of men? Well, guess what, pal? They fished you in. You're beached and landed, man. Beached and landed. Do you know why they always sent the missionaries in first? Why they always allowed the priests and the zealots to invade before the rest of them came? Because they knew what they had. They knew the subversive power of the Word. They'd seen it work before in Africa, India, Asia. They sent their emissaries, their scholared clergy first because even if they were killed they weren't really losing anything. There was always going to be another Word thumper coming along. Another starry-eyed pedant, gesticulating and murmuring Scripture. They knew that if they could rob a people of their belief system they could control them.

"So they sent these kind, humble lackeys to break their trail. And I will give them this. I'll give them the fact that some of those priests and missionaries were kind, maybe even good-hearted, but they were still nothing more than proselytizing stooges setting the people up for the kill. They killed belief, ritual, ceremony, self-respect, dignity, cultures and honor. Why? Because they believed their way was the only way. They believed everybody was created to be exactly like them. Anything different was less, was pagan, heathen, savage. So they didn't have the ability to offer choice. Choice was never part of it. They came and they preached and they set them up for the kill. They bred fear and subservience to a God of wrath and vengeance. The God they said was responsible for the death of their way. Their heathen, savage way.

"And you want to be a part of that? You're blind, pal. You're blind if you can't see that your involvement with the church sets you up to continue the spiritual slaughter of your people Not the Kanes but *your* people. Your blood, your history, your culture, your identity. They're setting you up. They *want* you to stand in a pulpit as an example that assimilation works. That it's okay to desert yourself, pretending to be someone else. That it's okay to strap on the wrappings of their way, losing yourself, forgetting yourself.

"They want you to be a fisher of men, Josh. To fish other Indians in. To get them hooked and landed too. Because you know what? Colonization doesn't have an end point. It can't be satisfied. It's not enough to colonize a people. If that was it all the horseshit would have ended a long time ago. No, it's got to go on until everything is colonized, the land, resources, air, water, all of it raped, depleted and spent. That's what they did in Europe. That's all they know. That's why they had to come here. Not because of some lofty romantic ideal of widening their knowledge of the world. No. They needed to find another place to go. Some to escape, some to recreate the same madness in a place with more room. That's why they came. Because they'd already soiled their own bed.

"You know what it says in Genesis — and I will give you Dominion over the birds of the air, the fish of the sea da da da da da da? That's what it's all about. Dominion. Control. Supreme power. Their God gave them that. Their religion gives them permission to go wherever they want and exercise *dominion*. From the

Latin *dominus*. Dominus means God, Josh. Their religion gives them the power to be God! That's what they believe. And as long as they believe that, nothing is sacred. No land, no people, nothing. Old colonizers never die, they just go and settle somewhere else."

He said all of it with a stridence and cadence I'd never heard from him before. Fervor — the first time I ever experienced fervor in a human voice. When he finished he spat over the edge and sat there immobile, sepulchral.

Perhaps in all friendships there comes a moment when the tug of individual lives, destinies and beliefs is so insistent, so pervasive that the weave of its fabric is tested. Those moments that test its tolerance arrive unannounced, threatening the permanence of everything, the warmth of fabric, the elegance of structure.

"I don't know any of that, Johnny," I said quietly, humbled by his oration. "But maybe I should. Maybe I need to look at all of it before I make a decision. There may be questions I still need to ask, answers I need to get."

He didn't respond for a long time. He sat and doodled on the rock with the small chunk of granite, sighing deeply every now and then, shaking his head. Watching his private struggle, I felt the powerlessness that's part of all relationships, all loves, when you know for dead certain that there's nothing you can do until an armistice descends on the battleground. When he spoke again it was *sotto voce*. He spoke, looking across the expanse of horizon, and I strained to catch it all.

"You know how you learn some things and you can almost feel the world rearranging itself all around you, like you'd never seen it that way before? That's how I feel. I read that book and it was like nothing was right. Not me, not my world, my life, nothing. So I read some more and talked with Staatz and his brothers until it was like I found myself in their anger. My voice. I feel guilty. Guilty because I can't rub off my whiteness. And it pisses me off. It *really* pisses me off because everything that I've learned, everything that I read about, was like a knife going into me. Into my fuckin' soul. My heart. I'm not supposed to be a whiteman, Josh, I'm not. I'm supposed to be an Indian. I'm not pissed off at you. I'm pissed off at them for the lies and the horseshit. For my bullshit life."

"It's okay, Johnny. It's okay," I said, laying a hand on his shoulder. "I'll read the book if you lend it to me. Maybe I'll get angry too. I don't know. We're supposed to be good, loyal and kind. We passed blood on it. So I'll read the book, okay?"

"You sure? It'll piss you off."

"I'll keep that in mind," I said with a grin.

"You won't be the same."

"Big deal. I'm not the same as I was ten minutes ago, thanks to you."

"Hey, what's a blood brother for?"

"You really think I'm an apple Johnny? A phony?"

"Nah. Not really. An apple wouldn't even look. Wouldn't question. You're more like a Viva Puff."

"A what?"

"You know, those little cookies that are all brown on the outside with a big white inside and red in the middle?"

"Great," I said. "Just great."

"**S**o you read the book?" Nettles asked, pouring more coffee.

"It was like being woken up roughly. Shaken out of slumber. There was a history in those pages I never imagined possible. I mean, we grow up in a Canada that's ordered and neat, a society that's ostensibly democratic, socialized and benevolent. At least that's what I believed until I read that book"

"And now?" he prodded, one eyebrow arched slightly, sliding a plate of sandwiches towards me.

"Now I still believe that it's ostensibly that way. If history has given us anything it's the ability to keep up appearances. Beneath the pseudo-rational sheen of things is a world a lot less glamorous, a lot less civilized, less rational, less healthy than we want to admit. People are still being belittled, disempowered, disenfranchised and assimilated. Did you ever hear the Spanish term *los desaparecidos*?" I asked.

"Los what?"

"*Los desaparecidos*. It means the disappeared. It's a term that rose from the civil wars in Central America. The regimes would round up those who they believed opposed it and they would disappear without a trace. The loved ones they left behind refer to them as the disappeared."

"So what's that got to do with this? Gebhardt was in Central America, was he? That where he got the military connections. Mercenary, was he Joshua?"

I laughed disarmingly. "No. Nothing like that. At least not that I'm aware of. I'm just trying to make a point."

"And that is?"

"That every society acts like a regime in some ways. They all create their disappeared. You don't have to be an Indian to be disenfranchised or disinherited, David. All of us are to some degree. You're what, English extraction?" I asked him.

"Yeah. Only extraction sounds like something you're yanked out of. You're saying society's like a big dentist yankin' us out of our backgrounds?"

He definitely had a way with an analogy. "I guess that's what I'm saying," I said, chuckling. "I'm willing to bet that you don't practice any of the things that set you apart as being decidedly British. Am I right?"

"I don't even know what decidedly British is," he said, "except maybe a good line for Red Rose."

"Exactly. You're disenfranchised. You're one of the *los desaparecidos* from your own heritage."

"And the point is?"

"The point is that we all surrender our identities to be a part of society. White, Indian, black, Russian, Czechoslovakian — everyone has to surrender some aspect of their cultural identity to be a part of society. There are no pure cultures here. Not anymore. There can't be because society demands that we assimilate part of it into our daily lives. If culture is the day-in, day-out activities we find ourselves involved in, then we're all disinherited from ourselves. None of what we're asked to do to function as Canadians these days was part of our pure cultural selves, you see?"

"Okay. But what does any of this have to do with this situation?"

"Everything, because that's what Johnny saw. He saw it in himself first and then he saw it in the lives of the native peoples. And it's what I saw after I read *Bury My Heart at Wounded Knee*."

"I'm not even on the same highway here, Joshua. Saw what?"

"Saw that history is about dissolution. That unless we're willing to act as warriors to save and preserve the hereditary truths we're born in, we all become the disappeared. Disappeared from our pure selves. It happened to the white races first and I think that's what colonization, as Johnny put it, is all about. The belief that you can recover yourself by starting over again. You can't, of course, but somewhere, somehow, the belief arose that there's salvation in geography. The more you occupy, the more you are."

"You got that from the book."

"Yes. Not as explicitly then. I've thought about it over the years but yes, I saw the effects of history."

"But it didn't change you like he said?"

"Oh, yes. Yes. It definitely changed me."

"How? You still became a reverend."

"I did. But up until that point I assumed I was supposed to lead people to *my* salvation, *my* sense of divinity. But *Bury My Heart at Wounded Knee* was the first book I read to convince me that if I were to preach, I would preach choice. I would preach about my own disinherited past, my own journey to my identity, the tools of both cultures that I used to get me to my Ojibway-ness, my Indian-ness, and my faith. You don't need to kill or fight to reclaim yourself, David, you just need to look in the right place for the gift of knowledge and of truth. But we all need someone to show us how to search. The truth you find is your own. The God you find is your own. I became a servant who was willing to preach acceptance instead of conversion."

He nodded solemnly. "The *first* book, you say. You read more?"

"Certainly. I borrowed all of Johnny's books, and he had a lot of them. Native newspapers, political tracts, *God Is Red, Prisoners of Grass, Red on White*, it was amazing the collection he had."

"And you read all of it?"

"Yes."

"And you still wanted to go to Bible college?"

"More than ever. The way things worked out, it was reading those books, realizing the hidden face of history, and dealing with the feelings born out of that exploration that convinced me."

"That went over well, I guess," he said ironically.

"Yes," I said with equal irony. "It went over real well."

T*he summer before we went fly fishing in the Hockley Valley was tough on me. You missed it entirely. You were so busy in your pastoral little world that you missed the action. That, of course, was the February that the AIM warriors squared off against the FBI in the town of Wounded Knee, South Dakota. Wounded Knee — life's ironies are so vaudevillian at times. Here I was being changed from the inside out by the history I was exposed to in* Bury My Heart at Wounded Knee *and suddenly Wounded Knee comes up in the news. You don't know how much I wanted to scram down there to be with those people in the sights of all those guns, how much I wanted to shoot back in anger, to seek redemption in a fusillade. But I couldn't. I didn't know enough. So I spent that whole summer with Eldridge Cleaver's* Soul on Ice, The Autobiography of Malcolm X, *Ralph Ellison's* Invisible Man, The Diaries of Louis Riel *and Harold Cardinal's* The Tragedy of Canada's Indians. *I read magazine articles on Bobby Seale, Huey Newton, Mao Tse-Tung, Che Guevara, the Weathermen and the Black Panthers. I started to learn that the process of*

becoming a warrior in this age was the process of acquiring information.

I began to realize the strength in Abbie Hoffman's assertion that in order to bring power to its knees you had to first understand how power maintained itself. The shackles of bondage are the shackles of ignorance, so I absorbed everything about as many revolutionary thinkers as I could. Going to Wounded Knee unprepared would have been like going unarmed, my presence no help to anyone. But I followed it as closely as the media tricksters would allow me and I seethed. Injustice is broad farce for the educated. Maybe that's how you learn to laugh in the face of danger. You have to learn to see it as the sophist buffoonery it really is.

The more I learned about the peculiarities of whiteman's power, the more I sensed that I was out of place. There I was in Mildmay, Ontario, slogging away for a few measly dollars an hour, shelling out vise grips, nails and baler twine when the real world needed warriors. But that's really the trick, the legerdemain that happens to keep us isolated from each other, politically hamstrung, and ineffective. They want us all to believe that the sole responsibility to our life and those we purport to love is the assumption of a role. We're encouraged to become something — doctor, lawyer, hardware clerk, whatever — and we're told that once we get there we've succeeded, we now have a function. Therein lies the smoke and mirrors. We get a function and then we get responsibility. The career, the mortgage, the car, the TV, the kids. We become responsible for maintaining it all, forgetting the broader, more critical issues like how much we're getting screwed and how deeply.

The critical thing becomes recognition and money. Money, money, money, the eternal carrot dangling in the faces of the mules who haul the wagon of power. People sell out who don't even know they're selling out. They pass on the ethics of a degree, a job, a future. I saw all of it, standing in the aisle of the old man's store, and I saw how easily we fall into the trap of sufficiency. That's when I knew what I would do. I would save everything possible so I could go and get my education. Not in some ivy-covered institution but in the streets, on the reserves, in the gatherings where the people went to learn how to survive. I was going to use the whiteman's capitalist system to finance my own agenda, and it gave me pleasure. The day I decided that was the day I was born.

Life's purpose is to create. We all do it in one way or another. Literally, of course, through art, more practically through work and education as we create our selves, but we all create in order to be. In order to become. That's what I believe. But the bigger lesson is to learn how to live creatively. To have creative relationships with those around us. The key is to recognize the breath of Creation, the God, if you will, in yourself and then in those around you. Living creatively is to recognize God in everyone and to honor and cherish that God. Indians believe that. So do other spiritual peoples.

There's a story about Columbus that says he was so taken by the spiritual nature of the people he stumbled upon that he believed them to be created in the very image of God. *Du corpus in Dio*, he was reported to have written to his queen. *In Dio*. And from that came the word *Indian*.

Proponents of the story insist that Latin phraseology is the real root of the word *Indian* rather than the awkward folksy notion that a seasoned navigator like Columbus could have harbored the thought that he'd landed in India. How he could have subjected them to the slaughter he did after that initial revelation was beyond my comprehension.

As I read and learned over the course of the long winter of 1973 and on into the languid spring of 1974, I shared my findings with my parents. They were as shocked as I was. They had grown up, as I had, in an educational system that taught the romantic notion of settlement, the scenario that featured the chiseled, bronzed countenances of Indians aiding their white brothers in adjusting to this new land in return for the favors of a Christian God, a worldly education and the munificence of civilization. Indians were the stalwart guides of the explorers, staunch, unblinking allies in war, the benevolent purveyors of corn, squash and furs, while the renegade factions among them were quickly brought to right by the firm, guiding hand of their white brothers. We had no idea of the details of Cortez's genocidal sweep of the Aztec, Pizarro's carbon-copy attrition of the Inca or the reincarnation of those methods in the colonization of North America. The idea that kidnapping, muti-lation, rape and savagery were the founding principles of the con-tinent's settlement astounded us. We were saddened, angered, and we sought solace in the ways we'd learned — the security of our faith and the ministrations of Jacqueline Kakeeway.

She listened as the three of us poured out our hurt over this newfound knowledge. She was the balm for our confusions and the remedy for the rise of political bile we felt inside us.

My parents took their first sweat lodge ceremony early in the spring of 1974. It was a special healing lodge for the three of us, along with Pastor Chuck. We were to sweat out the impurities of resentment, vitriol and malignant sorrow. We were to pray for the power of forgiveness, to sing the praises of a nurturing creation, seeking its continued guidance and teachings, and we were to med-itate on our most inner selves, mingle with our hurt and anger to discover why we had them. They lasted the whole four rounds, and we emerged from the womb of the lodge rejuvenated, whole, recom-mitted to the principles of the faiths we followed and were learning.

It had never once struck me as strange that my parents and my religious mentor would eagerly participate in a ritual so distant from their structured worship. We had learned, through the process of my reculturalization, that the underpinnings of faith, worship and spirituality remain constant throughout the length and breadth of God's world. We knew that praise was the gleeful noise of recognition. That prayer was the soft murmuring of a humble and contrite heart in the face of creation. That meditation was the heart in rapt anticipation of guidance, direction and insight. And that devotion was not so much to the God of our choosing as to the semblance of the God we discovered in our-selves, its growth and manifestation in our lives.

Our hurt and our anger had sprung from the realization that history had duped us and through its deliberate obfuscation had made us complicitors by our mute acceptance of it. We, like most people, had been innocent victims of a parade of misinformation that had started with the first scrunch of sand beneath a booted foot in the land of the Tainos. Our resentment was fueled by the awareness that the land we loved so dearly, the three hundred and twenty acres we had come to refer to as our hereditary farm, had never been ours to claim. The thieves' road that had begun in the 1400s had wended its way even to the heart of our cherished farmland. To deny that one salient fact was to shrug off history, to tacitly endorse its layered lie.

Our profound sorrow was driven by the recognition that we could not reorder history. For the remainder of our lives we would have to struggle to pacify ourselves with the desire to avoid recreating its vices in our own worlds. We claimed all of this for ourselves within the skin of the sweat lodge. Claimed it, owned it and let it go. And that, perhaps, is why I have never questioned Pastor Chuck's or my parents' quiet readiness for the ritual. Because, I believe, all spiritual warriors carry within themselves an ecumenic compass. It is lodged in the most private chambers of the heart, its pointer tremulous, sensitive to the pull of unseen redemptions.

My redemption began on December 29, 1890, when the Seventh US Cavalry, in an act of retribution for the debacle of Little Big Horn, murdered two hundred native men, women and children on the frozen banks of a creek called Wounded Knee. With the Gatling guns sweeping the writhing bodies, echoes embedding themselves like bullets in the trunks of the trees and cordite burning the nostrils of the soldiers, the blood of a people seeped through the ice and snow, sealing itself forever in the articulate bosom of the earth. This land is a palimpsest, but it requires the eyes and ears of the enlightened to hear its songs and see its scars. For the earth holds its dead in its arms forever and the songs of the people are borne on the sibilant voices of creek and river, the whisper of the grasses, the conversation of wind and leaf and tree, the stoic reticence of rocks. As I read the story of that slaughter when I was eighteen, felt wrath and fury kindling inside me and then tempered those flames with the spiritual qualities of the sweat lodge and the faith of my raising, I realized that a part of me had died and a part of me was born that frigid winter morning. I realized that history, when you know it, can either include you in the massacre or empower you to survival.

My innocence vaporized like small talk and was replaced by the harder rhetoric of maturity. That's what died on the frozen creek that morning of 1890. A people's innocence and mine.

Part of my heart is buried at Wounded Knee. Fragments of it are buried wherever the people were murdered, in murder's hundred nefarious ways, in the name of a conquest euphemized as settlement. Places called Batoche, Sand Creek, Sainte-Marie Among The Hurons and Hochelaga.

We all have our Wounded Knees — that was the seed of my redemption. The knowledge that our hearts reside in places where slivers of our innocence are buried. Emerging from the sweat lodge, I knew that when my body is returned to the arms of the earth you will bury my heart at Wounded Knee. You will inter it on the shore of Georgian Bay, lay it to rest in the middle of three hundred and twenty acres of farmland, consign it to the dust of anonymous battlefields and entomb it beneath a granite cenotaph that stands in the middle of the Hockley Valley, inscribed and elegized with the swirl and swaggle of letters formed by heart and hand. Everywhere I lived and everywhere I died.

I discovered healing that spring. Healing is understanding, and I knew two things for absolute certain after the experience of the sweat lodge. I knew that the problems of the world, both worlds, were spiritual as opposed to political and that their lasting resolution needed to come from spiritual ways and means. And I knew that I needed to continue on the path I had been directed in order to effect, in some small was, a migration to spiritual resolution. There would always be someone, Indian or not, taking the same painful path to their own redemption, kneeling at their own cenotaphs, harboring their own confusions. So I *would* become a preacher. A spiritual warrior. I would minister from the arch of a bridge that spanned two worlds, whose supports and columns rose from the bedrock of a shared acknowledgment of the sacred, the divine and the eternal.

For such is the kingdom.

Good-byes have a residue that you carry into everything that follows. It shows itself in peculiar places as your life and your world meander through their course. You'll find it in the face you swear you recognize, the snatches of song through the window of a passing car, the sudden slam of a screen door in summer, the perfect stillness of a child in slumber and the sudden ballet of cats' feet across a stretch of snow. That's the joy of living inhabited lives — the recurrence of the profound in the ordinary.

We graduated from high school in June of 1974. In the faces of my classmates were only traces of the children we'd been five short years before. We were men and women now, bulkier with time, fleshed and muscled with learning, weightier with courage. Our class was smaller, diminished by academic ennui, the call of farm and family, death, relocation. As the small roll of paper was slipped into our palms there wasn't a one of us who knew the person we would eventually be.

Ralphie was going to Minnesota on a hockey scholarship, where he would star and be drafted by the Chicago Blackhawks before a knee injury would return him to Carrick Township, lessened like all home-town heroes who never get beyond the population sign, where he would marry, raise children and die of a heart attack when he was forty-two. Connie Shaus married Victor Ringle, and they work a farm near Neustadt. Lenny Weber earned an agricultural degree at the University of Western Ontario and is making a killing at experimental farming on the family acres. Allen Begg set fire to a neighbor's house and in fear of serving time ran away and was never seen in Walkerton again. Chris Hollingshead became a Walkerton fireman, where it's said his tremendous height allows him to work without a ladder. Mary Ellen Reid became the first woman in Bruce County elected to the Ontario legislature. We see each other now and again, and she is still the genteel, refined woman she became after the debacle of our freshman year. As I moved from person to person at the graduation, hugging them, laughing and offering the usual promises to stay in touch, the residue of those good-byes settled easily into my psyche, to emerge and re-emerge suddenly and unexpectedly throughout my life. There was only one that remained to be said.

Johnny and I had become less and less involved with each other's lives over the course of that final year. A few times I had tried to let him know the reactions I was having to the books I borrowed but he merely shrugged. We'd go out now and then for movies, bowling and pizza, but each of those occasions was like a cursory statement, a nicety performed for propriety's sake. He'd never revealed any plans for college, work or travel, and I was curious to know what he had in mind. We arranged to get together for a few hours the Sunday after graduation and a week before I was scheduled to leave for Red Deer and a summer job with a wheat farmer outside nearby Airdrie.

He arrived in late afternoon. He'd filled out, tall, muscular and agile with a prowling leanness. He wore a red bandanna around his head. His long blond hair flowed down to the middle of his back, and he'd taken to wearing a scruffy beard. He smiled, chatted with my parents for a few minutes, declined the supper invitation he knew he always had, clapped me on the back and shepherded me out the door and across the yard towards the equipment shed. He seemed quietly jubilant, simmering with intent, and a throwback to the Johnny I'd known years before. Seeing him, a man, in the middle of the area where we'd invented the game as boys brought the realities of time crashing down around me.

"I'm leaving, Josh," he said, staring at me with the characteristic fire.

"Where are you going? You got a job?" I asked, not entirely surprised by the suddenness of the information.

He leaned on the rail fence and looked out over the acres. When he looked at me again it was with the face of a zealot. "Out there," he said, gesturing with one arm.

"Out there where?" I asked, slightly guarded.

"Wherever," he said and turned to look back across the land. "Wherever the people are."

"The people? Indian people, you mean?"

"Yeah. Our people, Josh. They need warriors right now. You hear of Kenora?"

"No."

"Well, it's gonna be the Wounded Knee of Canada, Josh. The Ojibway Warriors Society is going to take over a piece of land the town stole and turned into a park. They're gonna march in with guns and reclaim it. Me, Staatz and a couple of his brothers are gonna head up there and I want you to come too," he said.

"Why would I want to do that?"

"Because you're an Ojibway. And you're a warrior. You believe that, don't you?"

"Yeah, of course I do. But I don't believe in guns and I don't believe in violence. And besides ... I'm leaving too."

He looked at me hard. I could feel his life force like I did at that first meeting, only now it was a different energy, pointed and unrelenting.

"You're going to the Bible school. After everything you learned about the truth of things, you're still gonna follow through and capitulate. Surrender," he said derisively. "Hasn't anything sunk in? Doesn't any of what you've learned mean anything?"

"Yes. It means that there's a function for people like me. The ones who've had to struggle to reclaim themselves. The ones who've had to learn how to heal the rifts inside them. Who've had to ask themselves whether they're red or white, or even just who they really are."

"You asked yourself that? And what are you? Red ... or white?"

I stared back intently at him. "I'm red. I always have been. I was created to be an Ojibway male. I just happen to believe that I'm also supposed to preach."

"How can you? You've been to the sweat lodge! You've smoked the pipe! I haven't even done those things but at least I respect them enough not to dishonor them by turning my back on it all and reaching out to the whiteman way! There's frontlines out there, Josh, and the people need all of us to stand there with them. This generation, we gotta be the defenders of the way. If we don't fight, it dies, and when it dies, the people die!"

It was like I could see the chasm between us. My understanding was built on the tangible experience of healing myself of shame, confusion and sorrow, the palliative confutation of garbled emotions. Johnny's was forged in anger, resentment and a need to be anything, anyone other than the spawn of his father, a wounding deep and immeasurable. Maybe it was beginnings of the intuitive therapeutic sense I would develop that told me that this was a gap bridgeable only through a mutual healing. That as long as one of us continued to deny the source of the ache, confront and disarm it, we would be shouting forever across a yawning valley, believing the echoes of our youthful voices, our friendship, would one day call out answers. But they would be just that — mere echoes, dissipated and frail, insistent with the vocabulary of denial. Johnny needed to go and pursue whatever form of invention or creation that he would, and I needed to tell him that I would always be waiting, pacing the far rim of healing.

"You're right, Johnny," I said, quietly. "You're right. There are frontlines. There are battle lines everywhere. Survival means struggle. My father's battle lines are drawn here, across this soil, and his struggle is to keep it arable, to replenish as well as reap. For a while I thought that my lines were drawn here too. But they aren't. You say that the frontlines are *out there* somewhere and you want to go find them, stand on them, be a defender, a protector, a warrior. Maybe yours are, Johnny, maybe yours are. But frontlines are everywhere."

He looked at me, quizzical, keen, and I sensed he was fighting to retain his anger. He placed one foot on the bottom rail and leaned forward, arms folded on the fence.

"I can't stand on your frontlines and be effective," I said. "All I know, all I was raised in and all I've been taught, by my parents,

Pastor Chuck, Jacqueline, the pipe and the sweat, is that the spiritual solution is the only solution. When everything is said and done, every form of survival depends on spiritual survival. That's what I believe. And that's where I can be a warrior. So I'm going to follow through. Just like you are. And when I'm ready, when I've learned enough, I'm coming back to Cape Croker. I'm bringing back what I've learned and offering it back to the people. I'll offer back the lessons I've learned about finding God, about finding myself, about finding peace."

He nodded all the time I spoke. When I finished he stood up straight and shook himself briefly. The look he offered was neutral.

"And how will you *offer* your wisdom to the *dead*, preacher? How will you console *them*? You're right about one thing. This is a war of attrition. We've been under siege for generations and our frontlines are everywhere. But you know what? All you've done is create your own marketplace to keep on selling out. So, go and learn your whiteman religion and meet your whiteman God. But do the people a favor and don't come back. The real warriors will protect them. We'll shelter them. Oh. And when you stand before your Creator *just as you are*, I only hope He's as color blind as you! What does your Bible say? And I shall make you whiter than snow? Well, it looks like it's working, doesn't it? Too bad neither of you can do anything about the skin, though."

And he walked away.

He neither stopped to speak to my parents, who stood on the back porch, nor slowed in his car to take the turn onto Highway 9. He disappeared over Conroy's hill with a squeal of tires and the angry whine of engine.

His grandfather called the next day to say he'd disappeared overnight, and I wondered whether he'd bothered looking back at all, whether he'd watched the glimmer of Mildmay recede deeper and deeper into the depths of his rearview mirror until it, his past, his boyhood and me, fell away like a carapace, like the glass itself, settling in slivers within his psyche, the residue of good-bye.

"**G**ood-bye wasn't in his vocabulary, eh?" Nettles said eventually.

"What?" I muttered.

"Good-bye. The G-word. He didn't know how to say it. Never had to before. The abandoned ones are like that. They get so used to being left they can't handle being the leaver. They don't wanna feel like they're becoming like the abandoners who raised them. So they create a crisis just so they don't have to use the G-word."

"Are you saying he knew what my response would be?"

"Maybe not to the letter. But, yeah. He knew. Anger was his out."

"I've never considered that, but you could be right," I said. Nettles amazed me with the scope of his perception beneath the bumbling charm.

"You wanna know what I think, Joshua?" he asked. "I think he was pissed for a while. I think he got hot the moment you started going to the reserve to visit. What's her name? Jacqueline? Next thing you know you got a peace pipe in your kisser, takin' the sweat bath thing, beatin' on a drum, doin' the whole noble savage production number. Everything that Gebhardt wanted for himself. Far as he figured, he was supposed to be the Injun. The way he wrote the script, he was gonna ride across the prairie shouting the good news and glad tidings to you, not the other way around," Nettles said, lounging in his chair and lacing his fingers behind his head.

"You may be right," was all I could counter.

"Think about it. You gave him the only role he ever had. He brought you everything right from the get go. He brought you baseball. He brought you the blood brother thing. Hell, he brought you the whole Injun trip in the first place. Way he figured, *he* was the hunter and the gatherer."

"So the books and the political knowledge were his compensation?"

"Maybe not so much. Maybe he woulda latched onto that anyway. But I think the books and the warrior guy from the juvie joint were the ways he figured he'd be able to lead you again. He needed you, Joshua. He needed you to need him. You were the whole shebang. A brother. Someone to count on. Someone to share secrets with. Someone to care for. Then you went and grew up on him. Every needy person in the world takes everyone else's growin' up as growin' away. 'Cause they only understand one direction. Away. Gone. Finito. He figured you wouldn't need him any more. That you'd find your way to Injun without him."

It hurt to think our friendship had been built on emotional insecurity instead of the light and magic I'd always regarded it in. Still, there was credence to what Nettles said, and thinking about the way things had developed I realized that the distancing between us had begun as I edged closer to resolving my cultural quandaries. As Jacqueline had brought me closer to myself, she'd also, unwittingly, taken me further from my friend.

"So, in part, I suppose, I created him. This situation," I said, flooded with realization.

"Correctamundo. That's what he figures too. That's why he wants you here. This is like full circle for him. He's the warrior he always wanted to be. He wants you to see him in his finery, all the feathers and flash. He wants to tell you that he was right all along. Because you never went back, did you?"

"No," I said. "Not yet. I haven't felt ready. I've always gone back to visit, to maintain the connection to Jacqueline, but no, I haven't gone back like I said I would." I suddenly felt very guilty.

"He knows that, obviously."

"Yes. Obviously."

"Bingo. But there's more, isn't there?"

"Yes. I suppose there is."

"I figured there had to be. You saw him again and you fought again, didn't you? He drove the spear in deeper, didn't he?"

"Yes," I said, quietly.

"You wanna tell me about it now or do you wanna sleep on it? Your call, but either way you gotta spill the beans, Joshua. I need to know goin' in tomorrow where the ball's placed. It's fourth down here. Kick or try, you know."

"I'd like to think about it. I need to think about it."

"Fair enough. You know where your room is. Fridge is open twenty-four hours. And Joshua?"

"Yes?"

"I'm not tryin' to play the stiff prick here. I'm not tryin' to rip your memories apart on you. It's just that we're dealin' for life here and I kinda figure life is what's gonna diffuse this thing. His life. Yours. Shit, maybe even mine."

"I know, David. No offense taken."

"Okay. You need me, call me. Just wake me like my wife does."

"How's that?"

"Kiss me on the ear and tell me that you love me."

I laughed. "Sounds like a spiritual awakening to me."

Nettles chuckled. "Adds a whole different meaning to getting up in the middle of the night, doesn't it?"

"Yes," I said, "and probably in your case being raised from the dead as well!"

"Raised from the dead. That's a good one. You're okay, Reverend, you're okay," he said from the stairs.

Ben Gebhardt died in the spring I graduated from college. He never left the sofa in those final years. His wife, however, had earned an accounting diploma through correspondence, proudly hung her shingle on the front porch and taken over the books for most of Mildmay's small businesses. A young couple managed the hardware store now, and Elly Gebhardt ran her office the same way

she ran her life — silently, loyally, primly. Neither Johnny nor I
made the funeral. I was knee deep cramming for final exams and
Johnny had disappeared.

Shortly after, Elly had moved in with Harold, where she stayed
through his passing and until her own in the fall of 1988. Old Man
Givens's place was razed by a mysterious fire, and people still talk
about how she stood watching it burn, lingering there long after the
firemen and rubberneckers had abandoned it. There's a small park
there now where children play late into the indigoed stretch of
summer evenings. Johnny would think that ironic as hell.

My own family prospered. Len Wilton passed away suddenly in
the mid-70s and, being the last in the Wilton line, had bequeathed
the two hundred and forty acres his family had worked for generations to my father. The Wiltons and the Kanes had arrived in Carrick
Township at the same time and I guess Len figured my father was
the closest he could get to tilling the line of heredity. The Wilton
acres nudged the Walkerton townline. For a while my dad rented out
those acres, but as the population swelled the town fathers peeled
off more and more cash for expansion into the old Wilton spread.
By the time they were ready to retire from farming in the late '80s
my parents were secure. They rented out our acres, traveled and
lived comfortably in that old brick house. They never minded that I
would not farm the land. They were content to know that it would
remain in the Kane family, and it's still known as the Kane place
despite the tenant farmers who bring it to crop each year.

Pastor Chuck married Rebecca Norton after five years of
courtship. Rumor has it that he finally popped the question after
Rebecca had speculated loudly and vociferously at Hilda's Hair
Heaven that the only missionary position she was ever going to see
was the pastor's head bowed in prayer. I performed the rites of
matrimony. A Christian rock and roll band played long into the
night, and Pastor Chuck himself took over the drums for a wild set
that included his reworkings of "House of the Risin' 'Son'," "I Want
to Take You Higher" and "Proud Mary." They settled into the
manse, where they soon had two children, Seth and Holly. He still
preaches at St. Giles.

Jacqueline continued working on the reserve. She never liked the term medicine woman, preferring instead the humbler term elder, but she was known anyway as a strong medicine woman. In the early '80s she initiated a camp where women from every tribe and nation gathered to spend time in ceremony, meditative retreat and rest. It became so popular that they made a permanent site for it on a point on Georgian Bay. It's called Mindemoya, or Old Woman Lodge, and is filled to capacity year round with native and non-native women. She was a special guest at my ordainment, and she also performed the traditional Ojibway marriage ritual at my wedding and is the spiritual grandmother of my son.

Everyone who had been a significant contributor to my life was still an active and essential part of it. Except Johnny Gebhardt. He had existed through the years since the end of high school as pages of intermittent letters. He never left a forwarding address, never asked to visit, never followed the letters with a phone call. Still, he'd written. I felt like home plate in the baseball game of his life: something he needed to touch, but briefly, vital only in passing.

I believe those letters were his catharsis. His way of justifying his choices. His way of arresting motion, to fix it and hold it. Allowing me to inspect it, to see it, was to give it breath so it could move again, become real. He was like an artist who needed to leave something behind, something immortal. Memory is the only after-life possible, those letters said. He needed me. I recognized that finally. He needed me because I had been the only permanence he'd ever known. When our blood had mingled in that willow tree as ten-year-olds, we had sealed an eternal pact. For me, such loy-alty was as natural as breathing, the very construct of friendship, but for Johnny it had assumed mammoth proportions, a treaty between himself and fate itself, declaring that he would always count, matter and affect. The letters were simply his part of the deal. His conversations in absentia.

I'd been back to the Hockley Valley hundreds of times since that fall of 1973. I've gone with Shirley. I've gone with my son. I've wandered there alone. I've walked that ragged little trail through the frolic of nature and emerged upon the lip of that cliff as wide-eyed as always. I've dangled my feet over its vertiginous space and clambered down the fifteen feet to the narrow ledge that sits beneath two sets of names. I have reached up and placed my hand upon them, feeling the serrated bite of granite edges smoothed somewhat by time, and trailed my finger along the indented swirl and lilt of the letters, allowing the skin its memory. I touch everything with the skin of my returnings.

I wondered as I sat in the Nettles' den whether time had made him a pilgrim too. Whether he'd made the journey back through the valley and stood with his palm pressed against the letters that spelled out the boys and young men we were together. I wondered whether pieces of his heart were buried in significant places or whether his pilgrimages and returnings were limited to the landscape of memories, the sacred and the profound cached in anonymous places. I wondered what a life without monuments must be. How a heart without elegies beats. And I wondered how deep some aches might go when left untended, unspoken, unseen.

He had brought me everything. He'd brought me to the very edge of discovery. Watching me walk towards my self must have seemed like an act of desertion. Hearing me speak of teachings and learnings must have rung as sharply as the denunciations of this father. My statements of being and becoming were the ripping away of the thongs that lashed us together, and when I chose the divergent path of religion over the way of the warrior, the abandoning must have rung like the very trumpets at Jericho.

I hadn't heard any of it. I heard only ranting. I heard only anger. I realized then that the things we think we hear are only part of the story. That it's not so much the words themselves we need to strive to hear. It's the punctuation. Our hearts are buried in the punctuation.

Part Four

LIKE ARROWS

With the beeping of the alarm clock, the Nettles house became a frenzied place. Doors slammed, cryptic conversations were flung upstairs and down, radios blared, dishes clattered, phones rang and feet thumped. I might have preferred an hour or two of meditative time but still, I was grateful to be a part of a domestic hubbub.

Nettles drove one-handed, slurping coffee from an oversized plastic mug in the shape of Sylvester the Cat. While he zig-zagged between lanes I filled in the years. I had graduated in the spring of 1976 and begun my assistant pastorship at a small community gospel church in St. Catharines, Ontario, shortly after. Shirley and I were married in the spring of 1977. We were twenty-two. Jonathan was born in the fall of 1978 and I saw Johnny Gebhardt for the last time. He'd called my father from British Columbia asking for me to appear at his trial after the logging protest. I had flown out right away. We succeeded in getting him an acquittal and he'd emerged from the detention cell with a raised-fist salute and a smile.

"Same old Johnny?" Nettles asked.

"At first, yes," I said. "It didn't take long before everything turned ugly, though."

"Ugly how?"

He'd walked up and grabbed me into a long, enthusiastic hug, and I'd felt grateful and happy in the arms of reunion. We'd driven in his old Mustang to a small diner where he'd voraciously piled into a huge breakfast of sausages, eggs, pancakes, toast, cereal, juice and coffee, all the while denouncing jail food and rating the local police against others he'd dealt with.

"And just how did you acquire all this specific knowledge, Johnny?" I'd asked jokingly.

He'd laid down his cutlery and leaned forward to stare at me across the table. "It's the life," he'd said.

"What life?" Nettles asked.

"That's what I asked. He just smirked at me and shook his head, stuck a toothpick in the corner of his mouth, leaned a little closer and said — Indian life."

"What the hell is that supposed to mean?" Nettles said over the rim of his plastic cup.

"Again, that's what I asked, and he just smirked at me again in that downcasting way people do when they figure you're ignorant of the obvious. I've never forgotten what he said after that. Because it wasn't so much conversation as it was a statement, a manifesto a credo. Indian life is the only real life, he said, the only life that lets you see what this country is really all about. Its quaking political guts, he called it. When you press for your rights to equal treatment under law, your right to an education, your right to adequate housing, your right to make a living, your right to your language, then you discover your real rights as an Indian. When you press for your rights you get them read to you. You have the right to remain silent, the right to an attorney, the right to a phone call. *Those* are your Aboriginal rights.

"You live the Indian life and you see that. You see that white plus might equals right. When you take a stand, you call attention to the truth and they arrest you. They say you're obstructing justice. Canada doesn't care about justice. The law says as long as you're a good little Indian and stay at home and shut up we'll protect you, we'll serve you. Serve you with what? Serve you with a summons, serve you with notice that we're damming the river you fish in, that we're flooding your homeland so we can sell power to the cities, serve you with a letter that says your land claim's been denied, that you can't have the house you need, that your kids are being taken away for their own protection, serve you with the one hand that's reaching out with money while the other hand's sneaking something away. That's how the law serves you if you live the Indian life. The Indian life is about seeing all of that every damn day. There is no justice. There's just them and there's ... *just us.*"

I was surprised at how easily it all rolled off my tongue. Nettles too raised his eyebrows.

"Almost sounds like you're convinced yourself, Joshua."

"Well, I may have embellished some, but that was the gist of it," I said. "Fervor's like that. I've heard it from the pulpit and I've heard it on the street. It's all in the delivery. There's something in us that responds to it when the cause is right, or appears right. It's always been fervor over logic, or zeal over faith."

"And rhetoric over truth?" he asked sharply.

"And rhetoric over truth," I echoed.

Nettles regarded me carefully from the corner of his eye. "And you never considered that maybe what he was saying might have been the truth? That maybe underneath the fervor was reality?"

"Sure. I considered it," I said.

"And?"

"And he's right in a lot of ways," I said. "I don't think anyone can challenge the fact that injustice is threaded throughout our system. But political truth can't define you. Those kind of truths can change overnight. It's only the inside truths we discover and act upon that eventually define us as human beings."

"You're pretty good with the rhetoric yourself, Reverend," Nettles said with a small grin. "But what if you go in there today and you find out that this warrior truth he espouses is genuine for him? How do we disarm that?"

"That's just it, David. All we should be concerned about here is disarming it. Not discrediting it, not denouncing it, not exorcising it. Heck, we don't even try to validate it. Johnny, the Warriors in Oka, the militants, the yellers and the shouters don't need our validation. They need our recognition. So we disarm it, let those people go and bring Johnny out safely. We're not politicians and we're not ultimate judgment. We're just men," I said firmly.

"Men with a mission," he intoned.

"Yes. Joshua and his trumpet," I said quietly.

"David and his sling," Nettles said, patting the badge over his pocket.

"And John?" I asked.

"John with is voice crying in the wilderness." Nettles said almost sadly. "You wanna finish off about how that reunion turned out? We're almost at the office."

I sighed. "It was ugly. I was young and still had my pants on fire. It was my evangelical period."

I told him how the conversation had degenerated. My response had been to say that we were pretty lucky in 1978 to be living in Canada given the unrest and despotism raging in other countries. I'd said it was true that democracy, the parliamentary system and the justice system had their flaws, but they were all we had and it was up to all of us to make them work and make them accountable to the masses. Johnny had fumed through all of it. When I'd finished he looked gravely at me.

"You know," he'd said finally, "it's funny because you really *look* like an Indian. And I'd almost believe you are. At least until you open your mouth.

"It's not too late, though, Josh," he'd said. "You can still chuck it all. You can come with me and fight for the people. You don't even have to fight physically. Just tell them how close they came to getting you."

"I can't."

"Why? What is so big and important in their world that you can't come back to your own?"

"I'm married," I'd said. "I've been married for a year and a half and we're expecting a baby any time now."

His face had lit up. "Wow! Right on, Josh! Wow! She's a Cape Croker girl, right? You married an Ojibway. I knew it!"

"No."

"No? Well, where's she from? What band? What tribe, man?"

When I told him I saw the energy recede from his face like it had the very first day I met him. "She's not from any band. She's just a woman. A very fine, very loving, very beautiful —"

"Very white woman," he said bluntly.

"Yes. But I don't see her as white."

"You don't see *anything* as white!" he spat.

"Johnny, this isn't a color test. It's about love."

"And love is blind, right?"

"Yes. Genuine love *is* blind."

"*You're* fuckin' blind! And it *is* a color test. Everything is. Right from day one they're out to get your soul, and now they've come and got you with their women. That's your reward for selling out, Josh. Now you can fuck one of us like we've been fuckin' you! The only difference is, now you get kissed before you get screwed."

"Johnny, shut up!" I'd said, standing suddenly.

For the first time in my life I thought I would strike another human being. He looked at me as calmly as one who's faced down hundreds of threats and scratched and fought in a hundred alleys.

"Well, well," he said. "Is this spiritual backbone, Preacher, or is there really a warrior buried under all that white?"

I swallowed hard before I spoke. "Look, Johnny, you chose to walk out of my life four years ago. You don't know me now because you wouldn't stick around. You don't know what I felt, what I found, what I learned. You don't know what my motivations are, what my plans are. You don't know *me*!"

"Kinda makes us even, then, wouldn't you say?"

I stared.

"You don't know you either."

"I know myself well enough to know that I can't abandon a friend. That I'll fly across the country to be there when I'm needed because I took an oath — an *Indian* oath — in a willow tree a long, long time ago that I would always be loyal and good and kind. Being loyal doesn't mean you walk away for four years. Being good doesn't mean you disappear into your own life and never reappear in mine. Being kind doesn't mean you only reappear when you need something."

"I don't know about you," he said, "but I pledged to always be good and loyal and kind except in battle because that's different. Well, welcome to the battle, Josh." His arm swept the room. "It's all around you. Find some balls under all the shit you're carrying around. Admit that they got you and come into the battle."

"I can't," I said quietly.

Johnny sighed. "I know."

"What do we do now?' I asked.

He shrugged, gulped some coffee, wiped his mouth on his sleeve and looked at me with that clear-eyed gaze I knew so well. "I don't know. At least I don't know about you. Me, I'm out of here."

"Where will you go?"

"Wherever I need to go, Josh," he said cryptically.

"What about me?" I inquired.

"What *about* you, man? At least you're on the right question. Stay on that question for a while and maybe, just maybe, you'll start to come around to an answer. Maybe you'll start to see how hamstrung and hog-tied you are. You're lookin' for salvation but you're lookin' in the wrong place. Salvation ain't in no whiteman's heaven — it's in an Indian reality. Try it sometime. You might like it," he said bitterly.

"You tried it Johnny?"

"Yeah. I tried it," he said angrily. "I tried it. And you know what? I belong there. So do you. You know the story in the Bible about the apostles finding the blind beggar near the gates of the place called Beautiful?" he asked.

"Yeah, I do. Acts Chapter Three. He was crippled actually."

"Whatever," he said with an aggravated little wave. "Well you should study your own teaching, Preacher, because that blind beggar is you!"

"Me? How do you figure that?"

He grinned maliciously. "Let me paraphrase. The disciples are wandering around spreading the Word and they find this blind man begging from the people coming out of the temple. In fact, his friends carry him there every day. Right?"

"Not exactly, but I'm with you. Go on."

"Well, the blind guy figures these people are a good touch. Them being filled with compassion and care, of course. He's begging there every day. He gets a few coins in his outstretched palm every day and he figures he's got it made. The only thing he doesn't know is that he's at the steps of the temple. I'm on, right?"

"Yes. You're on."

"Well, he figures his saving grace is in those few coins. He eats, he drinks, he survives. But what he doesn't know is that he's near the gates of the place called Beautiful. The temple where he can find true salvation, a true saving grace. He's close to the place of beauty but he never knew. Right?"

"Right."

"Well, I'm no theologian but it seems to me that the question this parable is asking is ... how close have you been to the gates of salvation and missed it because you were blind? Am I right?'

"Yes."

"Well, you're the beggar, Josh. Jacqueline, you own Pastor, your parents, me — we all carried you to the gates! You were on the doorstep of your own salvation and you missed it because you were blind. You could have stepped across into a place of beauty. Your own identity. Your Indianness. Your history, your language, your ceremonies. But you stayed blind and were willing to settle for the coins in your palm. You're that beggar, Josh. And all I'm asking is how long are you gonna stay blind?"

He slapped a few bills on the table and walked away. I stood there, as alone as I have ever felt, searching for some words to keep him there, searching for the great lost chord of our friendship, to carry it to him so we could rest and replenish ourselves in the hushed note of its security.

But I found nothing.

"Did you have an answer?" Nettles asked suddenly.

"Then? No," I said, shaken from my recollection. "Now? Yes.

Only the most fortunate or the most desperate of us find an instantaneous salvation. Most of us have to settle for the developing kind. The kind that evolves slowly over the years. The kind of salvation that gets buttressed and supported by life itself, all the ups and downs and wounds. Grace lies within our wounds," I said quietly.

"Grace?"

"Grace. An unqualified gift. Salvation. Self-knowledge. Being carried across the threshold of a place called Beautiful," I said.

"And that place would be where, Joshua?" Nettles asked, wheeling into a parking lot I assumed was at the police station.

I heaved a huge sigh, preparing myself for the battle at hand and remembering the battle Johnny and I had fought twelve years ago. "It's the place your God assigns. Your own essential place in everything. Some of us call it heaven. Others ... well, others just call it belonging."

Staatz died.

He was only twenty-five and he's gone. I only knew him for eight of those years and he left me too soon. I still need him. There's more that he needs to tell me. More that I need to understand.

You should have met him. I know that now but then I was too selfish. You had the old woman and the reserve to turn to to help you find your way, but me? All I had was Staatz. We trucked around together for two years after I split from Mildmay and he showed me everything. We never made it to Kenora that first summer. We wanted to but we got turned away on the Trans-Canada. We hung around trying to figure a way to sneak through the back country but we didn't know our way around so we headed for Minnesota instead. We went to Red Lake to see a few guys that Staatz and his brothers knew and then we toured around the Minneapolis–St. Paul ghetto where the Movement was born. Everywhere we went people knew who he was. He was so young but he could talk, Josh. He could stand at the front of a room full of angry, volatile people and he would reach out and cradle all their wounding, all their passion. Take all their energy in his hand, acknowledge it, soothe it and reroute it into something constructive, energizing and strong. He burned with a passion that was incendiary, magnetic, and I loved him. He would talk and I would listen. He told the great and glorious story of the people. Not just the romantic kind about the way things used to be and how we all need to reconnect to that, but the gritty, uncompromising story about all the different kinds of hunger. The hunger for tradition, for culture, for language, for ceremony, for ritual, for a self-determining future, for freedom, for understanding, for a rightful place on our own land and for recognition of that rightfulness. All the various and sundry hungers of a people caught between the jaws of an omnivorous society that digests everything. He was my example of a warrior heart in action, and he was my friend.

Every now and then I'd be challenged by someone because of my whiteness. I'd be put down and accused of spying, of being a plant, of being a wanna-be. Staatz defended me every time. Not that he needed to after a while. I could have handled any rough stuff that came along and even a philosophical dispute. But he waded in and told them about my own warrior heart, my fearlessness, my dedication, my renunciation of my history and my culture, my defense of one of their own and the price I paid for it. He stood by me and he stood for me, and I like to think that I did the same for him.

We went to Movement meetings everywhere. San Francisco, White Mountain, Rapid City, Vancouver, Pueblo, Sabaskong, Maniwaki, Kahnawake and Washington. We met warriors from every tribe and culture. We heard their stories, learned of their ways, their histories, their struggles, their defeats and their victories. We moved among them and we saw that the Great Hoop of the People was strong but still required its warriors to fight for its survival. Everywhere we went he was welcomed like a great general. We were swept into closed meetings and secret discussions. We were included in everything, and it wasn't long before I was being listened to and respected. Staatz brought me into the circle.

But he died.

He came to my place one night when we were living in Seattle. He was drunk. He never drank. Said that warriors didn't use the medicine that destroyed their people, so I was surprised. Shocked, really. He shuf-fled into my room and sat in the one armchair that I had, cradling a whiskey bottle in his lap. I will always remember how that looked. The bottle engulfed in one huge brown hand, clenched like a hated thing but raised to the mouth like elixir. He sat there for the longest time staring at my wall, but you could tell he was looking far beyond it into an internal landscape I know now he'd carried around forever. Then he cried. Huge, swelling silent tears that rolled down his face and dropped onto that bot-tle in his lap. He cried and drank and cried and drank until that whiskey was finished and the bottle was slumped to the floor beside him. Not a word. Not a single, solitary word. Then, he wiped the tears away with the back of his hand and stared straight ahead of himself for a few moments and then whispered something so softly I couldn't make it out. I leaned forward to hear him and he repeated it. A drone-like rolling of syllables, thickened with drink and full of pain.

"They lied."

That's all. Just that. I asked him who "they" were and he shrugged and smirked. He lit a smoke and sat back in that chair and started talk-ing in a loose, unpunctuated ramble, eyes unfocused and empty. It was scary. A live haunting. He told me about his life on the Six Nations Reserve when he was a boy. How he and his brothers played among the hills and hollows of that place and felt it grow inside them until it had become sacred ground. He talked about a life filled with the realization of his place with his people, of belonging, of rightness, of balance and how that was disrupted one spring morning with the arrival of a bus that was soon filled with the sobbing bodies of children scooped up for transporta-tion to a residential school far away. How he was one of those children and the fear and terror he felt. He spoke of the nuns and priests who wel-comed them. How they were said to be home and how that word felt blas-phemed, wrong, like the words Sister *and* Father *would soon become. They were marched into a small room where they were scrubbed raw with harsh-smelling soap and powders, their clothing torn from their bodies disrespectfully and burned before their eyes. He told of being marshaled into a room with a picture on the wall of the man he would soon know as Jesus surrounded by his disciples. How he was told as they cut off his braids and long hair how it was heathen, evil, uncivilized and unworthy of God's heaven. He said he could never understand why the men in the pictures had such long hair. He talked about being beaten for using the language he was born to speak and being tossed into a small, cramped crawlspace for two days because he had dared to stand on the front porch of that school and sing the morning prayer song to the rising sun. And how later he would be forced to memorize prayer songs and sing them in a choir in a crowded church. How he was told Indian things were evil and needed to be cleansed from him and being strapped for asking how they planned to cleanse him of his skin.*

And he talked about the hundreds of midnight invasions. How he lay in his bunk with the blankets over his eyes listening to the creak of the floorboards as the good fathers worked their way from bed to bed over those long months. About the hands in the darkness, touching, fondling, groping. About the consummation of their holy crusade and the whispered "God loves you" as the violation was completed. They penetrated more than the bodies of those children those nights. They penetrated the protective sheath of history, culture and dignity. And then they disappeared back into their robes and Bibles, their commandments and their salvation. That was the true invasion of North America, he said. The invasion of spirit, mind and body. And then he walked out. No good-bye, no wave, no ceremony. He just left me.

We found his body in a motel cabin. He'd put a bullet through his heart because that's where all the pain was. He could fight in the street, he could battle on the frontlines, he could endure the strife of open conflict and he could lead others to discover their hidden sources of strength and survival, but he couldn't heal himself. He couldn't undo the effects of those late-night occupations of his soul. He went out the only way he could. Alone and miserable. I hated him for that. Hated him with all the pure invective we human beings reserve for those we love when they leave us. But it faded and in its place was just a hole. A vacant place inside of me that's never been filled except with the rage I feel for those who killed him. Because they murdered him. They poisoned him. They doused the fire of his spirit and left him to claw away for embers. He could only find them in the hearts of others and he worked at fanning them so that he might find a little warmth in the glow of their rekindling. In the end it wasn't enough.

And I guess, in a way, I'm looking for embers too.

Nettles ushered me into a small room, filled to cramped conditions with blackboards, flip charts, reams and reams of paper, and the cast-off plastic and paper of a few dozen suppers on the run. A large blueprint of the building Johnny occupied was spread out on two desks pushed together. The room he'd settled on was outlined harshly in red. Nettles beamed boyishly at a group of men in shirtsleeves and shoulder holsters.

"Mornin', Cap! Boys! Anything on the go today or should we sign off and golf a few holes?"

I was introduced to Chief Inspector Brian Dodge and Inspectors Ed O'Fallon, Terry Carleton and Art Hager. With Nettles they made up the brain trust behind resolving the occupation. They all regarded me suspiciously, as though the connection between preacher and Indian was an improbable one.

"Oh, don't fuss, fellas. He's a preacher, all right. What's the parish, Joshua?" Nettles asked.

I replied sternly, "St. Geronimo's parish of Our Lady of Perpetual Land Claims."

Nettles cackled and the line of men in front of us grinned uncomfortably.

There was a long moment of silence that rattled me a little, and then Brian Dodge began to review the overnight developments. There would be no forthcoming representation from either provincial or federal government, although the Calgary mayor had volunteered any assistance he might give, which was negligible. Local native groups had moved in to surround the building in a show of solidarity, but they'd been found to be an unaffiliated group from a local cultural school and posed no real threat. They'd been joined by a left-wing group of environmental slash race relations slash New Age crystal gazers working group. They were highly vocal but content to be photographed and quoted. Local media were hot on the story with splashy headlines in both local papers, and there'd been huge reaction to a radio phone-in show the previous evening that largely denounced the government over the Oka conflict and praised the irony of Johnny's action. Public support, it seemed, was high. The tactical unit was working on a route to the boardroom but it looked doubtful. There'd been no answer yet from technicians on the bomb squad over verification of the explosives taped to the doors, one of the female hostages was five months' pregnant and one of the men was on medication for clinical depression which he'd been without since day one of the affair. The perp had no identifiable kin, no known affiliations with known agitators or militant organizations and no ties to the Warriors behind the barricades in Oka. Unpredictable. Seemingly volatile. Handle with caution. Dodge rattled all of it off in an officious, military manner and then asked Nettles for updates of additional information.

He transformed before my eyes. The bumpkin was replaced by a consummate professional who gave a stern and disciplined reiteration of everything he'd been able to discern from what I'd told him. He was sharp and thorough.

"Subject is the product of a non-nurturing home. Alcoholic father, emotionally absent mother. Transient home life in developing years. Settled in rural southwestern Ontario by age ten. Prior to the friendship formed with Reverend Kane at that time there were no intimate relationships, no normal bonding patterns with family or community. Above-average intelligence with marked isolationist tendencies. Subject formed an attraction to Indians in early grade school years that bordered on obsession. Displayed fits of volatile temper. Acquitted of assault as a juvenile offender, served remand custodial time awaiting trial. While incarcerated he formed a friendship with a young militant which became the breeding ground for his politics. Following a normal high-school career subject immediately left the family and the community and traveled with the militant friend to various militant organization meetings and activities. Know affiliation with the American Indian Movement, degree unknown. Movements in last sixteen years unverifiable. Only known contact through letters to Reverend Kane, infrequent, transient. The letters reveal the mechanics of motivation to politicize. Off-the-cuff analysis: he's smart enough, motivated enough and tough enough to make things difficult but not impossible. We're fortunate to have Reverend Kane here. That's it."

"Profile?" O'Fallon asked.

"None," Nettles said. "All we have is a guy who's symbiotically attached to Indians. Thorough knowledge of politics and history with strident overtones but not fanatical. No nutcase. No loony. Rational. Competent. A little misinformed on the realities of political probability but overall a candidate for compromise. Provided."

"Provided what?" Hager asked.

"Provided the friendship factor with Reverend Kane here is as tight as it appears. They had a couple heated political and cultural disagreements. The reverend's approach has always been more linear, direct, simplified. Gebhardt's been more emotive, strident, personalized but adopted. But he never let go. They fought, he split, but he never let it go. There were the letters. Something in that friendship stayed with him and *provided* Joshua can get in touch with that, compromise is entirely possible."

"And if not?" Carleton asked.

"If not, we're off to the races," he said grimly.

"Okay," Dodge said, "so where do we touch down here? We got the phone line open, Gebhardt's waiting for contact with the reverend. How do we play this?"

Nettles coughed. "He wants to go in."

"No way," Dodge said. "We've got enough lives hanging in the balance here. I won't put up another one."

"You have to," I said.

"What?" Dodge asked sharply.

"You have to," I repeated. "Johnny won't have it any other way."

"Pardon me, Reverend," Hager threw in suddenly, "but who gives a shit what he will and won't have? We flew you all the way out here on his request. You're here, the phone's there, he's waiting. Let's dance!"

I could feel their tiredness. I sensed the weight of the stress of being the guardians of thirteen lives, the self-righteous anger that smoldered under their efficient ordering of movement, and I could appreciate the light they regarded Johnny in.

"I appreciate your concern and the way you've handled everything up to now. But I know Johnny. I know that if there's going to be a resolution here it's going to have to come his way. And his way is face-to-face. I need to go in there. I need to sit with him in council. He's likely got a pipe. I need to sit and smoke with him. Then we'll talk. He won't do it any other way. We have to respect his respect of ceremony. And mine," I said.

"You're joking, right?" Carleton asked.

"No," I said firmly, "I'm not. For all intents and purposes, Johnny's a warrior. He's a whiteman but he's still a warrior. He's got the warrior creed and he'll only negotiate out of that. We might not understand that but we have to respect it. We show respect to him and he'll show it back, it's that simple. I go in or I fly home. I won't be responsible for the outcome if you refuse to respect the tradition behind everything here."

"He's serious?" Dodge said to Nettles.

"Oh, yeah, Cap, he's serious."

"Then I guess he goes in. I don't agree. But if he's willing to take the risk, I've got hostages I need back in the daylight and a bad guy I need in custody. Dave, you're our phone guy. Reverend, I have to tell you, my concern is that Gebhardt just wants to even the score with you by taking you out with him. But, if you feel it's the only way, it's the only way."

I thought of our solemn oath. "Johnny won't hurt me," I said.

"I wish I had your faith," he replied.

"So, we make contact," O'Fallon said. "Tell him you're on your way. Get him to crack the downstairs doors. But if we have a shot, do we take it?"

The officers looked gravely at each other.

"No," I said suddenly. "I won't be used as a lure. I won't be a tool for assassination."

"But you know that this all might boil down to us having to do that, Reverend?" Dodge asked.

"Yes," I said, sadly. "I know. But he wanted me here for a reason. A reason bigger than simply being his mediator. Once we find out what that reason is, I believe we'll be able to disarm this whole thing."

"It still might be simple revenge," Hager stressed.

"Yes, it might. I've considered that, perhaps, I might be a symbol. That taking out, as you say, a sell-out preacher is an unimpeachable statement. But I don't think so"

"Your faith has some pretty iron balls, Reverend," O'Fallon said with a grin.

"Yes. The Holy Kahoonies, they're called," I answered to laughs all round.

Nettles and I moved to Dodge's office where we outlined the process for the negotiations. Nettles would maintain a phone contact with me while I met with Johnny. Because he had not requested a helicopter or a car, the police were assuming he did not plan to come out alive. They'd chosen to treat the situation as if Johnny was prepared to sacrifice everyone, himself included, and now me as well. While we were talking, the tactical team would still be shopping for an avenue of approach. I would not mention this, because if it came down to saving all the hostages' lives at the loss of his, Johnny would be eliminated. When the team had achieved an access route, Nettles would tell me the code words "No one has to die." Until then my focus should be on maintaining Johnny's composure and using the threads of our friendship to maneuver him to surrender. Any requests for money, cars, helicopters or whatever would be handled through Nettles and they would be prepared to consider anything for the safe release of the hostages. When there were no questions remaining, Dodge shook my hand firmly, wished me luck and we went back into the squad room.

"He's on the phone, Bri," Carleton said, holding the receiver towards me.

"Go ahead," Dodge said, laying a hand between my shoulders. "It's take-off time."

I closed my eyes and murmured a quick prayer. The phone felt like a sodden weight and as I raised it to my ear I caught Nettles's eye. He flashed me a thumbs-up and picked up another handpiece to listen.

"Johnny?" I said, rather shakily.

There was a small chuckle over the line and I had a flash of the reed-thin boy of twenty-five years before.

"Hey," he said.

"Hey."

"Bottom of the ninth here, Josh."

"Yeah, I guess."

"I had to go to the bull pen."

"Yeah, well, no shame in that. Everyone needs a good closer."

"Yeah. You comin' in?"

"Hey, wouldn't miss it! You want I should bring anything?"

"Nah. Well, yeah. They probably know about Mr. Svenson's medication. Bring that and maybe something for headaches. There's a few people here complaining about stress. See what you can do."

"Sure. I should be over fairly soon. You'll meet me at the doors downstairs?"

"Check. Actually, I'll send one of the others. Don't wanna give the boys the benefit of an open shot, you know?"

"Suggestion?"

"Suggest away."

"Let the pregnant woman open the door for me. Then let her walk. I'll reseal the door if you tell me how."

"Sounds fair. I didn't know she was expecting, otherwise I wouldn't have kept her. Deal."

"Good. See you in a few."

"Check," he said and disconnected.

The officers looked at me with a new respect. Dodge clapped me on the back and Nettles just grinned.

"Nice move," he said. "That's one less life we have to worry about."

"Two," I said.

"Yeah. Two."

"He agreed easily enough," I said.

"Yeah, he did. That's a good sign. You got any more you wanna tell me before we sink our choppers into this thing, Joshua? Now's the time."

"Yeah," I said, leaning back in my chair, "maybe just a couple things."

"Fire away."

I unfolded the last letter I'd received from Johnny.

*W*e are the children of someone else's history. We are born and we die under the shadow of a foreign sense of time. We carry within us the infertile seeds of promises sewn by the hands of greed. Withered and dried, they are lodged in our breasts like arrows, oozing their poisons, singing their histories.

Those are his words, not mine. I could never come up with anything that poetic or profound, could never touch the heart of the struggle in that way. All of us carry our woundings around within us like arrows.

I've just come out of the mountains. I spent the entire winter up there. I can't tell you exactly where but it's a special place, an alpine meadow high up in the Rockies. In the Long-Ago Time the People would come to celebrate the powers of nature. All nations would gather and the Great Hoop of the People would form in that meadow to restore itself through ceremony and prayer. Great stories were told, and even now you can feel the incredible power that resides there. Above it, the sky is a tremendous bowl, like a pipe bowl, the universe gathered within it. The mountains stand around it in a huge circle like a medicine lodge with all the natural world nestled between its ribs. The land veritably pulses with energy. I stayed in a teepee through the whole winter. I wanted to know how it felt to have your life so connected to the power of nature. To have nothing but a hide between yourself and the world. To have nothing but a fire, burning the wood you gathered, cooking the meat you hunted, for security and warmth. To have only your need for survival to lean on when the winds howled and the snow deepened around you. To feel the real power of this universe. To try to see and feel myself in the face of that power. They all said I was crazy but I needed to know what it was I was fighting for. Conflict isn't fighting unless you carry the weapons of belief and the tangible sense of the heartbeat you're fighting to protect. If you don't have that, all you have is politics, anger and bravado. Anger isn't courage. That's another thing he said once. Courage is born in humility, a humility born of the land. After this winter I'm starting to know what he meant.

There was always a thick bed of spruce boughs and hides on the floor to keep away the frost and the fire kept the inside warm and comfortable through even the deepest chill. I'd brought a pile of books and a small sketch book. My friends had helped me gather a few elk and moose hides that I wanted to work, so I had plenty of projects to occupy my time. Most days I would chop wood, rig a snare, hunt or just head out across the meadow on snowshoes or on foot if the snow wasn't all that deep. Most of the time it was.

I'd learned how to fletch arrows with feather and sinew from an old Cheyenne guy the summer before and I set to work doing that. I'd gathered the shafts and a thick switch of Osage orange that I wanted to make into a bow. When I left that meadow I had a handmade bow with a sinew string and thirteen fletched and sinewed arrows with a parfleche quiver. I made pair of moccasins too. But the thing that I learned the most from was sitting there night after night scraping and shaping the fluted length of a pipe stem.

Not just anyone can have a pipe. Being a pipeholder is an honor bestowed upon those who have proved themselves spiritually and morally worthy. But I'd learned that we can have pipes of our own. Not the sacred redstone pipes you see in ceremonies but harder gray stone pipes. So I sat down and began shaping the stem. It's a complicated process and it requires your utmost attention. I carry it with me in a pipe bag I made out of elk hide. Someday I want to either make a bowl or get fortunate enough to have one given to me, but for now, that pipe stem and the teachings it brought me are my most cherished possessions.

While I carved, whittled and sliced that length of wood into shape, I thought about nothing else except what it was to be used for. Maybe it's part of the mystic or monastic experience that says solitary work and musing on spiritual matters results in an enlightenment, an elevated awareness, an epiphany even. Christ had his forty days in the wilderness, after all. I began to see what this life of mine was all about as every inch of that pipe stem took shape. We all have a purpose here, some gift we emerge with that we carry into the great mix, and I'd assumed all along that mine was to be a warrior. I thought my life had prepared me for that — the aloneness, the bleakness, the loss and the anger.

But as I worked on that pipe stem I began to realize that I had no idea what my purpose was. The stem, as you know, is made of wood and symbolizes all living things, life in this reality. But the stem also symbolizes humility. It is wood after all, a finite thing, like life. Only when the stem is joined to the bowl does it become a sacred item. Because the bowl is faith. The bowl symbolizes the universe and all it contains, the eternal, the invisible. Humility and faith require each other to be vital energies. That's a spiritual law. You can't have one without the other. When the humility that comes from life is joined to an eternal faith, a reliance on the unseen, the invisible forces of the universe, it is a sacred union. The People used the pipe to symbolize that sanctity, that wholeness, and to anchor their lives with it. That's why a pipe ceremony is such a solemn ritual, because of the critical joining of humility and faith. I knew all of that but I'd never considered it in the context of myself. I'd been too distracted, too intent on the display of my allegiance, the great fireworks and fusillade of my loyalty, my worthiness, my mettle, my strength. I began to realize that courage without faith and humility is just the strut and preening of a fragile vanity. I'd been a strutter all along. Staatz's words came back to me again, only this time rife with meaning. Conflict isn't fighting without belief and the tangible sense of the heartbeat you're fighting to protect, he said. I got a tangible sense of that heartbeat through the storms and howlings of that Rocky Mountain winter. I felt the humility that the land and the unseen powers of the universe ask of us. I felt the tough, elastic resiliency that is born through recognition of that humility and the tougher sinew of a faith born of survival. I found courage. I found my warrior essence.

See, there's a conceit to this warrior thing. That's the big lesson I learned in that meadow. There's also something that you'd probably call grace. The conceit lives in the belief that you carry within yourself the

*power to alter things. To perpetuate the way of the People. Conceit tells
you that power is enough, life force is enough, grit, determination, force-
fulness are all enough. The conceit is fueled by bravado. Most of us, I
think, at least me, were being warriors of conceit.*

*But grace lies within the application of the teachings. The teachings
ensure the survival of the warriors, not the reverse. I lived under the warrior creed that "it's a good day to die." I believed that this meant that I
was brave enough to face death in order to fight for the People. I was
wrong. "Today is a good day to die" doesn't suggest sacrifice. It suggests
acceptance, humility. When warriors headed out for battle it was after
prayer, earnest prayer for the survival of their families, survival of themselves and for the well-being of their enemies. If you can face conflict
praying for your enemy as well as yourself, you enter that conflict armed
with humility, belief and faith, and if you come armed with those
weapons, it is indeed a good day to die. You can face your Creator knowing you've discovered wholeness, rightness and yourself.*

*Anybody can die in battle. In the history of the world, millions have,
but that doesn't qualify them as warriors. I know that now. The warrior
way is about a principled living. It's about carrying the spirit of the People
and their beliefs within you, acting upon them, living them. That's what
perpetuation is all about. It's not fighting to bring back the wigwam or the
buffalo hunt. They have passed like a shadow across the prairie grass,
like Sitting Bull said. But the spirit of them is still here and that's what we
need to fight to perpetuate. The tangible sense of the heartbeat. The
heartbeat that resounds in the sweat lodge, the pipe, the drum, the languages, the stories, the teachings, the connection with the land, the day-
in and day-out motions of the People. Those are the tangible things we
can pass on to the next generation, the things we can fight to protect. But
we have to live them first. You can't be a warrior without a tangible sense
of that heartbeat. You can't help soothe wounds without having felt them
yourself, without having eased your own pain. And that's the grace of the
warrior way. You become a fighter only when you know what it takes to
heal. Without that, all you have is politics, anger and bravado. If you
carry the spirit of those things within you, the tangible echo of that
ancient tribal heartbeat, then it doesn't matter what happens politically.*

It really doesn't. Because your spirit and the People's spirit will survive forever. In the end that's all we really have. Our cultural souls. Salvation? It's knowing that.

If I'm to fulfill this destiny of mine, I need to find somewhere to cultivate the faith, somewhere to learn what the mechanics of that are, how to live it. Funny, eh? I sound like you. I'm starting to think that maybe faith is a lot like inventing baseball. The only way to get it inside you is to get inside of it.

"**S**omehow I always thought it would be more," I said when I'd finished reading him the letter. "I thought for eight years that he'd eventually reappear but it would be more pacific, serene, spiritual. He sounded like he was on the verge of great discoveries. I have to confess that I'm at a genuine loss about how the man who wrote that letter got to be ensconced in an office building pointing guns and taking hostages."

"Me too. Guess he missed it," Nettles said.

"Missed what?"

"The Salvation Express," he said and gestured upward.

"It comes around again," I replied.

"It does?'

"Yes."

"Think this is the time?"

"We can only hope," I said as we headed for the car.

War zones shrink you. Perhaps there is in all of us a primal caution that reduces us to a Paleolithic prowling, a hunkering down on the haunches of our past, when the most elemental danger is found lurking at the edges of our worlds. We're perched suddenly on the point of fight or flight and our innate sense of survival responds with a shocking immediacy. We cower against the rocks and bushes. Peering around us with darting, feral eyes, nostrils flared and every nerve and sinew bunched taut, our bodies compressed, flattened, diminished for the pounce or the bounding away, we become physically lessened and spiritually more. It's a curious paradox, this outwardness and inwardness. We become ourselves because of it. It's not so much the lurk and leer of death that elevates us in the face of war as the tintinnabulation of life within and around us.

Life. The primal desire.

We entered a war zone that morning. We left the city and all I'd come to accept as normal behind us and slid silently into a panorama of tension. It's difficult to equate the words we use to describe society — civilized, democratic, just — with automatic weapons, bulletproof vests, camouflage, rocket launchers, helicopters and hordes of personnel. The flicker of police lights, the crisp bustle of movement, the frantic whir of chopper blades and the crush of the crowd beyond the police tape did not heighten things, they merely slowed them down.

I existed in a frame-by-frame world. Nettles handing me a bottle of pills. Dodge leaning close to talk with officers near the front doors. Waving us over. Nettles placing a hand over my shoulder. Cameramen hustling in a bow-legged trot. Native people under banners waving fists of encouragement. Officers kneeling behind cruisers with hands on their holsters. The police creating an opening in their huddle that Nettles and I eased into. All heads turning towards the glass doors. Frantic motion all around. A vested constable duck-walking with a hand-held radio, handing it to Dodge. Dodge gesturing to me. Nettles grim-faced, eyeing me. Sudden emptiness around me. The glass doors looming larger and darker with each step. A woman's face behind the glass, ashen, shaking hands peeling duct tape from the handles. The door cracking open. Stepping out. Eyes pleading. Gone. A yell of victory. The unmoving air of the lobby. Johnny's voice yelling something about the package on the floor. I tape it securely to the door handles and turn to see him, yards away cradling a rifle, pointing its barrel towards the elevators. We enter and feel the push of the lift. I see his eyes. Blue. Impossible blue.

The doors slid open on the fourth floor and we stepped out. He seemed taller than I remembered him, thicker with years but still possessing the same animal grace. A bold smear of red covered one half of his face, with two black wavy lines running from his hairline down beneath his chin. He wore a single eagle feather in his hair, which hung in two braids with a smaller, thinner braid on the left side. On his feet were a pair of fringed moccasins that reached to just below his knees. He had a bone and leather choker around his neck, and a pale chambray shirt under a fringed and beaded hide vest. The beaded designs were pyramidal, one on each shoulder, front and back, green, yellow and white. The colors of growth, enlightenment and wisdom according to the teachings of the Medicine Wheel. With the paint on his face, his features were stark, the boyish good looks I remembered hidden except for the eyes, which looked out at me strongly, directly and clear. We studied each other in silence. There was a smile at the edges of those eyes and I wanted to reach out and hug him to me.

He nodded. "Hey," was all he said.

"Hey."

"Welcome to my kingdom," he said expansively.

"Thanks. Any coffee?"

"Sure. It's instant, but what the hell."

"What the hell."

"You okay?"

"Me? Yeah. You?"

"All right. I haven't slept much. Spotlights through the windows all night. Feel like I should be doing vaudeville or something."

"The situation does have its burlesque qualities," I said.

"You're telling me. Let's get to the boardroom. I don't like keeping those people tied up any longer than I have to."

"They're not tied up all the time?" I asked, surprised.

"Hell no. We got cable, there's cards, food, this place is a country club. Tonight we're gonna tune in a ball game!"

"You're not afraid they'll run? Try to overpower you?" I asked.

"Nah. There's no heroes here. Everyone just wants to get home without holes. Besides, we have an understanding." he said.

"An understanding?"

"Yeah. Respect. They respect me enough to behave themselves and I respect them enough to let them have movement most of the day. The failure of that understanding is implied," he said and offered a crooked little grin and a small lift of the rifle.

"You'd shoot them?"

"Me? Are you crazy? No. It's them," he said, hooking a thumb towards the windows. "Outside. They're the dangerous ones here. They're the ones who wanna play out High Noon. That's our understanding. I'm their protection!" he said.

"You're their captor," I replied.

"Well, in a manner of speaking. I mean, I've got the detonator and all, but as long as I'm alive and well, the boys aren't gonna come crashing in here shooting and blowing things up in the name of justice, propriety and the ghost of Matt Dillon. As long as I'm okay, they're okay. And besides ... no one's got the joke yet."

"What joke?"

"You said it yourself, Josh. The situation's got its burlesque qualities. Only this isn't a burlesque so much as it is counting coup," he said.

"What are you talking about?"

He smiled, a warm generous smile that broke out of the starkness of the war paint as suddenly as inspiration through ennui. He put an arm around my shoulder and directed me along the hallway towards the far boardroom and the captives. My edginess lapsed somewhat in the boyish closeness.

"I don't know if you ever found this out. I think maybe you have to be pretty connected to the old way to have it given to you. But I'll tell you anyway," he said, ambling casually up the hallway. "In traditional times our men would go into battle to defend their territory. They went armed with the knowledge that life is the most sacred of things. Theirs, the world's, their enemies'. Knowing that, they entered those conflicts with the desire to simply touch their enemy. They carried short curved staffs decorated with furs and feathers to represent living things and painted with symbolic designs and colors to represent the spiritual world. Those sticks were called coup sticks. As the two sides converged the trick was to touch your enemy with your coup stick. It was seen as a far greater measure of integrity and courage to be able to reach out and touch your enemy than to take his life. Warriors then recognized that anyone could take a life. That's always been easy. It's much harder to grant life, especially to an enemy." He stopped to lean against the wall casually.

"But they needed something they could display as a symbol of their bravery. So when they braided their hair, they braided an extra little braid on the heart side. Like this," he said, grabbing the tiny third braid I'd noticed. "It's called a scalp lock — a warrior braid. When they went into battle the trick became to touch your enemy and cut off his scalp lock. Unlike Europeans, no one had to die for battle to be victorious, no one had to be crushed, or subjugated. They just took the warrior braid. The whiteman, of course, bastardized the tradition. He saw it as taking the whole scalp. Killing a warrior and dishonoring him by taking his hair. That's where the Hollywood notion of Indians taking scalps came from. Same with hair. They'd have us believe that Indians wore their hair parted neatly in the middle and braided. We didn't. We parted it on the heart side to remind us to always live heart first, not head first. Counting coup pretty much disappeared after settlement started. Our notions of courage and victory got swept up into the general mishmash like everything else. But it's still possible to count coup these days. You just have to use a little science, that's all." He winked at me.

"So, are you saying that no one's going to die here, Johnny? Is that it?" I asked cautiously.

"I'm saying no one's going to die. And that's the joke they haven't got yet!" He leaned in close to me and glanced over his shoulder, bugging out his eyes and arching his eyebrows. The old Johnny. He cupped one hand close to my ear and whispered, "Because there's no explosives."

"What!"

He grinned slyly. "There's no explosives."

"What about downstairs? I retaped the dynamite to the door handles myself."

"No. You *thought* you retaped the dynamite to the door handles. Anyone who was looking only *thought* they saw you do it. They only *thought* the entranceway was sealed and primed. But it's not real. Well, yeah, the dynamite is real, but the wires and stuff? I faked it. I'm no mad bomber, Josh. The only thing I ever blew up was a story or two." He grinned broadly. "You can learn anything from books, Josh."

I was flabbergasted. "But the commissionaires. The knapsack. The detonator."

He laughed. "It was all acting. Acting. Props. I created the illusion of a well-thought-out, well-prepared occupation and I played the part of a grim, rational desperado. That government guy Mueller bought it hook, line and sinker and he sold everybody into believing it. When I let those four hostages go I made sure they saw me painting myself, saw me checking ammunition, got a good long look at the detonator, everything. Right down to loading and stuffing the derringers in my moccasins. And they bought it all because it's perfect timing. Theater is timing. Everyone's so shook up over Oka and the firepower and the masked Warriors that the idea of one crazy waving guns and planting bombs in solidarity isn't so big a stretch."

"You have got to be kidding," I said.

"No joke," he replied firmly.

"But why?"

"Burlesque." He grinned. "Camp. Irony. Farce. A ludicrous representation. What better way to show the effects of a forced occupation than to perform an occupation yourself?

"Welcome to the frontlines," he said quietly.

"I'm lost here," I said. "I'm not sure I get what you're trying to tell me."

"It's a performance piece, Josh. Five hundred years ago they landed here and began a forced occupation of our land. They *invaded*. They wanted conquest. Why do you think the Spaniards called themselves *conquistadores*? Because they sought to conquer. To conquer the land, to conquer the people they found here. Only they called it exploration and discovery. Euphemism is as strong a weapon as bullets and steel, you know. But how can you be a conqueror when you get *welcomed* on your arrival? How do you call yourself a discoverer when you were lost in the first place? Columbus didn't discover America. It was never lost. He was! Can't you see the farce in that? The broad comedy?" He rattled it all off with piercing eyes.

"Sure. Okay. It's a tragic comedy. So?" I asked.

"So this occupation is built on the same lies. Rightness. Power. Destiny. The people who are the victims of this occupation, the apparent victims anyway, are in this room here," he said, indicating the boardroom. "They're sitting there hog-tied. Incapable of motion. All of their rights are gone. In all of this great country they're forced to stay in one small piece of it. They have no political voice. They're only recognized as humans when I bequeath a little humanity. They're under my *care* because I arrived here with power. I conquered. And I conquered with *lies*. I made them less by making myself more. And that's all okay to me as long as I can still believe that I'm right, that power gives me the right, that it's my destiny as a warrior and that history is a tool for justification. This fourth floor starting to sound a little like North America? Like Canada?" he asked.

I remembered the American Indian Movement's occupation of Alcatraz Island and how the manifesto they issued to the US government likened the conditions there to a typical Indian reservation. That had been theatrical, dramatic and effective as long as the occupation lasted. Once it was over, however, little was ever made of the action and it remained a small satirical footnote in the annals of the Indian movement. The idea behind Johnny's action was not new. It was bold, and definitely outrageous, but not new. I asked him how long the message would have credence once a resolution was reached.

"That's why you're here," he said. "I'm going to be seen as an eccentric at the very least. Probably more in the vein of a criminal sociopath with a warped sense of humor. That's what they'll try to make me out as. They'll discount anything I might say and any allusion I might draw to the truth of things. So I need a spokesman to make sense of it all. I created a caricature here with the war paint and the guns and shit. Right down to the little derringers in my moccasins. That's all anyone's going to be able to see after it's all over, and I need them to be able to see the *story*. The coup that's been counted here. I need you to tell them," he said solemnly.

"Why me?" I asked.

He looked at me from out of the war paint and I could see the pain that lived at the edges of his eyes. Pain that had always been there in various squints and creases and looks. Pain that I never fully recognized until that very moment. He held the look for what seemed an eternity and I could sense the struggle he was having bringing the emotions to language.

"Because you and Staatz were the only ones who ever knew," he said quietly.

"Knew what, John?" We were both surprised at the sudden propriety. I suppose it was my way of recognizing the unveiling of a truth, a solemnity reserved for confessionals and ritual.

"Knew that I was supposed to be a warrior. That I've done everything out of love and not obsession. That I'm not crazy. That I'm not a radical loony," he answered humbly, fixing me with those mesmerizing eyes.

"Staatz is gone now but they'll listen to you. You're a preacher, a man of faith. You have no agenda, no politics, no subversive tendencies. They need the message to come from a man like that and

I need you to help me finish this in a good way. They can't rush in with you here. They have to play it out and let me play it out to the conclusion I've decided on."

"And what conclusion is that, John?"

He grinned again at the sound of the name.

"You're frock is showing," he said.

"Sorry."

"Don't be. It's who you are." He looked away. "The conclusion is that nobody dies. Nobody dies. See, they think that we think like they think, and we don't. They think that this is about conflict, about flagrant challenge, about some zealous desire for revenge and retribution. But it's not. It's about resolution. So's Oka. So's every instance where the People have stood up and protected themselves. Always. Everywhere. Just like this. We walk out of here and we tell the story. Let the power of the symbol be the message. We make sure we know exactly what it is we're going to say and we walk out of here. Everybody goes home safe. Except me. I go to jail, but that's a sacrifice I was always prepared to make."

"And you want me to act as your spokesman? That's it?"

"No, not entirely," he said firmly. "I need you to help me figure out how we're going to get everybody out and not weaken my position. I can't appear to have an illogical script. It has to be a strong final act. When the curtain comes down on this baby I want them to be hungry for more. I need you to help me write it."

I was irritated. "You're making it sound like all we're doing is writing a play here."

"We are," he said and grinned. "We are. A human comedy. Because they won't listen to politics any more. They won't listen to leaders who speak in terms of human rights and moral obligation. Hell, they won't even listen to those who speak on spiritual terms. They being the politicians. They being the media. They being the people who consume the stories and consume the rhetoric. Everybody. Canadians. They don't listen any more. They need a story told in terms they can relate to. Something they can laugh about, cry about, pack around in their bellies for a while. Something that'll sneak up on them in the dark of their nights like they think Indians do. We don't necessarily need weapons and masks to make our point. It helps sometimes, sure, but what we really need is a story powerful in its implication. A palpable truth, you know?"

"But what if they miss it?"

"Some of them will. They always have. Shit, look how many people think that *Gulliver's Travels* was a cute story about giants and dwarfs. But some of them will get it. The learned, the enlightened, the creative, the inspired, the recovering wounded. They'll understand. And those are the kinds of people who can help change things. Those are the kind of people we need to speak to about our survival. The ones who understand intuitively that surviving isn't about going back, it's about learning how to pull out the arrows and heal. Everybody needs to heal, Josh. Not just the Indians."

"This whole thing is about healing?"

"Yeah."

"But you were the one who told me that what we needed to do was fight, to be warriors and fight. The only message I ever got from you has been warrior this and warrior that. I have to tell you that this plan of yours doesn't sound much like a warrior thing. It doesn't sound like you."

He gazed at me again for a long moment. "That's because I learned something about that. Something about warriors and something about me."

"You changed?"

"Yeah. Big time."

"How?"

"What?"

"How?"

"And you said you weren't a real Indian!" he said mischievously, and we both grinned at the old joke. "Let's go untie these people, let you talk to them for a while, reassure them, talk to your phone contact, and then I'll tell you all about it. Then we can work on getting us off this stage gracefully. Okay?"

"Okay."

"Great. Let's get to work. I only hope that you're not like me right now."

"How's that?" I asked.

"Gettin' kinda tired of my occupation!" he said and smirked through the paint.

We untied the hostages and Johnny introduced me as the chief negotiator, news that they greeted with relief. Several of them gathered at the coffee urn, all of them careful to avoid the windows. Johnny had secured couch cushions from various waiting rooms and these were strewn along the walls. Some people lay down to rest. A small group turned on the television, two or three others just sat numbly.

The news was being broadcast live from the front of the building. The reporter identified me and said that my arrival spelled a probable break to the standoff.

Nettles was cautious when I called him. I told him that we were just sitting now to plan and that I would get back to him when we had something concrete. I assured him that the captives were safe and healthy and that things were moving in the right direction. We agreed to have contact at least every hour. If I failed to make contact they would increase their efforts at finding an armed resolution. He stressed the word *resolution*.

As the captives watched in bug-eyed wonder, Johnny reverently assembled a small pipe, blessed it in the smoke of a sweetgrass braid, filled it with tobacco, lit it and offered smoke to the powers of the four directions, the earth and the sky, then smoked himself and passed the pipe to me. I sensed the discomfort of the people as they watched us and I realized in that moment how easily misunderstanding can breed fear. To uninitiated eyes the ceremony must appear heathen, pagan, prehistoric. To us, the acolytes, it was a ritualized joining to the divine. We placed ourselves in the circle prescribed with that pipe as its center. The circle of life. The circle of humble, honest belief and reliance on the eternal and the unseen. From such a position we could talk without fear. The story he told was compelling.

For three and a half years following our brief reunion in British Columbia he had wandered like a latter-day knight errant. Without Staatz he had to find his way around as best he could, and his journeys took him to a wide variety of settings, each with their accompanying angst and anger. Barriere Lake, Restigouche, Lubicon Lake, Temagami and Ottawa. He'd gone searching for a venue for his anger and they'd always been easy to find, and he had assimilated a lot of politics, rhetoric and resentment. From one confrontation to the next he brought his rehearsed diatribe and found acceptance, but never satisfaction. Then he'd decided that the search for fulfillment had to have more substance beyond the shouting and mere resisting. That was when he decided to spend a winter in the teepee.

He'd come out of the mountains with a hunger. A bona fide spiritual hunger, he said. He wanted to know more about the way. More about the preservation of the spirit of the warrior way he'd gotten a glimpse of with the help of the pipe stem. For a few months he'd traveled around and asked people at gatherings and powwows where he could go to learn more. Most of the answers were standard, like finding an elder, going to the sweat lodge, things he'd already done. Then he heard the story of Chief Tall Bear. Chief Tall Bear was chief of a small band of Cree in northern Alberta. He was a traditional person who practiced the old ways in all his affairs. He saw the effects of colonization on his people, in the way they changed their values, their beliefs, their morals and their behaviors with each incursion of the outside world. He watched the spirit of the old ways dwindling and dying amongst his people. He watched his language become replaced with English, watched as storytelling was replaced by television, as alcohol and drugs robbed young people of their spirit and their vision, as violence and abuse began to run rampant in his community, as despair and hopelessness led to suicides, as more and more people walked away from their communities and lurched towards the glittering promise of cities, only to return broken inside and crying. And he watched as another generation came into the world and learned nothing of their heritage and everything of the outside way. It sorrowed him so much that he decided to lead those who would follow away from the effects of that outside way.

One spring morning he left his reservation with a handful of believers and disappeared onto traditional land in the lap of the Rocky Mountains. There they set up a camp. At first it was a collection of teepees, but through the years it had grown into a log cabin settlement. On this land they revitalized the traditional way. They reperpetuated traditional child-rearing practices, spoke only their traditional tongue, taught only through story, ceremony and ritual. They hunted and gathered from the land. They performed the old rites. They held council fires and teaching lodges. They became a tribal people again. And as the years had passed, Tall Bear's Camp, as it was known, became a sacred place. People migrated there from every tribe and culture to experience the tribal way, to touch the heartbeat of their culture and carry it back with them into a world that only diminished that heartbeat. There was no electricity there other than the human kind that flows between people working together to preserve the truths that had sustained them though everything. Chief Tall Bear was a warrior in the truest sense, granting life back to his people, and he allowed the people who followed him to become warriors too. He'd died not long after the camp was established but his followers carried on his work. Johnny arrived there the autumn following his sojourn in the teepee. He arrived with a letter of introduction from a member of the Looking Horse family. Long ago a Looking Horse had been chosen to be the holder of the original pipe, the one that White Buffalo Calf Woman had brought to the People to teach them the medicine way. They were a respected family, and without such an introduction Johnny might not have been allowed to enter. Norville Looking Horse had been a friend of Staatz and his family and when Johnny told him about his winter in the moutnains and the glimpse of things he'd received, Norville had told him about Tall Bear's Camp. Johnny stayed there for six years.

The camp was tucked in the heart of the highest part of the foothills just before they lifted themselves up into mountains. The land was lush and rich. Without the disruptions of technology and invention the people lived as close to the traditional tribal way as possible. Everyone had a clan. Each clan had its own teaching lodge and each had its own area of responsibility to the whole. Johnny had entered as a member of the Beaver Clan. As a member of that clan he had learned to gather firewood and the responsibilities inherent in that role. Later he had become a hunter and learned the responsibilities of that function. He became a Caller, going around the camp announcing ceremony, activity or important news. And at the last he had been a helper or assistant to one of the elders. With each role he had been schooled not only in each task's relevance and importance to the collective but in the honor that resided in each endeavor. From the most menial to the most venerated, he'd learned the vitality of each function, how it gives life to the people. He'd learned the essence of the way. He learned to drum and sing. He learned to dance. He learned how to ask in a humble way for those things that escaped his understanding. He learned to listen. He learned to speak quietly and respectfully. And he learned how to pray. It had taken six years to learn those things but he'd stayed. The only times he ventured out was to attend a yearly ecumenical gathering on a nearby reserve and an occasional powwow. When he thought he'd learned enough he'd left with the blessings of his teachers, his elders and the people.

That had been two years ago. Now, he talked about how he understood his anger, had visited it, touched it, held it and let it go.

And he talked about me.

In quiet tones he spoke about the incredible love he'd felt for me from the very beginning. How he'd wished that my parents and I would come one day and carry him away into our world. He told me that all he knew of love back then had been tied up with all he knew of loyalty. Loyal meant you would never leave, never abandon, never choose another path and never change. He'd believed we would become Indians together, that we'd invent ourselves in that incarnation just like we'd invented ourselves as ball players.

Only after going back through everything during those six years in the mountains did he realize that it was himself he hated. Getting back at white people was getting back at Ben and Elly Gebhardt. All the yelling, the shouting, the finger pointing were the indictments he wished he could have leveled at his parents and himself. He was a warrior, all right — he'd just been fighting the wrong enemy.

He re-entered a world where little had changed. He'd traveled around and witnessed unrest and discontent. An anger born of frustration over human desires that went unrecognized, unheeded and abandoned, over breaches of trust that lodge like arrows in the breast of the people. Oka hadn't surprised him in its eruption, he said. Only in its delay.

It wasn't the People who had created AIM, warriors and warrior societies, he said, the whiteman had. They had made it all necessary through their denial of a people's integrity and worth.

"Their best device is history. They use history to qualify their subjugation of lands and peoples. But it's a purely selective device. They use only the parts they need to justify their exploitations. For instance, and this is a big one in terms of the People, they always say that if we were so strong in our cultural and spiritual way, why did we acquiesce so easily to the whiteman's religion? It must have been because we were simple savages in dire need of *real* salvation. Therefore, they were right to come here and convert us to their Christianity.

"But they conveniently leave out the essence of the story." He took a piece of paper and drew a small circle on it.

"See, in the Long-Ago Time, the natural world was the People's greatest teacher. The natural world manifested all the spiritual laws if you learned to look there. Truly spiritual people were those who learned the spiritual laws and practiced them in their daily life. Such people were held in high regard and the People wanted a special symbol that they could offer such persons to signify their special place in the circle.

"So they started with the circle itself, to represent wholeness and completeness. But that wasn't enough. So they put a long vertical line across the middle of that circle to represent a living relationship with the Creator." He drew a line down through the circle.

"Still, that wasn't enough. They thought about the examples they had seen in their villages. They knew that the spiritual ones reflected their spiritual relationship with everything around them, animals, plants, rocks, water and the People themselves. So they put another line horizontally across the circle to represent that relationship. Like this," he said and drew another line across the circle.

"A cross," I said quietly.

"Well," he said, "not in so many words. But a powerful symbol to them of someone who lived a life of harmony with the spiritual and the physical worlds. It was bestowed rarely because people who live in such a manner are very rare themselves. Those who received this honor might paint it on their medicine pouch or wear it beneath their clothing close to their heart. It was far too sacred a symbol to be displayed. And they were far too humble in the face of its implication.

"When the black robes arrived the People were amazed because they wore these symbols around their necks. They thought, These must be very spiritual beings because they wear this honor for all to see. These must be beings worthy of our honor, respect and attention. That's the real reason the priests were listened to and allowed to go about spreading the message of their Christian God. Not because of the rightness of the whiteman's religion or the power of their God. But because of trust. A trust with its roots in the divine. And they *knew*. The priests knew because once they learned the language and familiarized themselves with the iconography of the People they knew the real story, the real reason the land was opened in front of them. But it was never included in history because it didn't serve to justify either the continued invasion of land, mind and spirit or the impression of Aboriginal people as dull pagans. It would have only highlighted their breach of trust. So they buried it."

I was stunned. In all the time I had spent with Jacqueline she had never introduced me to this story. I was awed by the strength of the spiritual way that gave rise to the symbol and devastated by the abuse of that spiritual way that followed.

"Where did you hear this, Johnny?" I asked.

"In a sweat lodge one time. We were given the story to help in

our healing. Those are the only places you can hear those traditional stories. In places of healing," he said.

"But you're telling me here."

"Exactly," he said.

"**I**t's going well," I told Nettles when I checked in. "He's open
and negotiable."

"Glad to hear it. Glad to hear it. Sounds like no one has to die,"
he said pointedly.

"That's right. No one has to," I said while Johnny listened on
the extension.

"Any change in demands from in there?" Nettles asked.

"No. I need time, David."

"Take all you need. We're prepared to deal with it."

"I'll talk to you in an hour."

Secrets metamorphose. When we're children they sweep and
shift with the vibrancy of a world revealing itself like the colors
in a kaleidoscope. We press them to our chests like cherished
things, certain that they are our own vital discoveries, our own new
worlds unbesmirched by other eyes. They are our private joy. But
as we grow older and time works its harder, more practical magic
on our hearts and minds, our secrets become weightier things,
deeper and darker colors in a phantasmagoria of loyalties and
associations. They become our private pain.

As I hung up the phone I churned with uncertainty over the
pair of secrets I held. I wanted fourteen people to walk out of this
building safely.

As I watched Johnny move among his captives, asking each of

them about any discomforts or messages for their families, I knew his genuine concern for them. This was a man standing on and for belief. A man willing to fight for the survival of a people in the only way he knew. A people not his own except for the common unity of a way of faith and a way of being. A man brave enough, bold enough and strong enough to place his life in a sacrificial manner before an incredible opposition. A warrior. I was Indian enough to see the injustice that Johnny spoke of. There was indeed a farcical quality to the history of this land, and perhaps it might take a dramatic human comedy to bring the message into the living rooms.

"You know what I figure should happen in Oka?" Johnny said, approaching and folding a note pad into his chest pocket.

"No," I said, glad to be shaken from my mental stew. "What should happen?"

"Well, pretty much every Canadian, or at least pretty much every *white* Canadian, is insulted over the barricades. To them the Warriors are renegades, thugs, criminals. Right?"

"I suppose."

"And pretty much every white Canadian figures that although they might have a legitimate beef, they've no right to arm themselves and challenge justice, right?"

"Generally, yes."

"And pretty much every white Canadian figures they should be brave enough to show their faces instead of wearing masks, right?"

"Again, generally, yes."

"And they pretty much agree that it's a sad day for the country when their own army has to face-off against its own citizens, right?"

"Yes. Even more widely."

"And most of them are missing the farce, right?"

"The farce being?"

He grinned slowly. "The farce being that the Mohawks are defending sacred ground and their right to perpetuate their spiritual and cultural way. The army is defending a golf course and their right to inexpensive greens fees."

I chuckled. "Okay. So what should happen?"

"Well, I figure they should all walk out and face the army line. Just when the soldiers are getting antsy they should drop their weapons, pull out golf clubs and drive a few hundred balls at the ranks. And then just walk out. What a statement that would be!"

I laughed. He was right. It was farcical.

"Won't happen, though," he said, sadly.

"Why?"

"Because it can't. Because there's too much at stake there. That's why the farce is up to someone else."

"You?"

"I guess." He shrugged.

"Why?"

He sighed heavily. "Because if they take me out, Josh, it's just one life. But they'll still have to listen to me fall. Maybe it's hard for you or anyone to understand, but when you're a warrior you fight out of love. Love for your people, love for your enemy. Love for the ground we share. You can't fight out of hate, out of self-righteous anger, out of indignation or some jingoistic notion that your borders are everywhere. Those are just soldiers. I know you know that. It took me a long time to realize it but I know it now, and believe me, this is a good day to die."

"Because why?' I asked.

"Because I know the truth now."

"And that is?"

He looked at me with an unwavering peaceful face that shone through the slick ooze of paint. I had never seen that look on his face. "That I was always supposed to be a warrior," he said with dignity. "I was born with an Indian heart and an Indian mind. I was. I was if you believe that human purpose is to find your own humble place in the scheme of things, that salvation is a process. That we're not born to control but to belong. If you believe that your God is a living God alive in every thing and every body and that life is the most sacred thing. If you believe those things, then I was born to be and I *am* an Indian. Just as much as you, minus the blood and the skin of course, but just as much.

"I had the warrior thing wrong for a long time. But now I know the truth. And the truth is that being a warrior is living principled and moral ... and dying the same way. It's learning that the life all around you depends ultimately on kindness, respect, purity, har-mony balance ... and sacrifice. That's what being a warrior is all about. And there's another thing I know, too."

"What's that, Johnny?' I asked, humbled.

"I know that I'm a whiteman," he said with a slow grin. "That's *my* truth. The hardest one I've had to face. I'm a Germanic Caucasian male because that's what my Creator created me to be. I'm not an Indian. I never can be. I wasn't graced with that identity. As much sweat lodge time as I have, as much ceremony and ritual as I absorb and use, as much as I try to live the life, under the braids, the moccasins, the war paint, I'm still Johnny Gebhardt, *white guy*. My salvation lies in finding out what *that* means. Because I disinherited myself a long time ago. Tried to lose myself by redis-covering myself in an Indian motif. But I was created a whiteman and I need to explore that, and maybe cast it away once my explo-ration's over and return to the circle anyway. But I can't deny myself any longer. Can't go on living as a displaced person. Besides, I've never tasted Wiener schnitzel, never did the polka or visited the country."

He stood there looking out the windows and I knew how diffi-cult a journey this had been for him. Knew how treacherous denial's boneyard could be and how strong you become for the trek. I admired him with the pure exuberant zeal of boyhood that I knew whose secret I would bear, whose territories I would defend and whose blood I would protect with my own.

"Then I guess we'd better get busy getting out of here so we can get you on a slow boat to the Rhineland!" I said.

"Yeah. I'm about ready for home, wherever that turns out to be."

We sketched out a number of scenarios for surrender. The one we were leaning strongly towards had Johnny cropping his hair into a crewcut, borrowing some clothes from one of the hostages and negotiating his delivery to Nettles as the first released hostage. I would re-enter the building and return with the rest of the hostages, whereupon Johnny would identify himself in front of the TV cameras, making his statement and allowing himself to be secured in custody. He'd like it because, as he said, it showed that you never knew who the warriors were going to be. However, we decided that the identities of each hostage were quite likely known, especially to the tactical unit, who would need to know who it was they were supposed to be shooting at. Or at least we hoped they knew.

One by one we erased scenarios and settled on order. Or, at least, order in a fashion. Each hostage would leave the building carrying one of Johnny's handmade arrows. They would walk to the police line and wait there for the next one. When they were all safe and protected, I would walk out and lay his weapons down in front of the building. I would re-enter and we would walk together to make a statement of surrender in front of a television camera. I would follow him with a message about there never being any real threat on his part, about his compassion for his hostages, how they were representative of the captive situation of native peoples, and the necessity for everyone to look at the larger issue rather than focus on the criminality of this one situation. I would tell people that the demands he'd made for a special sitting of the House of Commons, for a United Nations tribunal, and for the withdrawal of the army from Oka were demands made to focus attention on the processes necessary for resolution, for the continued emancipation of all native people in the country. Only when we'd secured the right to speak would he allow the situation to defuse itself.

"And if they don't agree?" I asked.

He shrugged. "If they don't agree then we find another tack. If they don't agree it's just their way of telling me, telling us, that we still, despite everything, have no voice."

"But we will work towards finding another tack?"

"Of course. No one's going to die here, Josh."

"I know. But I think before we call Nettles we should fax the media and tell them exactly what the terms of surrender are. Arrange the scrum beforehand. That way, if it doesn't happen, they at least know the story."

"We should trust them?" he asked, eyebrows raised.

"We have to," I said simply.

"Josh, the media only want to hear from Indians when they're either dead, dying or complaining. We don't have to wear war paint anymore because the media paints it on us themselves whenever we push for something."

"But, Johnny, they're storytellers too. In our circle storytellers have a responsibility to tell stories like they receive them, accurately, without color or embellishment. We call it honesty. They call it ethics."

"You believe that?"

"We have to."

"Trust the integrity of the oppressor, right?"

"Right. In all his guises."

"Oooh, I like that! Okay. You wanna write the fax and I'll get busy figuring out what I want to say?"

As I watched him move across the room to a private place and begin scratching out his message to the world, I found myself saddened that I had missed the opportunity to be part of his migration to self-knowledge and truth. The mole journey we all must make to find our own salvation, to find the quality of light we reside in. He bent his head in thought, pen poised above the paper, and I uttered a silent prayer to the Creator watching over all of us that he be directed the words he needed, and that he be granted the ultimate reward of the true warrior. Peace.

I faxed the terms of resolution to the media. That's how I worded it. *Resolution.* I waited fifteen minutes before I picked up the phone to call Nettles.

He answered on the first ring. "You got me singing soprano here, Joshua," he said.

"What do you mean?"

"I mean alto's impossible with my nuts in a vise! We were going to discuss everything first. That's what our agreement was. What's up with faxing the press first?" he asked harshly.

"Expedience," I said. "The quick out, David. Johnny's not flexible on this and we don't have time to dillydally around trying to come to terms. Not with the shooters crawling through the rafters. Now everybody knows what's on the table. Now we can get busy and end this thing. Peacefully. Bloodlessly."

There was a lengthy silence at the other end. When he spoke again it was in a more conciliatory tone.

"Okay. How soon does he want to get this done?'

"Quite soon," I said.

"Okay. I'll push pause on the tac team. You rewind to the point about the statement. If this is going to be some radical swill-pushing, finger-pointing rhetoric, I don't think anybody needs it," he said.

"It won't be any of that. I expect him to come out with a measured response. It's like you said yourself, he's an articulate son-of-a-bitch."

He chuckled. "What do you mean, measured?"

"I mean, from what I can see, everything that's been accomplished up here has been accomplished through clarity, reason and with an obvious goal in mind. It's not slap-dash. Right now, he's gauging his response."

"What about you? What's your response going to be?"

"I'm simply going to tell people what I've seen here."

"And that is?"

"That is, right or wrong, I've observed a man with a sense of purpose. I will neither endorse nor denigrate that purpose."

"That's it?"

"That's it."

"And you have no idea what Gebhardt's message will be exactly?"

"No."

"Is he horning in?"

"Horning in?"

"Listening."

"No."

"Well, what about if we just keep the cameras pointed at him but don't actually shoot anything?"

"You can't."

"Why not?'

"Two reasons."

"Shoot."

"One, the media will expect a statement and they'll record it anyway. You can't stop that. Two, honor."

"Honor?"

"Yes. He's dropping all demands but these. He's willing to walk out and into custody. He's being honorable and all he expects from you is the same."

"You sound like defense counsel, Reverend."

"My integrity is on the line here too, David. And my life. I'm trusting that he'll allow me to leave unharmed along with all the others. If I can, can't you?"

"Look, Joshua, all I'm saying is that this is a guy who's crafty enough to establish this whole situation. He's a persuasive bastard. A grifter."

"I hear you. But I'm the one that's been up here, David. I'm the one who's talked with him, who's listened to him, and believe me, if you come across with an okay to what he's asking, no one gets injured. I'm staking my life on it," I said flatly. "Leave the cameras live."

"There's no vendetta? This isn't just some cooked campaign to nail you once you two are alone. No sense of that?"

"None."

"You're sure."

"I'm sure."

"Okay. I'll ring you as soon as I push it by Dodge. Me, I'd spring. But brass is brass."

"Try, David."

"I will. You be cool."

"Roger."

We didn't have to wait long. About ten minutes after I hung up, the phone buzzed and Nettles told us that Dodge had okayed the plan. First, there would be a swift tactical team response should anything amiss occur at any time throughout the release and surrender. While the hostages were being released I was to stand beside the door at all times, in full view of the police, to ensure my safety. When we exited he was to walk with arms raised behind his head and away from the weapons I had laid in front of the building. We would proceed to an area directly in front of a police van where Johnny and I would have the opportunity to make our statements to the press, which would be broadcast live over the CBC, and he would be arrested immediately after. I could, if I chose, accompany Johnny into custody, to ensure his safety. Nettles added that he had argued for that as a point of honor. I grinned and told Nettles that we would call as soon as we were ready to leave.

After a minute or two Johnny looked up at me with a half smile on his face. "It's almost over, then," was all he said.

"Almost," I replied.

He opened his duffelbag and removed a bow and a leather parfleche of arrows. He handed them to me and I studied them in amazement. The arrows were fletched with hawk feathers and glued with the same sinew that bound their tips to the shafts. The arrowheads were carved from pieces of bone, stone and antler. They were beautiful. The bow was a muscular-feeling piece of wood. Its length was rubbed to a dull sheen and the sinew that stretched from end to end thrummed with a primal basso energy. It felt like it had a song. The parfleche was decorated with the same pyramidal design that graced Johnny's hide vest, with the same green, yellow and white beads. The craftsmanship was exquisite, and I sensed that I was holding a part of a people's history in my hands.

"I want you to have these when it's over," he said.

"What?" I asked, surprised.

"They're yours. When I made these I hoped to get a sense of connection to the warrior essence. To understand how and why I chose to fight the way I did. I wanted to be armed with the old way. Only, to be armed the old way doesn't require weapons. But you *always* knew that. Intuitively, you always knew. This design you see is a mountain," he said, pointing to the parfleche. "The mountain is a symbol of faith — an enduring faith. And the colors represent the by-products of faith. I had to search for them, but you always had them. You were always armed the warrior way. I'm just sorry that I didn't know that sooner," he said with tears in his eyes.

I reached out and accepted his incredible gift. In the Indian way, you accept a gift with all the honor, humility and dignity with which it is offered. In that way you honor both the giver and the gift itself.

"I'm sorry too, Johnny," I said with a choked voice. "I'm sorry I didn't know how to reach you. That I let you leave without chasing after you and fighting for our friendship, that I didn't hear what you were trying to tell me."

"I'm sorry I couldn't tell you. And for denouncing your life and your wife the way I did. I was wrong, Josh. I apologize. Think she'd like to meet me someday?" he asked.

I smiled and wiped at my eyes. "Yeah. She would. Do you have an idea what my son's name is?"

"No. What is it?"

"Jonathan," I said, quietly. "Johnny to his friends. And to his dad."

"Good name. Can he hit?"

"Like a machine."

"It's only right. With a name like Johnny. Does he know about me?"

"Everything. Same with Shirley."

"Yeah?"

"Yeah."

"Josh, when I get out ..."

"We'll be waiting," I said, and he smiled.

We looked at each other openly and without fear. In his eyes I saw the energy and the life force, strong and resilient, directed now by compliance to a more benevolent spirit, a living force within him. In my eyes, he was not a warrior, a whiteman, a radical or a threat. He was my friend. Laughing Dog. Johnny Gebhardt. And as the moment stretched to its unspoken breadth he was as he had always been, a quality of light in which I stood.

"Me too," was all he said finally, quietly. And I knew.

❂

He scribbled away for about half an hour. When he'd finished I found an old IBM Selectric for him and for the next hour the clatter of the typewriter punched the time away. I gathered the hostages around me while Johnny typed his statement, reassuring them that the resolution of their ordeal was imminent. As a group we agreed that the women would go first. They were quiet, not even moved to question the idea that they would emerge carrying arrows. In their eyes I saw that hope has a light of its own. They looked around the room and I sensed they were seeing it in an entirely different way than they ever had before, that it would always represent something far deeper than simply another room they worked in. And so we are transformed by circumstance.

Johnny finished his feverish pecking and I made a call to Nettles to inform him that we were ready. We ran through the procedure one more time. I reiterated that the television cameras had to capture the entire event. Johnny would check to ensure that fact on a monitor at the commissionaires' desk. No broadcast, no resolution. There could be no alteration.

Nettles said they were eager to end it provided there was no hidden agenda on Johnny's part. I assured him there wasn't, and he agreed to our itinerary of surrender. We would move out within minutes and I would call from a downstairs phone to let him know when to expect my appearance at the doors.

"Good luck," he said brusquely and disconnected.

We told the captives our plan and they began preparing themselves for their return to the real world, tucking in shirt tails and primping hair, cosmetic alterations I found somehow amusing. Johnny distributed the arrows solemnly. A few hostages met his eyes: most just accepted the trim shafts and turned away towards the door. Finally, Johnny and I looked at each other, nodded, opened the door and stepped out into the hallway, Johnny first, checking for tac team members and then sweeping the barrel of his automatic weapon toward the far staircase. We approached it in a vague straggly line like kindergarteners on an outing, feet clumping clumsily along the nap of the carpeting. No one said a word. I traveled in the middle of the group with Johnny bringing up the rear. All along that passageway and on into the close quarters of the stairwell, I expected any minute a crash of rifle fire, the clatter of a smoke bomb or the swift, merciless slashing of an assassin ridding us of our captor.

At the commissionaires' desk I tuned in to the CBC broadcast from outside the building. It showed the doors in the distance and swept to the tops of buildings across the street to show snipers aiming at the doorway. For the first time I felt real terror.

"They're ready," I told Johnny.

"TV up and running?" he asked.

"Yeah," I said. "Johnny, there's snipers on the rooftops across from us."

"Figured," he said, matter-of-factly. "Probably more we can't see."

"We gonna be okay?"

"Sure! They can't kill me in front of a national audience."

"We're ready, then?"

"We're ready."

I called Nettles.

"Game time," I said.

"Good. Joshua — *be careful.*"

"David, nothing's gonna —"

"No! Nothing's secure until we get him in custody. No matter how much you think you trust him, this guy's dangerous! He's got a live audience now, he can make any kind of huge display he wants. *Be careful!*"

"Okay. I'm heading to the doors now."

"Joshua, I mean it."

"I know. See you in a few minutes, David." I hung up.

I moved towards the doors with the first woman. Swallowing hard and hands clasped in front of her chest, she looked at me with desperation, and I smiled reassuringly at her. The tape came easily off the door frame and I set the pseudo explosives on the floor. Johnny's handiwork was incredible. It looked for all the world as though the wires connected the dynamite to the detonating device. I toyed briefly with the idea that maybe it *was* real, and a chill unlike any I'd felt ran the length of my spine. I swallowed hard myself and pushed the door open. The woman stepped out to freedom, the arrow clutched tightly in her hand.

I watched as photographers scrambled for a shot. Beyond the cordoned area I could see people craning their necks, all motion stilled while the conflict unfolded before them. The woman walked unsteadily towards the line of police vehicles.

"Okay?" Johnny yelled from across the lobby.

"Okay," I said, waving the next woman to the door.

When the last man stepped out the door, I was a quivering bale of tension. I thought of Shirley and Jonathan waiting for me at home and of how far away that was from me right at that time.

I looked back across the lobby. We see each other so differently through the lenses of stress, and for a moment all I could see was the warrior, the caricature he had created, and I felt afraid, and very, very alone. Suddenly my fate was in the hands of a masked militant. A heavily armed and agitated rebel. I walked solemnly towards him, aware suddenly of the boundaries of faith that doubt and fear can prescribe around your world. I half expected each step to end in the eruption of the rifle he carried, the slam of metal against my flesh.

"Don't be afraid," he said and laid an arm across my shoulders.

We stood there for a moment or two watching the motionless line across the plaza. He gazed around him, exhaling long and slow, then looked at me.

"It's time," he said simply, unslinging the rifle and handing it to me. I felt a tremor of release inside my chest.

He handed me the pistol and the holster he wore around his waist. He reached behind his back and removed an army .45 from his waistband and handed it to me with an almost comical shrug. From inside his shirt he pulled a pair of grenades. They bore a threatening heft.

"Cement," he said. "I filled them with cement so they'd feel real."

He handed over a nine-inch stiletto from his waistband, two Chinese throwing stars form inside his vest and a thick, heavy knife from a pocket at the middle of his back. He handed each of them to me with a sly little grin. By the time he'd disarmed himself of additional magazines for each of the guns I was amazed at both the scope of his arsenal and the fact that he could have moved around with so much weight on his body. It was far too cumbersome for me and I settled on the rifle and the grenades for my first trip out.

I heard the click of shutters as I walked out. I heard the gasp of several people in the cordoned area and a vague rustle as people edged nervously away from the front of the crowd. David Nettles stood beside a van that had been moved into place since I last looked out and he nodded slow, solemn encouragement to me, indicating the presence of the riflemen with an upward swing of his eyes. I nodded. Television cameramen crouched, aiming their lenses at me as I swung around and headed back to the building.

I bent to pick up the remaining weaponry and Johnny sniffled slightly. When I looked up I saw a tear run down the unpainted side of his face.

"It's just another maze," he said, quietly. "Even after all I've learned, all I've been through, I'm still afraid that when I break out of the maze all I'm gonna find is another one."

"Faith is like that," I said.

"Yeah? Even for you?" he asked, wiping his eye with a knuckle.

"Even for me," I said. "Living with faith isn't about the absence of fear. It's about the presence of it. It's about always being poised on the diving board. Fear sends you back down, faith makes you soar."

He grinned. "You kept the letters?"

"Every one."

"Cool."

I clapped him on the shoulder and turned to load my arms for the last trip. I felt his eyes on me across the lobby and I knew that trust was the element of our friendship I'd needed to bring back. The feeling of sneakered feet above us in our maze. I could, if I chose, leave him in that building and secure my own safety now. Could abandon him to the forces of justice and perhaps even convince myself through the coming years that I had done the right thing. Those thoughts danced through my head as I walked out the door, and I thought too how easily the seeds of our own moral destruction can germinate within us, sprouted by the instinct for survival and watered by self-indulgent fears. I walked out and laid the weapons down beside the rifle and the grenades, looked briefly at Nettles, the implied safety of the right, the might and the law, and turned back to the building where my brother waited.

He stood just inside the doors, looking out at the scenario he'd created like an artist at a mural that only reveals itself fully on its completion. He handed me the bow and parfleche. There was weight inside the quiver, and when I looked I saw a beaded rawhide pouch.

"What's this?" I asked.

"My pipe," he said. "It's a good pipe. You have it. You're worthy."

"Johnny ..."

"No, Josh. You earned this. You told me a long time ago you'd come back to the People and bring them what you learned. Well, you learned the way of the pipe. Maybe not in the traditional manner, but you learned. You carry it inside you. You live it. So you take this pipe with you when you go back to them. Tell them about my search. Tell them about yours. And smoke it with them. Smoke it with the ones who need to learn how to make that mole's journey, Josh. The ones who need to find the gift of knowledge and of truth. You won't have to look for them. They'll find you."

"Johnny, I haven't gone back yet," I said.

"I know. But you will. You will."

"You're sure?"

"Never more. Just do me one favor."

"Anything."

"Every now and then, go sit and smoke it, alone or with someone special, behind that old equipment shed, up on the cliff in the Hockley and anywhere you feel I'd like. Someday we'll go there together and have a smoke, but for now, take the pipe. I'll be with you in spirit," he said, smiling sadly.

"No problem," I replied and reached out to touch his sleeve.

He hugged me then. Reached out and pulled me into a deep and encompassing hug that lasted forever, it seemed. We stood and we rocked back and forth in each other's arms. I closed my eyes and in the warmth of that embrace I saw us again as I would always see us, a reed-thin boy who could punch holes in the sky with a baseball seated beside a brown-skinned boy with shining eyes in the swishing arms of a willow tree, hands together, blood on blood, eternity ritualized in innocence, wonder and possibility. We released each other back into the adult world and he punched me lightly on the shoulder.

"Disarmed and cowardly, let's get on with it!" he said, reaching out to push the door open for me.

I stepped into the sunlight. The air on my face was invigorating. I closed my eyes briefly and pulled deep dollops of it into my lungs. Security a few steps away. The cameramen were scrambling to get the best shot and I looked at Nettles, who stood by the van, squinting our way. Johnny was just stepping though the door.

"Ah, shit, Josh!" he was saying with a laugh.

I turned. His face was animated through the war paint and as he cleared the doorway he bent suddenly.

"I forgot the derringers. Here," he said, reaching out towards me clutching the tiny pistols by their handles.

"*No!*" I screamed.

His eyes flashed in surprise and then even wider as his chest was blown open by a sudden rain of metal. He stumbled backwards against the door, slid slowly to the ground, leaving a wide red smear on the glass. He looked at me with a stunned expression, then slowly, as he slumped to the pavement, it was replaced by recognition, a half smile at the corners of his mouth.

The bow and parfleche clattered to the pavement and I dropped beside him. A pool of blood widened around him, slowly and deliberately. Behind me I heard footsteps hurrying our way and the yelling of officers controlling the crowd. There was a thick hum in the air and in my chest. I cradled my friend's head in one hand, the blood warm and sticky on the other that pulled the sides of his vest tighter around him as though to stanch the flow from his chest. He breathed raspily, a gurgle of blood seeping from his mouth. I looked up and saw Nettles and the other officers approaching with a gaggle of cameramen and photographers.

"Get away from him!" I yelled, hot tears suddenly streaming down my face. I pointed at Nettles. "You get them out of here!"

"Joshua —"

"No! *Get ... them ... away!*" I screamed.

I looked up and saw four snipers at the ready, weapons pointed at Johnny.

I looked at Nettles stonily. "You tell them to stand down," I shouted. "*Now!*"

He waved to the rooftops and the riflemen eased their weapons off their shoulders. He stood there looking blankly at me and I felt Johnny's hand tugging at my lapel.

"Josh," he whispered. "It's okay, Josh. It's okay."

His head slumped deeper against my chest and I pulled him

closer. Somehow I worked my way behind him and I pulled him as close to me as I could, his head now resting on my shoulder, my legs straddled wide alongside his and my arms supporting his head. I brushed his hair to the sides of his temples and watched as he struggled to breathe.

"Hang on, Johnny," I said quietly. "Hang on."

"No," he croaked. "I hung on long enough, Josh."

"The ambulance is right here, Johnny," I said, crying. "Don't worry. I won't leave you."

"I know," he said. "I know."

Hearing him groan, I hitched closer to him, pressing my body tighter to him so he could feel my warmth. At that moment all I could think of was that I didn't want him to be cold.

"Josh," he said, turning his head so he could see my face out of the corner of his eye.

"Yes, Johnny,"

"It's the bottom of the ninth."

"Yeah."

"You know what?"

"What, Johnny?"

"You know when they ... open the flap on the lodge ... and the light ... the light pours in?"

"Yeah."

"That's what it's like."

"Johnny ..."

"Josh?"

"Yeah?"

"You gotta go home now. You gotta go home."

"I know."

"Go home, Josh. Tell them."

"Tell them what, Johnny?"

"Tell them it's all about light."

"Light? What do you mean, Johnny?"

But Laughing Dog had made it home.

⊚

I don't know how long I lay there with the body of my friend clutched to me. I only know that it was long enough for me to realize how easily death displaces us. How departures leave us stranded here on a vain and uncompromising earth, alone in a territory without maps, without poems, featureless and foreign. How easily faith is numbed. How quickly you become exiled from yourself. I lay with my cheek pressed against his head, the warrior braid tattooing my face with its weave. I was vaguely aware of David Nettles coming into my view and of him kneeling beside me, gently pressing Johnny's eyes closed.

"Joshua," I heard, finally. "Joshua, we have to go now."

"What?" I asked thickly.

"We have to go, Joshua. It's over."

"Over?"

"Over. Come on," he said, taking my arm.

Over. I sat there running those two syllables through my mind. When I realized what he meant I looked up at him sharply. "It's not over," I said.

"Yes, it is, Joshua. He's gone. He's dead," Nettles said softly.

"I'm not," I said. "And as long as I'm not, he's not. You made a deal with me."

"A deal?"

"A deal," I said. "We get to make our statements. No statement, no deal."

"But, Joshua, we're past that now."

I said unashamedly though the tears that were coursing down my face, "If you think we're past it, you're not the man I thought you were."

He looked at me levelly, studying me.

"He wrote it down. I'm going to read it," I said. "I'm going to walk right over there and I'm going to flag down those reporters and either tell them I'm making the statement now or tell them you won't keep your end of the deal. They'll still get their story, David. I can tell it now, or I can tell it later."

"You're serious."

"Completely."

"Then I guess we'd better get over there. Can you make it okay?"

"I'll be fine. Get someone to cover him, okay?"

"Yeah," he said and waved towards the police line.

I reached into Johnny's vest and removed his folded statement, rose and walked with Nettles to the van that was supposed to have carried Johnny into custody. I didn't think about the blood on my shirt. I though only about Johnny and how this had to end the way he'd wanted it to end. I owed him that kind of loyalty. I'd pledged it.

Ed O'Fallon was clutching a handful of arrows. He handed them silently to me when we arrived at the van. A circle of reporters immediately surrounded Nettles and he explained that the perpetrator had capitulated on his promise to release everyone safely, that he had pulled a pair of concealed weapons from his boot tops, aiming them at Reverend Kane. He had been fatally shot by police snipers. He told them that I had requested the fulfillment of the terms of surrender, and then he stepped back and waved me over. A Canadian flag fluttered over the scene, and I thought how the fabric and texture of the country had been rent with the locking and loading of weapons in Oka and in the silent flow of blood from the body of Johnny Gebhardt. I stepped up, front and center to those cameras, and slowly unfolded the blood-smeared paper. I took a long, slow breath and disappeared into the words.

*W*e are the children of someone else's history. We are born and we die under the shadow of a foreign sense of time. We carry within us the infertile seeds of promises sewn by the hands of greed. Withered *and dried, they are lodged in our breasts like arrows, oozing their poisons, singing their histories.*

Indians die. They die from poverty, despair, futility, desperation, melancholy, assimilation, racism and hatred. Arrows fired from the bow of colonization. Arrows that seep their poisons into the life blood of the People. The poisons of violence, suicide, drunkenness, cultural alienation and racism itself. Thirteen arrows and thirteen poisons. We return those arrows and poisons to you today.

We return them because we no longer need them. We no longer need to suffer their woundings, their humiliations, their lingering malaise. We return them because they are your arrows. They did not originate from us. We no longer need them. And we no longer wish to die.

We know they come from you. Five hundred years has given us that knowledge. The People's troubles have manifested themselves throughout the entire brief history of your presence in this land and we say — shame on you. Shame on you for the death of vital cultures. Shame on you for the outlawing of ceremony and ritual, for the death of languages, for the rape and pillaging of resources and peoples, for the broken treaties, the suicides, the drunkenness, the violence, the poverty and the rejection of ourselves. Shame on you for five hundred years of arrogance, mute accep-tance and ignorance. Shame on you.

But, now, today, if we allow these woundings to continue, if we allow the poisons that seep into the life blood of our People to continue, if we allow the atrophy of our cultural ways, our languages, our teachings, our communities and our people to continue, if we allow our anger, our pain, our denial to continue to be inflicted on ourselves, then we say — shame on us. Shame on us for their perpetuation, knowing what we know.

So we return these arrows to you. There are thirteen. Respect, honor, faith, loyalty, sharing, kindness, trust, honesty, humility, acceptance, for-giveness, gratitude and love. These are the thirteen arrows we return to you today. They are the healing properties of our medicine lodges. They are the prayer poles of our Sun Dance arbors. They are the ribs of our sweat lodges and they are the spars that support the Great Hoop of the People. They are the foundation of our way. They are the reasons that we have lived, survived and perpetuated ourselves despite everything. They are the life blood we would fight to protect and we would die to honor.

Learn their healing properties and join us in the building of a new place
of healing within their framework. Within the framework of this country.
A new lodge where all can sit as equals.

That's what we are fighting for. That's what we seek to perpetuate.
That is what lies beneath the anger, the politics and the rhetoric. It is what
lies beyond the barricades, road blocks and occupations. Yet when we
stand together to protect ourselves, you call us militants, radicals, crimi-
nals. We are none of these.

We are warriors.

But you are not an Indian, you say. You are white. You would ridicule
me for that, denounce my statements, my feelings and my actions as those
of a confused and addled personality assuming roles not his own to play.
I know what I am. I know where I came from. I know where I no longer
wish to return and I know where I belong. So I ask you, what defines a
warrior? Is it skin? Is it blood? Or is it heart, mind or conscience? Skin,
blood and tissue do not think or act or feel. Only heart, mind and con-
science can accomplish that.

I am a warrior of conscience. A warrior of heart and mind. You don't
need to be an Indian to assume that role — just human.

It is my humanity that makes me a warrior. My humanity and its
instinctual craving for security, survival, community, love and justice.
When you live in a tribal way you learn that these instinctual urges are
felt individually but expressed and experienced collectively. Tribalism is an
expression of the needs of the one honored by the whole. We are all tribal
people. We all have, within our genes, the memory of tribal fires. Some of
us have distanced ourselves from that memory through denial of our pri-
mordial past, our civilized ways, our technologies, our science, our vast
and cumbersome learnings. But it lies within each of us like a latent hope.
A vague stirring of desire to be included in the warmth, the security, of a
community, a circle easing together around a common fire, safe from the
encroaching darkness. Perhaps we need to remind each other that we
have those old fires in common. That each of us carries in the private
chambers of our heart the embers of fires that burned on distant, ancient
hills. That each of us possesses the memory of drums, prayer songs and
offerings to the great and tremendous mystery around us. That each of us,
in the great story that is the history of our people, carries the memory of

the one, nurtured, protected and enhanced by the whole. That we were once warriors and we, all of us, once fought to protect that way. That we are human beings and the night is always around us.

I do not fight to dishonor, disrespect or disassociate myself. I fight to be included. For the People to be included. For all of us to be included in that circle of light and warmth that springs from a desire for common survival. That is not criminal, radical or savage. It is human.

We cannot change history. We do not seek to. We only seek to use its woundings, its poisons, its pains and its failings to strengthen us for the march forward. To form the framework for a new and stronger lodge for all of us. A medicine lodge where all may heal themselves.

So we give these arrows back to you. Our blood is on them, our tears, our longings, our private joys. Hold them. Feel their energy, their strength, and join us in the raising of this lodge, this circle of belonging, for the trail has been long, the battles thick and deadly and our spirits cry for the promise of rest.

There was silence when I finished.

I folded the paper and put it in my shirt pocket. And I made my statement. I told them what I had seen. And I told them a story about a great meeting between the Animal People and the Creator. And I told them it was Johnny's story.

"Because he knew," I said. "He knew that the process is the same for an individual as it is for a community, a culture and a nation. All it takes is integrity, purity, of heart and courage. Johnny believed that this country had that. That its people had that. He just wanted to remind us."

And then I took my arrows and walked away.

Go home, he said. Go home. Go and tell them that it's all about light.

While my wife took care of the needs of our congregation those

hazy yellow days of autumn, I surrendered myself to the arms of
the earth, the pull of its waters, the suspiration of its winds and the
quiet temperance of its moods, its graceful shifts of balance. I surrendered myself to the thick pall of grief that settled over me like a
morning fog and I knew somehow that the ripple and gurgle of the
waters of the Hockley Valley would be the balm that soothed my
achings and the elixir that slaked my parched and sere spirit. I
could talk to my God there. I could talk to myself. And I could talk
to Johnny.

I set a small tent upon the land and spent my nights listening
to a nocturnal world a skin away. I spent my mornings and my
evenings upon that ragged creek casting lines across the water.
And I spent my afternoons dangling my feet over vertiginous space
on a cliff grown less precipitous by age and caution. I gazed away
across those trees and glens and thought about the boys we were
and the men we had become. Laughing Dog and Thunder Sky. I
thought about the great journeys we had made and how, in the
end, the land bears our secrets, our sorrows and our happiness.
Everywhere we lived and everywhere we died.

You become eternal when you leave a light to shine for the trav-
elers to come. You travel through a personal darkness, seeking the
mysterious glow that hovers somewhere beyond your familiar territories. Step by step you make your way towards and away from
yourself. A simultaneous distance. Those who return have secured
themselves to an immovable, living body — a people, a culture, a
past or belief. The strand they return on is woven of filaments
peeled from that bulk, that weight, that heft. My strand had been
fastened to the tree of faith that had sprouted on three hundred and
twenty fertile acres near Mildmay. A tree that had stretched
upwards, grown more canopied, lush and full with the gentle water-
ing of a cultural way that was eternal itself. Johnny had no tree.

That's why I left the church late that fall. Not out of any lingering sense of guilt or even an adopted resentment. Not because
of white and not because of Indian. But because of Johnny. Go
home, he said. Go home. Riding in on the warm wash of light atop
that cliff came the realization that home is not a destination. It's

not a building, a patch of land or a country. It's not a moral stance, nor is it an ideological affiliation. It's just belonging. A critical and luminant joining to the heartbeat of Creation. A symbiotic attachment to all that is and all that will be. There are no churches in that seamless meshing of energies. Just heartbeats. Heartbeats and the ceremonies and rituals of tribal peoples joined in a cosmic dance directed and choreographed by the invisible hand of God in all his guises.

We moved to Cape Croker the following spring and I went to work with Jacqueline at Mindemoya Lodge, counseling women who needed help removing the arrows of a misdirected religion, one that sought to teach that salvation was a place you prepared for instead of a place you carried within you. I helped them cope with the fear of a wrathful, punishing and vengeful God and learn to walk the path of trust, simple reliance and humility. In time, we established a talking circle for men and I was asked to lead it. It grew by word of mouth and the incredible power of example that change effects on those around us. Five short years later, a similar camp for men was established a few miles down the road from Mindemoya. It is now filled year round with men seeking reconnection to themselves and their idea of God. It's modeled after a traditional camp in the Rocky Mountain foothills and it's known as Johnny's Camp.

My wife became the pastor of a small nondenominational church she established on the reserve. Now and then I speak there, and in the joining of sweetgrass, sage and the teachings of the Gospel I find an ecumenic kinship that nurtures me, encourages me and lends me faith. I know the difference now between what is spiritual and what is religious. Can comprehend text and subtext. I know the point where holistic and ideological diverge. I've learned to take the best parts of each belief system and create a living, vital relationship to the God I find in everything. If I am a preacher now, I am preaching the message that you find God fully in yourself first and then you become graced with the discovery that He, or She, resides everywhere. In every thing, in every body.

A big, big God.

My son sits in sweat lodges and he sits in confirmation classes. He has learned the way of the pipe and the way of the Gospel. He has learned the language of his father's people and the language of his mother's, the way of the Ojibway and the way of the non-Aboriginal world. He is as comfortable in tweed as he is in buckskin, and he knows that when the time comes for him to move out into the world, he is stronger because he has the best of two worlds to fall back on when difficulty comes. You don't fail when you offer choice, Jacqueline said one time, only when you don't.

And me, I spend my time talking about light. How it is the world we are born into. How everything is colored by it. How in the end we travel on it. I spend my time talking to other men, other warriors, about this thing we call God and how it is the belief that saves us, not the ritual. I tell them that it's the same for everybody. And when the universe and our humanity becomes confusing, weighty, difficult and wounding, we can fall to our knees, and whether those knees are clad in buckskin, silk, denim or nothing at all, we find we are in the shelter of a shared Creator, a common God who loves us, nurtures us and leads us to light. So I lead them through sweat lodges. I teach them prayer songs. I teach them to talk openly with the God they seek, to yell, to scream, to cry, to swear. Because faith does not require an extensive vocabulary to work — merely a heart. Together we learn how to make that mole's journey within ourselves and to celebrate what we find there. The light of a personal truth, the light of self-knowledge and the light that allows us to follow the strands of our histories to a place called home.

It's all about light really. It's all about light. And when I stand in the hushed light of evening, watching the waters of Georgian Bay unfold against the lap of the land and then wash back into themselves, I think of him and realize another truth. That the quality of light we search for, the one we hope defines and sustains us forever, is revealed only when the story ends. The light of our example. We leave it behind like a beacon for those who come behind us, to light their way over footfalls and caverns. Eternal light. Eternal life.

EPILOGUE

The People tell a story of how light came into the world.

In the Long-Ago Time there was only darkness. The Animal People moved around within it casually and unafraid. They spoke to each other quietly with honor and respect, for no one saw each other's differences and there was nothing to fear.

One day a strange and eerie glow appeared on the horizon to the east. The Animal People gathered to see if any of them had knowledge of what this mystery might be. No one knew. Owl, the wise one, volunteered to investigate the nature of this mysterious glow in the sky. He flew off, and the Animal People knew that if anyone could comprehend this thing, it was Owl.

He was gone for several days. As each day passed the Animal People grew more worried for their brother, fearful that the glow to the east had captured him and that he had paid with his life for knowledge of the mystery. Then, suddenly, Owl landed, safe and secure, in the boughs of a great pine tree. The Animal People cheered and gathered around the tree to hear Owl's tale of the glow in the sky.

But there was something strange about him. Owl had possessed the vision of the eagle before he left and now he sat in the darkness, blinking and blinking as though his eyes were failing him.

"What's wrong with your eyes?" the Animal People asked.

The story he told amazed and hushed them all.

Owl had flown directly east towards the strange glow. As he flew nearer the glow had become brighter and brighter. Finally, he flew right into it and the illumination was so great that it very nearly blinded him. That is why, to this day, Owl feels more secure and hunts more successfully at night and why he still sits high in branches of trees blinking and blinking, trying to comprehend the mystery.

Needless to say, the Animal People were filled with wonder. After a great long talk they decided that someone must go and return with some of this glow.

Beaver made the first attempt. She swam along the creeks and rivers towards the east. When she reached the glow she grabbed a pawful and placed it on her broad flat tail and began the long swim back.

But the glow was so hot that it began to burn her tail. Beaver bore as much of the heat as she could until finally she slapped her flat tail against the water in alarm to quell the flames and dove beneath the water. The glow had burned all the beautiful fur from her tail. And that is why, even now, Beaver slaps her tail against the water and dives whenever she's alarmed.

Raven volunteered. In the Long-Ago Time, Raven was a bird of brilliant plumage, but when he returned from the east he was burned to the black pitch he still wears today.

Many of the Animal People tried and failed. That is why there are members of the Animal world that prefer the safety of the night and darkness.

Finally, a tiny spider crawled forward and volunteered to try. The Animal People had great respect for bravery but they could not figure how a tiny fragile spider could accomplish what her stronger brothers and sisters could not.

"I will spin a strand from this tree to the east. If I am blinded I can follow the strand back to you and if the heat becomes too much, I will cool it with my tears," Spider said, and all the Animal People were humbled by her courage.

They did not see her for a long time. Many days passed and the Animal People were convinced that Spider had failed.

But one day the glow to the east seemed larger. Morning by morning the glow became bigger and bigger, brighter and brighter, and the Animal People sensed a great change was coming to their world. Soon the glow filled up almost the whole of the sky and runners were sent to investigate. They returned saying that it was indeed Spider following the strand she had spun and bearing the gift of the mysterious glow on her back.

When Spider finally made it back too, the world was filled with the bright glow she carried.

"Oh, that must be so heavy!" they exclaimed.

"No," said Spider. "It's Light."

She told the story of how difficult it had been to get to the Light. How fearful she had become and how much she wanted to quit and return to the safety of the darkness. But she sensed that Light was a great thing and she wanted to share it with everyone. So she had scooped a tiny bit onto her back and begun to return along her woven strand. The longer she kept the Light with her, the brighter it had become. Her tears had indeed kept it cool and soon she felt happy about the arrival of the Light. That is why, in the mornings when the Light arrives from the east, you can still see spiders' tears clinging to their webs in celebration of the coming of the Light.

The Animal People looked around themselves suddenly. They could see each other for the first time and they were scared. They ran off in many directions, and it was a long time before they learned how to trust each other again and to live with each other's differences. The coming of the Light meant that they had more to learn of each other and their world. But they learned it and they continue to pass on these teachings to each other, and especially to Man, the newest and strangest of the Animal People.

And that is how Light came into the world.